Braving Storms

Book three of Atlas Cliffs series

Angela van Liempt

Dawn Publishing

First paperback edition September 2024

Cover design by Natasha MacKenzie, Miss Nat Mack Studio @missnatmack https://www.missnatmack.com/

Chapter heading Illustrations by Whitney Law of New Ink Book Services https://www.instagram.com/newinkbookservices/

Character art Illustration by Alexandra Hutan Art https://www.alexandrahuta-nart.com/

Editing by Kayla Ramoutar

Tagline by Sara Flanagan

ISBN 978-1-7782544-7-5 (Paperback)

ISBN 978-1-7782544-6-8 (E-book)

Published by Dawn Publishing

www.dawn-publishing.com

This one is for you. Yes, you. Thank you for letting me interrupt your life with my stories of ghosts, magic, and romance. I'm happy you're along for the ride...

"I am not afraid of storms, for I am learning how to sail my ship."
Louisa May Alcott

One

The blades of the vintage fan rattled as they spun, trapped in the wire cage as though they longed to break free. Drew faced the fan, letting the gentle breeze brush against her damp tank top as it dried the perspiration on her skin. Opening the window in Gran's bedroom-turned-studio offered no relief from the suffocating heat of the late June heatwave.

With graceful flutters, a butterfly danced in a staggered motion, circling back to land on the sea-salt-coated glass. Drew sat back in the desk chair and tapped the end of a graphite pencil on her forehead as she stared at the tiny dark veins weaving through the butterfly's velvet wings. The absence of blue on the insect triggered an ache of grief deep in her chest. This butterfly was not a sign from Gran. Her laptop descended into sleep-mode and the graphic for Nico's garage that she'd been working on vanished from the screen. He'd been adamant about changing the name of the garage from DeSarro and Son to DeSarro's Autor Repair and Restoration now that his father was a silent partner. Snapping the laptop shut, she bent over the large sketchbook and repositioned the pencil. The gentle scraping as she shaded the detailed feathers of the raven in mid-flight zoned out her mind and calmed her anxious soul. She scribbled *D. Harlow* at the bottom right corner as the click of a door sounded from downstairs. She leaned back in the oversized chair, gripping the edge of the broad desk to keep herself from falling back.

"It's just me," Nico called, easing the rising panic as it constricted from her stomach to her throat. Nico was her anchor, keeping her grounded in the chaos. He knew how to make her feel safe, and he was by her side when she needed him. Life was sweeter with him in it.

Thuds sounded as he ascended the stairs and leaned against the door frame. His damp hair clung to his forehead, and his navy t-shirt hugged his broad chest. Pushing away from her desk, she stood, dropping the pencil, and wrapped her arms around his waist. She rested her chin against his chest as she looked up at him, inhaling the alluring blend of sandalwood and soap that surrounded him. "You sure don't smell like a guy who's been in a garage sweating all afternoon."

"I went home and showered." He shoved his phone in his back pocket and embraced her. The dimple in his cheek appeared as he smiled. "I texted to see if you needed a car, but you didn't answer, so I thought I'd come by."

"I'm bad with my phone."

"Very."

She ran her fingers through his hair and kissed him, letting her lips linger on his. They'd been back together for six months, and she still couldn't get enough of him. She wanted the feeling of complete adoration to last forever, but fear tickled the back of her mind when she thought too far into the future. Nothing and no one lasted forever. Their kiss deepened and a resurgence of fresh laundry and soap clung to her senses as he held her tighter.

"Your car needs more work. I can drive you and pick you up until I get it fixed," he said between kisses.

"I'll just get a ride with J to work in the morning."

He glanced over her shoulder and released her as he moved closer to the half-finished painting resting on the easel by the window. "Is that inside the lighthouse? I've never been inside, have you?"

"Once, with Gran when I was little." She stood beside him and folded her arms. The memory of being inside the lighthouse of Aurora had faded, but she'd never forget the fear. She'd stood in her rain boots, gripping Gran's hand like a lifeline as the icy ocean air whipped at her coat.

"Is it finished?" Nico asked. "It's really good."

It's missing something.

"I don't know if I'll ever finish it. I'm stuck."

"Is it one of your visions? I don't think the lighthouse has ever flooded before."

They both stared at the mellowed blues, grays, and blacks blended to form the ocean surging through the main floor, waves skirting the bottom of the winding stairway to a landing above. She'd considered painting Jack at the top where the beacon turned, or a silhouette of Aurora herself, but the woman was elusive, and she had no image of her to suit the lady of the lighthouse... and something was missing.

"It was a dream," she whispered.

"Should I be worried?"

His gaze broke her trance, and she tilted her head against his shoulder. "Nothing to worry about. It's just a painting."

"From a dream that *you* had."

"Maybe I'll have another one and be able to finish the top part."

"Is everything okay? Still just the one ghost hanging around? No one is trying to hurt you?" Nico's smile faded as his eyes cast downward on hers.

"Just the one, and she still doesn't know she's dead, but no threats. It's a nice change, actually. Maybe the dark days are over."

"Don't jinx it, Drew." He eyed her neck, detangling the chains of the amulet and butterfly necklace he'd given her, and holding the amulet in his fingers. "It's cold and still."

"That's a good thing, don't you think? No one on the other side is trying to drag me away, for now anyway."

Nico's hands moved to her face, and his calloused fingers rested against her cheeks. Hard working hands that held her whole heart. "The other side can't have you. I won't let anyone hurt you."

"I know." No one could protect her from the dead, not even Nico, if he had an army behind him. Stopping unseen villains was impossible unless they were alive and human. Dominic Sloan's wild eyes still flashed in her mind sometimes, sending a pins and needles sensation crawling over her scarred upper thigh as though her thoughts could trigger a physical reaction on the healed wound.

Nico's hands dropped to his sides, and he grabbed his phone from his back pocket. "Simon left this morning, and I've got to help Mom with a few things." He didn't lift his gaze from the screen on his phone. "My brother can usually talk her into anything, but he couldn't talk her into keeping the house."

This time it was Nico's family home that had turned into prime Atlas Cliffs real estate, and he wasn't the decision-maker. His parents' divorce was final, and his mom was downsizing. His brother had met a girl at university, and they'd moved in together a year ago.

Nico had been tight-lipped about his uncertain future living situation, and Drew had been giving him space, not pressing him to talk about it. Her boyfriend was in stark denial, holding onto the impossible hope his family home wouldn't sell or his mom would change her mind.

But neither was going to happen. Drew had spent enough time with Marie DeSarro to know she was ready to move on from Nico's father and the family home.

"What will you do if it sells?" The question was out before she could stop herself.

"No idea. I'll deal with that when I have no other choice. No offer means no sale. Did you want to come with me?"

"I'm going to finish up here. Hey, I'm almost done with your new business logo. I think you're going to love it."

His lips lifted into a half smile. "No doubt, thanks. The new garage is better than the one at home. I just got a 1969 Camaro from a woman upstate, and the extra space at the back is big enough to keep restorations separate." His smile dropped, and he glanced around the room. "Dad hasn't been around much.

I'm supposed to be putting in the hours under an experienced mechanic, but he's just been signing the forms."

"Tell him how you feel."

"Yeah, right. If only it were that easy." His phone vibrated in his hand. "Sure you don't want to come?"

"I'm sure. I'll see you later?" She hugged him, letting her fingers interlace with his.

"Count on it." He leaned down and kissed her, sending a pleasant shiver running along her bare arms before he broke away and headed downstairs. The door below clicked shut, leaving Drew alone. She resisted running behind him to throw the deadbolt. No one was coming for her, but letting go of the constant paranoia was proving difficult.

This was her one day off during the week and she didn't want to spend it worrying. She and Jasper alternated these precious days, and she relished every single moment, especially during the busy tourist season at the Tough Cookie as travelers flocked to the area.

She needed four minutes of solitude to get off the roller coaster of emotions.

Just four minutes.

Sinking back into the chair, she spun around and stretched her legs out, resting her feet on a fuzzy ottoman. The sun's rays poured into the room, making her mint-green toenail polish shimmer. The rattling fan's rhythm continued, its gentle tapping increasing and subsiding with each oscillation, pervading the otherwise silent house. She wanted to lock this peace around her and never let go.

A hushed voice pierced her ears, the whisper soft like the butterfly's wings as it brushed her face in a sudden burst of cool air—not from the fan. Bolting upright, she struggled to catch her breath, her heart pounding in her chest.

"Who's here?"

The soft whispers grew louder, turning into a woman's faint humming, reminding her of Iris. But there was no blood-stained dress swirling around, and death didn't weigh on the presence vying for her attention, unlike the stubborn ghost girl for the past month who refused to acknowledge she was no longer among the living. A cluster of glitter spun like a tornado from the hallway into the room.

Drew stood, sending the wheeled chair backward against the wall with a thud. Her breaths curled in a mist as the temperature dropped around her in a swift breeze, sending the curtains billowing in the air. She pressed her back against the wall for a clear view of the entity as it took shape in front of her. Layers of black cloth rustled as a gown cascaded along the floor, gradually forming the silhouette of a woman bathed in the glow of golden light that matched her skin, her black hair flowing around her face in a striking contrast. She radiated ethereal energy reminiscent of Gran, not fearful, but holding a sense of angelic power. The extreme opposite of Hathorne's chokehold of terror.

With her feet planted on the wooden floorboards, Drew remained fixated. She wanted to step forward and reach out to the woman, but held back, afraid to frighten her away. Who was this ghost whose essence was unlike the others she'd grown used to?

The woman glided toward the back of the room, tilting her head as she gazed at the floor-to-ceiling bookshelf. With a swipe of her hand, books shook, and one flew from the shelf, sliding across the floor to land at Drew's feet. Gran's *Book of Spells*. The cover swung open, and the pages flipped in rapid succession. Drew crouched down and reached for the book, but the woman held her hands out and shook her head in warning.

The book settled, spilling open to blank pages. A mesmerizing display of red danced over the crisp paper.

Call the quarters.

Seek shelter from the storm.

Seek bravery in the face of death, breathe in life.

Drew read the words out loud and grabbed the book, wobbly on her feet. "What is this for? I don't understand." Goosebumps covered her body in the room's chill.

The woman moved closer, her footsteps silent, until she was inches away from Drew's face. Singed, dark hair framed her gaunt cheeks, and the satin collar of her dress was melted and frayed. She extended her blistered hands, and Drew stepped back, flinching from the smell of burnt flesh, but the woman persisted with a calm strength, her silent words penetrating Drew's mind—"*I mean you no harm*"—until the voice halted, replaced by a high-pitched buzzing in her ears.

The woman's hands graced Drew's cheeks, their warmth encompassing her. A zap of electricity coursed through her, and she clenched her jaw, gritting her teeth as a barrage of visions fought for her attention.

The lighthouse beacon rotated over a raging sea as a fire burned below, its flames creeping toward a woman, the same woman with her hands on Drew. The vision unfolded like a movie, bringing the cliffs into focus as the woman held a glowing object in her hands toward a cloaked man.

Hathorne.

The woman moved closer to Hathorne and Drew followed, unable to stop herself. She was a bystander, receiving a glimpse of the past. He couldn't come through a vision and hurt her. She continued to trail the woman through seagrass and sand. Waves smashed against boulders below, tearing pieces of rock away. The air thickened with each step closer as the gray smoke surrounding Hathorne sucked the air from her lungs. The woman held the object high above her head and a radiant light flashed as she chanted a spell. Drew had used the same spell to banish him from the living world at Haven.

With a swift motion, the cloaked witch hunter conjured a burst of flames, setting the woman's dress ablaze and sealing her fate. Drew's stomach churned at the pungent smell of burning flesh and she struggled to swallow excessive saliva as a metallic taste covered her tongue. The woman's magic tethered her to the ground, rendering her unable to break free from her hold. A final blast of light shot from the object hanging from the woman's hands and the cloaked witch hunter vanished. Flames enveloped the woman, and she collapsed to the ground, her screams carrying over the crashing waves before she disappeared into a slump of ashes and soot. Seawater sprayed over the cliffs, extinguishing the inferno, sending gray mist curling up into the night sky. A cloud shifted, allowing the full moon to illuminate the object on top of the rubble.

The amulet.

A faint glimmer pulsed within the center of the jewel around her neck.

Drew sucked in air suddenly, as if someone had slammed her back inside her body, as the woman removed her hands. The anguish of grief ripped through her chest as though it were her own death and not the woman standing in front of her. Tears spilled from her eyes, over her cheeks as they gazed at each other, the hint of a smile crossing the woman's face. Her eyes sparkled as she reached a pale hand for Drew's neck and held the amulet in her hand.

"Aurora," she whispered. Her dress twirled around her as she faced the painting and her smile dropped into a deep frown. Her pale fingers grazed the canvas, and in a frantic motion, her hands covered her eyes as she vanished.

The goosebumps subsided and heat rushed through the air again as Gran's fan clanged with each rotation. Drew sucked in a breath and grabbed the back of the chair to steady herself.

Did I just meet Aurora? The original Atlas Cliffs... witch?

Bending down to retrieve the book from the floor, her hands trembled as she flipped through the pages. The red cursive message remained, but she couldn't decipher its meaning. Call the quarters? Shelter from the storm? She scanned the room, but she was alone, and other than a few books on the floor, nothing was out of place—*the painting.*

She swallowed a building lump in her throat. A pool of bright red marred the surface of the canvas. The thick, red liquid slowly extended over the lighthouse landing, dripping down the winding staircase. Among the monochromatic surroundings, the vibrant, blood-like crimson stood out like death.

Sharp heat pricked the skin on her neck, and she lifted the silver chain until the amulet dangled at eye level. The black gem had awakened from its slumber, a thread of light spinning from the center like a tornado, bursting with a life she hadn't seen since she had recovered the amulet.

Something was happening. It might not be the entire sisterhood, but someone wanted her attention.

Had Aurora awoken the jewel?

Two

With a relentless heatwave hanging over the town, Drew left the painting, Aurora, and her thousand pressing questions behind to join Nico across the road at Jupiter Cove beach. The refreshing cold water and ocean breeze brought relief as the afternoon shifted into early evening and the sky turned a mesmerizing shade of pink. As the tide rose, the waves grew larger, crashing against the shore with more force.

The water splashed over her thighs as she balanced on the choppy water. Surfing calmed her from a place deep within her soul.

Nico floated on his board beside her, the silence between them a soothing comfort, like they were the only two people in the world—living or dead. Piper had never been interested in more than lounging on the beach, and Shane had refused to go in the water with her. It had been almost two years since she had first reconnected with Nico while surfing solo, but these days, they came out together all the time.

Nico was her surfer 'ride or die.' They'd learned to swim together from the time they were kids, naturally progressing to boogie boards, surfboards, and wetsuits. She grinned at the memory of trying on their new suits and using the hose to pour water inside to see how long it would take the water to warm up as it ballooned at their ankles. He was the only person who matched her energy out on the water. They shared an unspoken admiration for the immense power of the ocean, testing its boundaries, but respecting nature's limits.

And out here, she could think. Really think.

If she drifted long and far enough, she'd end up at Neptune Point miles down the coast and come face to face with the lighthouse.

Aurora. What was she trying to tell me?

Water lapped at her surfboard, and she rose and fell as a swell rolled underneath her. Nico paddled closer until he could reach out and touch her board, giving it a tug closer. With one hand on his board and the other on hers, he leaned in close, his gaze locked on her lips. Her legs kicked in synchronized circles beneath the glistening water as she balanced her core over the center of the board. Their lips collided, igniting a surge of tingles that raced beneath her wet suit and spread across her skin. The taste of salt water lingered on her tongue as they parted, and he adjusted his body weight back to the center of his board.

"Are you ready to go in?" He brushed his fingers through his wet hair, flicking drops of water from his face.

"No. Out here is so much better." Her fingers had pruned from the water, but she didn't care. This was peace.

"Are you all right? You've hardly said anything since we've been out here."

She hadn't told him about the visit from Aurora earlier, or the painting. The dam holding her questions flooded back into her mind. Questions she didn't have an answer for.

Nico's board drifted away, and he pivoted, paddling back to her. His lips turned up, and he raised his eyebrows. "I'll take that as everything's good?"

Just tell him. He's used to this.

But for how long? When would her ghost visits be too much for him?

"I saw someone today, someone new." The words fell out of her mouth. "But I don't want to freak you out."

"You can tell me anything, you know that. I think I've proven that."

"I don't need you to prove anything to me."

Nico's mouth opened and closed, as if trying to find the right words to say. "Who'd you see? Now I'm curious, so you've got to tell me."

She adjusted her tangled, waterlogged ponytail and her board floated away as the choppy water pushed them apart. Kicking her feet harder, she reached her hands into the water to paddle back to him. "Aurora."

"Aurora?" His eyebrows furrowed, and he looked up at her, shielding his eyes from the sun. "The lighthouse woman? That's the ghost you saw?"

"She appeared after you left and now my amulet is..." She reached for the silver chain around her neck and freed the amulet from underneath the wetsuit. A thread of light spun inside the jewel. "Can you see it?"

Gripping her board, he pulled her close. "What does it mean?"

"I'm not sure." The blood-like warning appearing on the painting lingered on the tip of her tongue, but she struggled to articulate her unease as his smile faded and concern spread across his face.

"Is she like the dead guy who wanted to kill you—"

"No. Not at all. She was calm and peaceful, like an angel. She doesn't want to hurt me, Nico. I think she might want to..." *Warn me.* "Help me."

"That's good, right?"

"Sure, good. Great."

It didn't feel great at all. The red on the painting and Aurora's reaction before she disappeared felt more like a terrible, ominous sign. But she couldn't bring herself to scare him, not when life had been so sweet. She wanted them to always be this close, this secure, and her ghostly encounters would threaten that.

With a nod, he lowered himself back on the tail of his board, gripping each side as the front rose from the water. He redirected the board toward shore and positioned himself on his stomach, ready to paddle, but waiting for her. "Come on, let's go in."

Sliding back on her board, she pivoted around to face the shoreline. Lying flat on her belly with her legs together, she extended her arms, paddling with her hands close to the board. As she passed Nico, his muscular arms flexed as he drove them deeper into the water to catch up. She navigated with the waves, allowing them to carry her toward shore. Falling behind, Nico rode a whitewater wave the rest of the way in, a huge grin plastered on his face.

They carried their boards up to the beach and stuck the tail ends into the sand. Nico pulled the zip cord at the back of his neck, releasing his wetsuit. He peeled off the top half, letting it hang around his waist, his tanned skin shimmering in the sunset. He possessed the type of good looks that radiated from the inside out, and she had a hard time not staring at him. It didn't matter if it was first thing in the morning, sweating in the garage, or wading out of the ocean after a day of surfing.

He sat on the sand and toyed with the silver chain she'd given him for his twentieth birthday a few weeks ago. "I wish every day was like this."

Drew tried not to flinch, her own thoughts echoing. "Who says it can't be?"

"There's a million reasons why it can't be," he said. "But it won't stop me from trying."

"And that is one of the million reasons I love you." She unzipped her wetsuit, rolled the sleeves off her arms, and let it fall around her waist.

His gaze met hers. "I love you too."

She adjusted her bikini top and plopped onto the sand beside him. "Even though I see dead people?"

He laughed. "It's all part of our life, baby."

"But won't you get tired of it? There's always going to be someone who's stuck and needs my help. What if it interferes with plans and life and everything?" She pulled the elastic from her ponytail and untangled the wet strands with her fingers. She didn't even know what she was saying. Life beyond what they had now? The future? What did that look like? She chewed on her bottom lip—the skin stinging as she tasted salt.

With a flicker of curiosity, he glanced at her through thick lashes. His brown eyes turned amber as the sunlight hit them. "I'll never get tired of *you* or stop loving *you*. Lots of shit will interfere with life. If this happens to be one of those things, we'll just figure it out."

"It's not that simple."

"It is for me." He exhaled deeply and stood, reaching his hand down to hers. She grabbed it and he yanked her up before pulling his board from the sand. "I'm starving. Let's go find something to barbecue."

Simple as that.

THREE

A ngling her board under her arm, Drew's feet sank into the sand as she made her way toward the stone stairway up to the road with Nico at her side. She stuck her feet in a pair of flip-flops she'd left at the top of the rocky cliff, and he followed her across the street to her house.

Music flowed from the house as she walked up the driveway toward Jasper's VW Bus by the shed. Sand clung to her body, finding its way into every place imaginable, with a layer covering her feet. The scorching heat engulfed her, erasing any trace of the cool ocean air. She struggled with her wetsuit, forcefully using one foot to remove it from her other leg. Her bikini bottom slipped down a little, and she yanked it up, adjusting the sides as heat crept up her cheeks. Nico hadn't noticed as he discarded his wetsuit and stood in front of her, tying the string on his board shorts. She adored having Jasper as a roommate, but there were moments when she craved the privacy of having the house to herself... with Nico.

Her stomach growled in sudden protest. "Maybe J is cooking something in there." She turned on the hose and rinsed the sand off her feet and the wetsuit, doing the same to Nico's discarded suit before hanging them up on dedicated hooks inside the shed.

"I'll barbecue burgers or something," Nico's voice carried from the shed as he stacked their surfboards on the racks he'd built.

Taking the hose from her, he rinsed off his feet. With a mischievous smile, he covered the hose with his thumb and sprayed her legs.

Goosebumps erupted over her body as the icy water cascaded down her legs. "Give me that!" She broke out in laughter, and it felt *good*—like she'd put down a heavy backpack she'd carried on a hike all day. Engaged in a playful struggle, she wrestled the hose away from him and sprayed him back. Cold water ran down his body, leaving a layer of sand along the driveway. She flipped her head down and soaked her hair, gasping from the cold water over her scalp.

"Can you turn the water off?" She dropped the hose to the ground and squeezed the water from her hair.

The unmistakable thumping of a subwoofer grew louder, and Nico's gaze shifted to the road as a jeep pulled into the driveway.

"Isn't that Taj?" she said.

"Yeah."

"Were you supposed to meet him at Maze?"

"Not that I remember." Nico headed toward the jeep as Taj stepped out, shoving his keys into the pocket of his shorts. He leaned against the jeep as he talked to Nico.

Drew wound the hose back on the reel as Taj sauntered up the driveway beside Nico with the same worried look that Celeste sometimes had.

"Are you coming in after?" Nico eyed Taj.

"I'm meeting Piper. We're going to that drive-in thing in Portal Park."

Piper. The most adventurous, romantic person Drew knew. "I forgot about that," she said, grabbing a towel she'd left hanging over the door of the shed.

"How? She hasn't stopped talking about it. Man, the things I do for that girl." Taj folded his arms, his neat black twists shimmering in the sunlight. He tapped his fingers to the beat of the music coming from the house.

Drew wiped her face and shoulders before wrapping the towel around her waist and tucked a corner to secure it. "I'm going to change—"

Taj stopped tapping. "Actually, I need to talk to you."

Nico glanced at Drew and shifted back to Taj. "Talk later, man." He headed inside and the screen door creaked open, protesting on its hinges as it shut behind him.

She had spent a considerable amount of time with Taj since Piper started dating him, but he'd never looked so serious and eager to have a conversation with her.

Despite the heat, a shiver ran through her. "What's up?"

Taj paced, stopping to run a hand over the hood of Jasper's bus. Jasper kept it pristine. Not a speck of dirt was on the front, not even a dead bug. "He really likes this thing?"

"He's obsessed," she said.

"Cool. Sure."

She gestured with her thumb toward the porch. "You sure you don't want to come in?"

"This is one of those things... only you will get." He clasped his hands together as he surveyed the yard. "Okay. This is gonna sound weird."

"Please, I embody weird. You can't shock me."

"I think maybe I can, you know what I'm saying?"

Her eyebrows pulled together so tight her head hurt, and she released the muscles in her face. What could he possibly say that would shock *her?* "Try me."

"I've been having dreams. Wait, no. Dreams are fun, and you don't want to wake up from them. I'm having fucking nightmares... about you."

Okay. He shocked her. Aurora, the painting, and now Taj—son of Celeste, a magical witch in her own right—having nightmares about Drew. The lightness of the day shifted with a rush of fear.

She rubbed her arms as the tiny hairs stood on end. "I'm going to need you to elaborate. What sort of nightmares?"

"See? I told you I'd freak you out." He held his hands out, and his deep brown eyes widened. "I don't know what to do. It just started happening, and it's every night. I'm scared to fall asleep."

"What are they about?"

"Us. You, me, Piper, Nico, even Claudia's there. But it changes, and it gets too dark to see. And I can hear yelling, screaming, for help, like a bunch of voices, except yours is louder than the others, but I can't find you, and there's water everywhere." As he spoke, his voice lowered and his eyes wandered elsewhere, no longer focused on her.

"Where are we?"

"Neptune Point, by the lighthouse, and when I wake up, I can't breathe, and it just…" That look came over him again. The worried Celeste look. "Ends."

"Ends how?" The red on the painting flashed in her mind, and she swallowed saliva past her parched throat. She eyed the hose, debating turning it on and drinking from it.

He stepped closer to her. Cicadas buzzed in the trees, and crickets chimed in. "Everyone is just gone, and you scream, but it gets cut off. It ends." He wiped his eyes with the back of his hand. "There's other shit going on with me, too."

"What other shit?"

He turned up his hands, so his palms faced the sky. The setting sun bathed his brown skin in a golden glow. "It's my hands. Sometimes they'll burn for no reason. There's no rash and I sure as hell wasn't hiking and fell into poison ivy—nothing like that."

She touched his hands and a sizzling sensation popped along her tongue like she'd eaten a sour candy she used to love as a kid. A hum of electricity pulsed in her mind, on the verge of one of her psychic visions. Overwhelmed by a grave, foreboding fear, she recoiled, yanking her hands away, and took a deep breath.

"What is it?" he asked. "Why'd you pull away like that?"

Celeste would be able to help. "Have you told your mom about this?"

He shook his head before he spoke. "No. No, I can't."

"Why not? She's the best person—"

He leaned against Jasper's van and crossed his arms. "I don't want her to know, so don't tell her. She's got enough going on. I'll figure it out on my own." His gaze met hers as he looked down at her. "I just might need some help."

She rubbed her face with both hands. Could Taj have his mother's gifts? Drew's? Was it possible that he was like her, Enid, and Celeste... A *witch*? Stretching her neck from side to side to ease the growing tension, she held out her hands toward him.

He gaped at her with his face scrunched up. "What are you doing?"

"Come here. Let's do this."

He pushed away from the van. "Whoa. Do what? I don't want any of that witchy voodoo you've got going on."

"*Voodoo*? If your mom heard you say that she'd be pissed, and you might already have it. Give me your hands."

"They're sweaty." He wiped his hands on his shorts.

"I don't care."

Taking a step closer, she wiggled her finger, narrowing her eyes on his. "I can see things. Let me try."

He placed his hands on hers, and her breath hitched, almost choking her. The sizzling sensation flooded her senses like electric shocks. Her vision blurred, and she closed her eyes. The images tore through her mind like wildfire.

"What's happening? My chest hurts and there's a disgusting taste in my mouth." Taj's voice faded into the distance.

It's so dark. Why is it so dark?

As her breathing grew shallow, her pulse thudded in her ears, reverberating like the amplified beat of a stethoscope. Her body drifted like a feather falling from the sky. She held onto his hands tighter, desperate to see something, anything, to unravel the mystery. A flash of light burned her eyes, and a shadow appeared. She tried to speak, to ask them who they were, but no words came out. Her beating heart stopped. She fought to breathe, gasping for air, but suffocation took oxygen's place.

"Drew!" Taj yanked his hands away and grabbed her arms, steadying her as her eyes flew open.

The air was thick with humidity, making it difficult for her to breathe as she struggled to catch her breath. Tears crawled over her cheeks. "Did you see anything?" Her words came out in whispers.

"No, but look at your necklace."

She held it up as swirls of light spun through the center.

Taj raised his hands, and a subtle glow emerged from the center of his palms. "What's happening to me?"

"I don't know."

Dropping his hands, he tugged his phone out. "Shit, I'm late. I've got to pick up Piper." His chest collapsed as he blew out a breath. "I can't be like this, Drew. No offense, but I don't want to talk to dead people or be magical. I can't live like that." His tone softened. "I don't mean to hurt your feelings."

"You're not. It's okay." She'd been exactly where Taj was and hated every minute. Except she'd had years to accept it and he'd barely had days.

"It'll be okay, right?" He pleaded with his eyes.

I have no idea. "Sure, we'll make it okay. We will."

"Tell Nico bye for me but leave this out." He pulled his keys from his pocket and curled his fingers around them. "I had to tell you."

"I know, I get it." She hugged herself and shuffled her feet as the gravel cut into her skin.

"Do you think the nightmares are about whatever is happening to me?" He lowered his voice. "I don't get it, you know? Why now?"

"I'm not sure, but we'll figure it out, everything will be okay." Her voice exuded a confidence she didn't have.

He glanced at his phone. "Piper's texting, I'm so late."

She forced a smile. "Better not keep her waiting."

"I'll see you?"

"Sure, yeah."

"Thank you." His shoulders relaxed as he turned toward his jeep. The base thumped from the car as he drove away with a wave outside the window.

Stepping onto the porch, she plucked one of Gran's pink stones from a planter. She held it up to the light and rolled it in her fingers. The vision felt as if she'd detached from her body, plunging into an abyss of darkness. She couldn't shake the feeling that she'd just experienced the terrifying sensation of dying.

Four

As Drew strolled along the main street of her coastal hometown, a haunting feeling of uneasiness resurfaced, bringing back memories of the witch hunter who had once targeted her. With a pink box filled with cupcakes in her hands, she continued along the bustling sidewalk, a knot forming in her stomach, constricting with each step closer to Little Mysteries. Her mind drifted away from the witch hunter, banished somewhere on the other side, and shifted to Taj and his nightmares about her. It wasn't the darkness in the vision that plagued her, but the suffocating aftermath it had on her senses, like a glimpse into death itself.

A sudden distinct awareness of being watched engulfed her. Her senses heightened—her ears buzzed, her skin tingled, and her eyes searching for anything out of place. But she found no shadows, no threats, and no signs of danger lurking.

With school out for summer, screaming children packed the splash pad across the street in Portal Park, and teenagers soared back and forth over the skateboard ramp, attempting jumps. Tourists stood out in their matching nautical polos, oversized sunglasses and designer handbags, as locals moved past them with purpose, their steps quick and determined. Tourist season brought life to Atlas Cliffs, as regulars arrived by yacht or fancy cars to their vacation homes that sat vacant for the rest of the year. But every person within her view appeared oblivious to her as she approached the entrance to Little Mysteries.

Sweat beaded along her forehead and crawled down the small of her back, soaking through the black shirt she wore with the words *Tough Cookie* embroidered on her chest. Jasper had insisted the thicker cotton material was the most professional choice—a decision she'd agreed with at the time, but under the glaring sun of the Friday afternoon in a relentless heatwave, she cursed the uniform choice. At least she'd paired it with shorts.

She stared down the alley between buildings. The brick walls were nowhere near as high as buildings in Boston, but high enough to block out the sun and cast shadows.

Did something move?

Wasps hovered over a garbage bin and a mouse scurried from underneath a paper bag. Watching eyes from a hidden corner bore into her, their presence known only by the uneasy feeling that settled deep within her bones.

Thrumming vibrated against her neck, and she grabbed the silver chain until the amulet dangled at eye level. The spinning light swirled in the center, radiating along the surface. Was it Aurora's magic brewing around her? Or something more sinister?

Chimes jingled, shaking her from her stupor. Balancing the box of cupcakes, she trailed behind two customers as they entered Celeste's store, glancing over her shoulder toward melodic laughter erupting from a café's patio.

The magical shop greeted her with the hum of ceiling fans. In a fleeting moment of connection, Celeste gestured for Drew to head into the back room before turning her attention back to two women who looked almost identical except one had long, pin straight hair and the other had a spiky pixie cut that reminded Drew of Nellie. The ache of missing Nellie had subsided, and she appeared joyful in her new city with her daughter and grandchild. Jasper's new menu launch brought in a younger clientele, and each time they had talked, Nellie expressed her pride at how well the Tough Cookie thrived under his version of an organized-chic management style.

She headed for the back, cutting through shoppers examining trinkets, books, and incense sticks, catching an earful of Celeste's conversation with the two women. They were sisters and one of them had discovered she had cancer. They were seeking new ways of healing. Celeste offered gentle words of kindness without promises. She might have magic flowing through her, but she couldn't heal or save anyone from death. Fear of dying was ingrained in humans, fueling the need to survive and battle against the unknown, the unseen, the unexpected. Drew met the wandering souls on the other side of life through the veil to where the dead traveled. She didn't know where they went beyond what she could see and didn't want to know. Knowing the secrets of the other side meant her own death... Maybe fear of dying was woven deep within her own soul, too.

Drew crossed through the curtain of beads dangling from the door and placed the box of cupcakes on a large table shaped like a tree stump. The smooth wail of a saxophone resonated from a set of speakers mounted on corner shelves, and she swayed to the music as she wandered around the room. She picked up a book called *The Magical World of Crystals* from the shelf and flipped through it. A row of candles in elaborate silver holders with creeping vines engraved in intricate details lined the shelf, their wicks blackened but unlit.

Celeste would urge her to focus and practice with the magic still flowing through her veins. Drew placed the book back on the shelf and leaned over the candles. She'd conjured words of messages in Gran's spell book—how to bring dead flowers back to life, find her missing phone, a lesson on focusing her vision-showing technique—but the power she'd once held inside her had subsided with the loss of the sisterhood inside the amulet. The once vibrant explosion of fireworks in her hands had vanished, leaving behind the soft glow of sparklers.

She'd believed the magic inside the amulet would never return, but Aurora's sudden appearance had caused a shift. Change was coming, and she'd better be ready.

Closing her eyes, she inhaled, releasing the air slowly through her lips. Waking up the energy and urging the magic to flow through her was the simple part. A fizzing sensation filled her head, as though a soda can had popped open, and the bubbles traveled down her chest and arms, reaching her palms and fingers. Like a tiny firefly, the thread of light inside the amulet swirled and flickered, casting an enchanting glow. Releasing the silver necklace, she let the stone rest against her chest and hovered her hand over the candles on the counter, trying to coax the magic from her body. She visualized dancing orange flames and ran her fingers over the candles, opening one eye to check on her progress. Puffs of smoke burst free from the charcoal wicks, but no flames. She raised her other hand

and held both over the candles, imagining the fire igniting, its heat touching her palms, but nothing happened. Her eyes fluttered open, and she concentrated until wisps of smoke started to coil and dance around her. The wicks remained blackened without a flame.

She dropped her hands and tapped her fingers on the counter, stopping herself as she chewed on her lower lip.

Gran's voice, as elusive as a blue moon, whispered in her ear like a warm hug. "Timing is everything."

I know, Gran. I know.

She swallowed the lump in her throat. Grief stuck to her like glitter on Christmas decorations, impossible to get rid of and popping up over the house all year long.

The clanging of beads startled her as Celeste entered the room. "Didn't I tell you not to play with fire?" Her yellow maxi dress cascaded to her ankles, highlighting her radiant brown skin. She wore a matching fabric headband twisted at her hairline that held back the black coils that usually framed her face.

Celeste's soothing presence settled over her, calming her.

"You'd never say that." Drew poked at the curls of smoke over the candles, but the elusive fire refused to ignite. "It isn't working, anyway. Doesn't matter how much I try, my magic is pretty much gone. It's not strong like it used to be."

"It's not gone, silly girl. We've talked about this." As Celeste opened the pink box of cupcakes on the table, her delicate beauty mark shifted, and her lips curved into her signature half smile.

Drew sat on a stool next to her and leaned on her elbows. Holding up a black and white frosted cupcake, Celeste inspected the sprinkled silver stars and sparkling half-moons in the center. "Jasper's *good*. Tell him I said so, will you?"

"I will." He'd worked hard at making the Tough Cookie the trendy spot it had become. She couldn't have done it alone. "What are they for, anyway?"

"I'm having friends over for Summer Solstice, well technically, it happened last night, but we're celebrating this evening." Celeste closed the lid on the box of cupcakes.

"What do you all do for Summer Solstice? Make a huge bonfire and dance naked under the moonlight?"

"Why don't you come see for yourself?" Celeste smiled.

"I've got plans with Nico." Heat rose to Drew's face when she mentioned his name. He still made her stomach flutter and sent tingles over her skin.

"He's one of the good ones." Celeste's forehead creased as she leaned toward a fan on the counter. "This heat is going to take me out."

A star-shaped clock on the wall caught Drew's eye. It was almost closing time at the Tough Cookie. "I better get back soon if I'm going to help Jasper close."

"It's ninety-five degrees outside. Far be it from me to keep you from helping that poor man close up shop and get out of there. I would've stopped by and picked them up, save you from leaving."

"I wanted to come... I need to talk to you about something."

"I'm listening." Celeste pulled a stool closer and took a seat.

"I met Aurora."

"Aurora?" Celeste raised an eyebrow. "Lighthouse witch, Aurora?"

"She showed me how she died, Celeste. She used the amulet to send *him* back, just like I did, and he..." As she chewed her lip, the memory of the acrid scent of burned flesh came rushing back. "He burned her alive. I could *see* it like I was there with her, and she did something to the amulet." Drew held it up to show her the light.

Celeste touched the jewel. "It's back, I see."

Drew filled her in on the spell that had appeared and the bright red paint that looked so much like blood...

"It's strange, like a warning of some kind, but why the painting?" With a stern expression, Celeste locked eyes with Drew, her tone resembling a mother's warning to her child. "If I were you, I'd stay away from the lighthouse and keep that jewel close until you can figure out the message."

The temptation to tell Celeste about Taj's nightmare was strong, but she couldn't betray her promise. "It always comes back to Neptune Point, doesn't it?" Drew said. Celeste had sold the property, and a construction company had moved forward to rebuild the Keeper's house after tearing down the remnants of the old one after the fire destroyed it. "Have you been back?"

Celeste stood and tapped her fingers on the table's rough surface. "I did what needed to be done, what Enid wanted, and now, I keep my distance. If burning that old house to the ground hasn't shaken the curse away, I don't know what will, but if *the* Aurora has found her way to you, there's got to be a reason. Maybe she just wants to share her story and finally found a medium who'll listen."

"What should I do?"

"What should you do," Celeste repeated, exhaling through her nose. "That's a good question. Maybe nothing just yet; we've all got our own gifts. You've got your grandmother's book, that amulet around your neck, and a window to the other side no one else can see. You don't have to navigate this world alone anymore; you've learned a few things. What do your instincts tell you?"

Something horrible is about to happen.

Drew's stomach twisted in knots. She'd never thought of herself as someone who overreacted, but every ounce of her being urged her to proceed with caution. "Just like you said, I'm being warned."

"And this ghost who's currently attached to you—"

"Jules."

"The girl who doesn't know she's dead, yes?" With her back turned to Drew, Celeste opened and closed the cabinet doors lining the back wall.

"She's not really a girl, more like her early or mid-twenties."

"Is she the only one vying for your attention at the present moment?"

"Just her. Until Aurora."

The same eerie feeling of being watched nudged her again, but no one else was around. She'd banished the witch hunter to some otherworld abyss, and Ori was gone—despite her wish to have him back, if even for one more conversation.

Opening a small drawer in a display cabinet, Celeste carefully retrieved a blue, oddly shaped rock. The blue rock had streaks of white stone throughout, with gold pieces embedded along the middle. "Lapis lazuli. Hold it first."

Drew held it in her palm, clutching her fingers around it, but the stone remained still and cold. "Should something be happening? It's not working."

"Dear mother nature of all things, Drew, have some patience. Close your eyes and *feel*."

Tightening her grip on the small stone in her palm, she focused her energy, magic—whatever existed inside of her, toward the stone. "Did it work?"

"It's the stone of breath. Breathe."

One of Drew's eyes opened. "Breathe? Like on the rock?"

"Sure, on the rock, around the rock." Celeste folded her arms across her chest, fighting a smile. "Just breathe, honey."

Taking a deep breath, Drew exhaled over the stone in her hands. Heat surged beneath her skin and sizzled over the rock in a burst of sparkles before fading within seconds, turning the stone cold. Her eyes flew open. "Did you feel that?"

"Take it with you for a little extra dose of magic, will you? You'll know what to do with it when the time comes."

And back to cryptic Celeste.

Drew stuck it in her pocket. "Sure."

"Whatever all this is," Celeste said. "I'm here if you need me."

"I know you are." Drew pushed back from the table and hopped off the stool.

"You did good, sticking around this town, keeping the house. I'm proud of you, and your gran would be proud, too."

"I hope so, and this is the haunted town of witchy secrets, how could I leave all this behind?" Sarcasm laced Drew's words, but her lips curled into an amused smile.

Celeste rolled her eyes. "It has a way of pulling you back in, trust me."

The weight of regret would have been unbearable if she had gone through with selling the house. Life had somehow convinced her she was where she belonged, and things had been good... *calm* since her decision to keep the house and business. But amidst the peace, a relentless desperation clawed at her, urging her to hold on to the life she had built, unwilling to release its grip. Nothing was going to take it away from her.

Celeste crossed the small room and raised her hand above the row of pillar candles. Her stack of beaded bracelets jangled as she ran her hand over the candles, and tiny flames ignited on each as she passed by. "The magic is not gone."

"How'd you do that?"

"Focus and—"

"Intention. Right." Drew chewed her lip and stopped herself. The habit reminded her of her mother, and she didn't want to think of Joelle, or her persistent phone calls from a California jail.

Celeste waved her other hand over the candles, extinguishing them. She plucked the box of cupcakes from the table.

"The store is closed, and I'd like to go home to my air conditioning."

Drew followed her through the beaded curtain, but before they reached the front door, a sharp drop in temperature surrounded her. As welcome as the cooler air was in the heatwave, she braced herself for who was coming, but a certain ghost girl who refused to believe she was dead came to mind.

In one swift motion, Celeste snatched her keys and bright yellow purse from a chair that matched the vibrant hue of her dress and froze in place. "Is your friend back? Oh, she's nothing like Ori. Persistent one, isn't she?" She shook her head. "Lost. So lost."

"Tell me about it." The words slipped out sharper than Drew intended, but the lack of progress in helping Jules frustrated her. How could she help this one when the woman refused to believe she was dead?

"Honey, she needs to know the truth." Celeste switched off the shop's decorative stained-glass lamps.

"I've tried telling her, but she disappears crying."

"Then you're doing it wrong. Don't tell her. *Show* her."

"Show me what?" Jules appeared and followed Celeste toward the front door, trying to touch her arm, but her translucent hand went right through. Her bright jade eyes widened as she waved her arms, desperate for Celeste's attention. "Why is she ignoring me? So rude. I need to go home! If you're not going to help, can she?" Her husky tone hinted at a previous life as a singer in a rock band.

"She can't see you," Drew said. "I'm the only one who can see you because... you're *dead*." She softened her tone.

"Show her." Celeste stood near the front door with her hand on the handle.

Jules held her bare arms up to her ashen face, her lip quivering. Blood stains marked the collar of her t-shirt. She tried to run her hands over her hair, hanging just past her chin, but her fingers couldn't grasp the dark strands. "What's wrong with me?"

Drew moved close to the heartbroken dead girl and a burst of energy tingled under her skin from her neck to her hands. Jules covered her face, her shoulders shaking as she wept. This was the crying portion of the girl's visit.

Here we go again.

Celeste adjusted her stance, balancing the pink box, and raised an eyebrow.

"I'll try to show her." Drew rubbed her hands together and reached for Jules' face. Her hands passed through the dead girl's cheeks when she tried to touch them, leaving her with a chilling emptiness. The ghostly figure rippled like water and vanished, with Jules' anguished cries fading into a whisper.

Using her hip, Celeste pushed the door open. "She's gone, isn't she?" She held the door open for Drew to exit the store.

"So much for showing." The moment Drew stepped outside, intense heat and humidity clung to her hair and clothes.

"That girl is a mix of anxious terror, and a world of chaos, poor thing. Tragedy weighs heavy around her, like chains dragging her down, but she doesn't even know it. Keep trying. She needs help, and I'm afraid you're the only one who can give it." Celeste handed her the box of cupcakes and turned to lock the door.

With the box cradled in her arm, she stepped away from the door and shaded her eyes with her hand as she scanned the street. People filed into restaurant and pub patios, loosening ties, dress shirt buttons, and discarding suit jackets for a Friday after work, social hour before returning to their regular home lives with family, kids, houses, apartments... regular-people life.

As she passed by the alley between Little Mysteries and a high-end café for those who enjoyed paying obscene prices for a coffee, she caught a glimpse of a shadow out of the corner of her eye. She stepped to the side, pressing her back against the brick, holding her breath. Seagulls battled over garbage strewn in the alley corners as bicyclists zoomed along the parallel street at the end of the narrow road. A high-pitch ringing buzzed in her ears, growing louder before coming to an abrupt stop.

Silence fell around her, and a raspy, familiar voice spoke from beside her. "Danger is coming."

The voice belonged to Jack Morana, the dead lighthouse keeper, and Atlas Cliff's witch protector. But she hadn't seen or heard from Jack since the fire at Neptune Point when he had transformed from his usual raven appearance into his ghostly human one.

"Jasper won't be impressed if you drop those and he has to spend more time in that hot kitchen baking another dozen cupcakes." Celeste scooped the tilted box from Drew's hands. "What are you looking at?"

Drew blinked a few times to clear her vision, but no one was there. No Jack, no raven. "Nothing." She lifted her hair away from her neck, but no breeze or cool air arrived for relief.

"Where are you parked?" Celeste adjusted her purse, holding her keys in her hand. "I'm behind the building."

"I walked over. Nico has my car. It was making a noise." Drew stole another glance down the narrow alley again, but the jangle of a bicycle bell and a group of kids' laughter replaced Jack's raspy voice.

Celeste reached her arm around Drew's shoulders and gave her a quick squeeze, gazing in the same direction as Drew. "I've got to run before I melt into a puddle on the ground. Don't worry, she'll be back. You just have to—"

"Show her."

"Exactly. Bye, Drew." Celeste strolled down the alley toward the back parking lot, singing in a low, melodic tone.

Any other day, Celeste's singing would soothe Drew's soul like a lullaby, but not today.

47

FIVE

Spinning Drew's keys in his fingers, Nico held them up and leaned against the wall near the front counter of the Tough Cookie. "Fixed for now and parked out back, but I'm waiting for a couple parts, and I'll take it in once they arrive." He flashed a dimpled smile.

She couldn't resist that smile. It got her every time. Taking the keys from him, she ran her fingers over the rose gold compass he'd given her for Christmas and clutched it in her palm before grabbing his face and kissing him. Tingles ran from her chest down to her toes.

He leaned back with a mischievous gaze through thick lashes. "Are you off yet?"

"I've spent the last hour with Celeste, and I've got to stay and help J finish closing up, but I can't wait for tonight. Beach bonfire and barbecue." She tucked the keys in the pocket of the black apron around her waist and stood under the air conditioning unit. "I need cool ocean air, this heat is brutal."

Nico brushed a loose strand of her red hair out of her eyes.

"How are you getting home? Want to wait here?" she asked.

"Taj is on his way… unless you change your mind and want to come home with me now?"

"You are temping, but I can't." She'd bailed on Jasper twice in the past month, leaving him solo for the Saturday morning breakfast prep, and couldn't do it again. And she had a stop to make before heading home. She rubbed her forehead. "I have paintings to drop off at the gallery before Claudia sends me another reminder." With a tilt of her head, she looked up at him and smiled. "Go hang out with Taj. I'll pick up Piper and we'll meet you at the house."

Home. Gran's old coastal house had evolved into a gathering haven for her and Jasper's friends.

She followed Nico to the door, holding it open as a red jeep pulled up to the curb in front of the bakery. Taj waved from the driver's seat as he eyed her. If he'd had another nightmare about her, he hadn't messaged. She'd been walking a fine line between wanting to ask him and giving him space to figure things out on his own.

Nico leaned down to kiss her, his lips brushing against hers. The oppressive heatwave paled compared to the intense heat radiating between them.

"My favorite couple. Do you two ever stop?" Jasper teased as he carried a tray of sugar packets through the swinging door and placed it on the counter. "Hi, Nico." He smiled and waved to Taj through the window.

She patted Nico's chest. "I'll see you at the house," he said, turning to leave.

Locking the door, she flipped the closed sign to face outside and tidied up the front café, resetting the handful of tables along the window and back wall with mugs and saucers.

An alternative rock song blared from a speaker on a corner shelf as she entered the kitchen and helped Jasper scrub down the surfaces. When they were done, she wiped sweat from her brow and tossed the paper towels in a trash can on her way to the closet-sized bathroom. Closing the door did little to drown out Jasper's off-key voice as he sang along to the music, but he kept things fun and light.

Her shirt stuck to her, and beads of perspiration trickled down her back. Submerging herself in the ocean would be sweet relief, but she settled for splashing cold water on her face and neck, with a re-application of deodorant. She topped it off with a spray of subtle jasmine scented perfume she kept stowed in a bag under the sink.

Claudia wouldn't be impressed with her frayed cut-off shorts and simple tank top, despite her best efforts to look presentable for a stop at Tate Gallery. She angled her face down, examining her reflection in the mirror. Her freckles had expanded across her cheeks, blending in with her sun-kissed skin. In the dead of winter, Gran had affectionately called them *Bricini*, their vivid hues standing out against her pale complexion. Releasing the elastic holding her messy hair, she finger-combed the red tangles, smoothing the frizz from her long waves. She gathered her hair back into a neater ponytail, securing a strand of hair around the elastic for a more polished look.

Well, Claudia. This will have to do.

She exited the bathroom as refreshed as she could be without a shower.

Jasper hung his chef jacket on the hook by the back door. Judging by his wardrobe change of pinstripe shorts and a matching button-up shirt, with his wavy brown hair slicked back off his face, he had other plans that didn't include going home. "Ready to charge out of this Popsicle stand?

"More than ready. Big plans tonight?"

Jasper flipped a switch, engulfing the kitchen in darkness, except for the range hood light in the windowless space. "I'm meeting Danny for dinner before a 7:30 appointment."

"That's specific. What kind of appointment?"

He tapped his lips with his fingertips, not meeting her eyes. He was holding back, debating telling her something, and she had that sinking feeling things were about to change. She braced herself for his response. He'd been looking for a place of his own, but the search had died off over the past month. And as happy as she was that he'd found love again, a selfish part of her, the part she wished she could squash, didn't want him to leave.

"Just tell me, J. What is it?"

"I didn't want to say anything unless it was a solid plan. I like to keep the up in the air stuff, up in the air."

"It's me. You know I need the up in the air stuff. I need to prepare for when the up in the air comes crashing down to the ground. I can take it, whatever it is."

"Okay, fine. I'm telling you because you're like my sister, and I can't not tell you big things happening in my life."

She could almost hear the countdown of the next life change about to happen.

Three, two...

"I'm going to see a house with Danny, and not to rent, to own."

One.

"Drew, don't look at me like that."

She concealed whatever facial expression was giving her inner sadness away. "What? I'm not looking at you like anything."

"You know you are. You look like a child whose pet just died."

The urge to bite her bottom lip gripped her as she curled it between her teeth and released it, biting her cheek instead. "I'm happy for you. I really am. This is amazing news."

"Really? You mean it?"

She meant every word. He wanted this new life, and she wanted it for him. "I'm just sad to see you go, that's all."

"I don't want this to ruin your night—"

"It won't, it's not, promise. This is about you and your happiness. I'll adjust. I know how to do that, I've had practice." She embraced him in a hug. "And hey, I won't have to listen to you belting out songs you don't know the words to or clean up your half empty coffee cups all over the house."

"You lie. You love my singing."

"You got me there." She hugged him tighter before releasing him. "I'm going to miss you."

"Good grief, nothing is set in stone yet. We're just looking, okay?" Jasper placed his hands on either of her shoulders. "It's after 5, closing time. Go home and make out with that hot boyfriend of yours on the beach. Summer has arrived, my friend. If you don't stop and enjoy it"—he clapped his hands together—"poof. Gone. And we'll be in a snowy deep freeze once again."

And she'd be traveling back and forth to Boston for school again, missing Nico. He wasn't wrong about the poof, gone part.

Grabbing her cross-body purse from the counter, she draped it over her shoulders and followed Jasper to the back door. She picked up the stack of wrapped paintings and stepped from the air-conditioned kitchen into the sauna outside. The amulet thrummed against her skin; balancing the paintings, she held the stone up as vines of light swirled. Perhaps the amulet could pick up on her emotions like the mood ring Gran used to wear. She still had that ring, along with some of Gran's costume jewelry, in a music box on her dresser.

Citrus wafted from a tree-shaped air freshener inside Jasper's Volkswagen bus as he opened the door. He wiped the dashboard, despite there being no visible dust. Nico had replaced parts and restored it in good working condition after Jasper was ready to set fire to it over the winter. It's what Nico did; fix things that would otherwise be beyond repair.

Jasper closed his eyes, raised his head, and extended his hands. He took a deep breath and exhaled. With what air, Drew had no clue. The heat sucked the oxygen from her lungs.

"Do ya feel that?" he asked.

"Hell has consumed Atlas Cliffs?" Popping open the trunk, she placed the canvases inside, careful not to let them fall.

He dropped his hands to his sides and placed his duffel bag in the backseat of his van. "Not just the heat. Life around us is good. I love it."

"That's what scares me. When things go too well—"

"You panic. But I promised you I'd stay with you at Gran's for a year, and that won't change. If I move out, I'll pay up until the end of the year, and when you're back at college, I'll still help, just like always."

She shut the trunk and adjusted her purse. "That's not what I mean, and I won't let you do that. I knew it wouldn't last forever; I'll just miss having you around. Who am I gonna watch movies and eat junk food with?"

"Me, ya goof, or I'm willing to bet Nico would join you any day, any time." He tossed her long, red ponytail over her shoulder. "Look, we'll still do those things, but living with you was a temporary solution to a severe lack of affordable housing, and a deep need for connection. I'm not leaving town... I don't ever want to leave town. You, me, Piper—we're family now, Drew. You're stuck with us. Stop worrying and stop chewing your lip. You wanted me to call you out on it."

She released her hold on her bottom lip. "It makes me feel better." She unlocked her car and tossed her bag in the back seat. "Do you think you'll ever get married? You've only known Danny for six months, how do you know when it's the one?" She used air quotes. She hadn't thought of marriage with Nico or anyone, but she loved him—couldn't imagine life without him.

"Relationships are funny. They need time to grow, but at the same time, when you know, you know... you know?"

"You sound like Gran."

"I speak truth," he said. "When you know, you know, and trust me, six months, two years, or ten, I know, and if you're honest with yourself, so do you."

"I'm nowhere near ready for forever with anyone. I'm barely ready for forever with myself and the ghosts who won't leave me alone."

More like, no one will ever want forever with me... The woman who talks to dead people.

Jasper rubbed his smooth chin as he leaned against the van and crossed one foot over the other like he was posing for a high-end fashion magazine. "What are you so scared of? Nico's not going anywhere. He's been living above his mother's garage for how long? That might end when the house sells, but he won't leave this town or you."

The thought of asking Nico to move in with her had crossed her mind. But if he did, it would mean a much bigger commitment, and if their forever ended, it would break her heart.

"Nico will figure it out and I'll be there for him. We're still young, I don't want to make plans and promises that'll just end up broken."

"I was nineteen when I met Ori, and if he hadn't..." Jasper cleared his throat and looked down at his feet. The gray pavement contrasted with his white slip-on canvas shoes. He wiped his eyes and faced her. "If Ori hadn't died, we'd be *together*-together. Like the forever kind."

"I believe you would've made it too. I just... I don't know if a relationship that lasts forever will happen for me with all the baggage following me around. Wouldn't you get sick of your partner pushing you aside to help dead people?"

Jasper made a face like he'd eaten something sour. "Sweet, gentle, Jesus, no! What you can do, who you are, is a—"

"Freak of nature?" She smiled.

"A freak of nature who has a cool ass gift."

"Gift or not, it's who I am. But what does that mean for my future? Can I have a family with someone? Bringing kids into my world would be like the Wild West, and I don't even know if I ever want kids."

"The world is already the Wild West, Drew." Jasper crossed his arms. "Tell me something. When you think of Nico, do you feel like you can't get enough time with him? Can't get enough of laughing with him, kissing him? He's a dreamboat, and the man wouldn't leave your side if you screamed at him to go.

Doesn't matter how old you are, you love him, and he feels the same way about you. Don't over think, just go with it. The rest will work out."

"What if it doesn't?"

"It already is! Look. Can I break this all down?" He brushed away his dark waves from his forehead and swept a hand over her in a grand Jasper gesture.

"Do I have a choice?"

"Actually, you don't. I've stayed quiet for too long. We've been living under the same gorgeous Cape Cod roof now for months. I say this from a place of love, because I fucking love you, Drew. You're always waiting for the other shoe to fall off the horse and hit the ground. I think you're terrified of being abandoned, and you push people who love you away. But no one is leaving you again."

Phrases from countless hours of therapy overwhelmed her mind. Abandonment issues stemming from her mother leaving, her father's absence, and having to step up and help her grandmother take care of an old house instead of growing up like a regular teenager. "You sound like a therapist." Avoiding eye contact with Jasper, she grabbed her water bottle from her bag in the car.

"Not a therapist, a friend who's gotten to know you well. Do me a favor? Please stop worrying and let yourself be happy?

You're the copper-haired queen of a very impressive king-dom. Own that shit and have some fun."

Drew nearly choked on the water. Her eyes watered as laughter escaped. "I feel more like the court jester, but thanks. And I really am in a good place, I don't have a fear of *being abandoned*."

I don't think so, anyway... Do I?

Jasper smoothed frizzy hairs on her head and narrowed a gaze on her. "Just keep it in mind when your first instinct is to push someone who cares about you away."

"I don't push people away... At least, not anymore."

Living in the same house as Jasper had opened the door to her deepest insecurities, but he was wrong about the abandonment fears. Instead of pushing Nico away, she held onto him tightly, not wanting to let him go.

Jasper raised an eyebrow but kept silent, climbing into his van. He fanned himself with his hand and rolled the window down. "All right, rock star, have fun tonight." He made a peace sign with his fingers as he drove away.

As she fumbled with her keys, a cluster of tiny birds flew off a tree branch like a burst of confetti. Beyond the chain-link fence, a shadow darted, followed by a scream echoing in her ears. She spun around, but no one was there. Icy fingers wrapped around her wrist, hitching her breath. Stepping backward, she yanked her hand away from the unseen grip as a tingling sensation crawled under her skin, intensifying.

"Who's here?"

In a swirl of mist, Jules materialized in front of her. She had her hands on her hips and narrowed her gaze on Drew. "You're the only person who can see me, aren't you? Why is that? I try to talk to people, and they walk right through me." She held her hands up, but they resembled a mesh of mist like sprinkles. "*Through* me. I need to know what you know."

Drew exhaled a heavy breath. Continuous encounters with the dead shattered her hopes of hanging onto a long-lasting relationship.

Six

Drew braced herself for the crying and disappearing act, but this time Jules didn't vanish in a puddle of tears. She stood firmly in place, balling her fists at her sides. "Well? Can you help me or not?" Her captivating green eyes gleamed with their own inner light.

Every time Jules appeared, she paced back and forth, never allowing Drew to engage in conversation. Jules' eyes narrowed on her, not just open to listening, but demanding answers, and a debate raged in Drew's mind. She needed to make it to Claudia's gallery before closing time and deliver her promised art, but the ghost woman wanted to talk to her.

She lit up her phone. A half-hour window remained until the gallery closed at six.

The small parking lot was empty, but the sidewalk toward the front of the building bustled with people, and her skin burned under the scorching sun. She had to show Jules she was dead, but this wasn't the place, not with the Friday evening downtown crowd of people gathering for dinner and drinks along the waterfront, not unless she wanted a sudden curious audience.

"Drew, is it? That's your name, right? Isn't that a boy's name?" Jules resumed pacing, but this time with determined steps without tears. "Doesn't matter. That woman in the store said you could show me something, can you?"

Drew's ability to see visions had improved. Maybe it would work on Jules this time. "I think so."

"Do you think, or do you know? Because I'm sick of feeling like I don't exist with zero control on where I go, when all I want is to go home." She attempted to push her dark, chin-length hair behind her ears, but her fingers passed right through her head, unable to grasp the loose strands hanging over her forehead. "See? I don't get it. Why can't I *do* anything? And look at these dirty clothes." Her hands gestured over herself unable to make contact. "I should be wearing a linen suit in a law office, not... *this*."

"You were a lawyer?"

Jules stopped moving and stared at Drew. "Not were, *am* a lawyer—well, kind of. I'm in law school. Doing an internship this summer." Jules shook her head. "*That's* what you gathered from what I just said? Did you not hear that I can't feel my own body or find my home?"

Until this moment, Jules had kept her personality hidden under tears and a disappearing act, and the last thing Drew wanted was to drag this out for months, the way she'd done with Ori. Being around him had been easy compared to Jules. Drew would forever consider Ori a friend, but her doubts ran high when it came to the newest visitor to her ghostly world.

"You don't say much, do you?" Jules said. "Come on, what are you waiting for? Let's do this."

"Not here, not now."

Jules spun around. "Yes, here and now. What is happening to me, where is home, and why do I look like this?"

"You're dead. You're stuck somewhere in the middle, but you are not alive anymore. I've been trying to tell you, but you disappear."

"Stop saying that, telling me I'm dead." Wringing her hands and trying to pick at her fingernails, Jules paced back and forth again. But rather than vanish, she shifted into her human form. She glanced around the parking lot and glared at Drew. "Are you dead?"

"No. And your hands aren't doing the thing anymore. Try touching your hair."

"If you're not dead, how is it you and I are having this conversation?" The pacing stopped as Jules examined her hands and brushed her fingers through her hair. "How did I do that? Tell me what you know." She stomped her bare feet, and they echoed on the pavement. Her gaze turned downward. "I'm me again, but where are my shoes? The only time I would ever dress like this or be without even a pair of sandals is if I were walking my dog on the beach."

Sadness gripped Drew's chest and throat. This woman once had a life with a career and a dog, and she didn't know it was all gone. "You're always you, Jules, but you're not... alive anymore, not like you were."

The enchanting, throaty call of a raven flying by startled Drew as it landed on the roof of the Tough Cookie and ruffled the thick feathers along its neck. If Jack was trying to get her attention, he was doing a terrible job communicating. If she didn't figure out how to help Jules, the woman would vanish from sight again, perhaps spiraling into a fit of tears and confusion.

The constant bustling of people made it impossible for her to stand with her hands on an invisible entity's face. "Can you sit in the car?" Drew opened the passenger door.

Jules glanced from her to the door and folded her arms. "Why? I'm not getting in a car with someone I don't even know. I've seen Dateline."

"Jules, come on. Work with me here. I won't hurt you, I can't hurt someone who's already dead."

"Can't we just talk?" Dropping her hands, exasperated, Jules turned her back to Drew. "Forget it, I'll find my own way home—"

"Not without my help. Please, I can't help you if you don't trust me, even a little. I get it, okay? It's weird but let me try what the lady in the shop said."

"Show me?"

"*Show* you. Exactly. But see all those people?"

"All those people who don't know I exist." Jules hung her head, her chin touching her chest, tears erupting again as she reverted to her ghost-like appearance.

Drew's hand passed through Jules' arm as she reached for her. This wouldn't work unless she could touch her. "Can you focus..." *On being a human?* She couldn't hurt the crying woman's feelings. "Focus on me. Look at my hands, they're flesh and skin. Focus on your hands looking like this. Can you try that for me?"

Jules' head rose, and she stretched her fingers over Drew's hand, sending a chilled intangible touch.

"I can't do this," Jules muttered.

"Yes, you can." Drew stole a glance behind her, but the people walking by didn't notice, not that it made a difference anymore. She helped dead people. The locals sometimes gossiped about her with falsehoods of rituals and ceremonies, but their close mindedness was none of her business. She shut the passenger door and stood in front of Jules. "You can do this." She wiggled her fingers toward Jules. "Take my hands."

Jules concentrated on Drew's hands, but as she approached to grab them, she lost her balance and tumbled through Drew. "Do you have any idea how frustrating this is? If what you say is true, if I'm dead? I'm definitely in hell."

"Hell doesn't exist. Try again." Drew spun around to face her new ghost companion again and held out her hands.

"How do you know?"

"How do I know what? Come on, Jules, focus."

"That hell doesn't exist."

"I don't really know. I just don't believe it does." The memory of sending Hathorne to a realm she knew nothing about filled her mind, along with the screams of lost souls inside the witch hunter's portal. But the notion of a Heaven and Hell never felt right to her. It was something different, much more expansive and complicated.

Jules touched her hair and ran her fingers along her blood-stained t-shirt, looking up at Drew with widened eyes. "Why the blood? It feels like I don't exist."

Drew refused to allow Jules to succumb to tears again. This woman was going to understand she was dead, and remember something, anything, so Drew could help her find peace. Maybe Enid and Ori would be waiting on the other side for her. "You exist to me, okay? I see you, and I'm going to get you home." She wiped sweat from her forehead and held out her hands, this time with firm determination.

With closed eyes, Jules stomped her feet against the ground. She attempted to pick at her fingernails again as she counted down from twenty.

With a sigh, Drew released her hands and let them hang by her sides. Her face flushed with heat. At this rate, she would burn to a crisp.

"Twelve, eleven—" Jules said.

"What are you doing?"

"Shh. Counting. Focusing like you asked. Do I need to start over?"

"No, please don't. Carry on." Drew pulled her phone from her pocket. She had twenty minutes before Claudia's persistent calls started, asking where the paintings were, and Piper would be next, wondering why she hadn't shown up yet.

"Two, one." Jules reached her hands out, but as Drew reached for them, a quick flutter of movement turned the ghost woman's silhouette into a more human form, and she grasped Drew's hands tightly. Her eyes flew open, and she stared at her arms. For the first time since Drew had encountered her, a smile that could stop time spread across the woman's face, and her eyes took on a new ethereal light reminding Drew of Ori's angelic moments.

The amulet emitted a burning radiance, as if it possessed its own sun. "Come here." Drew inched closer to her, fixated on the ominous dark stains of blood stretching across Jules' shirt and down her side. The palms of her hands tingled, and she reached for the ghost woman's face.

Jules stepped back, her smile dropping. "What are you doing?"

"I know this sound strange, but I have to put my hands on your face."

Jules linked her arms across her chest, her eyes glowing with an otherworldly light as she glared at Drew. "Is this going to hurt?"

Drew recalled the times before when Jack and Ori had done the same. The intense sensation was uncomfortable, like the way her body ached after a long shift waiting tables or a day of surfing, but she always tolerated it, and she doubted the dead could feel pain. "It won't hurt you, but I'm going to show you."

I'm hopefully going to show myself what happened, too.

Jules dropped her arms. "Fine, go ahead, I'm ready." She lifted her hands as they glitched like a bad radio connection. "Better be quick. I don't know what's happening."

An explosion of fireworks shattered underneath Drew's skin as she placed her hands on Jules' face. Drew's breath hitched, and she coughed, almost choking.

Okay, maybe sometimes the pain is more intense than others.

Jules reached up and grasped Drew's hands against her cheeks. "Do you feel that?"

A sudden jolt shot through Drew's head, forcing her to close her eyes. She gritted her teeth as the electric current subsided. When it cleared, an image took shape, like a Polaroid photo from decades ago as the picture went from a white-out to a moving image of a car speeding around a turn, chased by a black sedan. With headlights the only source of light, the little hatchback, not unlike her own, spun out of control and careened into the guardrail. The black sedan pulled up behind it, the doors opened, and three men climbed out adjusting jackets, carrying guns as they swarmed the car. Smoke poured from the hood as the driver's side door opened and a young woman fell to the ground. She lifted her head, gripping her shoulder as blood pooled through her fingers and around her collarbone, soaking into her shirt. As she scrambled to her bare feet, Drew transported in front of her, staring into her terrified face.

She was witnessing Jules' death.

One man grabbed Jules by the hair and forced her to walk over the rocky cliffs as she begged them to spare her life. Her frantic screams echoed over and over, "Why me? Why me? What did I do?"

Drew charged at the men, reaching for the young woman, grabbing at her hands to pull her back, but her efforts were useless as the man pushed Jules over the rocks, sending her body plummeting into the black abyss below. The crashing waves masked the sound of her slight frame hitting the surface. The men pushed the idling car over the rocky cliffs to crash into the waves below.

Drew opened her eyes, ending the vision, and a throbbing ache permeated from her neck to her ears until she dropped her hands and leaped back. Fear shifted into panic as a sharp pain tore through her chest. She forced herself to take deep breaths as she leaned against her car door and slid down to the hot pavement with shaking legs.

Jules crouched beside Drew. Tears streamed over her pale cheeks. "I want to see more. Show me more," Jules begged, her voice shaking through sobs.

With her throat feeling like it was closing over, cutting off her airway, Drew couldn't speak.

"Please, keep going, Drew!" Jules pleaded.

"I can't." Drew wiped tears from her eyes.

"I died." Jules' body sparkled, and she locked eyes with Drew as a look of devastation crossed her face. "I'm really dead."

"I'm sorry, Jules. I'm so sorry."

"Who hurt me? Who would do this? I demand you tell me right now." Jules bounded up from the pavement, grabbing at her arms and head. "No, not again—" She vanished, leaving a fine mist in her wake.

The raven flew overhead and landed on the roof of Drew's car. Laughter burst out from the street as a group of teenagers walked by. Life continued around her, oblivious to the horror she'd witnessed.

The black sedan reminded her of one terrifying man, even though he hadn't appeared in the vision.

Dominic Sloan.

Sweat pricked along the back of her neck as she scrambled off the ground and yanked the amulet off her head. She presented the shimmering jewel to the winged creature. "Why are you here, Jack? Because this isn't helping."

With a shrill screech, the bird took flight and disappeared into the trees.

She'd convinced Jules she was dead, but what was her next move? How was she supposed to help her cross over when she didn't even know the way?

SEVEN

Emerging from her car in front of Tate Gallery, Drew adjusted her denim shorts where they stuck to her skin. The haunting vision of Jules' death pervaded her senses, haunting her with a sick feeling in her stomach, and she couldn't help but scan the busy boardwalk for threats. Tourists flocked to restaurant patios, snapping pictures of the bustling scene as they merged with familiar locals, all enjoying their tall, colorful drinks with umbrellas and lemon slices.

Her purse vibrated as she draped it across her body and opened the trunk. Her phone hadn't stopped buzzing with notifications in the five-minute drive from the Tough Cookie.

She retrieved it from her purse and responded to Piper with a status update, and Claudia with an, "almost there". Given the recent encounter with Jules, being five minutes late didn't seem so bad.

Atlas Cliffs lacked the anonymity of a big city. A young woman plunging to her death had to have made the news. Turning her back to the trunk, Drew did a quick search on her phone. She typed as many phrases as she could think of—"Woman dies in Atlas Cliffs", "Woman pushed off a cliff to her death", "Jules obituary"—but they all turned up nothing. When she typed, "Atlas Cliffs woman murdered," the search results revealed the names Iris and Dominic Sloan, formerly known as Ben Morana from Neptune Point. Panic tightened its grip around her stomach, and she closed the search window and locked her phone before tossing it back into her purse.

If Sloan had been involved in Jules' death, he was already behind bars, so what else was keeping her here? Unless no one knew who had murdered her. But if the woman once lived and died in Atlas Cliffs, there had to be a way to find out her name and who her family was—even if someone had covered something up. Perhaps it wasn't Sloan, but someone else who had killed her, leaving her family desperate for answers.

Until she could figure out the mystery, she would shake off the horrible vision, move forward, and have a fun night. Her

New Year's resolution had been to have more fun and less chaos. How could she live a normal life if she allowed the dead to consume her with theirs?

She stretched her neck from side to side with a cringe-inducing crack before removing the wrapped paintings from the trunk to add to her growing portfolio at Tate Gallery. The extra cash from selling her paintings covered some of the house's maintenance costs. Nico believed he could make a few repairs to the roof for another year, but she was trying to postpone using Gran's savings for as long as possible.

What was she going to do once Jasper left? She could rent out the room to someone else... but having a stranger live with her in Gran's house gave her a pit in her stomach. There'd have to be another way. She thought about Nico again and imagined him there with her, always, but the last thing she wanted was for him to agree to live with her out of necessity. They hadn't even talked about living together. He had his own shit to deal with between his mother selling the house, moving out of his childhood home, and running a brand-new garage in town with his father. She refused to burden him with more, and messing with an amazing relationship wasn't an option. Normally, nothing went this well for her. Plus, she loved Nico. She'd figure it out. Figuring things out on her own was one of her best attributes. Or so she'd like to believe.

She navigated the cobble stone walkway toward the entrance for Tate Gallery with both paintings in her hands.

"What are you carrying? I'd offer to help, but I'm not exactly alive," Jules' familiar voice chimed from beside her. Drew spun around, tightening her grip on the paintings.

Jules sidled up to her with her hands stuffed in the pockets of her baggy jeans, rolled up at the ankles. She was in her human form, and if people could see her, she'd blend right in with the locals except for the bloodstains and bare feet. Her solemn face triggered visions of moments before being thrown off the cliff, sending a shiver crawling through Drew despite the oppressive heat.

Jules waved her hands in front of Drew. "Hello, remember me? I know you can still see me. You sure look like you can. What are those?"

"I can still see you, and they're paintings." Drew adjusted the canvases in her arms. She had a feeling Jules would become a regular presence now that she was aware of the truth. The faster she helped her cross over, the sooner she could resume her summer of fun plans.

"You're an artist? Are you any good?"

Not really.

"Good enough, I guess," Drew lowered her voice, trying to make sure no one watched her talking to herself.

Jules' face twisted in a mix of curiosity and skepticism as she studied the white building with the door painted in a vibrant pink design matching the Tate Gallery sign hanging over a massive display window. "They hang your work here? The place with the hot pink thing on the door like a flamingo on drugs?"

Drew faced the front of the building and adjusted the paintings, tilting her head. Flamingo on drugs? "That's the one. She's a friend of mine. We sort of have a deal."

A couple strolled hand in hand, giving her an odd look, and Drew smiled and waved as they walked by. Leaning against a weathered pillar at the bottom of the stone steps, she positioned herself to shield her face from the prying eyes of curious onlookers.

Jules maneuvered around so she could stand in front of her. "You're lucky to have friends and a life still ahead of you. I feel like I've been asleep for years and suddenly I'm a restless ball of shit and can't find my way home, and the first person I meet informs me I'm dead." Jules paced back and forth with a death grip on her fingers as she picked at her nails. "I wish I believed you when you told me. I wasted time not listening, and when you showed me what I'd been keeping buried... it hurt. I'm angry." She released her fingers. "No, I'm more than angry. I'm a pissed off ball of *rage*."

Drew's phone buzzed again. This time, her ring tone accompanied the vibration from inside her purse. It had to be Claudia, wondering where she was, but she let it ring. "I'm sorry to hurt you, but I didn't know how else to tell you."

"Are you kidding me? I needed to be smacked back into my new reality, clearly. Look at me." Jules pulled at her T-shirt and looked down at herself. "I will find out who murdered me, evidence must exist somewhere. Do you think I've been dead for long?"

"Long enough that I couldn't find anything, but I'll keep trying." Drew positioned the paintings higher to cover her mouth as she talked. "Try to remember, okay? I don't know why you forgot, or much about how it works, but anything you can think of about your death, or who you are, it'll help."

Jules tucked her hair behind her ears. "I need your word that you won't lie to me if you find out something, and that you swear you'll get me out of this... stuck place, between where I am and where I should be."

Drew adjusted the awkward paintings. If the acrylic paint melted through the bubble wrap in this heat, Claudia would have a fit when she opened the protective plastic. "You have my word, I won't lie to you. You can trust me."

Jules narrowed her gaze on her and twisted her mouth. "Trust? Don't use big words unless you're ready to back them up. Do you solemnly swear you're going to help me, no matter the cost?" Jules lowered her raspy tone.

"You really do sound like a lawyer," Drew said.

"Almost lawyer, and I need you to say it."

"I solemnly swear I will help you no matter the cost, but right now, I need to get these inside the gallery before she sees me and comes running outside yelling."

She had made a lot of promises. The business, the house, college, Nico, now Jules, and even the occasional local begging for her to connect them with their loved one. She wasn't sure she'd be able to juggle all the balls in the air without them crashing down on her.

A woman slowed down as she walked by and glared at Drew. "Witch," she muttered under her breath. When Gran was alive, she had been a regular customer of the Tough Cookie. While she had her moments of rudeness, she had never been so direct before.

Jules' head snapped up, and she followed the woman. "What did you just say to her?"

The new ghost woman was a feisty one. "She can't hear you," Drew called after her.

With her face twisted in an appalled expression, the woman strutted away, tightly gripping an over-sized handbag. Someone would always judge her for what they didn't understand, but Drew was learning to brush off the ignorance.

Jules caught up to her as she climbed the steps to the entrance of the Tate Gallery. "Aren't you going to stand up for yourself? How can she talk to you like that? How can you let her?"

"Because it's true."

"What do you mean?" A smile spread across Jules' face. "You're a *witch*?" She ran her fingers over her hair. "Why didn't you tell me you're a witch? This is good. This is very, very good. You can definitely help me." She counted on her fingers, reciting a lengthy list of expectations she had of Drew, but as her voice faded, so did her presence.

Celeste's voice echoed in Drew's mind, like a distant memory from when they'd first met.

Be careful of labels.

The lack of understanding among some locals was palpable. Being labeled a witch didn't reflect the person she was, despite the terrible misconceptions surrounding the word. And did any of that really matter?

Let it go.

Fumbling with the door handle, Drew muttered under her breath. "If you can hear me, Ori, please show yourself. Doesn't have to be for long, I promise I won't ask you do to anything, I just miss you." She almost gave up with the handle and bent down to set the paintings on the stoop when the door swung open and someone reached their hands out, picking up both canvases before retreating with their back to her.

Wiping her damp hair off her forehead, she stepped inside the gallery. Her skin pricked with goosebumps as the cool air encompassed her bare arms and legs. Steps framed with a glass railing wound up to a second level, with floors so clean, lights reflected off the tiles. The man leaning the paintings against the counter had his back to her, but she'd know him anywhere. Turning around to face her, Shane raised an eyebrow over his icy blue eyes.

The last time she'd seen him, Nico had given him a bloody nose. "What are you doing here?" she asked.

"Hello to you too. I'm working here for the summer."

"Here? In an art gallery? Why?"

"I figured if I couldn't have you in my life, I could admire your artwork." He smirked at her.

Her mouth dropped open as she racked her brain for something clever to snap back at him. Was he going to be in Atlas Cliffs all summer? *Longer?*

"Jesus, Drew, relax, I'm kidding. I needed a job and Claudia offered. She's practically living with her boyfriend, so guess who gets an apartment for the summer?" He leaned against a counter made entirely of glass with an intricate sculpture of a castle inside the case.

"Don't lean on that, please." High heels clicked on the staircase as Claudia made her way down like a graceful... flamingo. It was all Drew could think about after Jules' comment.

Claudia had spun her blonde locks into a graceful bun, with a few wisps of hair framing her face. Her red painted lips complimented her porcelain skin, and she had lashes for days as her gaze swept over Drew. "It's good you're late. We closed ten minutes ago, and no one is here to see our featured local artist looking like a hot mess."

"I'm happy I can count on you for a boost of confidence, Claudia." Drew stuffed her hands in her pockets, taking a deep breath and biting her lip to avoid lashing out. "It's hot out," she added. She was here to drop off the paintings and leave.

"I'm so excited to see these." Claudia crouched down, careful to keep her legs together in her knee length sundress with metal clasps at the shoulders. She handled the first one like she was holding a fragile doll as she stood and carried it over to a large rectangular table. "Shane, bring me the other one, and be careful with it."

He wiped his hands on his black jeans—classic Shane, black jeans all year round—and handed Claudia the second piece of artwork, unwrapping it as he gave it to her. Drew hadn't expected Shane would be in town for the summer; his living in Boston for the rest of the year while she attended college had been close enough. She wouldn't be able to avoid him if he worked for Claudia at the gallery.

"Careful!" Claudia scolded.

Shane scowled. "Relax, Claudia, nothing's going to happen to it. If I'm going to work here, you can't breathe down my neck every time I do something."

Drew backed up, planning her escape. "If you don't need me, I've got to get going—"

"Wait! You're not leaving until I share my big news." Claudia's pursed red lips transformed into a broad smile, showcasing her impeccable white teeth, and her blue eyes sparkled under curled lashes.

For the first time, a striking resemblance stood out between Claudia and Shane. The same features that reminded Drew of the father they shared. She shuddered at the thought of Dominic Sloan, grateful he was rotting in jail a state away. She'd never wished someone dead before her experience with that man. He might be worse than the witch hunter, if such a thing was possible. The witch hunter embodied evil, but Sloan had chosen it.

Shane crossed his arms over his faded black t-shirt. Claudia must not have outfitted him with a new gallery approved wardrobe yet. Drew glanced down at her own style choice and crossed her arms. Shane observed her with curious eyes. Why did he have to come back to Atlas Cliffs? She tore her gaze away from him and focused on Claudia, refusing to let Shane think for a minute he'd gotten to her. She forced a smile. "What's your big news, Claudia?"

Claudia's heels echoed as she strutted toward Drew, sashaying across the grand lobby under a crystal chandelier hanging from the vaulted ceiling. Her outstretched hand displayed a ring with a diamond as large as one of Gran's garden stones. She wiggled her fingers and Drew grabbed her hand. "What the... is this?" Drew looked from Claudia's beaming face to the gleaming jewel on her ring finger. "Are you—?"

"Engaged! Yes!"

"Since when?" Drew asked.

"Since last night. It was a dream come true. He hired a private chef to cook us dinner, and there was a trail of rose petals leading to the bedroom filled with candles, and he got down on one knee—"

"And decided it was a good day to end his days of fun," Shane said. Drew rolled her eyes.

Claudia snapped her head toward him. "Asshole. I don't need a commentary, and so help me, I'll fire you as fast as I hired you." Claudia eyed him up and down. "And where are the new clothes I bought you? You can't work in the gallery dressed like that, Shane." She faced Drew and the Cheshire grin returned. "I want to wait until I'm twenty-one, but really, that's barely over a year and it'll be perfect for wedding planning, and we've known each other's families forever. I never thought Grant Salinger and I would connect after all this time." Claudia placed her hands on each of Drew's bare arms. "One more thing, but it involves you."

"How can there be more than that? Marriage is a big deal." Drew had hit her limit for talking about marriage in a single day, enough to sustain her until the following year.

Claudia brushed her left hand through the air, beaming brighter than the rock on her hand. The ring was so large, Drew didn't know how she could lift her hand in the air at all. "It is a big deal. But Grant's perfect for me, we're perfect for each other, a team, and when you find someone like that, you jump all the way in, you'll see."

Drew caught a side eye of Shane staring at her, his eyes burning into her soul, but she didn't meet his gaze. Jumping all the way in equated getting all the way hurt and broken. She wanted no part of it. Anyway, nineteen was too young to get married.

"Congratulations, Claudia. If you're happy, I'm happy for you." She braced herself for whatever Claudia had to say that involved her. "What was the more part involving me?"

"I'm throwing a party at the Atlas Cliffs yacht club the first weekend of July, and it's going to be a career break-through for you."

"I'm grateful for everything you've done for me, but I'm not interested in a fancy party." Drew folded her arms across her chest as though she could physically block Claudia from roping her into party plans.

"Well, get interested. I want you to be the featured artist. Influential people are traveling to our town for this, and trust me, you need to be there." Claudia held a hand up. "No... you *will* be there. You can do this, I'll help you." Her dress swished over her knees as she moved to the table and picked up one of Drew's paintings. As she held it in front of her, Drew tilted her head and eyed it over Claudia's shoulder.

The image flowed in a vivid array of colors, depicting an abstract center that wasn't abstract to her at all. She had created the clearing at Neptune Point, but in her vision, it wasn't the Haven that everyone knew. Inspired by a dream, the painting portrayed a different place that would've existed if she had failed to send the witch hunter away. The river churned with anger, and the portal swirled in a frenzied madness of blues and grays, and a shadow lurked among the trees, taunting her.

The second painting lay on the table in stark contrast to the first, radiating a kaleidoscope of colors and embodied light and safety. She'd painted a sunrise and sunset together, casting a golden glow, taming the shadows through the trees, and calming the river into submission. It pulsed with a magical energy, mirroring the unfinished canvas on the easel in her home studio of the Neptune Point lighthouse. She couldn't explain her muse for the paintings, but magic tingled under her skin and through her hands every time she grasped the paintbrush.

Claudia placed the painting back on the table beside the other and examined them together. She ran a finger across each canvas. "They're brilliant. Dark, but brilliant. I knew you had it in you. I want more of this haunting vibe. And I'm serious about the party. It's in two weeks and I need to know I count on you. There will be compensation, of course."

"I don't know, can't you choose another artist?" Drew asked. Although Claudia's compensation would help her with house repairs and tuition.

"She won't do that, it's you or no one," Shane said in a hushed tone.

"I can't believe I'm saying this, but he's right." Claudia held Drew at an arm's length and eyed her from the top of her red-haired head to her converse slip-ons. "You'll just need a dress, but I'll take care of it."

"Dress?"

She dropped her hands and narrowed a gaze on Drew. "Yes, dress. It's the gallery's official summer kick-off formal party, a welcome to Atlas Cliffs gathering. I'm going to let people know this town is back, we're cultured, and we feature unbeatable talent."

"You sounded like a travel advertisement," Drew joked, trying to cover up her unease.

Claudia rolled her eyes. "I'll let you choose the dress."

"I don't believe you."

"You can have a *say* on your dress. Nothing too frilly, promise. Classy, tasteful."

"I'm not the frilly type, Claudia." The last time she'd worn a dress was for prom.

Shane laughed. "You can wear sneakers, Drew. No one will know if the dress is long enough."

"No offense, big brother, but we aren't looking to you for fashion advice," Claudia retorted.

He tapped the top of one of the canvases. "I'm no art expert, but these are the best I've seen from you, not that I get a first look at anything you do anymore."

Drew ignored Shane's comment, as well as his observing gaze, and made her way closer to the two canvases, her sneakers squeaking on the glossy floor. Claudia would have them framed to perfection before displaying them on the wall.

Leaning over the table, Drew traced her fingertips over each painting. The gradual shift from dark to light symbolized a journey away from trauma and fear through the hidden veil to the other side, where no one else could see or understand. The grief of losing Shane had sent her into a downward spiral, and she'd given up painting. Reconnecting with art and going to college allowed her to express a dark part of her soul, and sharing this part of herself with the world hadn't been easy.

She rose, and Claudia stood beside her. "I'll need more by the end of the summer before you go back to college. But please trust me, you need to be at that party. This is your future we're talking about."

My future.

Others saw a bright future ahead of her, but all she could see was a void of uncertainty beyond today. Trust carried a lot of weight for such a small word. "All right, Claudia. I'll go. But I can just wear my prom dress."

"Absolutely not. Let me take care of that."

"No frills, no glitter, or bows—"

"No problem," Claudia said. "Stop worrying, I've got the perfect dress in mind."

Shane walked up the winding stairs, laughing and shaking his head.

Her phone vibrated inside her purse, and she dug it out, cutting off the blaring ring tone.

Piper.

"I'm on my way," she answered.

"I'm outside on my front step." Piper's smile was evident as she spoke with a palpable anticipation for the relaxed, fun summer they'd talked about for months.

But the summer break Drew longed for was slipping away like sand through her fingers.

Eight

The sky blushed pink as Drew rounded the turn along the coastal road toward home. She switched the air conditioning off and rolled the windows down, savoring the salt air as it rolled through the car off the ocean, gracing her skin with relief from the heat.

Piper held her hand out the window beside Drew in the passenger seat. "I never want summer to end."

"I feel the same way." The end of summer meant back to college, traveling back and forth from Boston on weekends, and missing Nico, surfing, her home. Atlas Cliffs went from being a town she wanted nothing to do with, to her safety net.

Shane had better not settle down here again. He wouldn't do that. He was a city guy, always had been.

"Is it possible to actually like Atlas Cliffs?" Piper mused.

"I saw Shane at the gallery," Drew said quickly. She needed to talk about it.

Piper let her head drop against the head rest away from the window to face Drew. She held strands of pink hair out of her eyes as the wind whipped through the car. "What the hell is he doing back in town? I mean, I know he and Claudia are family now, so I guess that makes sense, but the gallery? Doesn't sound like something he'd do."

"He's working for Claudia this summer. And he's different now, Piper. He used to be sweet to me, you know? Since last Christmas, it's like he's got a whole asshole thing going on."

"I hate to be the one to break it to you," Piper said. "Sweet wasn't a word I would use to describe Shane. He was never *friendly*—well, to you, maybe."

"Why didn't you say something?"

The house came into view, and Piper rolled the window up and smoothed her hair as she checked herself in the visor mirror. "I didn't want to ruin your happiness unless he was a shithead, and that's why he irritates me now. He cheated on you. That makes him a shithead." She snapped the visor back up and smiled. The tiny crystal on her eyebrow hoop sparkled in the sunlight.

The visions Ori had shown her of Shane with another girl, *Leah*, resurfaced in her mind. Gift or curse, she got to see first-hand what others could not. But those images shouldn't evoke anger anymore. She was happy, in love with Nico, and had let go of her resentment towards Shane—or so she'd thought until seeing him at the gallery stirred up feelings of betrayal.

Everyone was moving on, including Claudia. The massive ring on the Atlas Cliff's socialite's hand flashed in her head. "Claudia got engaged to Grant Salinger. Can you imagine Claudia *married*?"

"Sure, why not? I give it five years, tops. People who get married at nineteen don't stay married, not happily anyway. Look at my parents. They got married when they were twenty, before they finished university. I swear they have a business arrangement and nothing more."

"You think? Your parents seem in love to me."

Piper shifted her gaze out the window. "They're just always so formal and stuffy. I don't know how much fun they have anymore, you know? They're both workaholics."

"Maybe that works for them, maybe behind closed doors they're completely different—"

"Okay, I'm ending this conversation. I do not want to know what my parents are doing behind any doors." Piper laughed.

"Maybe Claudia and Grant will last. He's older, twenty-five? Six?"

"I'm willing to bet they don't last," Piper said.

"I'm not betting on Claudia's relationship, I'm happy for her."

Piper's chin dropped to her chest as she furrowed her brow. Drew smiled. "What? I'm happy for her. She deserves happiness, Piper. Did you know she's planning a party in a couple weeks? A Tate Gallery summer launch something or other."

Piper eyed Drew. "My mom told me about that party. It'll be impressive with all the fancy people at the prestigious yacht club, and I don't want any part of it."

Drew's chest tightened with anxiety, and she gripped the steering wheel with both hands. "You're coming, aren't you? It's cool she thinks my art is good enough to feature at this thing, but the thought of dressing up and socializing with a bunch of strangers terrifies me. What if they hate me? What did I get myself into?"

"They won't hate you, and it'll be good for you to put yourself out there, show your talent, network." Piper released an exasperated sigh, her teasing tone laced with playful frustration. "I'll be there, don't worry, we'll make it fun."

"Fun? Now there's a bet I'll take. When I think of *fun*, that isn't it."

"Bet away, friend, bet away. It's all mindset." Piper leaned back in her seat and twirled her hair around her finger. "You can have fun anywhere, anytime."

Drew parked in the driveway alongside Taj's jeep, and behind Nico's black '69 Chevelle. His dad had given it to him a couple months before his birthday and Nico had invested countless hours into refurbishing it to absolute perfection.

Her understanding of cars had expanded over the past few months, surpassing anything she had ever imagined, but when Nico talked with passion, she couldn't tear her eyes or ears away. Heat rushed to her face, and she suppressed a smile, thinking about him.

"You're not thinking about fancy parties anymore. Your face is as red as my sunburn, this is the tea I've been missing." Piper gazed at her with raised eyebrows and a mischievous smile.

Drew shut off the engine and took the keys from the ignition, leaving her window down. "There's no tea, nothing you don't already know. What about you and Taj? You two seem pretty serious. Do you think you'll last the long distance?"

"He worked his ass off and got into NYU for his physical therapy degree, so he'll be coming to New York this fall." Piper twisted another pink strand around her finger, her nails a matching fuchsia.

"I didn't know that. No more long distance?"

"It was his plan before we met—his dad is there, and I knew he was looking into it, but he just found out, or I would've told you sooner. I don't know what's next for me and Taj, but I sure am having fun now, and isn't that all that matters?" Piper dropped her hands onto her lap and reached for the door, her hand lingering on the handle. "You overthink, Drew. Nico's hot as hell and treats you like the queen you are. Roll with it. Don't worry about where any of it is going, just do *now*. I can't believe I've been home for a week and I'm this out of touch with the town gossip."

"You're lucky. I've been home for two months just trying to mind my business between the house, bakery, and the beach, but things keep pulling me back in."

Piper swung the car door open, but turned to Drew before getting out. "Ghost girl?"

And Aurora's warning.

"If you mean Jules, yes, and she's from here, she was in law school."

"Really? We should be able to find her, how many Jules are there? I'll start digging."

Sticking the keys in the ignition, Drew rolled her window up. "I think I know who killed her."

"Shitballs. Who?" Piper sat back in the car, letting the passenger door slam shut.

"One guess. He's rotting in prison and shares DNA with Claudia and Shane."

"*Sloan*? He killed the barefoot bloody girl? When? How?"

All pleasant thoughts of Nico and Piper's motto of *live in the moment* turned to stone, but the car was turning into an oven despite the cooler sea air rolling over the cliffs. "I'm going to give you the short version of how she died, and then I need to drop it for tonight, okay? It's been a lot of,"—*images of death*—"heavy shit, and if I keep doing this every time one of them wants my help, I'll never be able to just live my life. I don't want to lose what I've built here." She eyed the house with its patio lights flickering on and the sound of a guitar carrying over the summer evening air. "Remember my resolution for this year?"

"Less chaos, more fun."

"Exactly. *Fun.*" Every muscle in Drew's body tensed as she gave Piper the quick and dirty details of Jules' horrific murder in one breath, sending the amulet vibrating and her skin prickling.

Piper stared at Drew's neck and held the amulet at eye level. "How long has this been going on?"

Drew plucked the jewel from Piper's fingers. "Since yesterday."

"Looks like someone wants your attention again."

"I had a visitor."

"What kind of visitor?" Piper opened the car door and a gust of welcome air blew in the car. "I'm dying in here." She pulled at her white halter top and hopped out of the car. She shut the door and slipped her hands into the pockets of her black-and-white checkered shorts as Drew grabbed her purse and a backpack stuffed with her work clothes.

Piper sidled up to Drew and took the backpack from her hands. "Was it Ori? Gran? The other ghost girl, Enid?"

Using her hip, Drew closed the car door, taking a deep breath of ocean air as a breeze gusted by, offering her lungs a reprieve. "Her name is Aurora, the woman the lighthouse was named after."

"The original witch with the journal who kicked that witch hunter's ass?"

"That's the one."

"Okay, that's just cool as shit. Where was she? Did you go out to Neptune Point without me? I thought we were past the secret-keeping-do-everything-alone phase?"

She couldn't understand why Nico and her friends wanted to be a part of the dead's chaos, so being open with them about it continued to be tough. "She was here, upstairs in the studio." Drew stopped before she reached the front porch steps. "Whatever magic blew in with Aurora stuck around in the amulet."

"Sounds like a summer fling with adventure if you ask me." Piper's sly smile returned. "Bye-bye witch hunter, hello witch goddess bad ass."

"How about hello summer of surfing and beach fires under the stars with our boyfriends? Bye-bye everything else?"

Piper bounded up the porch stairs and bumped the swing, sending it swaying back and forth before spinning around. "You take the time you need to wrap your head around this, and I'll be ready when you are. This summer is going to be fire, Drew. And thanks again for saving me from working for my mother's law firm full time. Part time at the Tough Cookie will break it up. I can only stand so many days with her bossing me around." She opened the screen door, holding it for Drew before heading inside, calling out for Taj.

As Drew stepped on the threshold, a swirl of cold air danced around her, sending a cluster of sparks crawling along the palms of her hands. Heat rose from within the amulet along her skin and she stepped away from the door, letting it close. The wooden steps creaked under her feet as she moved down to the stone walkway.

"Jules?"

A gentle tumble of waves crashed along the beach across the road, and cicadas buzzed unseen around her. The sharp, earthy scent of freshly cut grass filled the air as she stepped closer to the edge of the walkway. Nico had mowed the lawn—his unwavering presence a constant in her life, always there to take care of things when she couldn't.

The icy mist whirled into a shimmering fog. A mourning dove cooed from the row of Gran's lilac trees as a car sped by.

"Who are you?"

With a graceful soar over the cliffs from across the road, the raven landed on the Adirondack bench in the front yard, ruffling its feathers as it settled. The air shimmered with a faint purple glow as Aurora emerged, her light wrapping around the amulet like delicate fingers. Aurora's hand brushed over the raven's back as she glided closer to Drew.

"Tell me what's going on, please?" Fighting against a building fear and her instinct to run inside, Drew stepped forward, nearing Jack's perch. "Why are you here?"

Smoke curled off Aurora's singed hair and the collar of her dress. "A storm is coming, but you will not brave the darkness alone."

"What storm? Who? I need more than cryptic warnings."

The raven lifted off the chair with a screech as Aurora's purple light swirled and vanished, dissipating into a mist that ascended into the sky, merging with the pink cloud cover. There had been no signs of storms, only scorching summer heat, but Aurora's warning weighed heavier than the weather. Desperate to fit the puzzle pieces together in her head, Drew rubbed her temples and closed her eyes.

The front screen door creaked. "You okay? I made burgers if you want one."

Nico's voice washed over her like a soothing balm, and she rushed up the stairs and into his arms, burying her face in his chest. She focused on her breathing, slowing each breath until her pulse stopped racing in her ears. The lingering scent of barbecue smoke clung to his shirt and skin, calming her nerves as he wrapped his arms around her and rested his chin on her head.

"What's up? Is she back?"

Drew nodded, forcing Nico to lift his chin over her head, but she couldn't bring herself to divulge the warning she'd received from Aurora. How could she when she struggled to understand it herself?

"Do you want to talk about it?" His voice was quiet as he spoke.

"Not tonight. I want to forget about all of it for tonight."

Nico pulled back, squinting his eyes as the last of the evening sun's rays beamed on his face. "Sure, but you promised you'd tell me if shit goes down again."

Stepping out of his embrace, she sucked in a breath. "I will, I promise."

I hope I can keep my promise.

She had spent months at college daydreaming of these summer nights when they could all hang out again, but those daydreams took a dark twist, leaving her unsettled.

Patio lights flickered on the row of crystals in the planter beside the doorway, sending a cascade of sparkles dancing along the porch boards. She leaned over to touch them, and a sudden vibration reverberated along her neck. Her fingers closed around the jewel.

I will not brave the storm alone.

Whatever that was supposed to mean.

Nico crouched beside her, locking eyes with hers. "Nothing is going to happen to you, I won't let it. You're safe, we're good, and we've got all summer together."

She touched his face, his faint stubble rough underneath her fingers. He'd do anything to protect her, but he wasn't a part of her hidden world, and she would do whatever it took to shield him from whatever darkness Aurora alluded to.

The screen door opened, and Piper stood holding a drink that matched her hair, filled to the brim with ice cubes and topped with a slice of pineapple and a cherry. "I've got a pitcher of this pink goodness, I dragged loungers onto the deck, and wondered where in the fresh hell my best friend is, only to find you two here bent down staring at stones? No chaos, more fun. Get your butts out back!" Piper swirled her drink with the straw and let the screen door slam behind her playfully as she left them on the porch.

Standing tall, Nico extended his hand with a smile that outshone even the most radiant of magic stones. Holding his hand, she allowed him to bring her back into his arms. The music played again from the back deck as she followed him inside, shutting the front door behind her.

Aurora hadn't returned, and from her view through the screened door, the coastal road couldn't be more serene if time froze. If only she could shake the nagging feeling that something terrible was closing in.

Nine

Stars peppered the night sky, and the moon was so full it looked like it might burst and send remnants tumbling over Jupiter Cove beach, sizzling into the vast ocean. Moonlight danced over the sea crests, and the cliffs appeared like mountains as they hugged the road. Drew scanned her surroundings for a sign of Hathorne's return or signs of nearby danger, but an intense magical instinct burning through her soul left no room for doubt—Hathorne was gone.

She was no closer to deciphering Aurora's *"a storm is coming"* omen.

Flames rose in the firepit, and a log snapped louder than Taj and Nico's strums on their acoustic guitars. Piper circled the rising flames with her whimsical pink beverage in one hand.

Drew touched her flushed cheeks that must be as red as her hair, and she silently cursed her ginger genetics as she sipped the rest of her own strawberry drink, savoring the sweet taste cleverly masking the alcohol. As she shook the ice before sticking the cup into the sand, a shimmer of tingles in the palms of her hands came in waves and she rubbed them on her shorts. The full moon had this effect on her ever since the night she'd sent Hathorn through the portal.

Piper plopped in the sand beside her and grabbed Drew's hand. "Holy hell. What is happening here? I thought you could control when they sparkled."

Drew pointed to the massive glowing ball in the sky.

"Gotcha. Full moon at night, magic takes flight." Piper stretched her legs out and wiggled her toes in the sand. "I keep waiting for werewolves and vampires to show up next. Like the shows on TV with the hot guys and golden eyes."

"I think dead people are quite enough," Drew said.

"I guess." Piper smiled and bumped her shoulder against Drew's.

The faint glimmer faded and Drew held up her hands. "It's going away."

Piper touched the amulet around Drew's neck, holding the black gem in her fingers like it was a delicate flower. "It's like a baby firefly, all alone in there. Is anyone else here?"

Drew took the amulet from Piper's fingers and examined it. The orange glow from the fire reflected off the shimmering surface, but Piper was right. A tiny thread of light flickered again, deep in the center. "No one is here except the four of us," she whispered, not sure if she believed her own words.

In a sudden burst, Piper jumped up and spun around, stumbling before planting her feet into the sand to anchor herself. She clutched her cup with both hands to prevent the entire contents from spilling over. "I want to help you figure out who the ghost woman is."

"Jules," Drew said.

"Jules, yes. Exactly." Piper's silver bracelets shimmered in the light and jingled together as she talked with her hands, keeping her cup from tipping over.

Nico's brows furrowed with curiosity as he looked at Drew. So much for a night without ghost talk. Keeping the chaotic part of her life separate from the peace she'd created wasn't easy.

"I'm sorry, I'm just excited. I won't say another word about it again tonight, I promise." Piper sat in the sand beside Taj, balancing the cup with expert precision despite her tipsy state.

Taj stopped strumming as he observed Piper with a grin, his face illuminated by the combination of light from the fire and the moon. For a brief second, he appeared magical, like his mother. If nightmares still plagued Taj, he remained quiet about it. Either he was in a world of denial, or he was keeping something from her.

Taj gazed at Piper. "How about we keep away from the ghost world and just enjoy summer? Last winter was enough danger, you know what I'm saying?" He eyed Drew.

"There's no danger, not this time, right Drew? Just fun paranormal stuff." Piper flashed a smile.

She appreciated Piper's enthusiasm for adventure and her willingness to help uncover the dead's secrets, but the night the witch hunter set the house on fire, almost killing her best friend, would forever haunt Drew's memory, and Nico would walk through a firing squad for her, but the ocean waves rolling up the beach served as a haunting reminder of Nico's near drowning in the Coda River.

Taj was right. Last winter had gone too far. She'd pushed the boundaries, walking the line between the living and the dead, dragging her friends along with her, and it almost got them killed. Promises or not, she'd never let it go that far ever again, and if the situation took a bad turn, she'd cut Piper out of her plan like snipping a dangling string. But if Taj fit into her witchy world of secrets and visions, Piper would find a way to be involved.

"We're surrounded by paranormal, Piper. I don't know why you want to go looking for it." Taj's voice cut through Drew's thoughts. "You all know who my mom is and what she can do, and we've all seen Drew use magic we never talk to anyone else about." Propping his guitar against a boulder, Taj got up and tossed more wood on the smoldering fire. Sparks exploded into the air as a blackened log snapped into pieces. Leaving her cup in the sand, Piper stood and wrapped her arms around his waist, letting him pull her against him. "All I'm trying to say," he continued, "maybe let's let the dead just be dead this summer." He eyed Drew.

If only it were that easy.

The flames danced and crackled, casting light over Nico's face as he observed her. "It doesn't work like that, Taj."

"Can you tell them to go away and leave you alone? Do you have any control?" Embracing Piper with both arms, Taj adjusted his stance by the fire.

Nico's piercing gaze held Drew's. "Sometimes, if I practice what your mom taught me and focus or use the book for a spell to block them. But it never lasts long. They'll always find a way." She reached for the amulet, and it warmed under her fingertips.

"That keeps you safe?" Taj asked.

"It's got a good track record." She offered him the most reassuring smile she could.

"Is there something you want to tell us?" Piper glanced up at Taj.

He turned his head away, breaking contact with her. "Just Mom's been hiding these small-ass crystals in my pockets, in my gym bag... drum case." Taj reached into his pockets, yanking the fabric out. "What the hell—"

"Looking for these?" Holding her hand out, Piper revealed two small crystal stones, one with a pale hue and the other as black as ink. She shrugged, glancing up at him with a fake look of innocence. "Back pocket."

Taj kissed her cheek as he took them from Piper's hand and held them out to Drew. "See? This is what I'm talking about. And I know she had something to do with that old house burning to the ground, but she won't say a word to me. You must know what happened. She tells you everything."

A rush of tingling erupted underneath her skin as she stood and let Taj drop the stones into her palm. Celeste had confessed Enid's wish to burn the house to the ground, and she had helped her friend. Drew would've done the same thing for Piper or anyone she loved, but she refused to break the unspoken agreement of trust and secrecy she had with Celeste.

Celeste never wanted her son to be part of this world, just like Gran had never wanted Drew to be part of it. But Taj, like

Drew, had ventured into the mystical unknown whether he wanted to or not. Maybe Celeste was aware of more than she admitted and had strategically placed crystals close to him for his protection.

Drew gave the gems back to Taj and rubbed her hands together to still the buzzing sensation. "The house was old, full of dust and mold... and investigators said rats chewed through wires, so it was bound to happen, eventually."

Without uttering a word, Nico stretched his legs and directed his gaze toward her, his eyes meeting hers. She knew him well enough to detect the skepticism in his expression. She trudged through the soft sand—still warm from the scorching heat and joined him on the chunk of deadwood. He put his guitar aside and draped an arm over her shoulders as she rested her head against his chest.

"Who bought the property out there anyway?" Piper asked. "I wonder who'll move into that house. I wouldn't want to live there."

"No clue," Taj said. "Probably some big city tourist looking for a piece of land beside the ocean with their very own haunted lighthouse."

"Maybe someday we'll have our very own piece of land, baby." Piper's laugh carried over the ocean's surf as she pulled Taj's hand, leading him away from the fire and toward the edge of the water, their shadows illuminated by the light of the moon as they walked hand in hand down the beach.

"What was all that about?" Nico's hand slid down Drew's back, sending shivers along her skin, melting the tension from her body.

"I don't know." Taj's secret wasn't hers to tell. She shifted her focus to Nico, overwhelmed by how much she loved him. Maybe Jasper was right and finding that special person had nothing to do with timing. Perhaps Nico would stick around in her world of ghosts and magic, and they'd defy reason, ending up together forever.

But happily ever after only happened in fairytales, and she was far from a princess.

The flickering light of the fire transformed Nico's deep brown eyes into a mesmerizing shade of amber. His chest rose and fell with slow, steady breaths, and she placed her hand over his heart to feel the gentle beats matching her own. Gone were their days of awkwardness, first kisses, and filling the silence with conversation. She'd become comfortable in her own skin with Nico and never wanted the feeling to disappear—her greatest fear hanging over her head like a storm cloud. He covered her hand with his, rubbing a thumb back and forth along her wrist. She melted against him, letting him hold her like he could shield her from an unseen darkness that lurked, waiting to pounce.

I don't want the other shoe to fall.

He moved his hand away from hers and shifted his position to face her. "I love you." His voice blended with the sound of waves surging and retreating over the shore.

His dimple appeared when he smiled down at her, the tiny crater casting all her worries away. It was easy to forget the horrors when she was with him.

She reached for his face and his hand moved to her neck, his fingers curling into her hair as his mouth closed over hers. His warm breath tickled her nose as she kissed him with growing passion. As their tongues explored, her fears dissolved. She wanted to pull him to the ground and make love right there on the beach, but Piper and Taj's laughter reminded her they weren't alone. They parted with shallow breaths, and she released her grasp on him to cradle his face. "I love you too."

Piper hurried across the road to collect her belongings from the house. "It's locked," she called. "I need keys!"

Drew took out her keys from her pocket as Nico offered his hand. "I'll run them over." She dropped the keys into his outstretched palm, and he dashed across the street up the driveway.

Taj hung back with Drew as they waited for a car to pass before crossing. "I had another nightmare. I just didn't want to scare anyone, including you."

She spun around in the middle of the road. "It scares me more when you don't tell me what's going on. Was there anything different or new?"

"Not really... well, sort of. One thing." Headlights glimmered from down the road, and they quickened their pace to the end of her driveway. "I heard a woman talking."

She swallowed hard. Piper and Nico's voices from the house carried over the crickets and rhythmic waves, and both she and Taj glanced toward the porch at the same time.

Drew kept her voice quiet. "What did she say?"

"I knew you'd ask, so I wrote it down." He handed her a folded piece of paper as the screen door creaked and Nico followed Piper down the porch steps.

"It makes no sense to me, but will you message if you figure it out because I'm starting to lose it, you know what I'm saying?"

"More than you know," she whispered.

Piper skipped toward them and hugged Drew goodbye before hopping into the jeep with Taj. As they drove away, Piper waved from the window, her pink hair flying around her face.

Clutching the note in her hand, Drew tried to hide the panic creeping into her chest. Could the woman be Aurora? An overwhelming need to read the note consumed her, but she trailed Nico onto the porch and sat on the swing.

"I'm getting water, did you want something from inside?" His tanned forearm flexed as he held his hand on the front door.

"Water would be great." Her parched mouth made her words come out softer than she had intended.

"You all right?"

"Yeah, just tired. Too many of Piper's pink drinks."

A smile crossed his face as he went inside.

Moths collided with the porch light as she unfolded the paper with trembling fingers, keeping a watchful eye beyond the screen. She could barely make out the scribbled words on the crumpled piece of paper, but there was no denying what she was reading.

Call the quarters. Seek shelter from the storm. Seek bravery in the face of death, breathe in life.

Aurora had spoken to him, too.

TEN

The night came alive with the chorus of crickets and the rustling of leaves among the towering oak and lilac bushes. Dark clouds slithered across the night sky, swallowing the stars as they wrapped the moon in a chokehold.

With the note tucked in her pocket, Drew swung on the porch swing as Nico shuffled around in the shed, storing the lawn mower. The floodlight's feeble reach extended only to the shed and driveway, leaving the front yard enveloped in shadows. She'd upgraded the outside lighting after Dominic Sloan's stalking days, but the wandering souls didn't trigger floodlights.

She stretched her legs, trying to rid the pins and needles sensation along her upper thigh. Nothing specific triggered the scarred injury, but the numbness worsened in stressful situations, or when fatigue set in, and she could check both off that list. She checked her phone to distract herself from Taj's note, but the only notification was Jasper letting her know he'd be staying at Danny's for the night.

Sliding her thumb along the silver chain of the amulet, she pushed the swing back and forth with her foot, her toe tracing a section of peeling paint on the floorboards. Jack and Aurora's warnings had gotten under her skin and consumed her mind, but perhaps she was overreacting and she had nothing to worry about other than an old Neptune Point curse coming back to haunt her.

Thunder rumbled, low and steady as a streak of lightning sliced through the clouds.

Turning the corner, Nico's eyes met hers, and a smile spread across his face. "Want to stay outside and watch?"

"Sure." She scooted over and patted the space beside her on the swing.

Taking a seat, he extended his legs in front of him, stretching them out further than hers. The rain tapping on the porch overhang intensified, flowing along the eavestrough and down the gutter, but they remained dry underneath its protective shelter. Nico lifted his arm, and she nestled against his warm body, curling her feet up on the seat as his arms tightened around her.

"Do you think it'll always be just like this?" she asked.

"Like what?"

She gripped his hands in hers and held them near her face. "I don't know."

"Yes you do. Just say what you're thinking."

She caught herself chewing her lip and stopped. "Don't you worry about what the future will look like? If you stay with the woman who talks to dead people? It doesn't ever weird you out?"

"Should it? It doesn't weird Piper out. Do you ever see that friendship ending?"

The cushions shifted beneath her as she turned around in his arms to face him. "Piper will move on with her own life with someone, be a big city lawyer, but that's a terrible example. You're not just my friend."

"I hope not. We already did the just friends thing, this is better." His lips curled into a smile, and she brushed her fingers along the indent of his cheek.

"I know what you're getting at, and I know you think everyone leaves, but the people who love you aren't going anywhere, dead people or not." He brought her hand to his lips and kissed it before holding it to his chest. "I'm not leaving. You believe me, don't you?"

"I believe you. I trust you with my life."

But when shit goes sideways, I won't hold your promises against you.

Thunder snapped like a whip, and she jumped. The wind picked up, sending tree branches swaying and leaves rustling against one other. Rain cascaded over the cars and streamed down the driveway as another bolt of lightning illuminated the darkened sky.

"Want to go in?" Nico glanced at her.

"Not yet." The electricity in the air pricked her skin as the thunderstorm unleashed its power, transforming the scorching heat into a crackling sizzle. The amulet pulsed along her neck as the heat and the storm collided, amplifying her magic.

"You hardly ever talk about the future," he said quietly. "Especially when it comes to you and me."

"I think about it all the time."

He knitted his brows together. "You do?"

"Of course I do. I'm not made of stone."

He pulled her closer, and she swung her legs over his. "I know you're not," he said. "I just worry you're going to regret keeping this place and want to leave."

"No regrets, I promise. I'm staying." She laced her fingers with his.

"I just wish you talked to me more about what you're going through. You get so quiet sometimes, and I know something's up."

Another gust of wind blew, rattling a loose railing on the deck, a chilling reminder of Aurora's storm warning. The haunting vision of Jules' death edged into her mind. Nico wanted her to tell him about the things on her mind and she had the perfect test. Who she was and what she saw never scared him, but her fears of sharing her terrifying experiences remained unchanged. "I think Dominic Sloan had something to do with Jules' death."

Nico froze, his body tense as if he were afraid to exhale. Seconds passed before he spoke. "He's in prison, Drew. He can't hurt you, or anyone ever again. Why do you think that?"

"She didn't know she was dead, so I showed her." She held her hands up. "Like how I showed you about the witch hunter." The memory of the night she'd spent in his place above the garage after the fire last winter sent goosebumps over her skin. It was the beginning of their journey to this moment, and if anything had gone differently that night, she might not be sitting here with him. The smallest moments turn into the biggest life changes.

He took her hands. "How could I forget? What did you see when you did the vision thing with her?"

"I saw her die." She swallowed to get rid of a building lump in her throat and bit down on her lip.

Nico stilled. "And you saw Sloan kill her?"

It hadn't been clear who had pushed her off the cliff, but the black sedan and those men... they had to be part of Dominic Sloan's ring. "Not exactly."

As she told him every detail of Jules' death, the weight of anxiety pressed down on her chest, making it difficult to breathe. She pulled away from Nico and sat up with her feet planted on the porch. A constant ringing in her ears replaced the sounds of the thunderstorm, making it difficult to hear anything else. Closing her eyes, she focused on taking slow, deep breaths, hoping to calm her racing heart. She wiggled her toes against the porch and gripped the cushions, toying with the frayed edges.

Nico crouched in front of her and placed his hands on the sides of her legs. "He's in jail and you're safe. Nothing's going to happen; I won't let it." His calm voice drowned out the incessant buzzing, and his cold hands pressed to her skin soothed the heat rushing through her, making her feel sick. Her heart rate slowed, and her breaths evened out.

She wrapped her arms around him, and he held her, guiding her up from the swing and into the house. He locked the door and turned the porch light off before following her up to her bedroom.

Rain clattered against the house, settling into a continuous rhythm. A powerful gust of wind rushed through the open window, sending the curtain sway in its wake, and cooling off her bedroom. Drew lay in bed, feeling the heat radiating from Nico's body against her back as he held her under the blankets. If she could freeze time and stay in this moment with him, she'd never leave the house.

She wanted to believe him. She wanted to believe that Nico could love her enough to keep her safe. But a storm with more impact than the one brewing outside was creeping into her life, and an alarm bell screamed inside of her like a blaring foghorn warning ships at sea of impending disaster.

She refused to let these precious moments with Nico slip past her, scared away by fear and worry. She clung to him, intertwining her fingers with his, and closed her eyes.

ELEVEN

Thunder rolled, and the house reverberated, jolting Drew out of a deep sleep. She wiped drool off her mouth as she rolled onto her side and tried to open her eyes. Her hair clung to her neck, damp with sweat, and she threw the blanket off. A rush of cool air sent a shiver over her bare skin. As she sat up, her head protested as a faint hangover throbbed behind her eyes. Her mouth was pasty and dry, and she reached for the glass of water on her bedside table. The curtains billowed and twisted as wind tore through the room. Nico's gentle breathing shifted as he stirred beside her on the bed, and she opened a bottle of ibuprofen, careful not to wake him. She popped the pain reliever into her mouth and washed it down with the last sip of water.

Chimes rang out from downstairs. *Chimes.* Gran's clock had never emitted a single chime throughout her entire life, and the eerie memory of its malfunctioning coincided with Gran's death.

What's happening?

In a rush, she leaped out of bed and threw on baggy shorts and the first T-shirt she could find in the dark. She tiptoed out of her bedroom, closing the door with a soft click before bounding down the stairs through the kitchen into the den. She pulled the chain of the desk light and stood face to face with the ornate, vintage clock. It was 3 a.m. The chimes fell silent, and she tapped the glass face. The amulet pulsed against her skin, and she grabbed it, holding it up to her face. Like a swirling tornado cloud, a tiny thread of light spun within the center, and her hands tingled in unexplained anticipation.

"Gran? Ori? Are you back?" She stared at the clock's face.

"It's just me." Jules' husky voice carried through the darkness. In the days when she was alive, she must've captivated people with her voice, commanding them to stop and listen to what she had to say.

"What are you doing here?" Drew asked, rubbing her eyes.

"I've never been inside your house." Jules strolled around the den, running her human fingers along the shelves. "It's dusty. And that jewel around your neck is lit like a Christmas tree."

Drew gripped the amulet in her palm to hide the light. "Things have been… happening."

"Anything you'd like to share?"

"Not really." Ori had been so much easier to deal with. So. Much. Easier. He'd been her friend. She couldn't see the same fate for her and Jules.

Jules tucked her chestnut hair behind her ears. "I can feel my hair when I'm like this and it reminds me of when I used to try to make it curly, but it never curled well. And my skin… I feel like a real person. It's too bad it won't last, there's people I'd like to haunt."

"What people? You remember?"

"I wish. I just thought it'd be the only thing fun I could do. While you've been living your exciting life on the beach with your boyfriend and friends, I've been working on a plan." She stopped pacing the room and tilted her head as she fixed her gaze on Drew's face. "I envy you. I hope you realize how lucky you are to still have your whole life ahead of you and not be stuck in purgatory."

Was Drew the lucky one? She'd escaped death twice in the past two years and survived, and yet this woman who should have her life ahead of her stood in Gran's den, dead and caught between the realm of the living and wherever paradise she should have found. "I don't know if luck has anything to do with it—"

"What then? And why me? Why would someone want to murder me? I don't know what I did, but I sure as hell didn't deserve to be shoved off a cliff and end up like this."

The twisted logic behind Dominic Sloan's murderous intentions was unfathomable. He hid behind a mask—burying Ben Morana and navigating through life as an undetected psychopath.

"Do you think your family had any, um, business dealings with a man named Dominic Sloan?"

"Who?" Jules took paper clips out of a mason jar on the desk and clipped them together, forming a chain. She paused, her wide eyes narrowing on Drew. "What do you know? Holy shit, do you know who did this to me?"

Drew stretched her neck from side to side. "I'm just trying to figure out the connection with what I saw of your..." *Murder, killing, torture*. No words captured the horror she'd witnessed in Jules' vision.

"Say it, Drew. My disgusting, brutalizing, horrific murder." With both hands, Jules crumpled the paper clips into a ball and threw them back in the glass jar. "I've got another question for you. How do *you* know him? The man you mentioned, Dominic Sloan, is it? Does *your* family have business dealings with him?"

No, but Nico's dad did.

"He ruined lives of people I love."

Jules sat in Gran's rocker and kicked her feet up on the ottoman. "Keep talking."

Drew bit her lip to stop herself from asking the dead girl to get off Gran's chair. The faster she helped Jules cross over, the sooner she'd be out of Drew's life. "What do you want to know?"

"Everything." Jules leaned forward with her elbows on her knees.

The conversation descended into a chaotic world of panic and anxiety. Ori had never pressured her to revisit the traumatic events that took place almost two years ago. She'd spent months working through—burying, really—memories of Sloan's attack and Iris' dead body with therapy and sheer determination. The last thing she wanted was to give a detailed play-by-play to a dead woman in Gran's den. She couldn't do it, wouldn't do it.

"It's late and I don't want to talk about it."

Jules' unblinking stare bore into her, as if she possessed the power to expose Drew's innermost thoughts she'd hidden behind cement walls. Few people would ever be privy to those feelings, and Jules wasn't one of them. Drew clutched the amulet, drawing strength from the warm energy radiating from the gem.

She was determined to find a way to send Jules to *paradise*. As Ori's voice echoed in her mind, sadness engulfed her. Grief struck in the most random moments—the smell of certain pastries Jasper made gave her the missing-Gran ache, or a word from the Ori dictionary sent her back months when he was her constant sidekick. The memories crashed into her mind like an unstoppable wave.

Jules waved her hands in grand circles. "Did you hear a word I just said?"

Why can't Jules be more like Ori?

"I need some intel," Jules said, her stunning green eyes wide and waiting for answers.

"Intel?"

"Intelligence. Background information. Stuff you know that I don't. I'll spell it out for you if it helps. How. Do. You. Know. That. *Man*?" Jules clapped her hands with each word like the rhythmic beat of a drum.

Drew sighed and sank onto the upholstered bench under the window, resting her aching head against the wall.

"I don't know where to start."

"I've got all night, hell at this rate, I might have eternity. Start at the beginning."

Drew's stomach churned and an intense burning sensation rose in her throat. Each shallow breath sent a prickling sensation coursing through the palms of her hands. Holding them up to her face, a faint glow shone under the skin of her palms.

"Tell her. She needs to know," an unfamiliar woman's voice whispered, soothing her from the inside out. Drew pulled her knees to her chest and wrapped her arms around them, pressing her palms against her bare skin. A calmness poured over her like warm water over her scalp and down her back. Her chest expanded with a deep inhale. As she exhaled through her lips, the amulet stilled. Everything was still. Her heart stopped racing, and her jaw unclenched.

Drew recounted the events from her past, each memory resurfacing with vivid clarity. She recounted Shane's tragic accident, which she had believed caused his death for months, and delved into the discovery of Iris's lifeless body in the tunnel at Neptune Point. Her story bounced from encounters with Dominic Sloan in Atlas Cliffs, the attic at the Keeper's house, and the lighthouse, ending with the shocking revelation of Sloan's identity as Ben Morana. In a sudden burst, the veil of calm allowing her to regurgitate the trauma fell to the floor. Her voice trembled, and she cleared her throat through tears as she rushed through the intense confrontation involving Dominic Sloan and the shooting in the warehouse.

She wrestled with the overwhelming urgency to vomit all over the den and clasped her hands over her mouth. She bolted into the kitchen and ran the tap, splashing water over her face covered in hot tears.

A hand rested on Drew's back as Jules leaned over the counter. "What's wrong with you?" For the first time, her voice quieted, softening with concern. "Do you need me to throw something to wake up lover boy? That Sloan asshole really did a number on you, didn't he? But you're still luckier than I am. You're standing where you are and here I am, a dead woman with no life left."

Drew cranked the tap handles off with unnecessary force, making the pipes creak, and spun around, gripping the counter. The ghost standing beside her had her on the verge of a breakdown, sending her back to a place she'd worked too hard to abandon.

"You need to leave, now." Drew stared into Jules' determined eyes. Even in her human form, her skin held an eerie resemblance to death, and her eyes gleamed with the same dazzling sparkle as Ori's.

"I'm not trying to be bitchy. That came out wrong. You're always working, surfing, painting, boyfriending—don't correct me, I know it's not a word and I don't care. My point is, you might be years younger than I was when I died, but we have more in common than you think. You hate the man who killed me as much as I do, and I don't even know him." Jules' animated hands accompanied her words. "You're also forgetting something, a *big something*. I can go where you can't."

Drew rubbed her burning eyes, unable to believe she was discussing Dominic Sloan again. "What are you talking about?"

"You're angry right now, but it's not at me. I did nothing to you except exist. I have no control over being here with you. And you can't see it now, but I can tell we're going to get along well, and as clear as turquoise water in the Caribbean, I need you, but you're going to need me, too."

"Why do I need you Jules? Please enlighten me instead of this poetic back and forth."

Jules touched Gran's teapot and ran her fingers along the counter. Drew resisted the urge to move in front of her, stopping her from invading her home... her life.

"All I needed to do was accept the truth." Jules gestured over herself. "I'm dead. But I'm not gone, and he's not paying nearly enough for taking me from what could've been. I was somebody, just like you are now. We're going to make him pay, but I need someone on this side to do it. That's where you come in."

"I don't know what you think I'm capable of, but I'm not going anywhere near that monster. You're going to cross over, but there has to be another way. He's in jail for murdering his siblings and Iris—"

"But not me. No one knows about me, do they? I barely remember my own family, why is that? It's like I've been in a messed-up slumber but instead of prince charming, I ended up with you."

The reasons behind the dead's detachment from their human lives remained a mystery to Drew, but the memories usually resurfaced, and it was a matter of time until Jules recollected her life in Atlas Cliffs. It had to be. "I don't know if it was him who killed you, any of those men could have—"

"It was him. I can feel it, and you know it too, and I'm not going anywhere until I know you're going to work with me. I want revenge."

Drew's past was coming back to haunt her, but there was no way she would allow Dominic Sloan to be a part of that.

There must be another way.

The digital clock on the microwave changed. She had to work in a few hours. Her patience for helping Jules had evaporated, and she had no choice but to put into action what Celeste had taught her. She'd been learning how to block the wandering when she needed them to go away.

She shut her eyes, imagining doors slamming around her, locking the path to her from the other side. The amulet thrummed against her skin, and she opened her eyes as the wind swept through the kitchen window, knocking a crystal off the ledge to the floor with a clang. Thunder clapped overhead as Drew picked up the sparkling stone and placed it back in place. Darkness enveloped the backyard except for flickering solar lights she'd strung along the cedar hedges. Closing the window, she waved her hand over the row of stones, and they glowed.

"Any chance you'd want to share some of that magic this way?" Jules' silhouette wavered like a ripple of water as she faded from human form into a ghost. "What are you doing, Drew? Stop! You're not getting rid of me that easy, I'll be back!" Her voice grew distant as she disappeared into a fine mist.

And I'll be ready.

Rain poured down in torrents, creating a curtain of water over the windows. Gran's butterfly shaped nightlights blinked off and back on as the power flickered. The house trembled under another rumble of thunder, and a flash of lightning lit up the room. A power outage silenced the steady hum of the house. With the fading glow from the amulet, her only source of light, Drew ventured into the den, searching through the cabinet for a flashlight. A thudding sounded from above her, and footsteps echoed down the stairs.

"Drew? Where are you?" Nico called out.

"In here." She fumbled with the switch on the flashlight, illuminating the small room as the door swung open and Nico bounded into the den wearing nothing but his boxers. His broad shoulders demanded attention, and she angled the beam of light over his tan skin. With a quick motion, he shielded his eyes and switched off the light on his phone. He moved close to her. "Did you have a nightmare again?" He scanned the room. "Is someone here?"

"She's gone."

"Who?"

"Jules."

"Did something happen?" His fingers brushed her skin as he held the amulet, sending goosebumps over her arms. "It has a mind of its own." Through his thick lashes, his eyes met hers, creating the familiar magnetic pull between them. Her hand dropped to her side, and the flashlight slipped from her grip and hit the floor, casting light along the dusty surface. The amulet's thread of light spun and flickered before performing a vanishing act.

Letting go of the stone, Nico stooped to pick up the flashlight. "What's going on?"

"She wants my help to... I don't know even know. I feel like she's never leaving and I'm not sure what to do." Her teeth grabbed her lip, chewing the tender skin. Nico ran a hand through his messy hair as his gaze fell to her lips.

She covered her mouth. "Don't say it. If the only thing I got from my mother is this bad habit, I don't care."

"I wasn't going to say anything. I've always found it hot."

"Hot? Fine, problem solved, I'm officially done fighting it."

Nico wrapped his arms around her. "You're not like your mother."

The room shook with the relentless drumming of thunder, and lightning pierced through the window. Drew flinched and gripped Nico's arm. He took her hand and led her through the kitchen into the living room. The rain blew sideways, slapping the window and soaking the window ledge. She pushed the curtains aside and pressed the window shut, locking the latch. With the streetlights dead, dark shadows danced among the trees. A sudden burst of lightning flashed over the cliffs, illuminating a silhouette soaring into the distance. The raven was as relentless as the thunderstorm.

Twelve

Drew bustled around the Tough Cookie, resetting tables, filling napkin holders and condiments, and wiping down chairs and surfaces. With animated hands, Piper engaged the last table of customers in conversation as she named destinations they should check out in Atlas Cliffs, but she left Jupiter Cover Beach off the list as one of the must-see places. A map wouldn't reveal the name, and none of the locals gave up that secret. Piper handled the influx of summer tourists like a pro, and they wouldn't have been able to keep up with the busy pace without her.

Stepping outside, Drew rolled down patio umbrellas and pushed chairs back against the tables. The rain dissipated, but the cooler Wednesday morning had long surrendered to the pervasive late afternoon heat seeping back over the town. A swirl of light moved across the street, and she cut through the tables toward the curb. The light shifted into a silhouette of a woman bearing a striking resemblance to Jules staring back at her. She blinked a few times, her eyes adjusting under the glare of the sun, but as her vision cleared, a trickle of people sauntered by, and Jules disappeared into the crowd.

Blocking Jules was no longer an option. The spell was wearing off.

She'd spent the past few days searching through news articles and accident reports for anything involving variations of the name Jules and came up empty-handed. Her strategy of blocking her was unraveling, and she couldn't keep holding her back with magic. Celeste had warned her about using magic to keep them away, but Drew refused to take part in any plan involving Dominic Sloan. Jules would have to let that go if she expected help.

A scruffy dog meandered down the bustling street, sniffing a garbage can before a pub owner chased it away. The dog limped; its tail drooping low as it tried to scurry down the street beside the Tough Cookie. It was slender, much thinner than it should be for its medium size, and the way it cowered away from anyone who walked by had to mean it was a stray, but her only experience with dogs had been Nico's years ago and she wasn't an expert.

Leaning over the wooden lattice divider, she called out in a gentle voice and made kissy noises. The dog stiffened and glanced up at her. Mud clung to its fur, making it appear a dark brown over black, but the lighter markings on its front legs resembled a pair of tall socks.

She opened the decorative gate for the small patio and followed the dog in between the narrow space between buildings, making kissy sounds again as she got closer. Its ears perked up, flopping over its head as it came to a sudden halt, emitting a low growl. Another growl escaped, this time more like a tired whine of defeat, and she stepped back. But instead of attacking, it crouched lower to the ground and slunk further down the street.

She knew nothing about animals. The potential of being bitten crossed her mind, but it looked more like a neglected animal desperate for food and shelter than a rabid dog. The Tough Cookie door chimes jingled, and she tore her attention away from the dog as the last customers exited the bakery. When she shifted her gaze back to the dog, it was gone.

I hope it doesn't die out here alone.

She headed back inside and flipped the sign to "closed". The air conditioning unit struggled to combat the oven's intense heat and maintain a cool temperature in the bakery.

Piper balanced a tray of pastries as she walked through the swinging door to the front of the bakery, carrying the aroma of vanilla and melted chocolate from the kitchen with her.

"Display cabinet. For the breakfast rush. Jasper's words." Piper's eyes widened as her gaze swept across the multitudes of glass encasements under the counter and built into the wall dividing the kitchen from the shop front. Jasper's decision to invest in refrigerated display cases proved to serve a purpose beyond appearance. They cooled with perfect precision, depending on the treats they held. "I'm going to get fired on my first day."

Drew laughed and took the tray from her hands. "Family doesn't fire family. You're great with the customers, better than I am, that's for sure."

Piper snatched a pen from behind her ear and stuffed it in the pocket of her apron around her waist. She fanned a handful of bills. "I'm in the money now, check out the tips. Tourist season kicks ass."

"It keeps us going. Now you can take me out for pizza at Maze tonight."

"Done. Wait, not done. Party planning with Claudia?" Piper stopped fanning her money.

"I'm her support person, or whatever she calls it." Drew placed each sugar-sprinkled pastry on the empty plates on the glass shelves. She re-arranged the display cards in wire holders, smiling to herself with a sense of pride at her graphic design skills with the bold, curvy lettering and colorful flowers.

Piper pulled a chair out from one of the turquoise tables, and plopped down, kicking her checkered Vans clad feet in front of her. "Why would you offer to help plan this fancy party with Claudia? Seriously. She's just going to use you."

Closing the cabinet, Drew wiped fingerprints off the glass. "I'm not really planning... she just wants to go over a few things. And she's not using me, she's been good to me."

"Because she features your artwork? You've got that backwards, friend. Your artwork brings people into her gallery." Piper held her hands out in front of her, inspecting her midnight blue manicured fingernails. "When's the party again? Maybe I'll be busy."

"Next Saturday, and you're going. Not for her, for me. I need you there. You're my social buffer."

Piper erupted into her infectious laughter. "Now who's using who? Bring Nico with you, he's good at peopling."

"He'll be busy helping Taj set up. You're coming, Piper." Drew balled up a dish towel and tossed it, missing Piper's face.

"Day one and you're fighting? Do I need to get HR involved?" Jasper strolled through the swinging kitchen door, holding out a plate of broken cookies in one hand and a large mug with the words, *I cast magic with flour. What's your superpower?* A gift Drew had given him for his twenty-fifth birthday the February past. Setting the plate on the table, he took a seat next to Piper. He adjusted the top buttons of his faded pink dress shirt and smoothed his navy shorts, having already changed out of his chef's coat.

His cologne masked the freshly baked pastry and Piper made a face. "Jesus, did you douse yourself? It's too much, J. Too much."

"It's Versace, and no. I did the standard three-spray on the pulse points and a step into the mist dousing."

"Big plans tonight, or more house hunting?" Drew asked.

"Danny is coming by after he's off at 7, but that's about it, and so far it's a nil on the house, but yes, we are still looking."

"You guys went from meet cute to in love in a hurry." Piper picked up a piece of cookie from the plate and popped it into her mouth. She stopped chewing and closed her eyes. "Okay, these are making up for your overpowering cologne."

Jasper reached over and slid another chair from the table. "Sit with us and have a broken cookie before we get out of here, Drew." He took a bite, picking up crumbs that spilled on the table with his fingers and sprinkling them on a napkin he'd laid out on his lap.

The chair scraped on the tiled floor as Drew sat and settled herself close to the table. The cookie was still warm as she broke it apart and chocolate melted over her fingers. She savored the sweet goodness and licked the chocolate off her fingertips. "These are like Gran's. How'd you get them so perfect?" The bakery was thriving; Gran would've been proud. Running the place came naturally to Jasper, and he never forgot to involve Drew in the decision-making process. They were a great team.

Jasper leaned back in his chair. "Let me introduce you to Maddie's Gems. I used her famous double chocolate cookie recipe and didn't change a thing. We'll choose a day of the week and a charity, and donate the money these babies bring in. Our way of giving back to this community."

Drew wiped her hands on a napkin and sat back in the chair. "I wish you could've met her." She wouldn't doubt it if Gran had a hand in guiding Jasper to the Tough Cookie. He embodied the work ethic Gran had stood so fiercely for.

"I feel like I already have somehow, maybe in a past life or something." Jasper smiled.

Drew grabbed another piece off the plate. "Why are they all broken?"

"Sometimes things fall apart, and you can't put them back together." Jasper crumpled the napkin from his lap and tossed it in a nearby trash can.

"That's depressing." Piper made a face, her forehead creasing.

"Not really. We're enjoying them, aren't we?" Jasper said. "They're just serving a different purpose, and the cookies we'll be serving won't be broken, don't worry."

"Sure you don't want to change careers and become a therapist?" Drew asked.

"Not a chance." Jasper drank from the mug and scrolled on his phone. "When is Claudia's big party happening? There's a tropical storm brewing in the Atlantic they're watching. It could turn into a hurricane by next week... *Francine.*" The name rolled off Jasper's tongue like a song.

Piper clapped her hands together. "Francine's gonna crash a party."

Another bright swirl of light on the other side of the window begged Drew's attention, and she glanced behind the blind.

"What are you looking at?" Piper grabbed the chain and pulled, opening the blind and a view of the busy downtown street. Jules stood with her arms folded across her chest, tapping a bare foot.

"Close it, Piper." Drew sat back in the seat.

The blind slid back down, covering the window as Piper guided the chain, observing Drew with serious eyes. "You've been acting like a fugitive on the run all day, skittish, spying outside like that. What are you looking for?"

"Jules is back."

"I didn't know she was gone," Piper said. "You just went quiet about the whole thing."

"I used a spell and blocked her, but it's not holding."

Jasper looked up from his phone. "Is that what you've been up to in the other room with the incense and random colors of flashing light? Welcome to the house of practical magic. Why did you block her in the first place?"

"I needed a break. She got too intense."

"Sloan," Piper said.

"Sloan?" Jasper's nose crinkled with the question.

Drew crumpled the napkins from the table and stood, tossing them in the trash. "Dominic Sloan."

Jasper picked up his phone and typed, nodding. "I can't find any news on him—"

"Ben Morana," Drew said. "That's his real name."

"Gotcha, I forgot about that." Jasper's eyes remained fixed on his phone. "He's been in jail for the last year and a half for murder, fraud, organized crime, wow, all the mayhem."

Mayhem was one word to describe his reign of terror.

Piper wiped the table and took the plate away as Drew filled Jasper in on her own version of the Dominic Sloan saga, involving the dead woman who wanted to make him pay. The distinct ring of her phone blended with the vibration on the counter, and she jumped up to grab it. Taj's name appeared on the screen, and she answered as fast as she could. "Hello—"

"You need to come out here." Taj's voice trembled, filled with an urgent and frantic tone.

Piper stopped and hung the dishcloth on a rack as she stared at her, and Drew turned away. "Where?" She focused on Taj's voice as it cut out.

"Neptune Point... the new house. That woman is talking and I'm not feeling what she's putting down. She told me to come here, but I can't see her, she won't stop repeating herself and I think I'm losing it."

"What is she saying?"

"The note I gave you," he said. "Over and over and over again, begging me to remember it. You need to come out here, please, Drew."

The part had arrived for her car, and she'd told Nico she would drop it off at the garage after work. "Can you drive to my house before Maze and we'll talk—"

"No, she's still here, man. You need to come see for yourself. I can't do this."

A tapping on her shoulder caught her attention, and she spun around, meeting Piper's inquisitive gaze. "It's Taj, isn't it?"

Drew stared at her blankly; she didn't know what to say, how to break her promise. But she needed her best friend. And she knew Taj needed her too.

"I can hear his voice through the phone." Piper scrunched her nose. "Is he okay?"

"Are you still there?" Taj's voice shook.

"I'm at work, but so is Piper. She's worried."

"She knows. I told her." White noise drowned out Taj's voice.

Drew dragged her teeth over her bottom lip and pulled her phone from her face to check the time. She could make it out there in under twenty minutes if she drove fast. "I'm on my way."

She hung up as Piper grabbed her arm and dragged her through the swinging kitchen door. "Where is he? I'm coming too."

"Neptune Point. Why didn't you tell me you knew?"

"Why didn't you tell me *you* knew?" Piper huffed as she flung her tie-dye backpack over her shoulder.

"He didn't want me to say anything."

Jasper shoved the back door open. "Where are you two going in a panic?"

"Neptune Point to meet Taj." An oppressive wall of sweltering heat took her breath away as she stepped outside to the parking lot and rushed toward her car. "Come with me, Piper.

Taj can bring you back to get your car after." She cranked the cool air on as Piper hopped in beside her, waving to Jasper.

As she pulled out of the parking lot, the red dripping over the landing of her painting tugged at her mind.

So much for staying away from the lighthouse.

Thirteen

Drew navigated the curve and sped across the bridge approaching Neptune Point. The sleepy rotations of the lighthouse beacon blended with the orange hue of the sunlight. Shimmering light reflected off the waves as they rolled against the rocky edges of the rough shoreline. The beauty surrounding Neptune Point masked the haunting fear lurking beneath the surface.

Piper rolled her window down and stuck her hand out the window, pointing. "There's his car."

Taj's striking red jeep gleamed under the sun, and he leaned against the door while Drew pulled up alongside him. There was no sign of Aurora, but the amulet pulsed against her skin and her hands burned as she clung to the steering wheel.

Unbuckling her seatbelt, Piper bounded out of the car and hugged him. He'd trusted Piper with his secret, but couldn't have told his mom yet, or Celeste would have called her. Unsure of what to expect, and pressed for time, Drew killed the engine and got out, joining them. Salty gusts rolled over the rocks and clung to her skin, cutting through the heat.

"I didn't know who else to call." Taj stared over the hill toward the lighthouse.

Piper shook his arms and with a gentle touch, turned his face to hers. "You're not in this alone, I told you that. I'm here, and this isn't Drew's first rodeo." She smiled, but her eyes revealed her worry.

Any frustration Drew had about driving out to this place again subsided when she saw the fear in Taj's eyes. "What happened when you got here?"

"Just whispers and humming, like a fucked-up lullaby." As he rubbed his face, the wind carried a melodic woman's voice over the hill. His head jerked upward. "That, do you hear that?"

Drew trudged through the overgrown grass toward the new keeper's house and ignored the sensation of the dry blades scratching her legs.

"Do you see her?" Taj asked as he trailed after her, Piper following close behind.

A flock of seagulls dove and screeched overhead, cutting through the woman's humming. "Not yet, but I can hear her." Drew moved closer to the newly constructed house. A blue tarp covered the front porch, and a tilted tractor stood off to the side in the sand. The distinct scent of fresh wood surrounded her, and stickers remained on each newly installed window and the front door. But as stunning as the house appeared overlooking the water, she couldn't think of a single local who'd move into this place given the history.

She left the house behind and made her way toward the lighthouse. A sudden blast of icy air enveloped her, and her body recoiled as a shadowed silhouette emerged. The sea air whipped through Aurora's black hair, tossing it over her shoulders as she glided closer to Drew. Her dress, charred at the edges, swirled around her feet while tendrils of dark smoke circled around her.

"She's here," Drew whispered.

Piper gripped Taj's arm as he stood next to Drew. He fixed his gaze in the same direction as hers, though she knew he could only hear the dead woman. "She's here? You see her?" He lowered his voice, muttering to himself, "I'm not losing it. I knew she was real."

"You're definitely not losing it." A centuries-old witch had returned with strange warnings, and she needed to unravel the dead woman's intentions before something terrible happened. Sand filled her sneakers with each step forward on the soft ground until she faced Aurora.

"What does she look like?" Releasing Taj, Piper advanced toward Aurora, oblivious to the dead woman's presence.

"Piper, stay back." Taj reached for her, but she continued forward.

"What do you want?" Drew cut around Piper, creating a barrier between her friend and Aurora. "You said a storm is coming, but what does that mean? How does the painting fit into any of this?" She held out her tingling hands, and a light sparked along her skin. "I can't protect myself if I don't know what's coming."

Aurora extended her pale, bony fingers until they wrapped around the amulet. Purple light emanated through the woman, surrounding them both.

Piper clutched Drew's arm. "What's that light from?"

"She won't hurt us," Drew said, keeping her voice steady.

Aurora tilted her head to the side, her dark eyes falling on Piper before shifting to Taj, motioning for him to come closer. The skin on her arm had melted in jagged patterns, leaving behind dark red scars covered in a purple hue when illuminated by her magical light. Her mouth moved in silent words, gradually becoming louder as she recited the spell from the note. "Call the quarters. Seek shelter from the storm. Seek bravery in the face of death, breathe in life."

"She's doing it again." Taj had positioned himself beside Drew.

"That's Taj, you're freaking him out," Drew said. "We need more than a spell, Aurora."

"Can't she just say what it is she wants to say? What is it with this woman and chanting?" Taj's eyebrows knitted together, creating a deep crease, highlighting the intensity in his eyes.

Piper crossed her arms. "Should we... run?"

"No, she's trying to help us, but her method is useless." Drew's heart pounded in her chest as she dared to step closer until she was inches from Aurora's face.

"She stopped chanting. Drew, is she still here?" Taj raised his voice over the surge of waves hitting the rocks.

"I think she is," Piper said from behind Drew.

The overpowering aroma of singed flesh assaulted Drew's nostrils, and her stomach lurched. The darkness of Aurora's eyes resembled giant pupils, but the purple light radiating from the dead woman seeped through Drew with a calming effect on her racing heart, like a magical spell. She lowered her voice as she spoke to Aurora, as though the woman had entranced her. "If you don't help me understand, I can't help you or myself." She released her breath, and the air misted in front of her. Aurora stood motionless, staring into her eyes, and Drew broke the connection. "I was wrong, you don't want to help us at all. Forget it."

A burst of fireworks crackled over Drew's skin and her mouth filled with the familiar metallic taste of magic. A high-pitched ringing permeated her ears and tore through her head before halting, replaced with a seagull's piercing cry echoing above her. Its desperate call abruptly cut off, and it plummeted to the ground.

Piper's scream cut through the surging waves and Taj bolted, crouching beside the bird.

The bird's webbed feet crisscrossed, and its chest quivered in shallow movements as a tiny pink tongue dangled from its beak. The bird's breaths slowed, and the once bright yellow rings in its eyes dulled.

Consumed by a fit of anger, Drew's outstretched hands reached for Aurora, passing through the witch's ghostly figure. "You killed it, why did you do that?" With angry tears pooling in her eyes, she dropped to the ground beside Taj.

As Aurora passed between them, she gave a slow nod in Taj's direction. "Breathe life."

Taj's head snapped up. "Did you hear that?"

"Breathe life." Drew choked through tears. "You want him to, what, fix a dead bird? It doesn't work like that. He can't bring it back—"

Aurora pressed her fingers against her burnt, peeling lips and leaned close to Taj. He flinched as she whispered once more, "Breathe. Life."

"Breathe life, you said? Like the woman's chant." Piper's eyes widened, darting between Drew and Taj. "Taj, pick up the bird."

"I'm not touching a dead bird." Taj covered his mouth as he eyed the lifeless seagull.

Aurora stayed close to Taj's side as though waiting for him to do something... do what?

Breathe life.

Drew placed her hand on Taj's arm. "Piper's right, pick it up."

"Do you realize how insane this shit is?"

"I wish I didn't." Drew sniffed back tears. "But I think Aurora's trying to tell us something."

He attempted to grab the lifeless bird with his hands without making contact. "What do I do?"

"Breathe life," Drew said.

"Like what? CPR on a bird? I'm not putting my mouth on..." He bent closer, making a face at the graying tongue hanging out of the seagull's beak.

"Look at your hands, babe. You're wasting time, pick it up." Piper scooped up the bird and handed it to Taj.

He held his arms out as Piper slid the poor creature into his waiting hands. "I can't believe I'm doing this, what do I do with it?" A purple light radiated from his hands, encircling the seagull. He coughed and inhaled sharply. "Drew, what's going on? I feel like someone lit a fire in my chest."

"Spells help me focus my magic, try saying the words you gave me on the note," Drew said. In her journey to learn her own magic, she never imagined she would have to teach someone else.

"Do I say the words she keeps repeating all damn day?" Taj stood, balancing the seagull in his arms.

The amulet heated against Drew's skin, and a powerful wave of magic pulsed in her hands. "Do it."

"Call the quarters. Seek shelter from the storm. Seek bravery in the face of death, breathe in life," Taj uttered Aurora's persistent words, repeating them louder a second time, and louder still a third.

With closed eyes, Aurora raised her hands and faced her palms towards the sky. "Breathe life." A beaming smile crossed her face as she spoke the words before vanishing into a burst of vibrant purple and gray sparkles.

Taj lifted his hand, directing it over the seagull's head, and the bird's chest expanded as it took in a breath. He held his arms out as the seagull flapped its wings and let out a screech before taking flight.

Piper flung her arms around Taj, holding him. "You did it! You really did it. You brought a dead animal to life."

"How?" He looked at Drew. "That's not possible, how is that possible?"

Drew pushed herself off the ground and brushed sand off her legs. "Magic."

Taj surveyed the rocky cliffs and forest leading to Haven, his gaze landing back on Drew. "It's quiet. She's gone, isn't she?"

"For now," Drew said. Taj could breathe life, but she still was no further ahead at understanding Aurora's storm warning or the red dripping over the painting.

"For now? You expect her back?" Piper asked.

Drew shrugged. "I don't have a damn clue, but I wish I did."

Jack had once been an eerie, constant presence in Drew's nightmares before he entered her reality with his warnings, changing her life forever. And now it was her turn to help Taj. Celeste's kindness and support meant the world to her, and as Taj walked up back up the hill beside her, with magic coursing through him, she made a promise to not let him face his new world alone.

Piper climbed into the passenger seat of Taj's jeep, leaving the door open. "Should you tell your mom about this?"

Taj opened the driver's side door and rested his hand on the frame, pausing. "Not yet, I've got to let this sink in or something. If she gets a weird vibe off me she'll panic." He glanced at Drew, narrowing his brown eyes. "You know she'll be all over me for this, and I can't just yet... You promise you won't say anything?"

Celeste might not panic, but he was right, his mother wouldn't leave him alone until she could fix it, and that might be an impossible task.

Taj must've sensed Drew's hesitation and clasped his hands together, like he was begging her. "I'll tell her, okay? Just let me do it when the time is right. I need to know I can trust you with this."

"You can trust me, I won't tell her, promise," Drew said. Celeste needed to know, but she wanted him to trust her. She fished her keys from her pocket and unlocked her car. Her phone came alive with notifications as it picked up cell service. She was late getting to the garage.

Taj lingered as he sat in his jeep. "I don't get it, why me? And what was the point of killing a bird so I could bring it back to life?"

"I think she needed you to know what you can do." Drew's stomach clenched in knots as the image of scarlet paint saturating the canvas on the lighthouse landing popped into her mind. It was obvious it signified blood. But whose?

Piper leaned over and planted a kiss on Taj's cheek, thumbing lip gloss off his face after. "You're going to be okay, we'll get you through this. Look how adjusted Drew is."

A sudden laugh escaped Drew. "Adjusted?" Her mind spiraled, thinking of the past few years of ghosts, death, murderous secrets, and trauma.

"Well, yeah, I think so," Piper said seriously. "You're strong and your gift is badass and cool." Piper's doe eyes connected with Taj's. "What happened today was a miracle. I love you."

Taj touched Piper's face and kissed her. He'd done the impossible... a miracle. He would adjust, just like Piper said. And magic or not, the connection between Piper and Taj was undeniable.

"Can you promise you'll tell me if anything else happens, nightmares, voices... anything," Drew asked.

Taj extended his fist through the open window, and Drew met it with her own. "You got it," he said.

Nico's name illuminated on Drew's phone screen as it rang. "Hey, I'm on my way." She eyed Taj as he started the jeep and reversed onto the road. "Something came up." As Nico talked on the other end, she started the car and rolled the windows down.

"All good, I still have a few things to finish up and didn't know if you were still dropping your car off... you didn't message me back, and I wasn't sure if I should leave without you." His voice sounded distant, and static cut through the connection.

"Nico, I'm losing you, I'll be there soon."

The call went dead, leaving silence on the other end.

Fourteen

Drew parked beside Nico's black Chevelle, her car no match for the muscle car. Across the road from De-Sarro's Auto Repair and Restoration parking lot, the ship-yard where her father worked bustled with activity. She hadn't heard from him in a few weeks, and was used to his absence, but as she got out of the car, the row of ships docked held her gaze like magnets.

She lingered near the edge of the DeSarro's property as dockhands dropped anchor on a small fishing boat across the road. The echo of commands shouted over seagulls' cries and scraping metal, but their exact words remained unintelligible.

With her fingertips, she curled her lip toward her teeth and the taste of salty air filled her mouth. Two men exited the larger of the three warehouses, gesturing to someone driving a forklift. Sloan's warehouse was at the opposite end of the expansive shipyard. The memory of the shooting pervaded her mind, and her body tensed. She hadn't been back to the warehouse, and never wanted to step foot near the building again.

Breathing through the vice grip on her throat, she searched for her dad, but he wasn't among the workers or expected home for two more weeks. Since they'd repaired their relationship, he always called as soon as his ship docked, and he never broke a promise.

Boots hitting pavement reverberated from behind her and she shifted her stance as Nico walked up beside her, looking at his phone. He'd unzipped his grease-stained coveralls, revealing a white T-shirt underneath. But what grabbed her attention was the somber look on his face. "Did you want to come inside? It's a hell of a lot cooler. I'm almost done, and we can go."

"Sure." She didn't bother forcing a smile. Not with Nico. "What's wrong?"

Sliding his phone in his pocket, he looked at her, his face lighting up, but not reaching his eyes. "The part came in for your car, but I won't get to it until later tomorrow."

She took the car key off its metal ring and held it out for him. "My key."

He took it from her with a smile, his dimple trying to charm her away from the tension in his jaw and the distant look in his eyes. Whatever was troubling him was bigger than parts for her car. "I didn't mean to hang up, the phone cut off."

"It wasn't you, it was me."

"Were you at work?" he asked.

No, but I promised Taj I wouldn't say anything.

She averted her gaze, shielding her eyes from the sun, and scanned the shipyard again. She had tried not to keep things from him, but it was unavoidable. "Yeah." Her face flushed as the lie escaped, but she faced him. "What's wrong? I can tell something's off."

With furrowed brows, he tucked her key into his coveralls' pocket and gazed at the shipyard. "I wouldn't have agreed to buy this place if that warehouse was anywhere near it, I didn't want to buy here at all. I tried to find a way to just keep the shop where it was. Dad and I got into a fight about it, and everything's been a fucking mess ever since."

The reasons behind the garage location and the decisions made to purchase the space had never crossed her mind. She was oblivious to the heated arguments between Nico and his father over it. "You never told me that."

"I know."

"I don't care that the garage is where it is, and I don't want you and your dad to fight over it because of me."

His jaw clenched, and a muscle twitched beneath his skin. "I see you looking over there every time you come. I know you hate it down here."

"That's not true."

He tilted his head, squinting as the sun reflected in his brown eyes, turning them into their captivating amber hue. "Mom got an offer on the house today, there's no chance of going back. I haven't seen her so excited about anything in a long time, probably not since before Dad got caught dealing with..." Nico shifted his gaze away from her. "Not since before everything went down with the business, maybe even before that."

His entire world was on the verge of a tremendous shift, and she would have to be there for him the way he'd been there for her, but she wasn't sure how to break through the unfamiliar walls he was building around himself. "I'm sorry, Nico. I know how shitty this is. It's going to be okay—"

"It'll have to be, I'll make it okay." He ran a hand through his hair and rubbed the faint stubble along his jaw, averting his eyes from hers.

Stepping closer, she extended her hand, longing to hug him and comfort him, like he'd done for her so many times, but he turned away and headed toward his shop behind them.

Above the three large garage doors, DeSarro's Auto Repair and Restoration sign proudly displayed its bold letters. Nico had never walked away from her before, and it left her with a deep ache in her chest and a twinge of emptiness.

Not everyone goes away, she reminded herself. *Stop torturing yourself and let that shit go. This isn't about you, it's about Nico losing his family home.*

As she followed him toward the entrance, she glanced over her shoulder. The sun reflected off the row of metal shipping containers and a wave of nausea swept through her, forcing her to take a sharp breath.

He's right. I hate this place.

If her car didn't need work, she'd ask him for the key back and drive home, away from this place, but her determination to support Nico outweighed any lingering effects of her past trauma.

Nico leaned on the glass door to the shop, holding it open for her, his heartbreak eyes peering down at her through his long lashes. "I'll make sure you get your car back as soon as I can."

"I know you will. I'm not worried about it." She placed her hand on his chest as she walked by. His T-shirt, damp with sweat, hugged his body, accentuating his broad chest. "Thanks for taking care of it for me. Just let me know what I owe you."

"Nothing," he said, his voice distant.

"What about the parts?"

"I've got you."

"Nico, I don't need you to—"

"I want to. If I can take care of stuff for you, I will." He let the door close behind him, and his biceps flexed as he slid his arms in his coveralls and yanked them back up, leaving the front open.

"I appreciate it, but I can take care of things on my own." The air conditioner over-compensated for the scorching heat as it pumped icy air on full blast, sending a prickling of goose-bumps over her skin. She rubbed her arms and crossed them over her chest.

Ignoring her comment, Nico disappeared into a storage room behind the counter and returned with a black zip-up sweater. "Turn around," he said as he held the sweater for her to slip her arms into.

A faint aroma of grease and cigarette smoke drifted from the sweater as she let the sleeves hang over her hands. "Thanks."

"It's just us in here. Sil's gone for the day, and I haven't seen Dad since lunch." Darkness flitted through his eyes when he mentioned his father. "The office is unlocked if you want to hang out in there, or you can come with me. I just need fifteen minutes to clean up, and we'll get out of here."

A topic change might lift him from his dark mood. "What are you working on? Can I see?"

A small smile graced his lips for the first time. "Of course you can."

She followed him through the door separating the shop front from the massive garage bays. A fan exchanging air wheezed continuously as she scurried around a red lift contraption underneath a raised truck on a lift of its own. "That won't crash down, will it?"

Nico sauntered toward the back of the garage. "It's resting on a safety catch. I promise you're safe in here with me."

She stepped over a grease stain on the concrete floor and came face to face with a motorcycle in the next bay. "Those are death machines." The ghost of a man with half his face missing had followed her around campus for two weeks before she figured out where his girlfriend lived. The memory of arriving uninvited at a woman's office building to reveal the whereabouts of her late boyfriend's intended engagement ring was something Drew hoped to never relive. At least she had helped him cross over.

Nico laughed. "It's not mine, but they aren't death machines, not if you know how to ride. Sil works on them—he used to work on ships with your dad. It's bringing in new business."

He led her to a sleek car at the back in a separate ventilated area with its own garage door facing the rear of the building.

"You finished renovating back here?" Her fingertips brushed over the pale silver sports car. As Nico turned on the fluorescent overhead lights, they reflected off the metallic paint, creating a shimmering effect.

"Dad gave me money to build this space so I can keep the resto cars separate from the day-to-day repairs. And this is my summer project. A 1969 Camaro." Nico opened the car door and leaned inside. "It's still got the original suspension but needs a new console and I'll replace those torn bucket seats. She just had a new paint job, champagne metallic. It's rare to find this color anymore. She's beautiful."

Afraid of leaving fingerprints, Drew pulled her hand away from the car. "She?"

"Oh yeah, with that power and beauty? This one's definitely she." As Nico spoke, the tension slipped out of him, easing his shoulders. He told her of the woman from upstate who vacationed in Alas Cliffs for the summer with her sister, who had heard about his restoration business and its growing reputation and entrusted him with reviving her cherished Camaro her late father had left her. He gently shut the car door and flipped the light off. "I'll put my tools away and we'll go."

Drew's fingers found their way into the pockets of his coveralls, and she gave a playful tug. Unable to physically make him move closer, his work boots shuffled along the concrete as he bridged the gap between them until they were inches apart.

Tilting her head to the side, she shifted her gaze until their eyes met. "Everything's going to be okay. I've got you, too."

He cupped her face in his calloused hands and held eye contact before bringing his mouth toward hers. Rising on her tiptoes, she leaned in and met him halfway, their lips brushing against each other. His warm breath mingled with hers as their lips connected, sending a shiver through her, tingling down her legs, intensifying the connection between them. Being in Nico's arms, kissing him, holding him close, was magic, like nothing she possessed, but he remained oblivious to the way he could make the world vanish.

His hands dropped from her face and trailed down her back until they found her hips underneath the over-sized sweater. She wrapped her arms around his neck, pressing her body against his, and he responded by pulling her even closer. He brought her with him as he stepped back, leaning against a workbench. His tongue had a lingering taste of spearmint gum. She slid her hands inside his coveralls, slipping them off his shoulders and tracing her fingers down his back.

The sudden slam of a door reverberated through the room, and the heavy thud of footsteps followed, echoing off the walls. Drew jerked her head away and untangled herself from Nico's embrace. Straightening up, he shrugged the top of his coveralls back over his shoulders and ran a hand through his hair. Her heart raced like a marathon runner, and beads of sweat formed on her skin. She unzipped the sweater and let it fall down her arms, clutching it in an anxious death grip.

Nico's father crossed the garage and placed a toolbox on a metal shelf. His dark, wavy hair clung to his forehead as he rummaged through a workbench near the motorcycle, not looking their way. "She can't be in here. It's a liability and if anything happens, you'd be in shit, and so would the business."

Drew glanced at Nico and watched as the tension returned with a vengeance in his temples and along his jawline. "She's fine."

Nick DeSarro narrowed his eyes at Nico. "She's not fine, she's a liability." He lifted his hand to wipe sweat off his forehead, revealing telltale signs of perspiration under the arms of his button-up shirt.

Drew had known Nico's dad for a long time, and his gruffness wasn't out of character, but a blade could slice through the tension in the garage. The amulet thrummed under her shirt against her skin, and she clamped her hand over it.

"Hi, Mr. DeSarro, I was just here for a minute to see the car. I'm leaving." She shot Nico a quick glance before heading for the exit.

"Nick." Nico's father softened his tone. "You've been around long enough, Drew. It's just Nick. I'm not that important."

She nodded in silent acknowledgement as she passed him. Gray hair had grown through his mustache and spotty goatee, and fine lines had deepened around his eyes. The troubled, distant look returned to Nico's face as he observed his father.

"I'll wait out front." Without waiting for Nico to respond, she stepped through the door into the front of the shop. She draped the sweater on the back of one of the waiting room chairs and stared through the window, between the auto parts signs, and an advertisement for motor oil. The sun beamed down over Nico's Chevelle, highlighting the black surface, and she touched the back of her chilled legs, imagining how nice the warmth of that seat would be. A picnic table sat empty on a grassy area near the corner of the building, shaded by trees.

She had her hand on the handle of the glass door, ready to walk outside, when the door separating the garage from the front room swung open, hitting the wall behind it. Nico's father bent down behind the counter and lifted a black duffel bag. "He'll be out in a minute, he's cleaning up. Did you want anything? Water? Coffee?" He gestured to a mini fridge on a small counter with a coffee machine and a wire holder filled with coffee pods.

"I'm good, thanks." Her knuckles paled under her grip on the door handle.

Holding the duffel bag with both hands, Nico's father headed for the back office. The door shut with a thud and a sharp metallic clang as music switched on, filling the air with the muffled sounds of an electric guitar and the steady beat of a drum. Nick DeSarro had always been the strong and silent type, but never this unapproachable and cold. Nico's family was falling apart, and there wasn't a damn thing she could do to help.

FIFTEEN

With her hand still gripping the shop's metal door handle, Drew shoved it open and stepped outside into the scorching heat. Squinting against the sun's harsh glare, she made her way toward the picnic table and sank onto the wooden seat. The shipyard across the road had fallen silent, leaving the seagulls' cries to fill the air and blend with the waves lapping against rocks. The dying seagull's shallow breaths and tortured cry haunted her mind. Taj had brought that bird back to life. Was that his own magic, or Aurora's power, flowing through him?

She resisted the urge to pick at the peeling blue paint along the side of the wooden table matching the trim on the building. DeSarro's Auto Repair and Restoration attracted both locals and tourists, and it was a significant improvement over the smaller garage at Nico's house. His father's instincts were correct; the building and location couldn't be more perfect, and any fear or anxiety that plagued her when she was near the shipyard were her own to handle, not Nico's. He had enough to deal with and would have to find a place to live unless he opted to stay with his mom. But that would mean traveling back and forth every day if she stuck with her plan to move in with her sister an hour away. He could find an apartment, or a roommate.

Or he could move in with me.

As she gnawed the inside of her cheek, her fingertips explored the rough, unfinished wood hidden under the layer of paint. A sharp pinch caught on her finger, and she jerked her hand back to inspect the source of the throbbing pain. A sliver of wood embedded itself underneath her skin. She squeezed and picked at it, wincing as she forced the tiny splinter from her flesh.

The bushes between the trees rustled as something moved beside her and she banged her knee on the table as she hopped up. "Ouch, Jesus!" Rubbing her knee, she focused on the scurrying action happening among the trees.

The dog from the Tough Cookie emerged from the bushes, its limp more pronounced as it settled on the dusty ground beyond the pavement, panting in the sweltering heat. Matted fur covered its floppy ears as its sad eyes locked on her. The dog's features up close triggered a nostalgic memory of a Lab-Shepherd mix she had once seen in a movie as a child.

"How'd you get here?" With slow, calculated steps, she approached, lowering to a crouching position a few feet away. The Tough Cookie wasn't far—nothing was in Atlas Cliffs—but the dog must've been on a steady prowl to find its way through the trees behind the buildings to get here.

The dog sat at attention, tilting its head from side to side as a whine escaped. She edged closer for a better look. Covered in dirt, the dog's emaciated torso revealed ribs through its fur. Its big brown eyes tracked her every move, whimpering louder as it limped in circles before collapsing on the pavement. With a groan, it rested its head on muddy front paws. Her heart hurt at the sight of the poor pup. She dared to reach her hand out, but the dog cowered.

"You've got no one to take care of you? You must be thirsty."

She glanced at the building for a hose, or water source. "I'll get you water and food." The dog lifted its head, its ears perking up. "I won't hurt you, promise." The dog sat back up, its tail wagging. Concentrating on a deep place of calm, energy coursed through her hands, sending a subtle tingling sensation as she held them low, palms up toward the dog.

The dog scuttled closer to her, stopping to lick the dried blood on its hind leg. Abandoned and broken, the sweet animal looked up at her with a mixture of hope and fear. It nudged her hands, now burning as a faint glow emitted from the center. The dog licked her fingers and she pet its head, rubbing behind its ears. The pup had no collar, tags, or any sign of an owner, and she had no intention of leaving it here.

She eyed the few cars in the lot—her car wasn't an option. The dog wasn't small, but not too big for the back seat of Nico's Chevelle. He wouldn't be angry if she used his car... his expensive, newly restored, clean car, to rescue a dog. A muddy, bleeding, injured dog. Nico once had a dog, Maisie. She'd died when he was fifteen, devastating him. His mother vowed to never have a pet again, but he loved animals. He'd know what to do, and she'd clean the seats.

"Will you bite me if I pick you up?" The dog blinked and nudged her hands again. She laughed. "I'll take that as a no."

If only she could communicate with animals the way she could with the dead. She stood and stepped backward toward Nico's car, gesturing to the dog to follow her. The amulet mirrored the energy buzzing under her skin as she continued to call the dog. "Come on. You can do it."

The dog limped forward, whining as it followed her. With a guttural screech, a raven dove over her head, its ink-black feathers shimmering in the sunlight. A gust of air off the water brushed her skin, cutting through the oppressive humid air. The raven soared over the cars and vanished into the distance, leaving no evidence of danger behind.

A drawn-out whine sounded from her feet, dragging her attention back to the injured dog. She pushed the button on the Chevelle's handle and the door opened. Folding the front seat forward, she patted the spotless red seat.

Shit. He's going to be pissed.

"Jump up. Come. Up." The dog stared at her and sat on the pavement beside Nico's car.

"You've got to help him." Jules appeared, leaning over the open car door.

Drew gasped. "You're back."

"You thought you could block me forever? I'm disappointed in you. So disappointed."

Drew let out a slow breath between pursed lips. Celeste had warned her the block-the-dead spell wouldn't hold up for long. "I needed time—"

"Well, you're in luck because all I've got is time. You got me good, I'll give you that, but I've got tricks too, you know, and you're not shutting me out again."

Jules folded her arms across her chest. Sunlight emphasized the bloodstains on her shirt, intensifying a pit in Drew's stomach. Guilt was winning. She'd used magic, creating a barrier between herself and Jules, and it had worked. But all it did was postpone the inevitable. She couldn't escape the dead forever. They'd find her, they always did.

Jules bent down and patted the dog on the head, and the dog did something no one else but Drew could do. It looked up at Jules, wagging its tail, *seeing* her. "Of course, you can see me, but no one else can. The punches keep coming." Jules stood with an eye roll. "Are you taking him home?"

Drew eyed the garage, expecting Nico to be there, but there was no sign of him. "I'm waiting for him to finish work."

"Not *boyfriend* him, *dog* him."

Drew patted the back seat again and called to the dog. "What do you think I'm trying to do?"

"I wish I knew." Jules gestured to the dog. "Have you tried picking him up?"

"Not exactly, but I was getting to it."

She was not getting to that part, but there was no way she'd admit that to her snarky ghost companion. Drew lowered herself to the ground, her arms encircling the dog's body, providing support for its hindquarters. A pungent odor like death mixed with a skunk's spray emanating from its fur overwhelmed her senses, forcing her to breathe through her mouth. As she lifted, trying to balance its awkward weight in her arms, the dog let out a wail. She struggled to keep a firm grip on it as it wriggled and thrashed, but she crouched, nearly dropping the dog on the back seat of Nico's car. "I'm so sorry! What did I do? Did I hurt you? Are you okay?"

Jules crouched beside her. "Did he talk back? Can you communicate with animals too?"

"Ha ha, Jules. Really? I'm trying to help it."

Jules rolled her sparkling, ghost-like eyes again. "He's obviously hurt, look at his back leg."

"I know it's hurt. I didn't mean to make it cry like that."

"Him," Jules said.

"How do you know?"

"Really? You can't see this is a male dog, Drew?"

Heat rose to her face, intensifying her burning skin from the sun as she glimpsed what Jules was talking about. "I see that now, thank you for pointing it out. I haven't spent a lot of time around animals."

"Mm-hmm," Jules said.

"Can you help me get him to lie down?"

Jules raised her arms, but they resembled a ghostly silhouette. "Of course I can do that for you. I'm an expert at dealing with this middle of the road nowhere existence."

"You said you had tricks." With a gentle touch, Drew pet the dog and adjusted him on the back seat. The dog licked

Drew's face, and she recoiled, but softened when her eyes locked onto the dog's pitiful expression with flattened ears and visible whites of his eyes as he looked up at her. She returned the front seat back in position, leaving the door open for air.

"You've got company," Jules said with her eyes glued to the door beside the garage. "Lover boy is coming. I didn't say it before 'causes I was mad at you, but I don't blame you for blocking me. I'd do the same thing if I had *that* around all day long." With a stern gaze, she pointed her finger at Drew. "But don't do it again. I'm just saying I get it."

"Would you please stop calling him that?" Drew lowered her voice. Another wave of heat rushed to her cheeks when her eyes fell on Nico's back as he shut the door behind him. Jules wasn't wrong, but *lover boy?*

Making his way toward the car, he slung a backpack over his shoulder. He had taken off the coveralls, leaving him in a T-shirt and jeans worn out to perfection.

Brown paw prints covered the red seat as the dog stared up at her. She made a mental note to pick up cleaner and one of Gran's soft rags.

"He doesn't look happy. Is he one of those guys who loses his mind if a drop of dirt touches his sexy muscle car?"

He absolutely is not one of those guys, but this won't be good.

With a furrowed brow, Nico approached, eyeing the open car door. "What's that smell?"

She held her hands out to stop him. "Before you freak out, I'm going to take care of it."

"I'm scared to look." He bent down and stuck his head inside the car. His eyes widened as he stepped back. "What the fuck? The seats are trashed. Where did this dog come from?"

Jules' smirk turned into giggling; a sound Drew never thought she'd ever hear from her. "Oh, he's pissed," Jules said.

Drew reached into the car and gave the dog a gentle pat behind his filthy ears. "Someone abandoned him, and he'll die if we don't help." She stood with her hand on the door frame. "Sorry I got your car dirty—"

"No you're not." Closing his eyes, Nico let out a frustrated breath through pursed lips and ran his hands over his tired face.

"I'm not sorry I let the dog in the backseat, but I am sorry about the seats. I'll clean them and you'll never know he was here."

Nico sighed; his eyes fixated on the dog. Silent seconds ticked by as though he were contemplating his next move. He extended his hand to the backseat and scratched the dog's ears. A small smile fought to break through, but it dropped when he looked back up. "He stinks, but he's not going to die. I might if I can't sell this car because the seats are ruined."

"You're selling it? You love this car, I don't understand, your dad gave it to you—"

"I can't keep it, it's just... business." He popped the trunk and dropped his backpack, closing it with a thud.

Nico positioned the seat forward, scrutinizing the dog as he ran a hand over the muddy paw prints stubbornly clinging to the vibrant, red interior. "Jesus, this better come off." He pushed the seat back in place. "The dog's in rough shape."

Dropping her arms to her sides, Drew made her way to the passenger side. "That's why he's in your backseat."

"I see that," he said.

As Drew flung the passenger door open, Jules rushed to her side. "Can you call him Henry? That was my dog's name... the day I died I'd dropped him home and had to run to the store for ice, or something... my memory comes through in bits and pieces and it's not clear, but I remember walking Henry on the beach." Pointing downward, she let her chin fall to her chest. "That's why the bare feet. I never returned home." In a sudden whirl, Jules disappeared as a radiant light surrounded her.

Slight relief coursed through Drew; Jules had finally unveiled a piece of her time alive. It might be a small memory, but perhaps more would follow, and Drew could help her sooner than she thought.

Oblivious to Jules, Nico reached into his pocket and pulled out a set of keys. "All right, let's do this. Get in, we'll find a vet that can check him out before they close."

Drew winced as the seat scorched the backs of her legs. The engine rumbled to life, and she yanked the door closed.

Nico cranked up the air conditioning, flipping the vintage radio on. "You okay?"

"I'm on fire, but I think I'll survive."

"You're on fire all right." He backed out of the space, reaching a hand back to pet the dog before steering toward town.

"What held you up for so long?" She hesitated to bring up the topic of the odd encounter with his father, and the discernable tension between them.

"I had more to do than I thought." He grabbed his sunglasses from the visor and put them on, hiding his eyes. "Look up vets that are still open. It's almost 7. Someone must be available."

"Think we'll make to Maze on time?" She dialed the number for the Atlas Cliff's animal hospital.

"For 8 o'clock? Not a chance."

Piper would not be happy when she showed up and found Claudia waiting with Drew nowhere in sight. She informed the vet receptionist about the dog situation and hung up before sending Piper a quick message that she'd be late.

The faint twitch along Nico's jaw returned as he drove, keeping his eyes on the road and not saying a word. A persistent feeling of dread washed over her like a rogue wave, settling in her soul like a dreadful premonition, but she couldn't figure out what to brace herself for.

Sixteen

"You're late." Claudia leaned back in her chair and picked at the lace trim along her V-neck top with her matching pink fingernails.

"We needed to take care of something." Drew approached the large round table near the stage. A growing number of people disrupted the usual quiet Wednesday evening at Maze. Taj's band were setting up for an impromptu concert sponsored by Tate Real Estate, and tourists and locals mingled together over pizza and beer specials, filling the room with a loud hum of chatter. Too loud for a discussion about party planning. Claudia's decision to gather at Maze when a text message would've sufficed baffled her. She had no intention of leaving the house at all until Nico and Jasper reassured her that the dog wasn't on his deathbed and would be fine in the bathroom, with vet medication, food, and water.

"You're here now, and that's all that matters. I'm featuring your art at the party, and I need you to sign a few things." Claudia's meticulously groomed eyebrows raised as she flipped through pages of a notebook.

Grant Salinger rolled the sleeves of his pressed linen shirt up and grabbed chairs from a nearby table. With a cool, confident stride, he approached Claudia, his commercial smile lighting up his face as he leaned over and muttered something in her ear. Her cotton-candy pink lips turned into a sly grin as she slapped his arm and laughed. The Atlas Cliffs ice-queen had found a king to rule alongside her.

I'm an asshole for thinking like this about her. She's been through stuff too.

It had been a long day, and irritability simmered underneath her skin.

"Are you good if I go help Taj?" Nico's arm encircled her waist, sending a shiver up her back. Staying home would have been a much better option.

"Go ahead, I'm good." She smiled, but he responded with a solemn nod. Worry had lurked in his eyes since they left the garage, and she wasn't sure what to do about it.

Claudia swept her blonde hair off her shoulder. "Sit beside me." She sat on the edge of the chair with perfect posture and patted the empty seat next to her.

Still unsure what Claudia needed her for, Drew stretched her neck from side to side and settled in the seat beside her. A massive half-eaten pepperoni pizza with a candle underneath keeping it warm, surrounded by glasses brimming with ice and a variety of drinks, adorned the round table. As Claudia talked about the party location, décor, and which of Drew's paintings she planned to feature, Piper waved from the stage, her pink ponytail bouncing as she jumped. She grabbed Taj and kissed him like she'd never see him again before bounding down the stairs toward the table.

"You're not paying attention," Claudia said.

"Yes, I am. You can use whatever paintings you want. It's cool with me, promise." She wanted to get this over with and get back home to the dog... *Henry.*

"I can't go on a promise of what is cool with you, Drew. This could be career-changing for both of us. Important people are going to be at this party."

"You're joking, right? It's Atlas Cliffs, not big city royalty."

Claudia clicked a black pen and slid documents over. "Read them over. I want your permission to use the lighthouse piece you're working on."

Drew took the pen and froze. She hadn't touched the painting since Aurora appeared and chilling crimson paint pooled on the lighthouse landing, resembling blood. She clicked the pen a few times, retracting the ball point and placed it on the table. "You can't have it, not that one."

"Can't have what?" Shane slid into the chair next to her and leaned forward with his elbows on the table. He eyed the paper and glanced up at her. "How's party planning going?"

Shane's presence at Maze shouldn't surprise her. She should expect to see him all over town this summer now that he worked with his sister. But it was jarring. She couldn't believe there was a time she loved him, and now could hardly stand being around him.

"Did you get fitted for your tux today?" Claudia held papers in midair as she raised her eyebrows at Shane.

"Tux?" Drew asked. "How fancy *is* this thing?"

"And I found a dress that will look perfect on you," Claudia continued, steamrolling on. "This will be the best thing that's happened to Atlas Cliffs in a very long time, and no one is going to mess it up." Claudia looked from Shane to Drew and back to Shane. "The two of you can deal with each other for a few hours, can't you?"

"I'm not the one with the problem." A smug smile crossed Shane's face.

Guitar riffs reverberated through the speaker as Taj settled behind his drums and shared a laugh with the bass player. Nico's demeanor shifted as he tinkered with the sound equipment, his usual banter with the band members replaced by a quiet and solitary focus. She chewed on her lip, welcoming the soothing habit.

Claudia folded papers and placed them in an envelope. "I need you to trust me on this. I saw that piece in your studio and it's good. Really good." Claudia stared at her with intense focus, and Drew straightened her back and folded a napkin into a small square. Aurora used magic on that painting, and she refused to let Claudia get her hands on it.

"Take this proposal, read it over. This might not be big city royalty, but big city buyers are coming to this function, and you and I are here to stay, so let's secure ourselves a solid place. It'll be fun, you'll see." Sliding back in the chair, Claudia crossed her legs, revealing the straps of her heeled sandals delicately encircling her ankles. With a gentle tap, she stole Jasper's attention next to her. "Oh, and one more thing. Jasper agreed to cater the desserts."

"What? Since when?" Drew's artwork was one thing, but she wanted to keep Gran's small-town bakery far away from big city manipulation.

"Since about an hour ago. You were late, you missed it," Jasper said.

Drew shot Jasper a glare as Danny arrived, bringing a burst of sunshine with his bright smile and genuine, happy-to-be-alive attitude. He made a brief detour to Drew, wrapping his arm around her shoulders in a quick hello hug, before finding a seat across from Jasper at the table. She never imagined nurse Danny, who'd seen her at her worst after a horrible car accident, would become her friend. It baffled her how he could work in the hospital, surrounded by death and sadness, and not become jaded.

Jasper leaned across the table. "I know what you're thinking, and if you really—like, *really*—don't want me to do this, I won't. But—"

"It's good for business." If she could read minds, Jasper's thoughts would scream, "it's good for business" after every Tough Cookie decision he made, and he'd be right. But Claudia's party reminded her of Dominic Sloan's world of power, money, and manipulating people to do whatever he wanted, when he wanted. The more Claudia pushed for control, the stronger the urge to retreat home and shut out the world took over. Jasper attempted to suppress a smile as he patted Drew's hand and returned to his seat.

"Which painting is she talking about?" Stage lights flickered off Shane's jet-black hair.

"The lighthouse." Her voice faltered as the red on the landing seared into her mind like a burning ember. With a firm grip, she crumpled the envelope and shoved it into her purse, hanging from the back of the chair. "You can remind your sister that it doesn't matter what proposal she gives me. I'm not letting her have it."

Shane laughed. "Yeah, right. You think she listens to me?"

"Doesn't she? Aren't you bonded now or something? You're spending the summer here." Her crankiness was bleeding out and she couldn't stop it.

"That's really bugging you, isn't it?"

Drew tensed and shifted in her seat to face him. "Not at all. You do you, and I'll do me. What role do you have at Claudia's fancy party, anyway? It isn't your scene."

"How would you know what my scene is?" Shane gestured his hands to his chest in a symbol of pride. "You're looking at the official host of the Tate Step into Summer Bash."

"Unless that hurricane makes her cancel it," she said.

"It's still early and Claudia's ready for anything, trust me."

"There's no way she'd let you host, Shane."

"You underestimate her. We're family now, we stand united. You'll see when you show up next Saturday night." Shane's voice dripped with sarcasm as he watched Nico weave through the crowd gathered around the stage and head back to the table. "Will he be joining you?"

"Yes, actually. Are you bringing anyone?"

"Yes, actually, why? Does that bother you?"

"Why would it? I want you to be happy." It wasn't the first time she'd said those words to him, but they'd never carried as much sincerity as they did in that moment. She never wished unhappiness upon him, no matter how frustrating he could be.

"No, you don't." He didn't take his eyes off Nico. "You moved on like I meant nothing to you."

Her cheeks flushed as anger burned inside. "How could you say that after everything that's happened?" she snapped. She was barely *functioning* when she thought Shane had died. It was never *nothing*.

In a bold move, Piper swooped in between them, cutting Shane off and bringing the conversation to an abrupt halt. "I heard you got a dog and I want to meet him."

As Nico approached, Shane pushed his chair back and rose to his feet. The two of them eyed each other without saying a word. Nico positioned himself behind Drew and Piper with his hand on Drew's chair. He was taller than Shane, but Shane held his ground, folding his arms across his chest. Nico had ended their last encounter by punching a drunk, belligerent Shane in the face, but that had been months ago.

Drew gripped the table to stand as Piper leaned down close to her ear. "It's like an episode of how animals behave in the wild."

She refused to mediate Nico and Shane's conversation and shifted her weight to lean back in the chair. The music made it impossible to hear any words exchanged between them, but Nico's face remained stoic when his lips moved.

"What do you think they're talking about?" Piper plopped into the empty seat next to her.

She tugged on her bottom lip with her teeth. "I don't know, but Shane is living here for the summer, so we're going to run into him, and we've all moved on. It's really no big deal."

Anxiety simmered inside her. *If it's not a big deal, why does it look like one?*

Taking a slice of pizza off the pan, Piper gripped a string of melted cheese extending onto the table. She devoured another bite and licked her fingers as she talked. "You've got the guy who faked his own death and cheated on one side, in a silent battle with the honorable man who would walk through fire for his woman on the other. My money's on Nico."

"That's ridiculous. They're just being friendly." There would be no way Nico could be friends with Shane. There was no way *she* could be friends with Shane.

Nico folded his arms across his chest, mirroring Shane as he talked.

"That doesn't look like what I would call friendly." Piper's giggling drew the attention of Jasper and Danny, who exchanged smiles across the table. Claudia observed Piper before she glanced up at Nico and Shane, who were engrossed in conversation.

"What's that about?" Claudia asked.

"We were just wondering the same thing." Piper grabbed a napkin from a pile on the table and wiped her fingers.

Claudia huffed as she watched Piper. They tolerated each other for Drew's benefit, but that was the extent of the friendship.

"I'll intervene." Claudia uncrossed her legs, but Drew rose from the table before Claudia started something that couldn't be undone. As she moved next to Nico, her hand found his and their fingers intertwined, ending the heated conversation. His thumb traced back and forth over her hand, sending a flurry of butterflies taking off in her stomach.

Shane's eyes diverted toward Drew. He started to say something, but cut himself off and shifted his attention to Nico before his gaze fell back on her. "I'm outta here. Tell Claudia I'll see her at the gallery tomorrow." Without waiting for a response, he walked away, navigating around the crowded tables toward the door.

"What was that about?" Drew asked.

Nico's thumb stopped moving, but the subtle muscle twitching resumed along his jawline. "Nothing."

"That was not nothing, Nico. It's not like he's a friend of yours. It wasn't about me, was it?"

She cringed at how self-centered she sounded, but she couldn't think of a reason Shane and Nico would have such an intense conversation, as if they were on the verge of a physical altercation.

With a gentle tug, he pulled her close, his strong embrace pleading for her to let it go. But letting go wasn't easy for her. Letting go meant dropping the proverbial ball and allowing heartbreak to creep in. Nico never held back from her, but he had buried something deep, and she was determined to uncover it.

"We were talking cars. I'm just trying to not be an asshole to him, that's all," he said.

She wrapped her arms around his waist and leaned back, locking eyes with him. "Talk to me. It doesn't have to be here, or now, but whatever is going on, you can tell me."

Releasing his arms, he reached a hand to her face and brushed her hair off her cheek. "I've got nothing to tell."

Her stomach clenched, and a familiar ache traveled up her body, reminding her of past heartbreak. Was this the beginning of the end?

She shook her head at herself; even for her, that was too dramatic. But she knew him, and he was hiding something.

Strings of lights flickered along the ceiling, casting a warm glow. The band shifted to a mellow tune, and Nico leaned down from behind her.

"Wanna dance?"

"I thought you didn't dance."

"I don't."

She slowly turned around and held out her hand. "Sure, but should I lead, or will you?"

"There's leading involved?"

"So I've heard."

He took hold of her hand and steered her toward a small open area near the stage. Her hands found their way around his neck and his around her waist. The drum's steady rhythm echoed in her chest, mimicking a heartbeat. Nico pulled her in closer, his fingertips grazing the small of her back beneath her shirt as they swayed together. If only she could bottle moments like this and lock them in her soul to revisit whenever she needed an escape.

Old habits begged her to pull away, shut down... run. Anything to keep from getting hurt, but the threat wasn't clear. And this was Nico. Her Nico. He loved her, and she loved him. There was nothing here she had to run from.

The song ended, and she and Nico parted.

"I'm going to help Taj take down the equipment." Nico looked through thick lashes at her. "Are we okay?"

"Of course," she said, dropping her hands from him as laughter erupted from the table. All eyes were on Grant Salinger as he paused his story telling to sip amber liquid from a glass tumbler. Claudia beamed at him. He allowed her to correct the details, patiently waiting for her to finish. They complimented each other like the sun and the moon.

As Nico walked away, an icy chill surrounded her. Her breaths materialized into misty puffs, lingering in front of her, and she hugged herself and rubbed her bare arms. A bright cloud of swirling light took shape. Memories of Hathorne's wrath came rushing back, sending a wave of fear coursing through her, but the light faded, and Jules emerged.

Jules halted with her eyes glued to the group at the table. "How do you know him?" Jules' voice was so faint that Drew had to move closer to hear her.

Drew covered her mouth to avoid odd looks when she talked to what others would see as a void beside her. "Who?"

"My brother."

Grant Salinger stood near the table, flipping open his wallet while engaged in conversation with one of the waitstaff.

SEVENTEEN

In a whirlwind of frustrated emotion, Jules lunged at Grant Salinger, passing right through him on the other side of the table. With clenched fists, she threw her head back and let out a scream so gut-wrenching and loud it pierced Drew's ears like a bolt of electricity through her head and she clamped her hands over them.

"What's wrong?" Piper's voice sounded muffled as she rushed to Drew's side, her face panicked.

Drew blinked rapidly and rubbed her temples until Jules' screams faded to an echo.

"He doesn't see me! He doesn't even know I'm here, does he? Grant!" Jules' desperate wails turned into sobs as she grabbed at Grant's arm, her ghostly hand going through him like she was air.

Grant handed Claudia her fuchsia clutch off the table, and she adjusted the little bow on the handle as he pushed chairs back in. Jules glared at Drew with reddened eyes that matched the bloodstains on her collar. "Do something! Please do something. I need my brother to know I'm here."

"Jesus. What's happening right now?" Piper whispered.

"You hear her?"

"No—look at the amulet." Piper brushed her finger over the glowing jewel.

With a firm grip on the vibrating gem, Drew grasped Jules' hand and her fingers curled around Drew's wrist. Jules reached out to Grant, and as she touched his arm, he spun around in confusion.

His eyes darted back and forth between Drew and his arm, but her hand was nowhere near him. "What the..." He rubbed his arm.

Claudia let her purse dangle on her finger. "Ready, Grant?"

Jules vanished, leaving behind a chilling scream that reverberated against the towering ceiling. A sudden coughing spell made Drew's eyes water, and Piper handed her the remnants of a drink from the table. "I'm not drinking that." Drew sputtered. Her head felt like someone was hammering nails into her skull.

"Drink it before you choke to death. It's mine." Piper brought the glass up to Drew's face.

Drew seized the glass and gulped its sweet contents. The group had dispersed from around the table, leaving no trace of Jasper or Danny. Nico wrapped cables with Taj by the stage as Piper grabbed Drew's purse from the back of the chair.

Grant stood observing her, still gripping his arm. "I, um. I thought I saw..." He held his thumb and index finger over his eyes. "Never mind. It's been a long day."

Drew wished she could say, *Your dead sister just walked through me to get to you.* But that's not how helping the dead cross over worked.

Grant scanned the room as he shook his wrist to check the time on his watch before turning back to Drew. "Hey, I saw your paintings at the gallery, and I've been meaning to tell you I think you're really talented. Claudia's excited to feature your work at the event coming up."

How could she tell him about Jules? *Your sister wants to talk to you, and in case you didn't know, she was murdered.* That would go over well.

"Thank you," she said instead. Informing Grant about the return of his dead sister would require a delicate approach, and Maze wasn't the place to have that conversation.

"You should let her showcase the other one she told me about. You don't want to miss out on the opportunity," Grant said.

Every muscle in her body tensed. "It's not ready, but thanks for thinking of me."

Piper handed Drew her purse. "Don't you have to get home to your dog?"

"Dog?" Claudia blinked so fast, her stunning wings for lashes almost took flight, but Piper's distraction worked.

"He's not mine, not really," Drew said. "I'm just helping him out. He's going to need a home once he's better. Are you interested?"

Claudia scrunched her face. "I'm not a dog person."

Dropping her hand, Claudia straightened her back and linked arms with her boyfriend.

Atlas Cliffs royalty.

Nico sauntered up to Drew. "I'm ready to go when you are."

"Oh, I'm ready," she muttered.

Claudia walked away from the table, but she stopped and spun around. "I'll message you about that dress, Drew." With a gentle clap, she pressed her hands together and raised them to her face, as if in a moment of deep contemplation. "And please, please consider finishing that painting for next Saturday."

"Bye, Claudia. We've got a dog to tend to." Piper waved in a sweeping gesture, and Claudia rolled her eyes as she turned and headed for the exit. "Why are you friends, again?"

"She really is a good person, and she wants to help, she just comes across as—"

"Stuck-up, bitchy, bossy—" With her hand raised, Piper listed off on her fingers all the ways Claudia was terrible.

"Who are we talking about?" Taj approached, carrying a symbol stand and a drum rack. "This is the last of it." Taj nodded to Nico, who took one of the stands off Taj's hands.

"She's just been through some shit," Nico said, tightening his grip on the metal stand. "I kind of feel bad for her. It's all superficial with her and having a shit father sucks."

"Except she was already like this before going through said shit, Nico. Am I right?" Piper held her hands out, wide-eyed, her anticipation palpable.

"She's been there for me; I see a different side of Claudia," Drew said tightly. Claudia's methods might be intrusive, and she frustrated the hell out of her, but she'd proven to be a fiercely loyal friend. When Joelle showed up on the front porch, demanding to be welcomed back into Drew's life, Claudia was the one who had shown up for her.

Little did Claudia know she was about to discover the horrifying secret that her father had stolen another victim's life and Drew would have to show up for her.

"I swear that's the only reason I try to be civil to her." Piper applied lip gloss and stuck the tube back in the pocket of her ripped jeans.

Taj adjusted the awkward drum stand in his arms as he headed for the door. "No comment, I barely know her. Let's get out of here before this crashes to the floor."

As Maze cleared out, a small group of patrons lingered at the bar, their conversations blending with the sound of clanging dishes coming from the kitchen.

Nico repositioned the stand in his arms and nodded toward the door. "After you."

"Want help?"

"I've got it. Go ahead."

The solar lights created a playful dance of illumination, zigzagging across the alleyway before splitting off toward the back parking lot, where they parted ways. Leaving downtown, Nico drove along the coastal road toward home with the windows down and a blanket of stars covering the night sky. The crisp sea air swept through the car, piercing through the intense warmth. The music's volume was a murmur above the sound of waves carrying the tide closer to shore, but Nico's thumbs remained still on the steering wheel, a stark contrast to his usual tapping.

She rested her head against the seat. "What were you and Shane really talking about tonight?"

He hesitated, taking a hand off the wheel to rake it through his hair. "Just small talk."

"Why don't I believe you?" The words caught, and she cleared her throat. "It didn't look like nothing... and it's not like you guys are friends."

"We used to talk at Haven when he first moved to town, we were just catching up."

With fewer streetlights as they left town, she adjusted her seat belt and shifted to get a better look at his face and read his expression.

"There's nothing for you to read into, trust me. I'm just..." His arm draped over the door frame as he stole glances at Drew. "I'm just dealing with some stuff right now, and I can't talk about it until I get it right in my head."

"What does it have to do with Shane?"

His Adam's apple bobbed, and he held his eyes on the road. "He's living in town for the summer and he'll be around. If you tell me you want nothing to do with him, I get it and I'll have your back every single time. But if he's back in your life—"

"No, he's not, Nico."

"It's a small town, and our circle isn't that big. I can't avoid him."

"So what? You're his *friend* now?"

The tires crunched on the gravel as Nico pulled into her driveway and parked behind Jasper's van. The engine rumbled as he threw it in park and faced her. "I don't want him to *not* trust me. I can't explain it right now. Please, just leave it at that."

She struggled to let it go. If anything, it had been her who held back, and after months of trusting him, trusting one another, the sudden shift in his behavior unsettled her. Being caught between her conflicting desire to withdraw and detach or hold on to him tightly for fear of losing him bothered her more than she cared to admit. "Do you want to stay tonight?"

The floodlight on the side of the house hit his face, illuminating his features. A trace of sadness hid in his expressive brown eyes, and his full lips parted and closed like he was about to say something and stopped himself. He cut the engine, dropping them into silence.

"I'm going home tonight," he said, his tone abrupt.

She bit her lip to suppress a growing lump rising in her throat.

When did all this vulnerability and fear sneak in, and how could she have allowed herself to fall this hard for him? The lump in her throat extended to a deep ache in her chest—the tightening grip anxiety loved to grace her with.

"Okay. Good night, Nico." She opened the car door and stepped into the humid evening air. A rhythmic chirping of crickets greeted her, and the comforting glow of the porch light guided her way back home.

As she shut the door, Nico opened his. "Drew." He caught up to her as she headed for the porch, but she kept her back to him, wishing there was a spell to suppress or numb hurt feelings.

She turned around to face him, forcing a smile to hide her inner turmoil. "Go home, I'm good. I have to check on the dog."

"Shit, right. I'm sorry. I'll come in and make sure he's okay."

"Jasper's here. He would've called if something was wrong." She refused to burden him with any more problems. "I'm the one who picked up a stray dog, I can take care of him."

He held her face in his hands. "Don't worry, okay?"

"I'm not."

His lips brushed hers, and she closed her eyes, breathing him in as she kissed him back. In contrast to the lingering moment in the garage, this one evaporated within seconds. She hugged him tight before they parted and he hurried back to his car, bringing the engine to roaring life.

He drove away, leaving her standing on the porch beside the row of Gran's crystals and the amulet pulsating around her neck, once again reminding her of Aurora's magic. Now that Jules knew who her brother was, she would return with a heightened urgency. Drew shifted her focus off her love life and her mind raced as she devised a plan to reconnect the Salingers one last time. Her soul's purpose would win. It always won.

Eighteen

The front door opened, and Henry limped onto the porch, wagging his tail. Jasper stood sipping from a mug with a tea label suspended from a string over the side. "He was whining at the door."

Drew crouched down and scratched behind Henry's ears. He was a fluff ball of dark fur, except for his two front paws that looked like a tall pair of white socks, and he no longer smelled like death. She pressed her face against his neck and inhaled a subtle hint of lavender. "Did you bath him?"

Jasper's face lit up. "Danny and I came home, gave him the next dose of his meds, and cleaned him up. It's our little welcome home surprise."

She hesitated for a moment before leaning close to Henry to hug him, unsure of how it would feel to embrace a dog, but he licked her cheek and rested his chin on her shoulder. The touch of his soft fur against her face was comforting. "He smells so good. See what a little love can do, Henry? You're going to be just fine."

"Love, food, and a big dose of medication... You named him Henry?" Jasper held the door open as she scooted Henry back inside, closing the door behind them. A cooking competition reality show was on TV, and a fan circulated air around the living room. "It's cooled off a bit in here."

"And yet, you're drinking tea." She helped Henry onto the sofa and followed Jasper into the kitchen. Danny smiled hello at her. "Henry is a good name, don't you think?"

"I think naming the dog is like keeping the dog," Jasper said.

"It's just a name." She tried to sound nonchalant, but her voice wavered. Keeping the dog wouldn't be practical, but how could she give him up?

Danny poured tea from Gran's floral teapot into a large mug. The lid still had the chip that Gran had glued back on. Grief's crushing ache clenched down on Drew's chest and unexpected tears burned her eyes, but she wasn't sure if she was responding to the teapot and missing Gran, or if Nico's distance was hurting her more than she expected.

"Sweetie, are you okay?" Danny placed the teapot between burners on the stove.

"J uses the electric kettle, so no one's used that pot since Gran." She took a breath and willed her tears to stop. "I don't know why I'm so emotional."

"Say no more. I will wash it and put it away. I'm so sorry." Danny gave Jasper a scrutinizing glance as he smoothed the sides of his classic Hollywood hairstyle. "J, you need to warn a person. All that is wild and free, the last thing I'd ever want to do is make you sad, Drew, I adore you."

"Don't pour it out, I'll have some." She placed her hand on Danny's arm. "She'd want us to use her things. I'm not upset, I don't know what's wrong with me."

Danny furrowed his thick, well-groomed brows as he poured the remaining tea into a mug. He placed it back on the stove with more care than handling an ancient artifact. "I am sorry for your loss. She was a beautiful woman."

"Thank you." What was bothering her had nothing to do with Gran's teapot, and everything to do with a growing unease stirring inside of her. Danny was the kindest person she knew, and the last thing she wanted was to make *him* sad. She gave him a quick squeeze, and he hugged her back before handing her the mug.

She sat in Gran's chair, holding the mug close to her nose, and breathed in the delicate aroma, somewhere between orange and lemon, but sweet, and every bit a reminder of Gran.

Henry slid off the sofa, collapsing at her feet. Placing the mug on the side table, she leaned forward and bent down to pet him. His tail thumped against the floor, and he stared up at her with pathetic eyes. "I need to find you a home."

"I think you already have, hasn't she, Henry?" Jasper sat on the sofa and turned the volume down on the television.

"I can't keep him," Drew said.

"Why not?" Danny sat beside him, adjusting the fan to blow in their direction, but the oscillating breeze couldn't budge a single strand of his trendy hairstyle.

"I go back to Boston for college at the end of August, work is busy..." Henry stared at her as she spoke, melting her heart. "I can't take care of a dog, I can barely handle myself."

Danny and Jasper shared a glance, their silent bond tangible, and she couldn't help but smile at the change in Jasper. He looked more content than she'd ever seen him.

"Any news on the house hunting?" she asked.

Danny's eyes widened. "You told her?" He leaned forward and tugged at a loose string on the hem of his polo shirt. "Nothing is happening yet. I don't want this to be a source of stress for you."

"I'm not stressed, I'm happy for you. But we're still doing junk food movie nights." She lifted the mug from the table and savored the blend of sweet and floral flavors. Leaving the place vacant while she was away and returning to an empty house would take getting used to, but she'd make it work, find a new roommate... or Nico.

Don't let yourself go there.

"Deal." Jasper bent down and scratched Henry's back. "What if we keep him?"

"*We?*" she asked.

"Yeah. Like he lives here," Jasper said. "I'll take care of him when you can't, but when the time comes that we find the perfect house, and you're in school or working, or need a dog sitter, he can stay with me."

With a yelp, Henry sat up and placed his front paws on the chair before falling back to the floor and licking his injured hind leg. "Is he okay?" She placed the mug on the side table and leaned over to help him.

Danny rushed to the floor and examined the dog's back leg with gentle hands, surrounding both her and Henry in calmness. "He'll be fine. It's a little raw, but the antibiotics will kick in." He held the dog's furry face in his hands. "Stop licking it or you'll get the cone of shame."

Danny helped Henry onto the chair where he tried to curl up on Drew's lap but was too big to fit. He gave up and nestled against her, tucking his hind legs against the chair.

"Where's Nico tonight? I assumed he was coming back here with you." Jasper stretched his legs out in front of him as Danny placed a blanket over the dog and sat back down.

"He went home." Reaching over Henry, she grabbed the mug again, holding it with both hands as she averted her eyes from Jasper.

"Did you have a fight?" Jasper asked.

She couldn't think of a single time when she and Nico fought. They talked, they vented, and sometimes they snapped at each other, but they made up, they kissed, they understood each other on a freakishly wild soul level. "It wasn't a fight. He's going through some stuff he needs to process."

"What was he talking to Shane about?" As Jasper raised an eyebrow, his face took on a similar look of curiosity that Piper often wore. "I sure didn't miss that unfold."

"Cars. Small talk." She chewed her bottom lip. The habit returning in full force, and she didn't care. "But I don't believe him."

"So that was Shane." Danny squinted his expressive eyes in thought. "Sloan's son who returned from the dead. Why is he back in town again?"

Drew told him about Shane's summer work at the gallery and Claudia's upcoming royal party—royal pain in the ass.

Jasper filled in details Drew missed and glanced back at her. "And he doesn't want Shane to *not* trust him? Something's up."

"That's what he said." Drew took a long drink of the tea before placing it back on the table beside her. "It doesn't matter, I'm letting it go. Nico's got a lot going on with his mom moving and the garage, and he'll have to figure out where he's going to live."

"Here isn't an option?" Jasper asked.

"I don't know." Her anxiety had crept in and doused her with self-doubting thoughts of her future and her present situation, involving a realm with the dead that no one else could see. "I just don't know what's going to happen. I have some things of my own to figure out right now, anyway."

"Mhmm." Jasper sat up, his tousled hair falling across his forehead, and leaned forward, resting his elbows on his knees. "Nico loves you. He'll talk, just give him time."

"I thought so too, but it feels like he's pulling away from me, like I might lose him, and I don't know why."

"That man isn't going anywhere, believe it. And whatever you do, don't shut down and break up with him because you think that's what he wants, or it's the only way to protect your heart from being broken. Make sure it's something you actually *want* before you jump. Regardless of what it is."

Her mouth dropped open. "I don't do that." She racked her brain for a better defense.

"Drew, I love you like my sister. And my biggest wish for you is that you will realize without a single doubt that those who love you, who really love you, will never leave, certainly not by choice."

Gran's rotary phone, the only landline plugged in, rang from the back den with a clattering, high-pitched ring. Drew's mother was the only person who tried to reach her on the land line anymore, especially after she had blocked the prison lines from her cell phone.

Maybe it's someone else, like Dad. Or a telemarketer... Anyone else.

Gulping the last of her tea, she shuffled from underneath Henry and rose from the chair. She dashed through the kitchen and into the den, grabbing the antique receiver off its base. The decorative hands-on Gran's vintage clock pointed to eleven minutes past eleven, sending a shudder ripping through her body as the visions of the witch hunter and Gran's death crept into her mind. "Hello?"

"Hi ginger-girl, it's Mom."

Joelle had never been her *mom*. Not in the way it counted. "You've got to drop the ginger-girl. I just can't—"

"You said that last time, I forgot," Joelle said.

The phone felt like a block of lead in Drew's hand, and she struggled to keep it up to her ear. A dryness settled in her throat as sweat pricked under her arms and behind her neck. She sat on the chair behind the desk and gripped the mason jar of paper clips. Joelle's calls with her forced cheerfulness still made Drew cringe. She could never forgive her mother for killing Ori.

"Is there a reason for your call?" Drew barely recognized her own business-like tone, but she couldn't warm the ice in her heart when it came to her mother.

"There always is." Voices echoed from across the line. "I just got on! Give me five minutes." Joelle's voice sounded muffled. "Fuck. I'm sorry, no privacy and all."

Right. You get no privacy, and Ori has no life.

She took a deep breath and pulled paper clips from the jar the way Jules had done. "Sounds like you have to go?"

"I need to know that we have a shot when I get out of here."

Drew crumpled the paper clips in her hand, and a sharp end dug into her skin. "You're getting out?"

"I'm in here for a felony hit and run, what do you think?"

"I think you deserve longer than what you got for killing Ori." The tight grip of anxiety and panic transformed into seething anger. "I have to go—"

"It's good you got to keep your grandmother's house, no plans to leave?"

What did she want? "Why?"

"In case I wanted to send you mail, you know, holiday and birthday cards. I know you're avoiding my calls, but I need you in my life. I don't know what I'll do if I can't keep in touch with my ginger..." Voices echoed through the phone again. "I'm going to group therapy and making a plan for when I'm released, because the day will come, Drew, and you're all I have."

A dull throbbing in the back of her neck spread to her scalp and behind her eyes.

I never want to see you again.

"Look, Joelle. I've told you, I won't be a part of your plans, not now, not ever. I can't do it."

Ignoring her, Joelle carried on with a rant, speaking through gritted teeth. "My mother disowned me, told me I was a disgrace, and she would have me arrested if I set foot on her property. She told me I ruined you and she hated you because you were a part of me. Can you imagine?"

Memories of the events in California the summer before raced through Drew's mind, like a whirlwind of scenes in a movie on fast-forward. She remembered arriving at the address on Joelle's letter and standing at the front door of an extravagant mansion. A woman had opened the red double doors,

Joelle's mother—Drew's estranged grandmother—and peered down on her with contempt, as if Drew was dirt beneath her shoes. It had only been after her mother's arrival in Atlas Cliffs that she had learned about the woman's identity. Joelle confessed the cruel woman had refused any connection with Drew when she was born, and that hadn't changed in the years since Joelle had abandoned her. Yet, somehow, the woman's hatred found its way to Drew on the other end of this antique relic of a telephone.

"It's tough when your own mother wants nothing to do with you," Drew said through shallow breaths. "I don't have to imagine it, I've lived it. But I'm not a kid anymore. I need to choose what's best for me, and it doesn't include you or her." Light from the amulet reflected off the metal paper clips as she tossed them back into the jar. She reached for the base of the phone, her fingers hovering over the two white buttons, ready to hang up and end the conversation.

"You don't mean that, you're a good person," Joelle said. "If you took a trip out this way, you could come to a group session, and we could work stuff out. That's what family is supposed to do. You're my daughter."

"I know who I am, and I know what family is supposed to do, but you're not my family." A wave of tears overwhelmed her, and she shut her eyes to stop them. She was determined to never cry over this woman again. "I'm hanging up now."

"I'll call you again soon, ginger… oops, *Drew*."

"Please don't bother." But the phone was dead. She'd worked hard to distance herself from Joelle, and there was no way that woman was going to weasel her way into Drew's life ever again.

NINETEEN

Rolling onto her back, Drew kicked the blankets off, letting the middle of the night breeze tickle her skin. Henry stirred at her feet, inching closer until he lay beside her. He let out a tired groan in the darkness and she scratched behind his ears.

"You can't sleep either?"

Sleep eluded her as her restless mind fought against its embrace, and she was on the verge of giving up trying. Dark thoughts overwhelmed her mind. Grief over Gran's absence made her chest hurt, the woman who was supposed to be her mom was a killer with no conscience who only cared about herself, J was moving out soon, and Nico's sudden shift in behavior caught her off guard.

She had more love in her life than she had ever dreamed possible but couldn't shake her fears of losing it all.

With a swift motion, she snatched her phone off the side table and glanced at the screen for notifications. It was strange that Nico hadn't messaged all evening. Her fingers tapped out the words, *everything okay?* But she deleted them. It was late, and perhaps she had gotten too comfortable with their daily back-and-forth.

But I love those conversations, even the simple ones.

Craving a distraction, she got out of bed and opened the curtains, unveiling stars sprinkled across the night sky. She pushed the window up as far as it would go, allowing the night sounds to pour in. With each surge over the shoreline, persistent waves brought in the tide, mingling with the buzzing and chirping of insects. A cluster of moths dove around the streetlight across the road. Their only focus was to latch onto the light, and strangely, she understood that desire. If she couldn't solve everyday life problems, she could tackle otherworldly ones instead.

"Let's go play with some magic."

Henry cocked his head to the side, perking his ears up. As she guided him off the bed, she could feel the prominent ribs underneath his fur, and she bent down to pet the top of his fuzzy head. "You're never going to starve again."

She took her time so he could keep up as he trailed her out of her room and down the hallway, limping to plop down in front of Jasper's closed door.

"This way," she whispered, patting her leg. He followed her into the art studio, and she shut the door behind them with a soft click. The heat in the room took her breath away, pricking her skin with sweat. She opened the window and turned on the fan, letting the cooler night air cut through the sauna in the room. She patted the plush chair for Henry and helped him up. He curled up and licked his front paws before resting his head and staring up at her.

She tugged the chain on Gran's stained-glass lamp in the corner, illuminating the painting underneath the window. The scarlet paint on the lighthouse landing had vanished. Her fingers traced along the canvas as her shallow breaths formed a misty haze over the dark swirls of blue and gray. The frigid air brushed against her skin, coming from a source other than the open window.

Spinning around, she waited for someone to appear. A sudden bright red soaked through the canvas, dripping before it pooled on the lighthouse landing. "Jules? Aurora?"

Henry's head shot up from his paws, and he stared at the bookshelf.

The amulet cast a stream of light over the painting as the red trickled down the canvas, coating the winding staircase. Reaching out, she touched the paint, tapping her fingertips together. The sticky substance clung to her skin as she glanced between her fingers and the painting.

What does it mean?

Trembling, she wiped her fingers on a rag and yanked the spell book from the shelf. Her palm tingled as she held it on the image of the hand with an eye in the center adorning the book's cover before opening to a blank page.

Henry leaped off the chair, stopping to lick his hind leg, and stared into a void behind her. A low growl escaped, turning into whimpers as his tail wagged. Sparkling mist swirled, and Aurora's black layers of fabric spun around, revealing bare feet, blackened and dirty.

The dead woman moved with the fluidity of water as she glided near Henry. Tilting her head back and forth, her hand drifted down toward the cowering dog. But he didn't growl or try to escape. He stared up at the ethereal woman, unafraid, letting her run her hands over his emaciated body. The book slipped out of Drew's hands and snapped shut as it hit the floor. She dropped to her knees and positioned herself between Aurora and Henry.

"Don't kill him like you did the seagull. Taj isn't here to bring him back."

She'd made mistakes about the dead's intentions before, but not this time.

Drew locked eyes with the dead woman. Small lights shimmered within Aurora's pupils, creating the disorienting beauty of stars during a dizzy spell. Curls of smoke dissipated in the air from her hair and dress as she crouched down beside Drew, reaching for Henry.

Flooded with panic, Drew covered the dog with her body. "No, please, don't hurt him. I won't let you do it."

Aurora placed a hand on Drew's back, and purple light surrounded them. White streaks like lightning cut through the bright color, forcing a burst of air deep inside her lungs. The vice gripping her chest eased and her jaw relaxed. An overwhelming sense of calm took hold, pushing aside the fear, and she sat up, backing away from Henry.

Wrapping her arms around Henry, Aurora muttered unintelligible words as she directed the peaceful light over him. The dog rolled on his back, revealing his belly, and Aurora's dress swirled around him, cascading down as she stood. Drew rubbed his soft fur, inspecting him. The injury on his leg was still visible, but it had become less deep and ulcerated. Squirming to regain his balance, he hopped up and circled Aurora before jumping onto the chair.

"He's not limping anymore. How'd you do that?" Drew sat next to Henry, perched on the chair's edge.

Aurora clasped her fingers together at her waist. Blistered scars marked her pale hands and arms. "My magic does not possess the ability to breathe life, only mend."

The pool of blood evaporated into fine droplets, lifting off the canvas, and Drew leaned closer. "Why does this keep happening? How do I make it stop?"

"You cannot." Aurora's entire being brightened before vanishing.

The spell book's front cover flew open to the first page. But the original image transformed from a dense forest with shadows lurking among the trees to a haunting view of Neptune Point lighthouse at night. Dark clouds concealed the moon and stars, but a single ray of light from the beacon streamed over a raging sea.

She dragged the book onto her lap and its pages fluttered like wings by an unseen force before settling on a blank page. Holding her hands over the page, she closed her eyes and focused on Gran, Enid, and Ori.

"Please help me. Tell me what to do."

Her breath caught in her throat, and she let out a sudden gasp. The taste of charcoaled ash coated her mouth, and she opened her eyes, swallowing repeatedly, desperate for a deep breath, but refused to move and break the spell as it took over and bold lettering charged across the page. Henry nestled closer to her and grew still, releasing hushed whimpers with his puppy-dog eyes glued to the book.

"It's working," she whispered.

The words appeared on the page like blood spatter.

Darkness awaits those who cause harm. Light returns after breaking ties that bind death to life.

The sensation of a thousand needles scraping along her palms tortured her skin, and she flinched in pain, yanking her hands back. The book snapped closed as thunder cracked, rattling the window. Lightning cut through the sudden cloud cover and lit up the room, casting shadows over the walls. A raven's screech passed by the window, and she scrambled off the chair. Rain erupted from the thick clouds, suffocating the starlight.

The amulet beckoned to her as its heat intensified against her skin. Grabbing the silver chain, she whipped it off her neck and held it up to the window. "What am I supposed to do with messages I don't understand?"

"The same man who killed me wants revenge." Jules spoke with conviction, and Drew turned away from the window.

"I told you we needed each other."

TWENTY

"This is the painting?" Celeste adjusted the buttons on her white silk blouse and placed her hands on her hips. The fan rattled as it swept air from side to side, sending sketchbook pages flying along the floor in Drew's studio room. Henry jumped out of the way and hid behind Celeste's legs. She bent down to pet him. "And you say she healed him?"

"Not fully, but he's not limping anymore. At first, I thought she was going to hurt him like she did—"

She cut herself off, remembering Celeste didn't know about Taj and the seagull.

Celeste held Henry's face in her hands and kissed his head. "Sweet pup. Like she did what?"

"I was just scared she wanted to hurt him, but she helped him."

"Have you found him a home yet?"

Drew gathered the papers off the floor and placed them on the small art table. "It's only been a few days."

"Perhaps he'll let you know where home is." As Celeste stood, Henry plopped onto the floor and rested his head on his paws, looking up at them.

Maybe he already has.

How could she adore an animal so much in such a short amount of time?

With a big exhale, Celeste tilted her head as she surveyed the painting. "What do you mean, *blood* appears?"

"It sure looks like blood. It's bright red and drips down along here." She gestured to the space on the landing. "It's sticky like paint, but it isn't paint, it can't be, and isn't blood sticky, too? I swear it was here last night, but it just disappears." She ran her fingers over the empty lighthouse landing.

"And the dead woman, Jules," Celeste said. "She was here?"

"Sloan wants revenge, Celeste. That's what she told me, but she vanished before I could ask her anything. I think she's annoyed with me."

"For what?" Celeste's distinct coils danced against the tops of her shoulders as she leaned back and gave Drew a scrutinizing look.

Drew chewed her lip. "I blocked her a bit too long, I guess."

"I see." A sigh escaped Celeste's lips as she folded her arms. "I told you to be careful doing that."

"It just gets to be a lot," Drew said. If she could find a way to block the dead from contacting her, she'd regain control of her life. "Why do I have to be so careful using it?" She tried to hide her hesitation.

Celeste spun her rings on her fingers, drawing Drew's eye. Celeste never fidgeted. "Imagine a talented pianist. This person plays and people stop and listen. Their fingers are magic over those ivory keys, bringing to life a sound that has never fallen on ears. Their music touches souls, changes perspectives, brings people together. Or imagine an artist, gifted with an ability to bring color to the world, breathe life into images, and emotion into hearts for a shared experience." Celeste glanced at Drew's painting. "Imagine a force blocking music, inspiration, creativity. The world would fall silent and gray."

"But how does that relate to blocking the dead?"

"You're missing the point, honey. You bring *souls* together." Celeste reattached the delicate loop on a button holding her luxurious silk sleeves up. "You've got magic running through you all the time."

Drew should be used to Celeste's poetic speeches, but she failed to understand the deeper meaning. "Are you about to tell me how with great magic comes great responsibility or something?"

Dropping her hands to her sides, Celeste moved close to Drew, her deep, amber eyes connecting to Drew's soul. "You've got it. The same way you have a responsibility to never cause harm with your magic."

"Blocking doesn't cause harm, does it?"

"What if Jules can no longer get through to you and stops trying? She'll be stuck in between worlds for eternity. All I'm saying is just use it sparingly, you understand? They're not all going to be as stubborn as this one."

Guilt weighed on Drew like an itchy wool blanket. "Noted."

Celeste picked up the spell book from the chair. "Did you ask the book? You could summon for help."

"I tried last night, look at this." Taking the book from Celeste, Drew flipped to the page with the crimson lettering. "'Darkness awaits those who cause harm. Light returns after breaking ties that bind death to life.' Does this have to do with Jules or Dominic Sloan? If I help her cross over, will it all go away? He used to be Ben Morana, so he's tied to the lighthouse, right?"

Celeste leaned over Drew's shoulder and touched the lettering. Removing her hand, she rubbed her fingertips together. "Strange. It feels... wet, but nothing."

"My brain hurts," Drew complained. "I can't figure it out."

"Aurora, *the* Aurora, came to you with what appears to be a warning through your painting."

"It doesn't just appear to be, it *feels* like a warning, all of it. The raven, the way she speaks to me in weird, cryptic phrases..." *The dead seagull.* "What do you think I should do?"

Celeste observed Drew and stared back at the painting.

"Please, Celeste. I'm stuck," Drew said.

"They come to you through the medium closest to your heart. For you, it's art, but it's visual and communicative. For Maddie, it was her garden."

That made sense. And for Taj, it was probably touch. Sound? He needed to talk to his mother.

"What's yours?"

Celeste moved her body from side to side, her arms floating in the air with a quick spin, and tapped her ear. "Music, sound."

Her ability to remain carefree in the face of crisis baffled Drew. "I still don't see how knowing this stuff is going to help me understand what those words in the book mean."

"Try calling for help."

"I doubt the original Atlas Cliffs witch has a cell phone."

"You're impossible. You have tools now, magic. And you know that's what I meant. If Aurora is the one you need, you can use a spell to call her back." Celeste held her hands out. "Give me your hands."

Drew placed the book down and extended her hands. Celeste turned them over, revealing Drew's palms. She lifted the amulet off Drew's neck, placing it in the center of her hands, draping the silver chain across them. Closing her eyes, she held one hand under Drew's and the other hovered over the amulet. "I summon thee, spirit of the sea, whose name bears light to guide those in need." She repeated the words until a golden strand of light spread from the center out, spinning faster and faster. Heat emanated from the onyx gem, seeping into Drew's skin, sending a crawling sensation over her hands.

Celeste's eyes opened, and she smiled. "Take it from here, honey."

"I don't know what to do."

Celeste touched Drew's cheek. "When are you going to trust yourself? You can do this."

Drew took a deep breath and exhaled slowly, focusing on the painting. She encompassed the amulet with both hands and repeated Celeste's words. "I summon thee, spirit of the sea... whose..."

"Whose name bears..."

"I summon thee, spirit of the sea, whose name bears light to guide those in need."

"Again." Celeste placed her hands over Drew's, and they spoke the words together.

Henry's bark broke Drew's concentration, and she clutched the amulet to her chest. "I don't think today's the day. It's not working."

Celeste patted Drew's arm. "It will. When the day is the day, it will." She winked. "Trust me." She glanced at her watch. "I should get back, but if you need me, I'll be here." She pointed to Drew's amulet. "I think someone else is here, too."

"Aurora?"

"Maybe, maybe not. The essence of the sisterhood hasn't left you. You've got pieces of Gran, Enid, even Ori." Celeste turned to leave.

"Has Taj... said anything?"

Celeste paused and directed her attention toward Drew. "About what? New York?"

He hadn't told her. "Yeah, New York." Drew returned the amulet back around her neck.

"He'll move in with his father, and it'll be good for him." Shaking her head, Celeste exhaled a slow breath. "Who am I kidding, it'll be good for his dad, too. My boy fell in love. Who am I to stand in the way of that? Your friend is lovely. She's got quite an aura around her. Full of passion and loyalty, and she's good to my son. So, yes, I know about New York."

"What happened? Between you and Taj's father?" Drew hit her forehead with her palm. "You don't have to answer that, it's not my business, you just never talk about it."

"It's all right, Drew." Celeste smiled. "We simply wanted different things, always did. His business grew, he was in demand and loved big city life. It wasn't an easy decision to part ways, but I have no regrets. We started as friends, and still are, but I realized I wasn't *in love* the way I should've been." Celeste's face lit up with a mischievous grin. "And dating has its moments, but it can be fun."

"Who are you dating in Atlas Cliffs?" Drew dared to ask. Whomever captured Celeste's heart would be nothing short of legendary, with enchanting charm and an irresistible appeal.

"Currently, no one, but let's just say it's been interesting. On that note, my time is up here." She exited the room and waved over her shoulder. "You'll be okay, Drew. Just call me if you need anything, you understand?" Her expression mirrored that of a mother's concern.

"I will."

She squeezed herself onto the plush chair beside Henry and picked up her phone as she absently stroked his soft fur. Her phone's weather app displayed notifications of the approaching hurricane wreaking havoc in the Atlantic that Jasper had mentioned, advising Atlas Cliff's residents to prepare for potential landfall along the southern coast over the next week. Displayed beneath the article were practical suggestions, including a list of essential items to have on hand, tips for handling a widespread power outage, and a reminder to store patio furniture. A quick search told her a hurricane hadn't hit Maine in decades.

If only ghost warnings came with the same clear set of preparations.

TWENTY-ONE

The condo structure boasted balconies stretching as high as the town's building regulations permitted. As expected, Claudia's unit was one of the penthouses on the top floor. Trying on a dress for Claudia was the least of her priorities, but Piper had offered to cover for her at the Tough Cookie so she could meet with Grant. If the dress business dragged on for too long, she'd miss the appointment she'd scheduled with him under a made-up name. He wouldn't be expecting her, and he sure as hell wouldn't be expecting to hear about his dead sister's return.

The weight of the truth lingered in the air as she prepared herself to tell him about Jules. She still hadn't figured out the best approach, or how much to tell him. If Grant knew his sister's killer was his girlfriend's father—or someone he'd hired to do it—would Claudia's life spiral? Maybe it was best to keep that detail from him and save Claudia from more suffering.

By helping the dead woman find her paradise, she would sever Jules' hold on her and release herself from the burden of Dominic Sloan's revenge. The man was incapable of hurting her from behind bars, and she refused to let Jules' exaggerated statement get to her.

A gust of chilled air cut through the humidity of the afternoon heat, stopping Drew as her hand reached for the door handle.

"I thought you were going to see Grant." Jules pursed her lips, locking her sharp gaze on Drew.

"Hello to you too. Where have you been? You drop a bomb on me like Dominic Sloan is out for revenge, and ditch me for two days?" Drew released the door handle and moved away from the entrance off to the side of the building.

"I wanted you to see how it feels. Not so good, is it?" Jules rolled her wide, bright eyes and tucked her hair behind her ears. "I wish I mattered more to you, that's all."

Balancing magic with the burden of responsibility required a set of skills Drew had been struggling with. "I'm sorry I hurt you. You do matter to me. Helping you matters to me."

"Who are you talking to? It can't possibly be me you're apologizing to." Jules twirled around, placing a hand on her forehead as she scanned the parking lot filled with luxury cars and the occasional confused onlookers who had to be wondering why Drew was standing there talking to herself.

Maybe she needed to work on her apologizing skills, too. "I can say it again if it helps."

"Yes, yes it would definitely help me to hear you say those words again." A rare smile crossed Jules' face.

"I am sorry that I hurt you. Why do you think Sloan wants revenge?"

"I saw him. He was talking to some guy. You know, the glass with the phones like in the movies?"

A wave of nausea washed over Drew as her stomach twisted, threatening to purge the breakfast sandwich she'd eaten earlier. "How do you know we're talking about the same person? How can you be sure it was Sloan?"

Jules lowered her voice to a husky whisper, though no one could ever hear her. "Well, for starters, I heard the man tell the guard at the front desk he was there to see Sloan, *and* when they each grabbed the phone to talk, he was fidgeting with an ID around his wrist with his name on it. Like I told you, I can go places no one else can. And I went to see the man who murdered me. I tried to mess with him, too. Threw his pillow across the room and tossed his mattress. I think I rattled the asshole."

"Jesus." Drew leaned against the brick building and steadied her breaths. "Why do you think he wants revenge?"

"Because he told the guy if he didn't help him, revenge would... how did he put it?" Jules tapped her lip. "Something like revenge would bleed into his family, with or without him. Whatever that means."

"But he's in a maximum-security prison, he can't do anything." Panic burned like indigestion into the back of Drew's throat.

"Maybe not, but I thought you should know."

Drew cleared her throat. There was no way Sloan could slither his way back into her life again, absolutely no way. "Any idea who the guy was, the one who went to see him?"

"Now that, I didn't find out, but I can go back."

Drew's phone buzzed inside her purse, and she'd bet her house Claudia was messaging again. "I'm late, but I made an appointment to see your brother after this. Just please, let me see Claudia and get this dress out of the way?"

"As long as we have an understanding and you promise not to ignore me, I will give this time to you."

"I promise," Drew said as she made her way to the front entrance again.

"I don't know. I'm losing faith in you." Jules picked at her nails at the same time Drew caught herself gnawing on her bottom lip. Perhaps the two women had more similarities than she had previously believed.

Leaving Jules behind, she stepped through the glass double doors and the unmistakable scent of polished leather and fresh paint overwhelmed her senses. A chandelier of icicle lights dangled from the ceiling. Large potted plants sat in each corner, and pristine, golden mailboxes covered the back wall next to an elaborate security system. Fidgeting with the zipper on her crossbody purse, Drew yanked it open and rummaged for her phone. A camera above her head shifted its position. She'd felt more at ease on the beach when she'd spread Gran's ashes than in the lobby of this pretentious place. Scrolling to the most recent text from Claudia, she ran a finger from the bottom of the list up, searching for suite 611, C. Tate & G. Salinger.

A security guard peeked out of an office door. "Can I help you?" A military-style cut defined his gray hair, and a small piece of tissue was stuck to a razor cut on his cheek, with a speck of blood at the center. His expression appeared familiar, but she couldn't place him, and despite exuding the long-time local vibe, he seemed unfamiliar with her, too.

"I'm here to see Claudia Tate, but I think I found her."

The man picked up a phone and held his hand up, exposing a heavy chain link bracelet with a unique charm attached, but he moved too fast for her to make out details. "Allow me." He glanced at a gold-faced clock on the wall, its missing second hand leaving an eerie silence in the room. Her phone confirmed the same time displayed in Roman numerals on the clock.

11:11.

The man grabbed a pen from his chest pocket and jotted something down behind a desk before hanging up. "Head up to the top floor. She's waiting for you."

Drew pushed through the doors on the faint buzzer's signal and stepped into a hallway with tiled floors resembling Tate Gallery. She pressed the arrow pointing upward and waited as the hum of a motor lowered the elevator car to the main floor.

Busying herself with work and shifting her focus to helping the dead wasn't proving to be as good a distraction from Nico as she'd hoped. She checked her phone for any sign of him, re-reading his one-word messages and responses they'd exchanged since the night he'd driven her home after Maze. And he'd returned her repaired car the night before but asked her to drive him back home. His reassurances were sincere, and his affection hadn't changed. He still kissed her hello, and goodbye, but the goodbyes were more frequent than the hellos and the gap between them was breaking her heart.

It's only been two days, don't panic. He's got a lot going on, I know what that feels like.

With a ding, the metal doors opened, and she stepped over the threshold and pressed the button marked 6 before jabbing the door close button to prevent anyone else from joining her. With a jerk, the elevator carried her upward.

"Fancy place." Jules appeared beside her.

No icy warning came this time. Drew closed her eyes and took a deep breath. "Why didn't you wait outside?"

"I was bored."

"Can't you be bored for twenty minutes *outside*?"

"Do you hear how bossy you are?" Jules rolled her eyes and stared straight ahead.

"I'm not bossy."

"A little compassion would go a long way," Jules said. "I thought we just covered this downstairs."

With another chime, the doors opened, and a foyer with black velvet benches and pristine white walls greeted her. The bright glow of tear-drop lights guided a path to the left or to the right. A quick glance at a label plate above a mahogany desk adorned with a bouquet of fresh flowers told her that suite 611 was to the right.

Jules strutted out of the elevator and ran a human hand over the desk before rubbing her fingers together. She leaned down and put her face in the middle of the bouquet. "You need to smell these."

Drew slipped into the hallway before the elevator doors could trap her back inside, fighting the urge to slip back in and punch the button for the lobby. She wanted to escape this elaborate display of wealth, run to Nico's garage and confront him into telling her the truth.

Clutching the phone as a lifeline in her hand, she made a quick pivot to the right, toward Claudia's condo. A whirlwind of cold air surrounded her, and Jules appeared in front of her. "I know you can hear me, do you not ever just stop and smell the flowers? Like ever?"

"My grandmother had gardens, I love flowers." Drew halted and faced Jules. "You've got to make up your mind, Jules. It's stop and smell the flowers, or I hustle and help you."

"Both, you can do both." Jules' fingers wrapped around Drew's wrist in a gentle grip.

Bracing herself for a jolt or a vision, Drew tried to pull away, but Jules held tighter. "What are you doing?"

"Your grandmother, she died, right?" Jules maintained eye contact with Drew as if she possessed the power to enchant.

"Last year."

"Were you close?"

"She raised me, she was like my mother." Drew's eyes burned with tears, and she blinked quickly to stop them. "What do you want from me?"

"You miss her a lot, I can see pain in your eyes. I'm sorry she died. See? I can say it, too."

Drew brushed away tears from underneath her eyes. This woman might be the death of her. "You really want me to go smell those damn flowers?"

"Absolutely I do. Hustle with a side of smell the flowers." Jules pulled her wrist, leading her back to the foyer. "Put your face in there, go on." A smile spread across Jules' face, the rare moments increasing.

"Just let me go try this dress on so we can get out of here."

Jules pointed to the flowers. "I need you on the same page as me if we're going to work together, and I stop and smell flowers."

"Funny, you don't strike me as a stop and smell the flowers person." Drew leaned in and inhaled the exotic floral arrangement of blues, pinks, yellows, and deep purple. The bouquet featured a cluster of white roses, their pure beauty drawing all attention to the center, but they reminded her of death. "These are for funerals."

"No, they're not. They mean everlasting love," Jules said. "I miss luxurious things. I'll have to settle for living vicariously through you until I leave here and go wherever I'm supposed to be... that place better be amazing, is all I can say."

Jules' parents, the Salingers, had owned a brick laying company, but Drew had heard little about them in years, and her online search since finding out Grant was Jules' sister hadn't shown results other than the company had shut down nearly eight years earlier after a horrible car accident took the life of their daughter, but no name was mentioned, which she couldn't comprehend. She hadn't found a website, family history, an obituary... it was as though someone had erased the woman from existence.

A twisted pang of guilt struck her. Drew had a lifetime of experiences ahead of her, but Jules would never have the chance again. She leaned closer to the bouquet, closed her eyes, and inhaled the powdery, sweet aroma. "They do smell luxurious. Look, just give me twenty minutes with Claudia, and we'll go see Grant."

"Can I at least come with you?"

"Does it matter if I say no?"

Jules bounded down the wide hallway. "Probably not." Her bare feet padded along the carpet's swirling pattern of blues and grays like the sea.

Drew followed her and knocked on suite 611 with a pink heart framing the peephole. She didn't need the number to know this was Claudia's place. The door opened and Claudia stood beaming. "Come in, I'm so ready for you."

"I'm just here to try on a dress, nothing to be ready for." Drew stepped inside the large entryway, and Jules trailed behind her. The enormous living room boasted elaborate leather furniture, and everything was white from the sofa and chair set, the kitchen cabinets, to the reflective tiled floor. She slipped off her sneakers and tiptoed over the plush carpet, afraid to dirty anything.

"Do you want a sparkling water?" Claudia held up a green bottle.

"No, thanks, I'm good. Just point me to where the dress is so I can get this over with."

"It's not as bad as you think it'll be."

"My art is the only reason I'm doing this."

"Our friendship means nothing to you, does it?" Claudia feigned exasperation. "Trust me, okay? I want you to succeed." She emptied the bottle into a glass and bubbles fizzed as she pressed her red lips against it and took a sip.

Exploring the condo, Jules picked up a banana from a wooden bowl and put it back. She continued around the room. "I could definitely live in a place like this."

Oblivious to Jules' presence, Claudia tilted her head to the side and a strand of her blonde hair escaped her messy bun. She slid her hands into the pockets of her loose mini dress. "I know you think this isn't who you are—"

"I don't just think, I know."

"For Christ's sake, Drew, stop it, would you? Selling yourself short like that constantly. I usually let it go, but it's starting to piss me off."

Her words smacked Drew like a bomb over her head. She opened her mouth to say something smart, or witty, or defend herself. "I don't sell myself short." It was the best she could come up with.

"Yes, you do. I'll be right back." Claudia walked with a bounce in her step down a hallway.

"She's got a point." Jules stood on her tiptoes, looking closer at a row of photographs along the mantel.

"No, she doesn't," Drew whispered, staying alert for Claudia's return.

Jules ran her fingers along the framed pictures. "How old are you, twenty?"

"Not till January, why?"

"Own your shit, that's why. You're a talented artist and this girl wants to throw a party honoring you? Dress up, put a smile on your face, and *own your shit*. What the fuck is this?" Jules picked up a picture from the mantel and held it up. She rushed faster than a human toward Drew and angled the intricate frame in Drew's face. "Why is my brother in this picture? Is he? Are they?"

"Holy hell. Why is that floating?" A dress bag slipped from Claudia's grasp and fell into a pile on the floor. "Explanation, please! It's moving!" She tripped over her feet and fell to the floor with a thud. "Shit, ouch."

Drew rushed over to Claudia and crouched down, offering her hand to help her stand. "Her name is Jules. She's—"

"Dead. You can say it. I'm dead, tell her. Tell her who I am." Carrying the picture, Jules moved closer, her body enveloped in a glow of light. Her human form shifted into a ghostly silhouette and the picture crashed to the floor, the glass shattering.

"Dead!" Drew yelled. "She's dead. Jules, stop, you're scaring her."

"What's going on? Jules? That's her name?" Claudia's voice trembled with hysteria.

"Tell her who I am." Jules stood inches from Claudia's face, but Claudia remained oblivious to her presence.

Drew inhaled a sharp breath as she stared at Claudia. When Grant discovered that the woman he was going to marry was the daughter of his sister's killer, Claudia's life would implode.

"Tell her!" Jules' face reddened as her scream echoed throughout the spacious condo, for Drew's ears only.

"Her name is Jules Salinger." Drew's gaze remained fixed on Claudia's stunned expression.

245

Twenty-Two

Claudia stopped picking up pieces of the broken frame and froze. "Grant's dead sister is in this room?"

Drew took the picture from her trembling hands and placed it with the pieces on the counter. "Where's your broom?"

"My what?" Claudia stared in Jules' direction at what must appear to be nothingness.

"Broom. For the glass?" Drew pointed to the shards scattered across the kitchen floor.

"I don't have one."

No broom. What did she do when she needed to clean a mess? Maybe Claudia Tate didn't clean.

Stepping over the mess, Claudia opened a narrow door beside the fridge. A vast space lit up with the flick of a switch, revealing a pantry. She grabbed a small handheld vacuum and handed it to Drew, her face as pale as Jules' and her thick lashes blinking over wide eyes. She was clearly terrified, and maybe in a state of shock.

Drew vacuumed up the mess as Jules paced back and forth across the tiled kitchen. "Your friend is dating my brother? Of course, she was there the other night, she was there with him."

Jules continued to mumble under her breath as Drew turned off the vacuum and placed it back in the pantry. "Jules is in the room, and she needs my help. I'm going to see Grant after I finish here to tell him about her."

Claudia sat on the edge of a plush bar stool and gripped the edge of the island countertop. "She died in a car accident, I don't know... like eight years ago, I think."

"Eight years? I've been dead for eight years?" Jules picked at her nails again.

"I didn't tell you that detail yet." Drew eyed Jules. The shock spread through the room like wildfire, but she was about to make it worse. Claudia needed to know the truth before Grant found out.

"It wasn't just a car accident, Claudia," Drew said.

Claudia's head snapped toward Drew. "What do you mean?"

Jules scrunched her face, disgusted. "I was murdered." She enunciated the last word, dragging it out.

"We think your father killed her—"

"Think?" Jules' mouth gaped open. "Wait, *father*? Her father is Sloan?"

Claudia stood and leaned over the counter with her face in her hands. "Jesus Christ... she was in a horrible car accident." She clenched her hands into tight fists and slammed them on the counter. "Don't do this to me, Drew. Not again."

"Your father threw me off a cliff." Jules glared at Claudia inches away.

"Is she still here?" Claudia asked.

"She's telling you he threw her off a cliff." Drew used the calmest voice she could muster. "And he did... or one of his men did, but I saw it."

Lifting her head, Claudia wiped tears from her eyes. "How did you see it? Never mind, you're a witch and you have visions, I get it." Her nose crinkled as she sniffed. "He'll leave me, we can't tell him. My father is dead to me, anyway."

"Claudia, I have to reconnect him with his sister—"

"Fine, but you will not breathe a word of this to him, promise me you won't tell him. Do you know how hard I've worked? How long it's taken me to get out of my father's shadow?"

"The woman my brother is with is my killer's *daughter*?" Jules gripped the sides of her head as she paced again. "Break them up, you've got to tell him and make him leave her, he can't stay with this woman."

The chaos in the room spiraled, and Drew had to make a choice, Jules or Claudia.

I'm sorry, Jules, but I have to do this again.

Drew focused on blocking Jules, putting walls up, plastering them shut, and locking a key. Anything she could think of to drive her away.

"What are you doing?" Jules held her hands up as they faded into a veil of mist. "We had an understanding, a moment of friendship. How could you?" Her voice trailed off, taking her with it.

"Your pendant is on fire." Claudia pointed at Drew's neck.

She lifted the silver chain, and the light spun in overdrive. A last burst of sparks exploded in the center before plunging the onyx amulet into darkness.

"She's gone," Drew said. "Jules was there at Maze the other night, that's where she saw him."

"He can't know about my father's involvement, Drew. I'm *your* friend, not Grant or Jules. Please don't tell him."

"I can't promise he won't find out—"

"I'm coming with you."

"Claudia, let me do this—"

"Absolutely not. If this was Nico's brother, or one of his parents, would you let him go through this alone?" Claudia's face reddened and her eyes filled with tears.

Drew's heart clenched. "Absolutely not."

"That's what I thought." Claudia grabbed tissues and dabbed the corners of her eyes, not waiting for Drew to respond. Sniffing, she plucked the dress bag from the floor and lifted it as high as she could. "I need you to try on this dress. The party is days away, and I refuse to be the town's joke. I've come too far." She handed Drew the bag. "The bathroom is down the hall on the left."

Taking the dress bag, Drew headed for the bathroom. The crack in Claudia's armor mirrored something inside her. As hard as it was to believe, she had more in common with Claudia Tate than she cared to admit. She understood the persistent fear of failure and protecting the delicate balance of forging a life of her own, far away from her tainted mother.

The bathroom was spotless, with a large clawfoot tub under the back window. She hung the dress bag on the hook at the back of the door. Cool air blew from a decorative grated vent in the ceiling. She ran her fingers along the marble tile framing two sinks in the broad vanity. The mirror was a piece of art by itself. She eyed it closely and touched the crystals embedded along the sides.

Were those real diamonds?

She half-expected a message to appear in the mirror, but nothing happened. Her own reflection caught her attention, and she placed her hands on the vanity. Freckles trailed over her nose, tapering off along her cheeks. The lights from the mirror danced in her green eyes, and they sparkled like emeralds. Her copper hair appeared striking under the light's glow. Maybe this party could be her scene. Drew Harlow. Artist.

"How are you making out in there?" Claudia's voice rang out on the other side of the door.

She jumped and unzipped the dress bag dangling on the bathroom door. "Give me a few minutes."

Or more if I can't get this thing on.

Carefully, she slid the delicate silk straps off the hanger. The vibrant royal blue dress had a simple v-neckline, and a bodice made of the softest silk and lace she'd ever touched. The intricate floral lace embroidery flowed down in a cascade, adorning the thin layers of tulle. She yanked her Tough Cookie collared shirt over her head, shook off her plain black shorts, and stepped into the dress, slipping the straps over her pale pink bra straps. She spun around, trying to zip up the back of the dress, and a knock sounded at the door.

"Can I come in?" Claudia's voice echoed from the hallway.

"It's not locked."

The door opened, and Claudia clasped her hands over her mouth. Her diamond ring picked up the light and sent a burst of sparkles along the wall. "This isn't your scene, my ass." She stormed into the bathroom and turned Drew toward the mirror. "Look at your fine self."

"I can't get it zipped." Drew dropped her hands and lifted her eyes to face herself in the mirror as Claudia pulled the zipper up.

With gentle fingers, Claudia released Drew's hair from the elastic, letting it tumble down her back and over her shoulders, concealing the bra straps. She looked older, and the dress didn't overpower the way she thought it might; it complimented her skin tone and red hair. She felt like she'd stepped into the woman she'd always wanted to become, and confidence surged through her. "The dress is beautiful."

Claudia sat on the edge of the counter. "You make it beautiful."

"I can't afford this—"

"It's on me. Wear it and keep it, or don't. Return it, pass it on, whatever floats your proverbial boat, but when I saw this, I just knew it would be perfect for you. And it's even long enough you can wear whatever,"—Claudia waved her hands and rolled her eyes—"sneakers you want on your feet, and no one will know. And check it out." Hopping off the counter, Claudia took Drew's hands and guided them to the hidden pockets on either side. "It's got pockets."

Drew and Claudia locked eyes through the mirror's reflection. Claudia embodied an unapproachable snob most of the time, but these rare glimpses were the reasons Drew held onto their friendship. Claudia was generous and kind when she wanted to be, and her fierce support never faltered. "You're a good friend, Claudia. Thank you."

Claudia smiled at her and squeezed her hands, but her face turned serious as she glanced at the smart watch attached to her wrist. "We should go see Grant."

"Unzip me."

Reality came crashing back into Drew. A desire to procrastinate gnawed at her, delaying the inevitable emotional reunion with Jules and Grant. But too much time had already passed, and Piper would wonder where in the hell she'd disappeared to.

She held the front of the dress as Claudia guided the zipper down with expert precision, glancing at Drew in the mirror again. "I feel the same about you. You're the only real girl friend I have."

"You're a good person," Drew said. "Maybe let people see that once in a while."

Claudia turned to leave but looked over her shoulder. "Not a chance. And don't you dare tell anyone. Let them think what they want, I don't care."

Yes, you do. We both do.

With the dress secured in the dress bag and draped over her arm, Drew followed Claudia down to the lobby.

The security guard came out of the small corner office and nodded. "How's the party planning coming along?"

"It's beautiful chaos, Mr. Salinger." Claudia directed sad eyes toward Drew.

Salinger?

"That storm they're tracking is going to be stronger than they thought. They think it might make landfall as a tropical storm or category one hurricane. The mayor put out a statement and everything. I hope you have a back-up plan."

"There's always a back-up plan," Claudia said. "I've got it under control, and I doubt it'll be as bad as they're saying."

"Famous last words, Miss Tate. Famous last words. My son has certainly found his match." His voice trailed off, and he gave a small salute, shaking the charm on the heavy chain link bracelet. This time, Drew had a clear view of the heart-shaped charm with the letter 'J' in the center.

"Have a good afternoon." He ducked back into the office, out of sight.

"Why didn't you tell me he's her father?" Drew pushed open the glass doors and stepped into the stifling heat. Dark clouds rumbled overhead, and light rain speckled the pavement.

"Grant first, okay?" Claudia dug keys out of her purse.

"I know that, but he's her dad, he's got to know—"

Claudia spun on her wedged sandals. "Grant first. I don't know how all this works, or what's going to happen, but that man in there didn't just lose his daughter. His wife died two years ago. You talk to dead people. Have you seen her, too?"

A sudden memory of the unfamiliar woman's voice echoed in her mind, reminding her of the night in the den with Jules. *Tell her. She needs to know.* She'd been the reason Drew told Jules about Dominic Sloan. Was Jules' mother the reason she'd returned from her eight-year slumber in between the living and dead?

"I know what I'm doing." Drew unlocked her car. "You need to let me do this. You might know party planning and dress shopping, but I know this world."

Claudia flinched as though someone had slapped her, and Drew wished she could take back her hurtful words. They didn't come out the way she'd intended. "I'm sorry. I didn't mean it like that."

Standing with her car door open, Claudia hesitated and looked up at Drew. "I'll meet you there." She slid into the large sedan and drove away.

Drew climbed in her car and started the engine, opening windows to keep herself from suffocating until the air conditioning kicked in. "It's time, Jules. Come back."

The car connected to a shared playlist she had with Jasper via Bluetooth, and music started playing through the speakers.

Jules appeared beside her in the passenger seat. "Sorry must be the word of the day. You did it again, and you promised me you wouldn't."

"I had to, and I'm sorry. See? I'm getting better at it already." She pulled onto the main road a few cars behind Claudia at the traffic lights. "She's not like her father, she's a good person and loves your brother."

"I saw the big rock on her hand, I assumed as much." Jules shifted her gaze out the window and tapped her fingers along the dash. "I like this song. I remember it, and it makes me happy."

Drew stole a glance from the road to Jules. "If you were dead for eight years before you found me, do you remember anything about where you were or what it was like?"

"Not really, it feels like no time passed, nothingness, except..." Jules' eyes widened, and she clasped her hands over her mouth, shifting toward Drew. "The man inside the building today was my dad, wasn't he? How'd you make me remember?"

"I didn't do anything," Drew said.

The more time Ori and Enid had spent with her, the more memories resurfaced, but Drew remained unaware of the soul's secrets.

Dropping her hands to her lap, Jules' skin glimmered, and her eyes sparkled. "My mom's dead too. I can feel her around me, with me, but she's not on your side. And if you ask me how I know, I won't have an answer, just that there's this strange pull, like a dam opening, and the water wants to take me with it."

As the song ended, Jules disappeared, leaving an empty seat behind.

This never gets easier.

Twenty-Three

The sun disappeared behind a thick blanket of dark clouds, and the rain poured down in sheets, creating an angry symphony of tapping against the car. By the time Drew parked, Claudia had already arrived and left her car. She held onto a sliver of hope that Claudia would have the sense to wait for her to get inside before telling Grant about his sister. Jules' ghostly silhouette blended with the shadows as she leaned against the doorway.

Maybe once Jules reconnected with her brother and father, she'd be able to move on without involving Sloan. But Jules had told her he'd met with someone and spoke of revenge. Her stomach tightened again, the knot extending to her chest.

He's in jail and he can't hurt me.

But he could get someone else to do it for him.

Jules gestured to Drew, and she bolted from the car, taking shelter from the rain beneath a stone overhang at the entrance of the prestigious building.

"Okay, let's do this." As Drew reached for the door handle, her phone vibrated in her pocket. It wasn't the brief buzz of a notification, but the lingering ring of an incoming call. With her heart racing, she reached for the phone, anticipating Nico's name to fill the screen.

Piper.

"I'm so sorry, it's taking longer—"

"Did Nico get hold of you?"

She clutched her chest, feeling as though her heart had come to a sudden halt, sinking into the pit of her stomach.

"Are you still there?" Piper asked. "He stopped by, looking for you. Something seemed wrong."

"What did he say?" Drew's heart started hammering in her chest.

"Nothing, he just came in looking for you, and took off," Piper said.

"Where'd he say he was going?"

"He didn't. Why wouldn't he just call or message you?"

A steady hum of chatter sounded through the phone. Jules gestured toward Drew again, and in a blink, she disappeared through the door. If Drew failed to show up in a few minutes, Jules and Claudia would be livid. She gripped the phone against her ear. She couldn't go to Nico until she helped Jules and Claudia. "I'll find him, don't worry. He didn't say anything?" Drew repeated.

"Nothing." Piper raised her voice over the background noise.

It was the lunch rush at the Tough Cookie, and Taj and Piper would be swamped. Three options weighed on her shoulders. Run inside with Jules, find Nico, help Piper at the bakery… or somehow manage all three. It suddenly hurt to breathe, as if the air was being sucked out of her lungs, and she thought she might faint. She swallowed the panic down and stepped out from underneath the shelter to let the rain hit her face. Anything to bring her back into the moment. "It sounds busy, I can come help, I'll try calling him—"

"It's a busload of tourists and they love me. J's here and he's got the new pastry chef back there. We've got this, just go."

"Are you sure?"

"Yes, I'm sure. I'm hanging up now. Call me as soon as you find out what's going on."

The phone went dead, and rain dripped down her forehead and soaked into her Tough Cookie shirt. She knew what she had to do; Nico would have to wait. She couldn't leave Claudia and Jules inside with Grant.

Stepping inside the office complex, Drew walked past Tate Realty on the first-floor triggering memories of her meetings with Anna Tate and signing papers to sell Gran's house. She released a tight breath and praised herself for keeping her home. She remembered that the elevator moved at a glacial pace, so she abandoned it, sprinting up two flights of stairs. She stumbled onto the second floor, surrounded by busy law offices, garnering stares as people in suits, dresses, and starched dress shirts looked up from computers and paperwork.

With a smile, she passed by a reception area and a man rose from behind a desk. "Do you have an appointment?"

"Yes, actually—"

"She's with me." Claudia stepped out of an office down a narrow hallway.

Drew hesitated as she reached the door with Grant Salinger's nameplate, catching her breath. She went in and took a seat across from him, the large desk between them cluttered with files. Jules' ghostly silhouette hung back by the large window overlooking the harbor.

The leather seat reclined as Grant sat back and clasped his hands over his chest. "You must be my *Melinda Gordon* appointment."

"It was the first name that came to me." She tugged her bottom lip with her teeth. Her damp shirt pricked her skin, and she sat upright so her back wasn't touching the chair.

Claudia shut the office door and sat in the seat next to her. "I told him his sister is back, and he thinks I've lost it."

"I'm disappointed in you, Grant," Jules said. "I'm standing right here." She glided across the room to stand behind Drew, sending an icy breeze around her.

"I've heard the rumors. People call you a witch, and you claim to talk to dead people—"

"I don't *claim* to do anything to anyone, people can say whatever they want. But your sister has been with me for the last two months, Grant."

"What are they, ghosts? I don't believe in ghosts," he said.

"I used to call them Wandering Souls, but ghosts, dead people, they're not all that different from us," Drew said. "All I know is I've been able to see them my whole life, they find me—usually for help, and it's just part of... me."

"Drew's my best friend, she's not lying," Claudia said.

The words smacked Drew in the face. *You're the only real girl friend I have.* Underneath that diamond exterior, Claudia was just a girl trying to find her place in the world. Like Drew. And she'd been there for Drew more times than she could count. She wouldn't tell Grant about Sloan, not yet. Not until she had to.

Grant loosened the top buttons on his dress shirt and rubbed his temples. His sandy hair stood on end as he ran his hands over his head before shifting his attention back to Drew. "I can't believe we're doing this here. I just graduated from law school and I'm trying to make a good impression, get my foot in the door. If it gets weird, we can't stay in this office."

"I'm not leaving." Jules moved closer to Grant.

"She doesn't want to leave." With her elbows on the armrests, Drew intertwined her fingers across her waist. She couldn't rush a reunion like this, but Jules would not cross over anywhere until she connected with her brother and father.

Claudia uncrossed her legs and rose from her seat, crossing the small space toward Grant. Lowering herself, she encircled him with her arms. "It won't get weird, and if it does, we'll leave. Let Drew help so your sister can find peace, right, Drew?" Desperation filled her eyes as she glanced at Drew.

"I can imagine how strange this might all seem, but it's normal for me." Drew dropped her hands onto her lap. "Usually once they get the chance to say goodbye, they can cross over, but I can tell you now, Jules won't go anywhere until she sees your dad again, too."

Looking panicked, Claudia hugged herself and rubbed her arms. Drew wouldn't be able to keep Claudia's father out of this for long. Sharing her truth might be the only way for Jules to cross over. If Grant loved Claudia enough to marry her, he'd have to acknowledge her struggles to overcome her father's history of murder and realize his fiancée was a victim too.

"Cross over?" Grant asked. "I can't do this, this—this is... Do you hear yourself? How can this be real life?" Holding his gaze to Drew, he gripped Claudia's hand.

"It is real," Claudia murmured. "Just let her help."

Jules tried to reach for Grant's hand but passed through him. "Don't let him make me leave. Tell him about the time he spray-painted my bike purple because I hated yellow, and our parents refused to buy me a new one until I could pay half."

"You painted her bike purple once," she said.

Grant let go of Claudia's hand and gripped his desk. His tanned complexion paled, losing its sun-kissed hue. "It was yellow and she hated it, but didn't have enough money for a new one."

"She's beside you." Drew stood and edged closer to the desk. "She's trying to touch your hand, but it's not working."

He held up his hand, examining it from every angle. Stepping back, Claudia created a space around him, her hand pressed to her mouth.

Pushing the chair back, he got up, letting his arms drop to his sides. "My parents loved your grandmother. She helped them after Jules died. I'll give you one shot to show me what you can do, but if this doesn't work, you leave and never speak of it to anyone, deal?"

"Of course, deal," Drew said.

Adjusting his posture, he rolled the sleeves of his shirt and cracked his neck, making Drew cringe. "If you really think you can connect me with my sister, who's been dead for the past eight years, I'm ready."

"Are you ready, Jules?" Drew reached for her transparent hand. "You've got to focus and take my hand."

"You don't even have to ask." Jules' body rippled, and shifted, revealing her human shape. "What do we do now?"

Drew clasped Jules' hand and a jolt of electricity surged through her head and down her neck, leaving behind the unmistakable metallic taste of magic. As her amulet thrummed underneath her shirt, a burst of sparklers erupted in her hands. "Give me your hand, Grant."

He hesitated, his gaze fixated on Drew's face, and Claudia stepped forward, taking his hand and placing it in Drew's.

His eyes shifted straight to Jules. "Jesus Christ. It's really you?" Grant's eyes welled with tears.

"Of course it's me, you had me worried for a minute. Still as stubborn as ever." Jules threw her arm around Grant, not breaking the connection with Drew.

As he held his sister, his tears erupted, streaming down his face. "I miss you. I wish you were still here. Nothing is the same without you, Dad is getting by, but barely, and Mom is gone." His voice caught as hugged her tighter.

Drew's legs trembled and a wave of exhaustion threatened to pull her down as she stood shoulder to shoulder with Jules, willing the connection to keep flowing between them.

Jules placed her hand on Grant's back. "You're strong, and so is Dad. I'm okay, Drew's helping me. But I need to talk to him. Drew, promise me we'll talk to my dad?"

"I promise." Drew's promises were never-ending these days, overwhelming her with uncertainty. The amulet's steady pulse faded until it stopped and the sensation in her hands subsided. The rapid, magical current slowed, and a buzzing filled her ears. "I'm losing the connection."

"Please don't go, not yet." Grant clung to his sister as her silhouette shimmered into a swirling mist before she vanished.

Releasing his hand, Drew collapsed in the chair and leaned forward with her elbows on her knees. A surge of pain and sorrow swept over her like it always did after she connected the living with the dead. Her heart raced erratically before settling back into a normal rhythm, leaving her breathless.

Grant placed his hands on the windowsill and Claudia rushed to him, wrapping her arms around his back. As he reached up, his hand found hers and they entwined their fingers around his waist. "The rumors are true," he said. "I don't know what to say. How can you do that?"

Pulling away from him, Claudia smoothed out her sundress and wiped her eyes. "Did it work? Has she crossed to a peaceful place?"

Claudia wore the same expression on her face as she did that night in the warehouse when her father threatened Drew with a gun. "She won't leave until she meets her dad again." Rising from the chair, she steadied her wobbly legs. "I'm sorry to run out of here after what just happened, but I have to go... I'm late for something."

"Wait." Grant rushed toward the door before she could open it. "Will we do this again, with Dad? When?" Straightening up, he wiped his brow. "I owe you an apology. I misjudged, and I'm sorry."

"You wouldn't be the first, and you won't be the last," Drew said. "Thanks though, but it's really okay." She gripped the door handle and hesitated. Jules would be back for her father. "We'll figure something out soon but talk to him first so he's ready."

"Of course, yes, that's a good idea," Grant said. "Here let me get that for you. I can walk you out—"

"I know my way, maybe you two can talk." Drew locked eyes with Claudia.

Just tell him the truth.

Her magical talents didn't include the ability to communicate through telepathy.

Claudia's gaze remained fixed on Drew. "It'll be the day everything changes for him, getting to be with his daughter again. I'll message you."

Twenty-Four

Dialing Nico's number, Drew sprinted from the office building to her car, stepping into a puddle as the rain pelted her hair. Shaking the water off her foot, she slammed the car door shut and turned the key in the ignition but sat still as she struggled to catch her breath.

Remnants of Jules' emotions clung to Drew's soul, consuming her with the dead woman's overwhelming desperation for another chance at life. A deep ache throbbed in her chest, shooting waves of dull pain down her back. Collapsing against her seat, she shivered as the icy blast of air conditioning hit her skin. Nico's voicemail answered, and she ended the call.

She turned the air down and covered her face, giving in to the sadness and letting the dead woman's grief release from her body as the tears took hold.

Taking a few deep breaths, she peeled out of the parking lot onto the street. Pedestrians scurried along the sidewalks; their faces hidden behind a multitude of colorful umbrellas. With a sudden jolt, the car hit a pothole and collided with a puddle, propelling a burst of water over the sidewalk. A woman shrieked as a man gave Drew the finger.

Why wasn't he answering her calls or messaging? She loved Nico, but sitting back in silence while he distanced himself from her wasn't an option. If they couldn't talk to each other, the relationship wouldn't last. She'd find him and ask him for the truth.

The Bluetooth finally gave up trying to connect to her phone, and the radio turned on, blaring a news update about the impending Hurricane Francine, still too far in the Atlantic to predict impact, but expected to move along the New England coast.

She wove through traffic toward the garage, her eyes darting between the road and her phone as she dialed him again. He went looking for her at work, but wasn't answering her calls? He never left her in the dark like this.

As rain poured down on the windshield, the wipers swept back and forth, trying to maintain a clear view of the road.

Pulling into the parking lot at DeSarro's, she rushed out of the car up to the front doors and yanked on the handle, but found it locked with no lights on.

She ran toward the garage windows, cupping her hands around her face to peer inside. The vehicles were stationary on the lifts, their hoods raised, with no signs of activity or noise.

Where are you, Nico?

A deep voice boomed, "Who's out there?"

She hurried back to the shop doors to find Nico's father standing with the door ajar. He eyed her up and down. "Come in."

With her hair drenched and her clothes clinging to her, she brushed past him and made her way inside. The harsh blast of cold air conditioning sent a chill over her skin and shivers through her.

"Here." Nico's dad tossed her the oversized, smoky sweater sitting in the same place she'd left it days earlier.

Sliding her arms in, she zipped it up and hugged herself. "Have you seen Nico?"

"Not since this morning." His attention shifted to his phone. "Excuse me, I've got to take this." He left her alone in the front entrance and shut the door to the office. The tone of his voice changed as he talked, but the office muffled his words.

A disorganized stack of papers lay in a pile behind the counter, and Drew glanced from the office to the stack. The computer monitor displayed the old DeSarro and Son screen saver, flickering as it bounced across the screen. With Nico's father still on the phone, she flipped through the pages only to find unfamiliar invoices for parts and labor displaying prices and names. She opened desk drawers filled with pens, wrenches, business cards, and a large bottom drawer that held stainless steel cups with the old logo.

"Looking for something?"

She slammed the drawer shut and stuffed her hands in her pockets. "I was just—"

"Mm." Tucking his phone in his back pocket, he sat in one of the waiting room chairs. "Go grab a towel from the cabinet in the bathroom."

"I'm fine, I should go." She pushed damp strands of hair off her face and headed for the door.

"When you find Nico..." Pausing, he rubbed his face with both hands. Leaning forward, he placed his elbows on his knees. His forehead creased and the lines between his eyes grew deeper as he focused his gaze on her. The pain in his eyes was reminiscent of the way Nico looked when he was hurting.

"Is he okay? I can't get a hold of him."

"Everything I do is for him. For my family."

His unexpected openness caught her off guard, leaving her unsure of how to respond. "I believe you. Do you know where he went?"

"He won't see it that way. He'll blame me."

"Mr. DeSarro—"

"Nick."

Right, first name basis.

She'd always called him Mr. DeSarro, unlike Nico's mother, Maria. She'd always been the sweet, warm soul who had welcomed Drew into their home since her father had brought her to live with Gran all those years ago.

"I don't mean to pry, but I'm worried about him. If there's something going on, please tell me. I love your son and just want to be there for him."

His gaze fell to the floor and a rare smile spread across his face, softening the lines. "He's got his mother's way, you know? Thank God he doesn't take after me."

"Don't say that, he loves you."

"Look, Drew. I fucked up a lot of things. That's not gonna be Nico. He's a good man, and I won't let him struggle. Not for a fucking second. Especially not because of my mistakes. You say you love him?"

Another wave of shivers coursed through her, and it wasn't from the freezing room. Her bond with Nico was unlike anything she dreamed possible. It was as though her soul recognized his, woven together since they had met as kids, and somehow, their paths had always been destined to merge. "I do love him."

"Then promise me you won't leave him when shit gets tough." His words held the weight of a dark premonition.

"Is there something I should know?" A palpable silence settled between them, accompanied by the lingering smell of smoke and oil.

He reached into his pocket and pulled out a key. "Can I give you this? He's not talking to me. He took off out of here, pissed off."

She reached for the key and a surge of electricity surged through her as her fingertips brushed against his palm, flooding her mind with a whirlwind of vivid images. Covered in shadows, a man wearing a dark jumpsuit, buttoned down to expose a white undershirt, sat on a cot with his hands on his face and iron bars obscuring Drew's view. Like a movie camera zooming in closer, she peered through the bars. With a sudden motion, the man dropped his hands and raised his head, shooting her a piercing glare. Cold, murderous eyes looked her up and down, sending a rush of shivers along her spine. He stood and took a step forward as his lips curled into a menacing smile. In a fast forward transition, he sat across from a man, each holding a black phone against their ears, and the ID bracelet around his wrist like Jules had mentioned.

Dominic Sloan.

Guards led the other man away, and the view changed, panning like a camera from the visitor's back to his face as he exited the room in the prison. Unable to breathe, Drew sucked in shallow breaths. Her heart shattered into a thousand pieces. The man at the prison with Sloan was Nick DeSarro.

With the key digging into her skin, she leaped back as an icy blade coursed from the top of her head to the pit of her stomach, extinguishing the fire. She swallowed to unclench the grip on her throat as fragments of light surrounded her in a burst of fireworks Nick DeSarro wouldn't be able to see. Her breath hitched, and she coughed, almost choking.

How could he do this to Nico?

"You need a drink of water?" he asked.

Gripping the key in her hand, she steadied herself. "What's this key for?"

"Don't lose it. You should leave now."

"Why did you visit Dominic Sloan in jail?"

His jaw dropped, before he clamped his mouth shut. "I don't know what you're talking about." His phone rang, startling her, and he pulled it from his chest pocket. "I've got to take this. DeSarro. Yup." He left her behind as he closed himself away in the office again.

When had Nico's father gone to visit Dominic Sloan, and why?

Struggling for air, she bent over with her hands on her thighs, battling panic and fear. That monster could never come back into her life.

Not ever.

TWENTY-FIVE

Drew sped away from the garage, heading through town. The vision couldn't be right, it just couldn't. But from the nightmares of Jack Morana, Iris's murder, Ori's visions of Shane and Leah on the boat when she'd believed he was dead—they'd never been wrong.

She called Nico's cell phone again, with no answer. He could be at Maze with Taj. She drove down the alley beside Maze, parked and shut the engine off. Taking the key from the ignition, she flung the door open, but her seatbelt snapped her back against the seat as she tried to get out.

Think, Drew. Think!

She couldn't figure out why Nico had stopped by the Tough Cookie looking for her, but the encounter with his father suggested he could've discovered something. Panicking wasn't his style, but neither was avoiding her.

Unbuckling the belt, she freed herself from the car and ran to the entrance as rain pelted her skin, grateful for Jasper's choice of black shirts instead of see-through white. She yanked the large door handle and stepped inside. Music played through the speakers, interrupted by a broadcaster with the latest news and weather forecast. More on the heatwave, thunderstorms, tracking Hurricane Francine, and basically... impending doom. Air conditioning did nothing to cool the room with the number of people gathered at tables and the pizza oven emitting heat.

Their usual table sat empty as Drew scanned the room, desperate to see Nico's broad shoulders sitting somewhere and finding him nowhere. She knew him better than this, and if he discovered anything close to what she'd just found out about his father, he would avoid any place as crowded as Maze on a Friday.

As she turned to leave, a different man with shoulders not as broad as Nico's, and a curious blue-eyed gaze, caught her attention.

Shane.

Drew remembered the girl he was sitting with all too well—the same girl from Ori's vision, and the girl he'd cheated with, Leah. Did it count as cheating if she had believed he'd been dead for months, but was actually miles away on a boat with someone else? Leah's dark hair tumbled down her back in a neat ponytail as she picked at her pizza. Shane stood and leaned down to say something to her before making his way toward Drew.

"You're soaked," he said.

"You're observant. Have you seen Nico?"

Dumb question. Of course, he wouldn't have seen him. Shane shook his head. "What's going on?"

Still unsure of what the two had talked about at Maze the other night, she weighed her words. "I'm not sure, but I can't get hold of him, and Piper said he was looking for me. He's not here, I'll just go."

Shane reached for her arm, and she spun around. There was a time his touch had a profound effect on her, but not anymore. All she felt was a deep worry for the man she loved.

"He doesn't want you involved." Dropping his hand from her, he folded his arms across his chest.

"Involved in what?" Warmth from the amulet graced her neck and her skin pricked with electricity. Was Shane keeping secrets too? "I knew the other night was more than small talk about cars." Why would Nico trust Shane over her? Anger rose, overpowering any lingering sense of hurt.

"Shit." Shane's expression twisted into a grimace. "Would you just let this one go for now?"

She narrowed her eyes at him, anger burning her cheeks. "What would Nico say to you but not me?"

"This isn't about me, I'm not the asshole you think I am."

"I don't think you're an asshole. I just—"

"I was a victim too, you know. My life was ruined too. Fuck. We actually liked each other at one time, didn't we? Or is that just forgotten?" Shane glared at her, holding his stance.

A few people paused and looked up from their half-eaten lunches with curiosity. Leah leaned back in her chair, staring in their direction as her fingers scrolled on her phone. Her gaze glanced back at her phone when Drew made eye contact.

She didn't have the time or energy to rehash her relationship with Shane, either alone or with an audience. Stepping closer to him, she lowered her voice. "How could I forget? My reminder is sitting in a booth behind you, and I'm trying to help a dead woman who was..." *Murdered by your father.* "Nothing is forgotten."

Shane's forehead creased in concentration. "You're a liar."

"Excuse me?" She clenched her fists, desperate to shout the words, but she resisted, not wanting to draw any more attention than they were already getting.

"You have forgotten, and you don't care. You forget how awesome we were together. We had fun, we laughed, we were... you know. Together. Everything fell apart, but it wasn't my fault, or yours. Shit got real dark on that boat, and I'm sorry I fucked up, but I can't take it back. Hate me if you want, Drew, but I'm not the enemy, and neither is she."

Drew made eye contact with Leah again, but this time, Leah didn't look away. She rested her elbows on the table and placed her phone down. The sting of the betrayal burned in Drew's chest, but she shoved it aside. She had no regrets or longing to be with Shane again, and their relationship would have ended no matter what had happened. Shane had been an escape from her loneliness, and someone to be broken with. Their relationship had taught her about loving herself enough to trust again. The emotions tied to the months she had thought he was dead and finding out he'd been with someone else had faded into an imprint—a stamp to close their chapter.

"I do care," she whispered. "And I don't think you're an asshole, not usually, anyway. But I need you to tell me whatever it is you're hiding."

Shane scratched his chest and twisted his mouth. He looked everywhere but at her.

"Shane, come on. I'm not an idiot."

He rubbed his jaw but said nothing. She gnawed at her bottom lip to keep from screaming in frustration. "Good talk," she said. "I've got to get out of here."

"My biological shit ass of a father isn't the only dad who's a fuck-up. Did you forget the reason Nico owns that garage by himself?"

His father was involved with Dominic Sloan again. The extortion and blackmail from the last time had kept him from doing jail time, but his reputation took a nosedive. "Of course I didn't. But Sloan is in prison now." She reminded herself as much as Shane.

Shane pursed his lips together. "Life didn't exactly stand still while he's been in there." He shook his head. "I talked to Nico earlier. He was chasing a lead, that's all I know. He doesn't want you involved in any of this, and I agree with him, so please, let it go, okay? There's nothing you can do. There's nothing any of us can do."

She turned away from him and headed for the door.

"Drew, come on."

"He's home, dear," Gran's soft voice murmured in her ear.

With her heart racing and tears spilling from her eyes, she kept her back to Shane and waved over her shoulder without turning around. Nick DeSarro was in over his head again, and she'd be damned if he was going to take Nico down with him.

TWENTY-SIX

Rounding the coastal road toward home, Drew slowed as she approached the street leading to Nico's. No one was behind her, and she pulled off the road onto the gravel shoulder. The view from the windshield cleared with each swipe of the wiper blades.

She grabbed her phone and dialed him again, letting it ring until it switched to voicemail. The only notification was from Piper checking in. She should keep going and make sure Henry was okay, but a mix of worry and anger consumed her. Before she could change her mind, she turned down the familiar street and drove up to the large garage beside Nico's house.

With a forceful gust of wind, the car door slipped from her hand as she opened it and swung back on its hinges. She got out of the car and sheets of rain blew sideways, soaking her hair against her face. The gray afternoon sky stole light from filtering in through the windows, shrouding the garage in darkness. It was barely 2 p.m., but it resembled the onset of evening. Another gust of air surrounded her, this time cold like a winter swell off the ocean.

"Drew!" Maria DeSarro called through the pounding rain. "He's up there!" She stood on the back deck, holding the door open.

Drew cut across the driveway, stepping into the backyard toward the wraparound deck. "Have you talked to him?"

Maria stepped further outside, her eyes puffy and her face red, remaining sheltered under the eaves as rain beaded along the chestnut painted boards.

Drew shielded her eyes from the rain as she looked up at Nico's mom. "Are you okay?"

Maria smoothed the dark curls from her face. "I'm fine... just worried about him. Come in, out of the rain. I'll get you a towel." She stepped back inside and propped the screened door open, displaying a stack of boxes with a roll of packing tape on top.

She was giving up her family home and life as she'd known it. Drew knew that feeling of sadness and loss all too well. She'd almost done the same thing months earlier.

"If you need help, I don't mind." The rain and thunder drowned out her words as though trying to silence her from saying the wrong thing. What did she know about raising a family, navigating a messy divorce, and leaving everything behind to start over?

Rain battered her, streaming down her face, and chilling her skin. At least it offered a break from the sweltering heat. Nico's mother reappeared and handed her a plush towel.

Standing on her tiptoes, Drew gripped the top of the deck's wooden rail and wrapped the towel around her as rain seeped through it. "Maria—"

"You look like a drowned rat. For goodness' sake, get in here and dry off."

Drew glanced at the stairs leading up the side of the garage to Nico's small place. "Thank you. I appreciate the offer, but I'm here to see Nico."

"Well, you better get your butt up there. Want a change of clothes? I can get you a T-shirt—"

"I'm good. Really."

Maria smiled at her. "I know you are. You've grown into a strong woman. Maddie would be proud."

Drew had known Nico's family for so long, she'd forgotten that Maria had watched her transition from a little girl into a grown woman. "I just wanted to say... to tell you... I'm really sorry you have to sell the house. And if there's anything I can do, I will."

Stepping out from under the eaves and into the rain, Maria leaned over the railing. "That's sweet of you, I might take you up on it. He's lucky to have you." She moved back underneath the protective shelter of the house.

Fear surprised her as it curled around her insides. Maria would be furious if she knew the truth about her ex-husband.

"There is one thing you can do for me," Maria raised her voice as the sky crackled with lightning, followed by a snap of thunder.

Shivering, Drew pulled the towel tighter under her chin in a failed attempt to warm herself. "Anything."

Maria pointed toward Nico's apartment above the garage. "Get out of the rain." Her eyes widened, and she shook her head as she headed back inside.

Drew bounded up the steps on the side of the garage, taking them two at a time until she reached the door. She knocked with a swift thud of her knuckles and waited. If footsteps were coming from inside, they were no match for the heavy rain surrounding her. She leaned over the rail to press her face against the kitchen window, but her heart sank further into her stomach. His mom said he was home, and the car was in the garage.

Where are you?

The railing protested with a loud creak as she leaned over, and she could feel it shifting beneath her weight. Her foot slipped and her arms flailed as she fell, still gripping the towel. Strong arms slipped underneath her, pulling her back onto the small porch landing. Nico's bare chest pressed against her back as he held her in his arms. She gazed into his eyes as rain streamed down his thick lashes.

"Are you okay?" he yelled over the torrential downpour.

"Where have you been?" The anger boiled over.

Releasing her, he pushed the door open for her to step inside ahead of him. With gasping breaths, she dropped the sopping wet towel into the kitchen sink and faced him.

Wearing a pair of worn-out jeans and nothing else, he grabbed a pitcher from the fridge and filled a glass with water.

His forearms, marked with faint traces of grease, flexed as he reached for a blanket on the sofa and draped it over her shoulders. "I've got to fix that railing. Are you sure you're not hurt?"

"No, I'm not hurt. I was worried, and you didn't answer any of my calls, you've barely messaged in days. What the hell, Nico?"

"My phone died, and I stopped in to see you at work, but Piper said you'd gone to see Claudia about a dress or something." As he stood across from her, his chest rose and fell in rhythm with her own shallow breathing.

She pushed her bottom lip into her mouth and tugged it with her teeth. "You're not wearing a shirt."

He laughed. "No kidding. I was as soaked as you are when I got home. Do you want one of my T-shirts?"

"I want you to tell me what's going on." As she held her lip between her fingertips, her teeth grazed the soft flesh of her cheek, seeking comfort that never came.

His expression turned serious, and he shifted his eyes away from her. "It's nothing for you to worry about."

"If it's nothing, then tell me."

Crossing the small kitchen, he gently pried her fingers away from her lips and held her hand in his. "I can't do that. Just trust me."

"Like I trusted Shane? You talked to him, but you won't tell me? Why are you keeping secrets and staying away from me?" She tugged her hand from his grasp, her heart heavy with the weight of regret for her uncontrolled cutting words. She trusted him with her life, but she'd believed he trusted her enough to talk to her when he was struggling with something.

He ran his hands through his damp hair. "That's not fair. I'd never do to you what he did, and you know it. And how is this any different from the secrets you keep from me?"

"I'm not keeping secrets from you." Her eyes filled with tears, and she looked away so he couldn't see them. She had made a habit of hiding things from him, even when she'd promised she wouldn't.

She could feel her walls threatening to build up again, prepared to embrace her heart and keep it safe. Shield it from the cruel, unrelenting sting of being left behind or forgotten.

Abandonment issues. Childhood trauma. She could almost hear her therapist's calm voice in her head. She clearly should be back in that woman's office.

Holding back tears, she took a deep breath, swallowing the lump in her throat. She refused to let those fears win, especially when it concerned Nico. But if he no longer felt the same way anymore, she had to find out.

"I'm sorry, I didn't mean what I said. You're nothing like Shane." She adjusted the blanket over her shoulders, grasping the soft fabric in her fingers. "Have your feelings for me changed? If you're having second thoughts about us, I'd rather you just say so instead of avoiding me."

"What? No, of course not." His gaze connected with hers, the hurt in his brown eyes unmistakable. "Second thoughts about us is the last thing I'm feeling. Why, have yours changed?" He turned away from her and gripped the back of the sofa. "We've been here before, and you left."

She wiped her eyes as the persistent lump in her throat resurfaced. "We aren't there again. This isn't like what happened after high school. I thought I made my feelings for you obvious. You've been the one avoiding me."

He moved closer, bridging the gap between them, and the tension in the air intensified. "I can't talk about it."

"Maybe I know more than you think. You're not in this alone." She suppressed her tears.

"Fuck, it sure feels like it. I've kept it all together, the business, the go between with my parents who hate each other, all while Simon is away at university. I'm supposed to be doing my apprenticeship, my own college—my *future* that no one seems to give a shit about. But I'm just figuring it all out by myself, and now *this*."

"Now what? I want to be here for you." Her chest tightened, and the words came out hushed.

He leaned against the back of the sofa with furrowed brows as he scanned the small living room. "Why is it okay for you to avoid telling me stuff, but you're mad at me if I do it?" His tone carried sadness rather than anger. "You just said you know more than I think, so why don't you let me in on what you know?"

The torment in his eyes awakened her own buried heartbreak. With a soft click, the small window air conditioning unit interrupted her thoughts, sending a cool breeze in the room and goosebumps over her bare skin. Shivering, she gripped the blanket tighter around herself. "I promise I'll tell you whatever you want, but if we're together, really together, you can't just ditch me because you've got shit going on that you don't think I can handle. How am I supposed to help if you don't talk to me?"

He held his hands out, frustrated. "See? You're avoiding talking to me. I'm scared if I tell you, you'll get involved, and it's not safe—"

"I can take care of myself." She released her grip on the blanket, and it slipped off her shoulders to the floor.

With a huff, Nico suppressed a smile, but his dimple gave away his amusement. "I'm aware. But no amount of magic can fix this." His smile faded, taking his dimple with it.

He stared at her with that all-encompassing-can't-live-without-you look, and she longed to grab his arms, wrap them around her, and never let him go. The breakup from a year ago had become a hazy memory, drifting further into the past. She had no desire to be anywhere else in the entire world, and the last thing she ever wanted was for him to feel the weight of loneliness.

His forehead creased as he reached out and hooked a finger in the belt loop of her shorts, pulling her closer. Her pulse raced and her breath hitched. With her arms wrapped around his waist, she tilted her head up, feeling the warmth of his hands as they clasped around her back.

"Your clothes are wet." His lips were inches from hers.

"I don't care. What did you tell Shane that you won't tell me?"

"Don't you find it weird talking about him like this?"

She angled her face away from him, but his hands still held her. "You're stalling. No, it isn't. We're so beyond all that now, it's like the weird never existed."

"I don't want you to worry about stuff you don't need to worry about."

"Don't do that," she said.

"What?"

"Be cryptic. Not with me. Never with me."

His lips grazed hers, waking up a cluster of butterflies in her belly. Heat from his body melted into hers, warming her skin underneath her wet shirt. She kissed him and his fingers trailed along her arms. She leaned back, breaking the connection, and he exhaled.

"We've been through so much," she said. "I'm not letting this go. Tell me your secrets and I'll tell you mine."

Releasing her from his arms, he half-sat on the back of the L-shaped sofa, with his legs stretched in front of him. "I'm ashamed to tell you. I don't want to drag you down with me."

"It's me, Nico. You and me. We've got this, whatever it is."

Thunder rumbled, growing farther in the distance, and as the rain subsided, the pinging on the metal roof faded away.

He played with the silver chain around his neck. "Dad's involved with Sloan again."

He knows.

And if she wanted him to be honest with her, she'd have to do the same, and she would, but she wanted him to tell her everything first. "What makes you say that?"

"I don't know all the details, but I'm trying to find out." Extending his arm, he took her hand. "Sloan tried to kill you, I can't let you be involved with this. I've been staying away until I could figure it out, but it's taking longer than I thought."

She squeezed his hand, sweat forming on her palm. Fear tightened around her, threatening to knock her off her feet, but she held steady. "What have you found out so far?"

"Not much, but ever since Dad helped me open the new shop, he's had wads of cash. Stacks. I walked in on him in the back office, stuffing it into a safe built into the wall."

Shane's warning was right. Life hadn't stopped for Dominic Sloan. "Is there any chance your dad earned that money legally somehow?"

Stop making shit up and tell him. Why is this so hard?

"From what?" Nico let go of her hand and crossed his arms. "Business picked up since everyone thinks he's stepped away, and I've had more resto work than I can keep up with, but he's got money flowing in like fucking *water*. I see the books and he's not getting all that cash from my jobs. I'd bet the garage he's working for Sloan again, and he's not alone, he can't be. Prison hasn't stopped that man from throwing his power around."

She tried to think of a scenario that would prove Sloan wasn't behind any of this again and would remain trapped in his cage forever. "If there are others, maybe it's not Sloan. Maybe it's money your dad had buried from last time."

A laugh escaped Nico. "Buried? Like the mafia?"

"Yeah, isn't that what people do?"

"I don't know, but I'm going to find out." Pushing off from the sofa, he reached into his back pocket and retrieved his phone. "He left his phone on the work bench unlocked. I took pictures with my phone, but he came back, and I didn't have time to see much. He's so damn angry all the time, and you know my father, he's never been a phone guy, but suddenly he's on it all the time. What's up with that?"

He held out his phone, and she leaned over it. "It just looks like a conversation about tires for a mustang."

"I thought so too, but look at the pickup date," he said.

"That's the night of Claudia's party."

"Exactly."

She locked eyes with him and could swear she glimpsed a flicker of relief in his expression. Relief that he could share what he'd found out. "So how does Shane fit in to all this?"

"He asked me."

"Asked you what?"

"If I really took over my dad's business. He was digging for information. A guy has been coming around the gallery asking questions."

Her defenses crept up her back, a knot forming in her stomach as she thought about the determination and work Claudia had poured into getting the place up and running. The gallery was growing in success, and if all this was true and Claudia's father slithered his way back into their lives—Drew couldn't let that happen. "Claudia doesn't know, does she." It wasn't a question.

Nico fidgeted with his chain again and shuddered, goosebumps appearing over his skin. "No, and please don't tell her." He flicked off the air conditioner and faced Drew. "Dominic Sloan will never find his way back into our lives."

And if Sloan somehow returned, what would it take to remove him from their lives?

Death.

Drew shook the ominous thought from her mind. Anger replaced the butterflies in her stomach like a swarm of wasps, and anxiety rose in her chest.

Nico led her to the sofa, and she collapsed into the plush cushions. Her summer break was nothing like she had envisioned.

Sitting beside her, he flopped against the back of the sofa and folded his hands over his head. "This is my shit to deal with, Drew. I need you to stay away from all of it. Don't come to the garage again until I figure it out."

Too late, I'm already in the middle of it.

The vision of Nico's dad with Dominic Sloan flashed through her mind. He'd been honest with her. Now it was her turn. "Your dad went to see Sloan in jail. I'm just as involved in this as you are."

His intense eyes widened. "How did you... When?"

"I went to the garage looking for you and your dad was there." She reached into the pocket of her damp shorts and handed him the key. "When he gave me this, I saw it in a vision. He told me to hang onto it, that you'll need it."

Nico took the key from her fingers and let his head fall back. He'd glimpsed the strange world she was a part of and didn't question it when she told him strange things like ghost conversations and visions. But she still couldn't bring herself to tell him about the blood red on the painting. Not yet.

"I followed him last night. He met up with this guy they call Hayes. I remember him from the time they kicked the shit out of Dad in the garage. I never told you this, but I scrubbed his blood off the cement floor the next day. Took me two hours and a lot of bleach. The stain is still there. I covered it with a storage cabinet."

Resting her head against the cushion next to him, she took his hand, holding it in both of hers. She swallowed through tight breaths, fighting back a wave of nausea. A high-pitch buzzing rang in her ears, growing louder before fading.

"This is going to be fine. I'll fix it." His voice sounded far away. "But my feelings for you haven't changed, they never will."

"Mine won't either. We'll fix it together." The how part eluded her, but she had help on the other side, and magic coursing through her body. Searching for an anchor in a building panic attack, she squeezed his fingers.

"Do you ever wonder how in the hell all this happened? How did we get here? My parents are divorced because Dad chose that life over his family, and he's doing it again. The business is mine now, and I can't let him destroy it or I'll have nothing."

"Sloan is in jail. He's not going anywhere. We can talk to Detective Porter—"

"No police, Drew. Please, not yet." He rubbed the faint stubble along his jaw. "It's my dad, you know? I've got to be sure. I just need time to figure out what's going on. What would I even say to her?"

Prickling sweat gathered behind Drew's neck and her chest tightened.

I'm having a heart attack.

The familiar, suffocating panic returned out of nowhere with a vengeance, consuming her with its pulsating presence and gripping her insides with a relentless force. She let go of Nico's hand and sat up, placing her hand over her chest, using as much pressure as she could, desperate to make sure her heart hadn't stopped beating.

I'm not dying. I'm not dying. I'm not alone, I'm safe. Oh my god I might be dying.

She was losing the battle, and if panic had a face, it would smirk with pleasure at her. Placing her elbows on her knees, she leaned forward, hanging her head down to hide her hyperventilating breaths. Dominic Sloan couldn't have a hold on Nico's dad again, he just couldn't. Not from prison—*impossible*. She gripped the amulet, its warmth radiating along her skin as it pulsed with slow beats in contrast to the blood thumping along her temples.

Nico crouched in front of her. "Look at me." As he spoke, his calm voice drowned out the incessant buzzing that plagued her ears. He took her hands. "Squeeze them as hard as you can."

She gripped his hands until her fingers paled and lifted her head. Hot tears mixed with sweat stung her cheeks.

"You're safe." He smiled at her. "I've got you."

She threw her arms around him and held him against her. He stood, lifting her with him, the warmth from his embrace bringing her heart rate and breathing back to a steady rhythm. She longed to escape their family's darkness and leave the dysfunction behind, even for just a short time. She wanted to let desire for the man she loved with every breath of her soul take over. Reaching her hands up to his face, she pulled his lips to hers, kissing him as though her existence depended on being connected to him. As he gripped the bottom of her wet shirt and pulled it over her head, his fingers brushed against her skin, igniting a trail of shivers down her back and a fiery heat that spread from her belly to her legs. He interlaced his fingers in her hair. A hundred sparklers ignited over her skin, only it wasn't from her magic. He possessed magic of his own that required no supernatural help. With his lips lingering on hers, he stepped backward, guiding her along with him. In a clumsy haze, they stumbled along the short hallway into his bedroom, leaving a trail of discarded clothes behind them.

He tenderly guided her onto the unmade bed, and she pulled him with her as she sank into the sea of blankets. His breath was warm as he trailed kisses along her chin, to her neck, and back to her lips. She melted against him, desperate to be as close to him as humanly possible. If she could shut the door and seal out the chaos of their world, she would stay in this moment and never leave.

I want to hold on to you... us, forever.

But a sense of dread brushed the corners of her mind. A storm was approaching, unlike anything a hurricane could unleash, and she was powerless to stop it.

Twenty-Seven

With Henry by her side, his leash taut in her grip, Drew stood waiting for Claudia in the lobby of her upscale condo building. "Are you here, Jules?"

Emerging from a mist, Jules materialized as a ghostly silhouette. Henry's tail wagged, and he barked. "Hang on." Jules shut her eyes and her body transformed, unveiling her chestnut hair, framing her pale skin. She opened her eyes wide and the jade-green glowed with more vibrancy than before. "Do you have any idea how freaking excited I am for this? What if I don't go anywhere and stay here with you?"

That had never happened before, and Drew wasn't about to entertain the possibility now. Her responsibility was helping the dead cross over. It was the only way she could maintain her mental health. If the dead attached themselves to her forever, she'd burn out with unbearable exhaustion. "That's not the deal, Jules. Nature will take over on this one."

Jules stifled a laugh. "You think I'm serious and I'd want to spend eternity by your side, begging you to connect me with people?"

"You know you love me," Drew joked.

Shrugging, Jules scrunched her face. "I sort of might."

The light banter provided a welcome distraction from the constant worry of Nico's dad's involvement with Sloan over the past couple of days. But when Jules and her father connected, Drew's instincts told her that the truth behind Jules' murder would unravel, and the weight of Sloan's presence would haunt her again. Claudia had kept Grant in the dark until Drew showed up, allowing fate to take its course. Drew begged her to change her mind and talk to him, but there was no changing Claudia's mind on any-thing, *ever*.

The glass doors opened, and Claudia gestured to Drew. "No one is in the office today to buzz you up." She raised her eyebrows. "You brought your dog?"

"Claudia, this is Henry, Henry, Claudia," Drew said. "If you want me to stay, he's coming with me. No one's at home and I feel bad leaving him too long."

Claudia held the door open. "He better not dirty my floors." Henry tried to lick her hand as he pranced by her and she recoiled, making a face of disgust as she pressed the elevator arrow up.

"See? He likes you," Drew said.

"Is she here with you now?"

Jules sidled up beside Claudia. "She's uptight, but totally my brother's type. It's too bad her father is a murderer. If I know Grant, he's going to have a tough time with that little tidbit."

"Maybe you can help him accept it," Drew muttered under her breath.

"What did you say?" Claudia asked.

"She's beside you." Drew led Henry inside the elevator, and he sat on her feet, resting against her legs. Reaching her hand down, she gave him a reassuring scratch on his head.

"Doesn't it creep you out?" Claudia covered her mouth as she whispered. "Can she hear me?"

"Of course I can hear you, I'm dead, I'm not oblivious." Jules stood in front of Claudia with her hands on her hips, but Claudia was the one oblivious to her presence.

Jules dismissed Drew's glare with a gesture and an eye roll. Jules and Claudia were more alike than either would ever know.

She turned her attention back to Claudia's question. "Sometimes it does, but not like it used to. It just depends on what the person wants." If others like the witch hunter made frequent appearances, "creeped out" would be an understatement. "Jules just wants to reunite with her family so she can move on, and maybe they can, too."

As the elevator doors opened, Jules hurried toward the table with the bouquet of flowers. Drew bent down and inhaled the sweet powder fragrance before following Claudia down the hallway. "Are you okay?" she asked before Claudia opened the door.

"Why wouldn't I be? Whatever happens today, I'll land on my feet like I always do. I'm sure you get it." But Claudia's lips quivered, and she turned her head away. As she reached for the handle, the door swung open, and Grant stood in the entryway.

The man from downstairs sat on the white sofa as Drew entered the spacious condo, this time wearing a short-sleeved dress shirt and gray pants instead of the security uniform. He held the charm on his bracelet between his fingers and stood with tears in his eyes.

He wiped his hand on his pants and extended a shaking hand. "I'm Noah Salinger. I'm sorry I didn't recognize you when you were in last time. I haven't seen you since you were..." He held his hand up above knee high. "It's been a while, but the red hair should've triggered something."

Drew shook his hand and gave him her warmest smile, despite her nervous energy. "I didn't remember you either, but Gran spoke highly of your family."

"After the accident"—he struggled to speak as his voice choked up—"Maddie was a blessing." Crow's feet framed his green eyes, resembling Jules' but without the striking light that she possessed in hers. "Is it true?" he asked. "I wouldn't be here if it weren't for Grant; he's adamant this is real."

"I'm not a cruel person, Mr. Salinger. I would never make up something so horrible. Your daughter and I have become close in the last couple months." Drew dropped Henry's leash, and he followed Jules around the vast living room.

"Oh, just say it, Drew. Friends. We have become friends. And your dog loves me, don't you, Henry?" Jules crouched down and stroked Henry's fur.

"She says we've become friends, and I guess she's not wrong."

Claudia settled on a plush stool next to the expansive island and adjusted the silver buttons on her white T-shirt. Fidgeting in her seat, she stared at Drew with pursed lips and wide eyes.

So help me, if Grant gives Claudia a hard time about her father, I'm going to lose it on him.

Grant pointed at Henry. "What's the dog doing? Is he going to make a mess on the area rug?"

"He's with Jules," she said.

Jules' father held the arm of the loveseat to steady himself as he pet the dog. "What's his name?"

"Actually, it's Henry." Drew spoke softly, considering her words. "Jules wanted me to name him after her dog, and it just felt right."

Noah sat on the loveseat and covered his face. A gold ring adorned his ring finger. "Henry. He passed three years ago, but he lived a good life, I made sure of it."

Jules crouched in front of her father and tried to take his hands. "Thank you, Dad. I love you."

Anguish seeped into Drew's soul, and the amulet's heat warmed her neck. The reunion had started, and she had to move forward or risk losing the connection. "I know how strange all this is, but I'm just here to help her move on from the stuck place she's in. She got to be with Grant, but she can't leave until she does the same with you, Mr. Salinger."

"Noah, please. It's just Noah."

"It's time." A woman's voice spoke in Drew's ear, accompanied by a bright light that spun beside her, mirroring the glow of the amulet. The woman's outline took shape inside the radiating light, too bright to make out her features. "It's sure nice to meet you, Drew. Thank you for taking such good care of my daughter. I'm Olivia."

The voice belonged to the same woman whose calm presence had nudged Drew to confide her traumatic secrets to Jules in the den. "Olivia is beside me."

"Mom?" Jules left Henry and ran into her mother's open arms. The light enveloped Jules, but she maintained her human appearance.

Noah rose and approached with cautious steps as Claudia hopped off the stool and stood between Grant and his father.

"My wife is here?" Noah's voice shook. "But I don't see anything." Tears streamed down his face.

"Take Drew's hand, Dad, that's what worked before, right?" Grant said.

"Let me show him." Jules grabbed Drew's hand and a fizzy burst erupted along her tongue as electricity surged from her head into her chest. Drew held her hand out to Noah.

"She wants you to see."

As Noah's cold hand grasped Drew's, a comforting warmth flowed from her palms and enveloped his hand. He gasped as Drew bridged the gap, dropping the veil between the dead and the living, allowing him to see his daughter and wife again. Sobs escaped him as Jules wrapped her arms around her dad, clinging to him, and whispering, *I love you so much* over and over again. Their emotions swirled and clashed within Drew, and she struggled against the welling tears as she fought to keep the connection between them.

Claudia sat on the edge of a nearby chair; her cheeks streaked with mascara coated tears. Henry dashed to her side, curling up against her feet, and she reached down to rest her hand on his head.

"Grant." Noah reached for his son and their hands clasped together.

"Mom? You're really here?" Grant choked through tears.

Olivia placed one hand on Grant's cheek and the other on Noah's, and her brilliant light encompassed them. "Your girl is perfect for you, Grant. Strong. All of you need to hold on to each other, time is short, but we'll see each other again. Love sees to that."

Tears streamed over Grant's reddened face, but it was Noah who spoke. "We will, that's a promise."

"I know where I'm going now, it worked, Drew." Jules beamed.

The amulet's light dimmed, and the electricity dulled. "I'm losing them. I can't hold on much longer." Drew eyed Jules as the young woman's body shifted into an ethereal light resembling her mother. The blood stains faded and her face radiated peace. "Say hi to Ori for me," she whispered.

"Wait, hang on, Drew, please." Jules reached forward, clasping Grant's face with both of her radiant hands, and bent forward, close to his face. "I need you to know my death wasn't an accident. Dominic Sloan murdered me." Jules glanced past Grant toward Claudia. "She's suffered enough, Grant. Don't you dare fuck this up and blame her. Promise me."

A sick feeling mixed with exhaustion swept over Drew as the connection between them faded. The truth broke free, falling to the ground like shattered glass.

Grant shifted his gaze to face Claudia, who stared up from her chair with devastation etched across her face. "What did she say?" She made no effort to wipe away her blackened tears.

"Your father murdered my sister," Grant said, his jaw twitching.

Claudia closed her eyes for a moment. "I know. I found out the day we went to your office, but I was too scared to tell you. He's ruining my life every day, and I can't make him stop. When will it stop?" Claudia slid off the chair to the floor, her cries echoing through the room, and Noah crouched in front of her, patting her trembling hands.

"It isn't her fault, Grant," Jules' voice trailed off. "Promise me you will try to understand." She released Grant, and the light dimmed, swirling before it vanished, taking Jules and her mother with it.

"I promise," Grant said, letting go of Drew's hand.

The amulet stilled, turning cold. Silence hung heavy in the air, broken only by the sound of Claudia's heartbreaking sobs.

Drew's legs weakened, forcing her to collapse on one of the pristine chairs and let her head fall back against the soft cushion.

"I knew it was him." Noah helped Claudia to her feet and gave her a sorrowful smile. "He blackmailed me for years. Not even closing my business kept him away. He forced us to keep her name from the public, let the accident be forgotten, or he threatened Grant would be next. And it all started because I wanted what I thought he could give—power, money, but none of that matters. I couldn't keep my family safe, and I'm to blame. He promised me a life of hell, and he got what he wanted. He took everything from me, *everything*." Noah looked at Drew as he gripped the "J" charm on his bracelet. "So many days I didn't want to live anymore, but today, you gave me back a piece of myself. I made my girls a promise, and I won't break it." He hugged Grant and patted him on the back as he released him, wiping his bloodshot eyes.

Pushing herself up from the chair, Drew approached Claudia as she gripped the counter. Pain emanated from Claudia's eyes as she stared at Grant, her vulnerability on rare display. If Grant stormed out of this place, Drew was ready to help Claudia pick up her broken pieces.

Grant walked toward Claudia, leaving inches between them as she maintained her gaze on his face.

What was he going to do? Anyone in town could see the way Grant's eyes lit up whenever Claudia entered the room. The man's devotion to her was unwavering. He'd confront an entire army on her behalf if he had to. Piper joked about it all the time. Would he leave her over a murderous father she had no control over? Over a monster who'd done nothing except leave his daughter's life in shambles? Drew stepped forward as frustration built inside her, ready to come to Claudia's defense, but Grant surprised her.

Hovering over her, he cradled Claudia's face in his hands. "I love you. I'm still here, we are still us, this isn't your fault. I believe that, but I need you to believe it too."

Claudia leaned into him, burying her face against his chest, crying as he held her. The diamond ring on her left hand caught the light from the chandelier above their heads, casting sparkles on the wall.

I never thought Claudia would be the person to challenge my jaded ideas of marriage and love.

She disagreed with Piper. If these two could get past this shit? They could probably make it through anything.

TWENTY-EIGHT

Collapsing on her living room sofa, Drew swung her legs up and propped a pillow under her head. Henry curled up on the floor beside her. She couldn't stop the tears the entire drive home, and still had no control over them. Her soul absorbed all the grief, heartache, and pain, leaving her heavy with sorrow—the toughest part of reuniting the dead with their loved ones.

But Jules was gone. Wasn't that what she'd wanted? To rid herself of the persistent, snarky ghost who refused to leave her alone, but challenged her to face her own hang-ups even when she didn't want to?

Emptiness settled in her chest, and her throat ached with sadness. She rolled onto her side and reached down so her hand rested on Henry's back. The dog who had adopted her as his new best friend. She hadn't looked for a new home for him, and she couldn't imagine giving him away to someone. Henry wasn't going anywhere; this was his home. She didn't care how she made it work, but she couldn't let him go.

Wiping away tears, she held up her phone and clicked on Piper's new message.

Need company?

With Jasper at work, coming home to an empty house was lonelier than she'd expected, but she didn't want to burden Piper and ask her to drive out to see her. If she was ever going to lead a regular existence, she'd have to learn to deal with the aftermath of the dead on her own.

I'm good, just chilling with Henry. Thanks though. She typed back, adding a heart emoji and placed her phone face down on her chest. Her fingers brushed against Gran's blanket as she raised her hand over her head, and she tugged on a loose string. Would Jules meet Gran on the other side? Maybe they all gathered around a golden table and traded stories.

Wallowing in grief dragged her down so far into an abyss, she wanted to wrap herself in a blanket despite the warm day, curl into a ball and drown in her tears. Fatigue weighed on her body, but she forced herself to sit up. The parting clouds allowed a stream of sunlight to filter through the window, casting a playful dance of light on Gran's blue butterfly figure on the mantel.

I need to breathe.

Jupiter Cove beach was the haven she was seeking.

Sliding her feet in flip-flops at the door, she called to Henry, and they headed across the road for the beach.

The wind danced across the water, creating ripples and carrying specks of sand as it brushed against her hair. With careful steps, she guided Henry down the stone staircase, making sure he was steady before tossing a stick for him to chase. His limp didn't slow him down as much anymore since Aurora's healing touch, but instead of running back to Drew, he snatched the stick and settled on the sand.

She walked until her bare feet sank into the cool, wet sand and waves rushed over her calves. Two people floated on surfboards in the deeper water, and a few small groups down the beach had set up with umbrellas and folding chairs, basking in the sun as it peeked and hid behind the clouds.

Claudia's party was days away, she was no closer to solving Jack's and Aurora's warnings, and Nico was supposed to be confronting his father about Sloan. A constant sense of unease had settled in her chest, but standing in the water as it numbed her legs with sand clinging to her skin and inhaling sea air somehow allowed her to breathe.

A deep rumbling of a car's engine got louder, and she shifted for a view toward the road as Nico's black Chevelle rounded the turn before disappearing behind the rock wall. She sent him a message letting him know where she was and made her way up the beach to wait for him.

As he bounded down the stone steps, his gaze swept the surroundings until it settled upon her. Henry's back end moved side to side as he wagged his tail with the stick in his mouth, and Nico bent down to scratch both sides of the dog's face.

Brushing the hair out of her eyes, Drew approached him. "How'd it go?"

"You don't want to know."

"I really do."

He rose and threw the stick for Henry. "How are you? Did it work?"

"She's gone, it worked." The ache returned, but she took a deep breath and let it go.

"Are you tired? I remember you saying it always drains your energy or something."

"Yeah, I'm okay. I'm glad you're here." She slipped her arms around his waist and pulled him close as he rubbed her back. "Want to go back to the house?"

"Only if you're ready."

"I want to hear about your dad." And the Sloan conversation wasn't one for public ears. She called to Henry, and they headed back to the house.

She filled Henry's bowls with food and water in the kitchen as Nico opened the patio door and sat at the kitchen table. He leaned on his elbows and rubbed his face. "I called your detective friend—actually, she told me it's *Sergeant* Porter now, and she's meeting me here. I hope it's okay, but I can't have her come to the house, not with Mom there, and the garage is out of the question, obviously."

"She's coming here today?" The last time Drew had seen Valerie Porter was to have her mother arrested. If anyone deserved to be promoted, it was her.

"You don't have to go out and talk to her," Nico said. "I'll do it."

"It's fine, I just wasn't expecting it."

"All I've got are the screen shots of Dad's phone with the date, and a gut feeling. But you had the vision, we know he met Sloan. If I do nothing and something happens, I'll never forgive myself. I don't know what else to do." He dropped his hands to the table.

With her leg tucked beneath her, she sat across from him and leaned forward, grasping his hands. His jaw tensed and worry etched his forehead.

"I'll be with you, no matter what. We'll figure this out, it's what we do," she said.

Gran's antique phone pierced the air with its shrill ring, echoing through the den. Drew closed her eyes and chewed her lip.

"Are you gonna get that?" Nico stood, but she grabbed his arm to pull him back.

"No."

"Well, do you want me to get it?"

"It's Joelle, I know it's her. She's the only who calls that phone, and I don't want to talk to her. Every time I do, I just hang up feeling awful."

Nico sat back down with his eyes locked on hers. The empathy in his brown eyes was palpable. "What do you want to do?"

"I want to unplug the phone, but for some stupid reason, I haven't been able to do it. Isn't that weird?"

"What isn't weird these days, you know? If you want to unplug it, go for it. If you change your mind, plug it back in."

Disconnecting the phone felt like a finality, but severing ties with her mother was what she needed. Maybe not forever, but until she had the courage to deal with her without losing herself again. She rose from the table, entered the den, and unplugged the phone from the wall, startled by the chiming clock.

Leaning against the door frame, Nico eyed the clock. "I didn't know the chimes worked. I never hear them."

"It's sort of a new thing. Maybe it's a sign from Gran. I haven't figured it out yet." The doorbell rang, and Henry barked. "Are you sure about doing this?"

"I have to do this."

With a presence that commanded authority and in full uniform, Valerie Porter had a grave look of concern across her face as she stood on the front porch, flanked by an officer Drew didn't recognize. Henry charged outside as Drew opened the front door and the officer bent down and scratched behind Henry's ears. The man looked like a small mountain as he scanned the road with his hands tucked under his vest before they both entered.

The mountain officer remained standing near the kitchen entrance as Sergeant Porter joined Drew and Nico at the table. Nico answered her questions and showed her the screenshots he'd taken from his father's phone.

Sergeant Porter talked as she made notes in a lined book. "As for Saturday night, we already have a plan for a police presence at the Tate event. I was hoping the hurricane would be enough that she'd have to cancel, but it seems to be downgraded to a tropical storm and won't make landfall until later than expected, so the mayor has given the go ahead. In any case, given what you've shown me, Nico, we'll be on alert for any unusual activity."

"What about the prison records? Did you confirm my dad went to see him?" Nico asked.

As she wrote in her notebook, Sergeant Porter's gold hoop earrings brushed against her radiant brown skin. Light streamed through the kitchen window, highlighting her intense dark eyes as she raised them to look at Nico. She radiated a captivating mix of beauty and badass—that hadn't changed. "There were no records of Nick DeSarro visiting Ben Morana, or Sloan, as we all know him."

"How is that possible?" Nico looked at Drew but didn't mention the vision.

What could he say? *My girlfriend saw it with her psychic ability.* They'd get curious stares, and the police would dismiss them.

Sergeant Porter eyed the mountain officer.

"Detective, find out the identities of all Sloan's visitors since his incarceration, and take Mr. DeSarro outside for a statement. I'll be right along."

"On it, ma'am." The detective scribbled on his notepad and tucked it back in his vest pocket.

The chair scraped against the floor as Sergeant Porter stood. Nico rose to his feet and joined the mountain officer toward the front door, their statures resembling each other, surprising Drew.

With the click of the screen door, Sergeant Porter crossed her arms and eyed Drew as she leaned against the counter. "How have you been? All this must be hard on you."

"It brings up a lot."

With an exhale, Sergeant Porter straightened her back and tucked her notebook away. "You still have my number if you ever need to talk." She stepped out of the kitchen.

Drew recalled her last conversation with Valerie Porter at the police station. Sergeant Porter had believed Drew about her visions, the ghosts, all of it. If telling her own truth could help the situation, she had to disclose her vision. "Wait. I have something to tell you, and I'm only doing this because you'll take me seriously."

"I'll always take you seriously, Drew. You have my word."

"It doesn't matter what the prison records show, Nick DeSarro met with Sloan in jail, I'd bet my life."

"And you know this how?" Sergeant Porter relaxed her arms as she approached Drew.

"I saw them together, in a vision, when I was at the garage with Nico's dad. I couldn't hear what they talked about, and I don't know why he was there, but I did see it, it happened."

"Thank you for trusting me with this." Sergeant Porter's brows furrowed as she placed a gentle hand on Drew's arm. "We're on it."

She stood with Nico on the porch as the two officers drove away. There was no evidence of any collaboration between Nico's dad and Sloan, but between her confession of the vision and the list of visitor's names, perhaps they would discover a clue about Sloan's associates.

Someone other than Nick DeSarro.

Drew's phone buzzed on the mantel where she'd left it after the beach, and she ran inside to grab it.

A text from Taj.

An old guy showed up last night and told me he's coming. What the hell is that? I'm not sleeping. Nightmares haven't stopped. I'm scared. What do we do now?

Who was coming?

She typed back, desperate to ease his mind. *I don't know what it means, but I'm trying. Don't panic and let me know if you get anything else from him. Please talk to your mom, she can help.*

Her words did nothing to settle the pit in her stomach. How could she fight back against a threat she couldn't see coming?

TWENTY-NINE

Closing the Tough Cookie at three on a Saturday never happened, but Jasper and Danny had an appointment with a realtor, and Drew offered to close the bakery on her own. She brought Henry, keeping him in the office until the customers left, so he wasn't alone all morning.

Jasper had written out a to-do list on a piece of baking themed stationery and left it on the counter near a row of cabinets. With Henry at her heels and her mind consumed with Claudia's party that evening, she picked up a pen and checked off each item as she went through the bakery cleaning display cabinets, closing the cash till, and printing out the daily sales report.

She'd have to rush home, shower, do something with her hair and makeup, and the dress was pressed and waiting on a hanger. Was she forgetting anything?

She pushed the chairs against tables and grabbed the chain to lower the blind over the large window. Rain pinged the glass and ominous clouds lined with streaks of black rolled along the sky. Treetops swayed in the wind as people ran from stores to their cars. Hurricane Francine might have weakened into a tropical storm and the forecast hadn't expected it to make landfall until the early morning hours, but as far as she could tell, the storm had moved along the coast, landing on Atlas Cliffs. The mayor had approved the party to proceed, on the condition that the Tates would end it by 11, sending Claudia on a mission to reassure everyone not to worry and that she had taken care of everything. But the storm wasn't waiting for hours to arrive. Francine wanted to grace Atlas Cliffs with her presence early, and Claudia should cancel the step-into-summer bash, gala... whatever she was calling it.

Drew and Taj had planned to meet the next day after he'd called her in a panic about worsening nightmares with ocean water that turned red as it surged inside the lighthouse. She had to return to Neptune Point and back to the lighthouse, the center of the warnings.

The amulet pulsed, and she lifted the onyx jewel to eye level as a bright light spun deep inside.

Get through this night and keep the magic close. I'll figure this out with Taj tomorrow, no dead seagulls required.

Holding the swinging door open, she called Henry to follow her into the back kitchen. She inspected the temperatures on the fridges and freezers and double-checked that the ovens were all off, shuddering when she passed Jasper's cartoon image reminders to prevent fires in the kitchen. The dark memory resurfaced of Sloan setting fire to the Tough Cookie, leaving the kitchen in ruins and Gran fighting for her life in the hospital.

She took the trash out through the back door, leaving it ajar as she tossed it into the large bin at the back of the parking lot near her car. A gust of wind roared through the trees, stirring up dust and sand, creating a dramatic contrast against the gray sky.

As she headed back inside, a raven screeched past her face, so close its wings brushed through her windblown hair. With the wind threatening to carry it away, the massive raven dipped its wing toward her, tilting its head before letting out a high-pitched call, sending a warning through her chest to her core before flying skyward into the distance.

In a hurry to retreat inside, a sharp pain shot through her foot as it collided with the bottom step. A tingling sensation traveled down her neck and arms, settling in the palms of her hands. The amulet's pulse intensified, and she wrapped her fingers around it as she stepped inside, slamming the door behind her. Henry greeted her, bolting through her legs, and sat by the door to the kitchen.

"We're leaving, I just need my purse... Where's my phone?" Taking off her apron, she rummaged for her phone, hanging it up when she found the pockets empty. "I'm so bad with my phone."

And now I'm talking to myself.

A thud reverberated from the front café, and Henry barked at the swinging door.

"What is it, boy?" she whispered. Fear pricked at the back of her neck and her mouth went dry.

Did I not lock the front door?

Henry's ears perked, and his nose twitched as he sniffed the air. A low growl rumbled from his throat, and he stood still as he glared at the door. Silence enveloped the bakery, interrupted only by the hum of the air conditioner kicking on and Henry's continuous growling in front of her. His tail stopped wagging as it lowered between his hind legs with a vigilant watch on the door.

It must just be a customer who thinks we're open.

Her ears had their own pulse as she grabbed her purse off the stool and rummaged through it for her phone. Where had she left it? No one living or dead was in the bakery, but she'd give anything to have Ori at her side. A rhythmic buzzing vibrated from the other room, followed by a steady tapping, and Henry tilted his head to the side with another growl.

The tapping turned into knocks, one after the other, slow and steady, like knuckles rapping on a wooden table. Dread tightened in her gut as she moved closer to the swinging door leading into the front café and placed her ear against the door.

The relentless knocks persisted. Someone was in the other room. It had to be a customer. Who else could it be? She was overreacting. Her gaze swept the kitchen for her phone and a sudden reminder stuck her. She'd left her phone on the front counter when she'd filled the cooler display cabinet with Jasper's Irish pastries for the next day.

With a deep breath, she shoved the swinging door and stepped through to the other side. The window rattled from the force of the wind, and as the storm stole the daylight, an eerie dimness engulfed the front café.

"You're looking well, Miss Harlow." Dominic Sloan flattened his clenched hands on the table as he leaned back in the chair. He glared at her from underneath the brim of a ball cap he'd pulled over his overgrown hair.

With a menacing bark, Henry charged at him, but he shoved the dog aside with a heavy boot, and Henry let out a startled yelp as he sought safety behind Drew's legs. She took a sudden step back and collided with the wall, inhaling sharply. Outside the window, a group of tourists in raincoats hurried along the sidewalk, their shadows disappearing behind the lowered blind, unaware of the terror unfolding inside.

"The sign said you were open, so I turned it to closed. I thought we could talk privately." Sloan's deep and calm voice had an eerie undertone of madness.

How could she forget to lock the door?

"What are you doing here? How are you out?" Her voice shook as she spoke.

"I'll ask the questions." He gestured to the seat across from him. "Join me."

A quick vibration sounded on the counter, and the screen of her phone lit up with a notification. She darted over and grabbed the phone, ready to call for help as red alerts and missed calls and messages flooded her screen. She caught glimpses of warnings as she fought to keep her eyes on him.

Riot breaks out... One guard dead... Man escapes in the early hours... Armed and dangerous.

And countless messages from Nico, Claudia, Piper. She opened the keypad and pressed 9. Then 1.

"You're a smart girl, Drew." He glared at the phone in her hands. "That's not a smart move."

Henry whined behind her legs, and she reached down to touch his head and urge him to stay. She had to press one button, and the police would swarm the place. *One button.* Her thumb hovered over the keypad displayed on the screen. Sloan stretched and the gray jacket he wore opened, revealing a gun with an elongated addition attached to it secured at his waist. She placed her phone back on the counter, keeping her hand on the only lifeline she had.

With his ears flattened, Henry advanced toward him, growling. Sloan grabbed his gun and aimed it at the dog's head. "Do something about that, will you? I'd hate to dirty your clean floor."

Grabbing Henry by the collar, Drew dragged him toward the kitchen. "Don't touch him." Her eyes burned and her chest ached. She pushed Henry through the swinging kitchen door, latching it closed.

She swallowed thickly. "What do you want? You're free now, why come back here?"

He narrowed his gaze on the display cabinet and the cof-feemaker, its timer set for the Sunday morning breakfast rush. "Black coffee. And a piece of Irish Whiskey cake."

How dare he request service like a paying customer? Magic thrummed like a burst of firecrackers under her skin, and she held her hands up, willing them to shoot flames in his direction.

But it didn't work like that. Her magic, fueled by a mystical book, wove spells of protection, allowing her to connect with both the living and the dead, sharing visions of warnings and premonitions. She'd banished a witch hunter to another realm, but could she kill someone with her magic?

"You always make your customers wait?" His voice grated against the silence, like dragging an anchor across concrete.

"You are not a customer. You're a murderer."

"Says the witch who talks to the dead." He folded his fingers together. "Coffee. I don't have all night."

"Or what? You'll pull out that gun and kill me, too? Like your brother and sister, and your son's mother? Or how about Jules Salinger?" Every muscle in her body constricted as she clenched her fists.

He laughed, cutting it off with a sinister smile. "My sister fell victim to your world, and poor Ezra paid the price for her negligence. That didn't end so well, now did it."

"I'm calling the police." With a firm grip on her phone, she stole a quick glance downward, her mind locked in a battle between life and death. Make the call, or not.

"You will do no such thing." He straightened his jacket before standing up from the chair. His looming presence exuded power and strength with every step closer.

Henry barked from the back room. An umbrella leaned against the door frame behind him—no match for a gun. But she couldn't let him get away, free.

His piercing eyes shifted to the door. "Keep that dog quiet." He moved the blinds and peered outside where a rusted station wagon was parked against the curb. "Go ahead, make the call, but you're not the only stop I have this evening. You don't know a reputable mechanic on this side of town, do you? I've been having some car trouble."

Not Nico.

With a slow exhale, she turned on the coffeemaker and grabbed a small plate from the cupboard behind her, keeping watch through the reflection in the glass cabinet doors as he returned to his place at the table. She opened the display case and, using a pie server, plopped a piece of cake on the plate. Her palms sweat as she held the metal server in a death grip with the energy buzzing underneath her touch through to the handle. She could charge him and stab him with its metal point. *Man dies by pie server.*

"You won't get the chance to try." He sat motionless with unblinking eyes, as though he could hear her thoughts.

She released the server, and walked the plate over to him, dropping it with a clang on the table.

Here's your cake, you fucking asshole.

Turning the plate, he ran a finger along the edge and glared at her. "Coffee. Black. And do you expect me to eat with my fingers like I'm an uncivilized animal?"

Now he was insulting animals. With anger burning in her chest and magic coursing under her skin, she grabbed a mug from the cabinet with one hand and the coffee pot with the other. Hot coffee sloshed as she poured, spilling over the mug and burning her hand. Flinching, she dared to turn her back to him and pulled a paper towel from the holder on the wall.

Don't lose it, keep him here, call the police.

They had to be swarming the town, searching for him.

"I'm waiting." The deep tone of his voice cut through her like a blade through butter.

She carried the mug and a fork to the table, wanting to dump it on his lap, but set it in front of him, not taking her eyes off his smug, lined face.

Steam coiled like a snake as he lifted the mug to his lips and drank the dark liquid. "Sit."

"I'm not sitting with you." Her words escaped through gritted teeth.

He kicked the chair across from him out. "Sit."

Henry barked again from the other side of the door.

"I'm not talking over that noise. Silence it, or I'll do it for you," he seethed.

"He's a dog, I can't control him."

Sloan stood, grabbing his gun. Throwing her arms in the air, Drew jumped in front of him. "No! No. I'll take care of it." Tears burned her eyes, threatening to spill over, but she choked them back. She reached behind her and unlatched the door, opening it a crack to grab Henry's collar. If he broke free and attacked, Sloan would shoot without hesitation.

With calculated steps, he moved closer, folding his arms across his chest, the gun still in his hand. "You've got five seconds. Five. Four."

Pulling Henry along, she shoved him into the back office and yanked the door closed, sending him into a barking frenzy. The amulet thrummed and pulsed against her neck, and she tucked it under her shirt.

I can't be alone, I just can't.

"Two." The sound of grinding metal echoed as he cocked the gun behind the door. "One."

Bursting through the kitchen door, she sent it swinging back, and it slammed against the counter. Henry's barks turned into whines as he frantically scratched at the office door.

"Sit." Sloan pointed to the chair with his gun, and every muscle in her body screamed for her to run, to fight, but she obeyed.

THIRTY

Sitting in Gran's bakery, sipping coffee and eating pastry, was the monster she'd believed had vanished from her life—the murderer who had once tried to kill her. An overwhelming urge burned inside her to reach across the table, grab his gun, and shoot him.

"You'll be a bleeding pile on the floor before you can even think of begging for your life." He dabbed his mouth with a napkin, folded it, and placed it on the empty plate.

"They're going to find you."

"Perhaps. But I don't work alone. It takes a village to accomplish extraordinary events."

"Why not run? Get as far as you can? Ruin lives in a new town someplace far away?" She clenched her fists in her lap, her nails digging into her palms. What was he going to do with her? If she walked away from the Tough Cooke, what would the cost be?

He threw his head back and let out a guttural laugh. She thought she'd vomit all over him. "You're a funny one, aren't you?" His face contorted, reddening with anger. Leaning with his elbows on the table, his eyes bore into hers. "My family's legacy is rooted in this town, and I won't let a witch take it from me or my family. You burn my childhood home to the ground, I will rebuild. You expose what was never meant to surface, I will snuff you out. Do you understand?"

His sister had been a witch too. Sitting across from her was a living, breathing Hathorne.

The amulet's energy seeped into her skin, flowing through her, leaving a metallic taste in her mouth as it coursed through her veins. "How can you hate something you know nothing about?"

He clicked his tongue. "Delusion has gotten to you, too, I see."

"What do you want from me? You want me dead?"

"It's simple, really. My lovely daughter is having a social gathering." He folded his hands on his chest as his lips curled in a sinister smile. "A name change will not remove the Sloan from her blood."

"She hates you. They both do." Drew's anger boiled as she forced herself to swallow the small amount of saliva left in her dry throat.

"Hate is a strong word." He leaned across the table and lowered his voice. "Under no circumstances should my daughter cancel this event. Your boyfriend isn't as dumb as I had pegged him, such a shame. He's poking around, interfering, and I don't trust that he will obey his father's commands and stay away." Sloan sipped his coffee with a slurp. "Ah, that's good." He placed the mug on the table and folded his hands together, glaring at her with soulless eyes. "Now, back to the DeSarro boy. He's attending this lovely event by your side, I presume?"

"Yes, a decision I'm currently rethinking." Her stomach lurched again, sending bile into her throat.

"Quite the opposite. You will attend and keep him with you. He is not to leave the building. When I get what I want, I will fuck off. Do you understand Miss Harlow?"

"I can't do that. I can't keep track of him inside that building, and the storm is getting worse, they could still cancel it, if the mayor decides, there will be no choice—"

"That is where you are gravely mistaken. I am giving you a choice to live. A choice to keep your boyfriend alive."

She folded her arms across her chest, feeling the sharp sting as her nails dug deeper into her burning palms. A rapid thumping escalated in her ears. "And what's stopping me from going to the police and telling them exactly where to find you?"

He sat back in the chair and put his hand on the gun. "I'm happy you asked."

She doubted that happiness was an emotion this monster was capable of.

He continued. "The Arlotts have a daughter who's a friend of yours. You took her cousin into your dead grandmother's house, correct? There's also a new store in town owned by a *witch*, but in my humble opinion, it should burn to the ground."

Her hands tingled with an unfamiliar energy, pulsating with a darker sensation. *Rage.* A desperate urge to scream ran through her like a freight train, something loud enough that she'd draw the attention of pedestrians walking by outside, ending his reign of horror, and perhaps her life. A woman beyond the window ran with a toddler in her arms, shielding them from the wind and rain with an oversized raincoat, and Drew suppressed her temper. If he had nothing to lose, he wouldn't care who he hurt around him.

Dominic Sloan tapped the gun on the table. "DeSarro's boy is growing into a fine young man, with a shiny new car Nick bought him, and that garage is coming along nicely. Do you know how to wire a bomb, so no one knows it's there?" A laugh escaped, and he put his hands up. "Don't worry, I don't either. But lucky for me, I have people who do."

She gripped her shirt with sweaty, burning hands that wanted to reach around his neck and beg her magic to choke him with superhuman strength. She was going to get herself killed.

"If you want to fuck off out of here, you won't touch them." The words flew from her mouth before she could stop them.

He stood with the gun in his hand and slammed his fist on the table. The plate slid off the table, shattering across the floor in pieces, and Henry's barks resumed from the back office. She pushed her chair back and gripped the seat until her knuckles turned numb. He loomed over her with his hand raised.

As he moved to strike, she leaped out of her seat, taking a quick step back. "If you hit me, they'll know."

He snorted back a laugh, halting it as fast as it escaped his throat. Grabbing her shirt collar, he curled the fabric in his fist. The amulet and butterfly pendant's chains dug into her skin, and she gasped for air that refused to fill her lungs. Tears burned over her cheeks, and he bent down until he was inches from her face. He held the gun to her head, staring at her with disgust, his rancid breath filling the space between them. "You will go to that party. If you speak of this to anyone, I will know, and I will kill you. But not before I make you watch the life drain from your boyfriend's eyes."

"I can't move with that gun to my head." Fury burned through her like wildfire.

He gripped her tighter and, in a sudden motion, flinched and yanked his hand back, shaking it as a red mark formed. "What the hell did you just do to me?"

The amulet scorched like a hot coal against her skin, but she didn't move.

With sweat running down her back and her hands trembling, she fumbled backward and gripped the counter with one hand and her phone with another.

"You never know who's watching." Tucking his gun back in his waist, he turned away from her and headed toward the door. With his hand gripping the door handle, he paused and cast a smug grin over his shoulder. "Don't fuck this up. I'd hate to see you or that boyfriend of yours get hurt." With a wink, he slid outside, leaving the door ajar behind him.

With a forceful gust of wind, the door swung open, sending a framed picture of Gran flying off the shelf. When it hit the floor, the glass cracked, sending shards flying in all directions. She bolted to the door, struggling against the wind as she slammed it shut, securing the door with the deadbolt and chain.

Henry's frantic barks echoed from the back office, and she ran through the swinging door and flung the office door open.

She dropped to her knees and threw her arms around him as he licked her face and whined.

With her face buried in her hands, she leaned against the wall and let out gut-wrenching sobs. What would she do? He had men watching her and her friends. Were they planting bombs in Nico's garage? What had Nick DeSarro gotten himself involved in?

Her stomach lurched again, and saliva returned to her mouth with a vengeance. Scrambling to stand, she rushed to the bathroom, bending over the toilet just in time to throw up.

With shallow breaths she ran the cold water, splashing her face and rinsing her mouth out. Streaks of mascara smudged her eyes, and she wiped at them with her fingers. She gripped the sides of the vanity and stared at herself in the mirror.

"What do I do now?" As she held the amulet up to the mirror, a soft glow emanated from its surface, casting a warm light on her face. "Does anyone hear me?"

Where are they when I need them?

Thirty-One

"You look like a goddess, Drew. Seriously." Jasper stood behind her as she gazed into the full-length mirror in her bedroom.

"The dress is beautiful." The bodice's stretchy material was comfortable, and the tulle skirt floated to the floor, concealing her sneakers as Claudia had promised.

"No, darling, you are." Danny tousled her wavy hair, framing her face with a few carefully arranged strands. "Perfect. Okay, I need to get ready, or we'll be late. See you there?"

"Thank you, by the way." She had struggled to get ready for the event, knowing who was in town, waiting for an opportunity to make her life hell.

"For what? It's nothing," Danny said.

"If I was left to my own devices, it wouldn't have ended up like this." She faced the mirror. Sweeping mascara framed her green eyes with curled lashes and she'd even agreed to a peach lip gloss.

"You can do this, Drew. They're going to love you." Danny gave her a squeeze before dashing out of her room.

Henry lifted his head off his paws from his spot on her bed and barked, making her jump.

"He approves," Jasper said.

She crouched down and kissed Henry's head. "I think I love you," she whispered.

"The moment that dog entered this house, I knew he wasn't ever leaving." Jasper adjusted his powder blue suit jacket as the doorbell rang. "I'll get it."

A swift breeze tossed the curtains against the wall from the open window as the raven flew by, letting out a screech. Lifting her dress, Drew climbed onto the window bench and slammed it shut. Jack wasn't the only ominous sign tainting the evening. Amidst the torrential rain and approaching powerful gusts of wind, a dark car had followed her home, speeding by when she turned in her driveway.

She was being watched.

If she didn't go to the party, if they all stayed away and she called Sergeant Porter... *Not before I make you watch the life drain from your boyfriend.* Sloan's words haunted her, and her stomach churned again.

Hourly updates kept everyone checking the news nonstop. Authorities had been pursuing Sloan through New Hampshire, but they were all wrong. A man bearing a striking resemblance to Sloan was leading them on a wild chase. The monster had strategized to use a decoy.

They had to catch him and throw him back in jail, or make life drain from *his* body. But if they caught the real Sloan, would he alert his men to unleash havoc? Nick DeSarro couldn't be one of those men; he would never put his family in danger. Except he'd done it before, and Sloan might not have given him a choice.

A gentle knock broke her from her thoughts, and she pushed off the bench as Nico stepped inside the room and leaned against the doorframe. He had his suit jacket draped over his arm, his white dress shirt displaying a few wrinkles. He went without a tie; he hated ties. He tolerated suits when needed, but Nico and fancy things outside of the car world were like oil and water. And she loved that about him. She bit her bottom lip and her eyes watered out of nowhere.

Nothing can happen to you. Nothing can happen to us.

She inhaled and exhaled slowly as he approached. "You look amazing."

"So do you."

He encircled her waist, interlocking his fingers at the small of her back. "Are you sure you're okay with going tonight with him out there somewhere? You could just say you're sick or something."

Nothing can happen tonight.

"I need to be there." His face was smooth under her fingertips—he'd shaved for the event. Standing on her tiptoes, she covered his mouth with hers, and he held her close as their kiss lingered. His warm breath tickled her face, sending shivers through her body. She pulled away to gaze into his brown eyes. "Do me a favor and stay close tonight, okay? In case we have to leave because of the storm."

"What aren't you saying?" He stepped backward. "We shouldn't be going tonight. I told you, he's not where they think he is."

"We have to go tonight." Panic rose from her twisted stomach into her chest.

Nico sat on the edge of her bed, letting the jacket hang on the floor. "Everything about this is wrong. I was at the garage early this morning and Dad was there. He's hiding something, I think he helped him escape. Remember his phone? It's all happening just like it said, today. Tonight."

She sat beside him, her body tense. "Did he say anything?"

"He loaded up a rusted piece of shit station wagon with duffel bags and when I told him I knew he was working with Sloan, we argued. He denied it, but it was weird. Before he left, he grabbed me, wouldn't let me move, and said he loved me. Made me promise I'd stay with you at this damn party tonight. He's killing me, Drew. Why is he doing this to me? To my mom and brother?"

The station wagon. Nico's dad had given Sloan a getaway car.

Reaching across his lap, she took his fingers in hers. "Sloan won't get away with this. I promise you." She had to do something. She would make it through this party, keep Nico safe, find Sloan and take care of him the only way she knew how. Treat him like the witch hunter.

Nico's eyes darkened. "You know something, don't you? I thought we were done keeping secrets."

"I'm not keeping secrets."

Shit.

They had a relationship based on trust and didn't lie to each other. But she would keep Nico safe come hell or high water. Even if it meant lying.

The vivid painting of the flooded lighthouse, perched on the easel in the other room, burst into her mind, igniting an overwhelming desire to go back.

Releasing her fingers, Nico touched the jewel resting against her neck, emitting a unique purple light.

Aurora's light.

"Promise?" he asked.

"I promise." The lie burned her tongue, and she swallowed it down like a pill sticking to her throat, averting her gaze from his. "We should go." She stood and took his hand, pulling him toward the door.

Attendants greeted guests as vehicles arrived under a stone carport for valet parking. Adorned in rain slickers over uniforms, the hired attendants battled a barrage of wind and rain, parking cars behind the Atlas Cliffs yacht club.

Nico navigated the Chevelle beside a row of vehicles near the entrance. He moved fast, getting out and opening the passenger side door before she could ask questions. The drive over would have been completely silent between them if not for the rumbling engine. The rain hammered against his jacket as he bent down and locked eyes with her, his gaze brimming with an unfamiliar intensity.

He doesn't believe me; he knows something's up.

Wind churned around them as she took his outstretched hand and got out of the car. Cooler air collided with humidity, the impending storm threatening to unleash hell over them like a beast stalking its prey.

"I'll park and meet you inside," he said. "I'm not letting valet take my car in case we need to get out of here."

Consumed by the urge to tell him the truth, her heart pounded inside her chest as though it could move up her throat. She wanted to scream until she had no voice left that Dominic Sloan was watching every move she made, using her in his twisted plan for escape, but if she uttered a word, this party would be over in the worst way.

Guilt gnawed at her like a blade scraping her insides at the thought of that monster running free. But if she didn't play along until she could execute her own plan, everyone she loved would become a wandering soul, including herself.

Leaving Nico behind, she lifted the cascading dress and ran up the steps toward the grand entrance. The howling wind drowned out the melodic tunes emanated from the speakers as it whipped at her hair. When she turned around at the top of the stone steps, Nico had disappeared to park the car.

The doors opened, and she followed a procession of women holding their hair in death grips, dressed in finery, and wearing more jewels than celebrities attending an award show. Men stepped inside, smoothing out their exquisite suits, and adjusting ties wrapped around their necks tighter than shackles. Those who were Atlas Cliff's locals carried an air of tension as

Sloan's escape dominated hushed conversations with theories of where he was going, wishing for his death or capture, and fake sounding sympathy for Claudia and Anna Tate.

She recognized store owners who had kept family businesses running for decades like Gran had done with the Tough Cookie. These guests acknowledged her with nods and tight smiles, knowing her connection to Sloan. They quickly turned their attention back to their champagne flutes and shook hands with newcomers, welcoming them, but still followed her from the corner of their eyes as she walked past.

A man in a black funeral suit with slicked back hair leaned against the wall near a coat rack, staring at her as he talked on a phone. The purple light brightened as it spun deep inside the amulet and her skin erupted in goosebumps with a wave of unease engulfing her.

She ducked past a gazebo, ignoring the fragrance of fresh flowers as she searched the crowd for threats.

"About time you made it." Shane appeared out of nowhere, standing in front of her wearing a tuxedo like he'd been born for this life. Maybe he had been.

"Where's Claudia?" she asked.

"Running around here barking orders at people. Don't worry, she'll find you." He beamed at guests and directed them with a gesture toward the main room behind them.

Lit candles in glass holders on tables, strands of fairy lights woven through black and white mesh draped along the walls, and a massive chandelier sent light dancing like pixie dust over silver and glassware transformed the room into another world.

She stood between the ballroom and the entrance. "I've never been inside before."

"That's about to change." Shane was at her side. "Tonight could change everything for you if you can forget about my convict of a father and let it."

The smirk on Shane's face took her back to the vision Ori had shown her when he was on the boat with another girl.

"There you are, handsome." Speaking of the other girl... like dark magic Drew had no control over, Leah suddenly linked arms with Shane and glared at Drew.

Shane's smirk vanished. "Leah meet Drew, Drew... Leah."

Leah had swept her raven hair into an intricate side braid with a clasp the same crimson as her gown.

Drew extended her hand toward Leah with a small smile. "Nice to finally meet you." Perhaps a hint of sarcasm escaped, but how could it not?

A gust of wind burst through the doors as a man and woman entered, shaking rain off broken and bent umbrellas, cursing under their breath. They owned a coffee shop near Casting Spoon and had run friendly competitions with Gran over the years. The woman gave Drew a wave as she hung up a bright yellow rain jacket. But it was Nico standing behind them who captured Drew's attention, stealing it away from any lingering feelings of betrayal brought up by Shane and Leah's appearance.

He narrowed his eyes on Shane as he strode up to Drew. "It's a little wet out there." He rubbed the arms of his suit jacket, the rain speckles absorbing together into soaked patches of fabric.

Drew slipped her fingers into Nico's hand as Shane introduced Leah, twisting his mouth to the side. Witnessing his discomfort brought her a profound sense of gratification. She wanted him to find happiness—she really did. But she'd be a bigger liar than she was earlier if she denied the betrayal didn't carry a hint of a lingering sting.

"I'll tell Claudia you're here," Shane said, tugging Leah's hand to pull her away.

Nico leaned his head close to hers. "You okay with all... *that*?"

"More than you know. He was an asshole for doing what he did, but I've moved on. We both have. I need you to believe that."

"*That*, I believe." He glared at her through lashes, still damp from the rain.

He knew she was keeping something from him. She could read it on his face.

Dropping his hand from hers, he gestured at the luxury surrounding them. "Look at this place. Look at us."

"What's that supposed to mean?"

"There's a hurricane outside, and Sloan is out there with nothing to lose... What the fuck are we doing in here?"

"It's a tropical storm," she said.

Folding his arms across his chest, he pursed his lips and eyed her. "Does it matter what kind of storm it is? It's worse than they thought. Aren't you concerned he's using this party somehow? Everyone is inside this building, Drew. I don't like it."

"You've seen the reports people are posting. He's probably escaped to Canada or somewhere by now—" The lies tasted sour in her mouth.

"That's bullshit and you know it." He shook his jacket off and gripped it with both hands. The buttons of his white shirt pulled against his broad chest as he ran a hand through his damp hair. He moved in close, and heat burned in her stomach, sending a ripple through her. He lowered his voice. "Why won't you tell me the truth?"

"There you are! Oh my God, I've been wondering where you are!" Claudia snatched Drew's arm and glanced up at Nico. "Hi Nico, I hope you don't mind, but we've got buyers—art *buyers*, and they want to meet you." Her smile widened, making her teeth appear whiter against her red lips.

Nico exhaled, not taking his eyes off Drew. He leaned down with his lips against her ear. His breath tickled her skin, and she wanted to grab him and run out of this place to the car and never look back. He held his phone up. "If you need me, send a message and I'm there." He watched her with his hands in his pockets as Claudia dragged her away.

What if Nico was right and Sloan was using the party for more than a distraction from his escape? Where had he vanished to?

Thirty-Two

A small group gathered around Drew's paintings, beautifully displayed with their own wall space dedicated to her art. Anna Tate stood in the center, waving her hands around as she talked and pointed to specific details on each piece of Drew's heart and soul hanging for everyone to ogle.

Her heart thudded in her chest like a drumbeat as Claudia guided her closer. She was a small-town local girl. Why would anyone want something she'd created?

The details and memories of each painting would remain forever etched in her mind.

She'd been with Shane at the time she'd created the ghostly silhouette holding the swing from falling and coming to terms with leaving her childhood behind without ever having her mom. The two abstract pieces still sent a shiver through her. A blend of colors transitioning from dark to light, reminding her of a realm she knew nothing about. The end of one chapter and the beginning of another. Claudia had left a space on the wall for the missing piece sitting untouched in her studio at home. She'd fought to feature it until hours earlier, and Drew continued to refuse to let her have it.

"I'd like to introduce you to the artist, Drew Harlow." Anna Tate beamed as she clasped her hands together, like a mother showing their child off.

How could everyone be so cheery, oblivious to Sloan's looming threats? The man in the funeral suit had followed her into the grand room, taking a seat near the exit. He adjusted his suit jacket and eyed her before scanning the crowd and landing where Nico stood with Taj. The man's jacket was loose enough to conceal a gun with no one noticing.

Her legs begged her to run. Grab Nico and run. Her fingers grazed her phone tucked inside her pocket.

Claudia took over the conversation, maintaining eye contact with Drew. "The paintings are all for sale and bids for silent auction are underway."

A sudden burst of pink hair, elegantly styled, and impossible to miss, captured Drew's attention. She waved, and Piper waved back with both hands as she approached.

Piper's short black dress matched her fingernails and Claudia made a face as she eyed her up and down. "We're busy right now."

"I'm not staying." Piper walked past Claudia to hug Drew. Piper lowered her voice. "You hanging in there?"

"I can do anything for an hour. Once this is over, we're leaving."

"Don't worry, already ten steps ahead of you." Piper followed Drew's gaze.

The funeral man stood and downed a glass of champagne and gave Drew a curt nod before weaving into the crowd. She took a deep breath and placed her hands on Piper's arms. "Look at me. We all need to stay inside until this is over, all of us." She gestured across the room toward Nico and Taj. "Keep an eye on them and if anything is weird, come find me or message."

"Of course. You're scaring me." Piper's eyes widened. "What the hell is going on? Did you *see* him?"

She could trust Piper without raising suspicion. Nico would take matters into his own hands and ignore her warnings.

She forced a smile as the man skirted the crowd near her. "I saw him today, he's here, in town, I'm just not sure where. If

I don't keep you guys inside this building, he said he would... He made threats. Promise me you won't breathe a word."

"Jesus, why not tell the police?" Piper leaned close to Drew's ear. "He shot you. You can't just let him be free."

"He has people here *watching*, he'll know. We stick it out here for a bit longer, and I'll call the police as soon as we're safely away, but not before."

The man talked on his phone again, diverting his watchful eye, and Drew gripped Piper's hand. "Please, promise me."

Piper gritted her teeth. "This sucks. It really sucks. How do you know he's not coming here?"

"I don't, but he really wanted me to keep Nico away—"

"Nico? I don't get it, what does he have to do with this?"

"His dad is involved again," Drew said as the man joined a group of people close by, taking a seat with a smile plastered on his face as he shot her a menacing look. What was he doing? "You need to walk away, I think he's watching us."

Piper spun around. "Who's watching us? You're freaking me out."

Drew shook her head to hush Piper, silently begging her to walk away.

With her hands up, Piper stepped backward, nearly bumping into a server with a tray of drinks. "Keep us all together, inside. Got it. Should be easy enough." Piper tapped her phone.

"Where's yours? And don't you dare leave this room behind my back, either."

Drew edged the top of her phone from her pocket. "Right here, like a lifeline."

Claudia cleared her throat, cutting in. "If you're looking for Taj, he's talking to Nico and Jasper at the dessert table."

"I know where they are." Piper gave Claudia a brief salute before turning her attention back to Drew. "Take care of yourself, I'll stick close."

Drew caught Nico's gaze as he glanced in her direction. He'd left Taj behind and was engaged in an intense conversation with Shane. His expression mirrored the seriousness of the night at Maze. At another table, Jasper served decorative slivers of cake to guests before handing a piece to Leah as she smiled at him.

She rejoined Claudia as she fielded questions from people who otherwise wouldn't give Drew a second glance. Each time she glanced at her phone, the seconds stretched out into an agonizing eternity.

"Well, color me proud." Celeste approached the art display. Her golden gown hugged her to elegant perfection as she sashayed up to the paintings. "If one could paint with their soul, this is what the result would look like."

A woman talked about custom pieces and Claudia stepped in and smiled her cover girl, red-lipped smile. "There will be a lighthouse piece coming, right Drew?"

Jesus, Claudia, what are you doing to me?

But Drew smiled back, widening her eyes. "Of course there will be. Just say the word and I'll get right on it."

Suppressing a smile, Celeste licked her lips and arched an eyebrow, her amusement evident. The woman held her eyes on the paintings, ignoring them both. "Good. Very good." She flicked a card from her breast pocket and handed it to Claudia, flashing a quick smile before walking away.

"I told you this would be worth it. No way was my father going to stop me." Claudia's face reddened as she stared straight ahead, unblinking. Snapping herself out of her stupor, she shifted toward Drew. "You look fantastic, by the way, I knew that dress would be perfection."

Drew lifted the tulle of her dress, revealing her white slip-on Converse. "I've got my running shoes on, just in case."

"Usually I'd make fun of you for it, but not tonight." Claudia's smile vanished, and she looked off into the distance, swiftly composing herself to greet more guests.

Celeste stuck around. "I cannot believe we are here with everything going on, even mother nature is fighting back."

"Mother nature is nothing compared to that monster." Drew bit her lip, stopping herself from saying more.

Celeste raised an eyebrow. "Care to elaborate?"

"Nothing to elaborate on." She avoided Celeste's curious eyes. "I just wish they'd catch him and this whole thing was over."

"If you know something they don't—"

"I don't."

Celeste hugged her with her hand on the back of Drew's head. "I'm heading out, but you know where to find me."

"You're not staying?" Drew pulled away, her face giving away panic. "You have to stay."

"I came for you, I saw, and I will talk to you later." She glanced across the room. "You sure you're all right, honey?"

The man watching was nowhere in sight, but she couldn't take the risk that he wouldn't be observing Celeste like the others.

"Just uneasy, that's all," Drew said.

"You'll be just fine. And you are surrounded in here." With a sharp inhale, Celeste closed her eyes as she touched her ear. "Oh yes, you are surrounded."

A young couple stopped to admire Drew's paintings, interrupting her conversation with Celeste, and Claudia relayed her Tate Gallery speech, praising the local talent. When Drew turned back to Celeste, she was gone.

If anything happened to Celeste… She tried to smile through rising panic and talk to the couple, shaking their hands with sweaty palms as they left.

Claudia looked at the gold watch around her wrist. "You did it. You're free for the night."

"It's over?"

"See? Not so bad."

Grant strode up to Claudia and kissed her, placing his hand across her back. With a serious expression, he scanned the room. "What's next? We have to be gone by eleven."

Drew acknowledged him with a nod before walking away. She hadn't seen him since reuniting him and his father with Jules. He'd seen her gift, and there was a vulnerability that lingered afterward.

"Drew," he called after her, and she stopped, taking a deep breath before turning around. "I wanted to thank you again for what you did for my dad," he continued, "and for me."

"You're welcome, it's what I do."

Frowning, he leaned in and cast a quick glance around again before opening his mouth to speak. "He killed my sister, and I will not let him get away. I want you to know I'm well connected in this town, and I can confirm he's nowhere near Atlas Cliffs. I don't want you to worry."

Claudia sidled up to Grant, linking her arm with his as she turned her attention toward Drew. "I'm proud of you tonight, you did good. Don't leave without saying bye, okay?" She pulled him away, leaving Drew standing near her art display alone.

Grant was clueless. Who did Sloan have working for him on the outside? Someone was misleading the police about Sloan's whereabouts, but where had he gone?

"You've got big problems, they're gone." Jules' ethereal silhouette appeared beside her, tilting her angelic face to the side as a golden glow surrounded her.

"It didn't work?" Drew's hand flew to her mouth to hide her shock.

"Oh, it worked beautifully, but I had to warn you."

"Wait, gone?" Frenzied moments of Sloan's threats in the bakery washed over her, the gun aimed at Henry, and held to her head. *But not before I make you watch the life drain from your boyfriend.* "Where's Nico?" Drew hurried across the room, her steps purposeful and the intensity of her concentration drowning out the awareness of her feet against the floor. Her eyes widened in terror, darting between faces, searching for him. Nico's tall stature was unmistakable in a crowd, but he was nowhere to be seen.

"He's with Shane," Jules' voice echoed over the music from behind her.

Drew spun around. "How do you know?"

"I was there, beside him, Drew. He escaped, just like I knew he would." Jules' soft features held love and compassion. "The monster who stole my life is walking free. But you won't be alone."

The light enveloped Jules and she vanished. Panic surged through Drew's chest, clenching like a corset being yanked too tight to breathe. Couples stared at her as they danced, averting their eyes when her gaze landed on theirs. Nothing mattered to her except finding Nico. Sweat gathered at the back of her neck and trickled down her back as a ringing buzzed in her ears.

They left.

And she had to find them.

THIRTY-THREE

Drew marched over to Leah, who was sitting by herself at a table, her face illuminated by the light from her phone. "Where's Shane and Nico?"

"That's what I'm trying to find out. He left me here."

With Piper at his side, Taj approached Drew. He cracked his knuckles with each hand, a somber expression on his face. "They took off."

"Tell her." Piper paced back and forth and twirled strands of pink hair in her fingers, winding them until her skin turned red.

Taj released his hands. "Nico's car is gone. I already checked."

"Where did they go?" she asked. But she already knew. Ben Morana had one place in Atlas Cliffs he had a deep connection with, long before he'd become Dominic Sloan.

"Neptune Point." Taj's words echoed her thoughts. "I'm going to find them."

"I'm going, you stay here," she said.

"I'm calling the police." Piper held her phone up and dialed, heading toward the lobby.

Taj watched Piper walk away and lowered his voice as he turned back to Drew. "I have a bad feeling. No way am I letting you go out there alone."

He'd been the one having the nightmares. She couldn't take the chance of Taj getting hurt... or worse, if the haunting visions were about him. Celeste would never forgive her if Drew involved her son. "Do you have any of your mom's stones with you?"

"What? That's where your mind is right now? I'm leaving. Keep Piper here, okay?"

"Wait." Fumbling in her pocket, Drew handed Taj the blue stone Celeste had given her. "Take this."

He glanced from the stone to her. "What's it for?"

"Lapis lazuli, the stone of breath... Her words. It's better than nothing, take it."

He took the blue stone from her palm, but as his fingers graced her skin, a jolt of electricity flooded her senses. She clenched her teeth as a burst of metallic fizz crackled along her tongue, gripping his hand to hold on to the connection when the same vision edged her mind. This time, the sound of howling wind and rushing water echoed in her ears as she descended into darkness.

"I can't breathe." Taj yanked his hand away, gasping for air. "What was that? The nightmare is coming true, isn't it?"

"I don't know, I don't know..." She struggled to speak, taking shallow breaths and suppressing her fear.

Taj tucked Celeste's stone in his pocket. "Please, stay behind. I'm begging you, do not go out there, Drew." Holding a hand up, he broke away from her, running for the door.

I have to go out there. I need a car.

Lifting the layers of her dress, Drew sprinted after him, almost crashing into Claudia.

"Why is everybody running away?" Claudia said.

"Do you have your car here?" Drew grabbed Claudia's arm, pulling her toward the door. "I need your keys."

"I'm not giving you my keys. Where are you going?"

"Keys, Claudia! I don't have time for this."

Claudia wrenched her arm out of Drew's grip and stood with her hands on her hips. "Make time. I'm not handing anything over until you explain yourself."

Taj turned back to them, his keys in his hand. "Your escaped father is at Neptune Point, and Shane and Nico took off after him." He narrowed his eyes at Drew as he walked backward toward the door. "Stay here. If what I've been seeing comes true? No, just fucking no. Stay with Piper, she's talking to the police." He didn't wait for Drew to respond as he shoved the doors open and disappeared into the thunderous wind outside.

Drew tried to chase after Taj, but Claudia clutched her arm in a death grip, and Drew spun around to face her. "He won't hurt Nico, or another person I love again. Over my dead body. I'll *steal* a car if I have to." Shaking from Claudia's grip, she reached for the door, struggling to open it as the wind created a vacuum effect.

With both hands, Claudia helped Drew pull the door open, her face inches from Drew's. "He's my father. We go together."

Crumpling handfuls of her dress, Drew followed Claudia down the stairs, grateful for her sneakers. The wind took her breath away as it bent trees sideways and tossed heavy rain, pelting her face in a sea of bullets.

Claudia effortlessly ran in high heels, guiding Drew toward the front, where a luxurious sedan was parked in one of the VIP spots. Claudia assumed control of the driver's seat and Drew hopped into the passenger seat, slamming the door as the dashboard illuminated and the engine hummed to life.

The back door swung open, and Piper leaned in, wiping pink strands of wet hair off her face. Mascara ran under her eyes. "I don't think so! Not without me."

"Get in!" Drew yelled. This was a bad idea, but she didn't know what else to do.

Before Piper's door could fully close, Claudia sped away. Tires squealed as she steered the car over the manicured lawn to get ahead of a line of cars. Sirens wailed in the distance, but the highway ran alongside the yacht club, and they could avoid traveling through town.

The speedometer climbed as Claudia adjusted her weight, pressing her foot down on the gas pedal. "What do we do once we get there?"

I stop him somehow.

"I'm working on that part. Just drive as fast as you can." Drew bounced her foot, still clutching her dress in her clammy hands.

Claudia's phone rang through the Bluetooth, the name displayed as "my love", and she clicked reject.

"You're not answering, *my love*?" Piper leaned between the two front seats. But what would usually be a joke wasn't. Her expression was grave, without a hint of a smile.

"This is my family bullshit, not his, I can't drag him into it. I thought the police had him. Grant said they were close, that's what they kept telling Mom and me." Claudia gripped the wheel and accelerated faster, dominating the empty road. The wind shook the car, pushing it toward the shoulder of the road.

"He came to see me today. If I didn't do exactly what he wanted..." Drew banged her head against the headrest. "He's got people watching, he told me he'd know if I went to the police. He made me keep Nico from leaving the party, and we all know how well that went." Tears burned her eyes and her words caught in her throat. "He threatened Piper, Nico, Celeste... asked me if I knew how to make a bomb, because he" —she lowered the tone of her voice to mimic his—"'sure had someone ready with one.' If anything happens to Nico, I'll die. It'll be all my fault." She wiped her eyes, refusing to give into a crying fit of rage.

I let this happen; I don't deserve self-pity.

Claudia darted her eyes from the road to Drew, back and forth. She turned on the wipers to battle the rain. "Why didn't you tell me? How did Shane and Nico know where to find him? Why did they leave without telling us?"

"Would you have really kept it to yourself?" Drew strained her eyes to see through the pitch-black outside. Her ears burned, and a shudder slid along her wet skin. "I don't know what they found out or how, but Nico's dad is involved."

Slamming her hands on the steering wheel, the car swerved as Claudia took her eyes off the road to glare at Drew.

"He is *my* father, *my* problem. After everything we've been through—after Grant's sister? You don't get to decide what you keep to yourself, Drew! This isn't always about you and *your* ghosts. Other lives, alive people's lives, are at stake too." She tightened her trembling hands on the wheel, refocused on the road, and pressed hard on the gas pedal.

Lost in her own chaos, Drew had failed to recognize the pain her friend was silently carrying. Sloan might've been in jail, but his terror hadn't stopped haunting Claudia. "I didn't realize—"

"And another thing." With a clenched fist, Claudia struck the wheel once more. "When are you going to start trusting people, especially your friends? You don't have to do this alone. We know you better than you think we do, what's it going to take for you to see we aren't out to get you, that we just want to help and be there for you, like you've been there for us? For me?"

"Preach, Claudia," Piper said from the backseat. "How in the fresh hell can Claudia Tate put my thoughts into the perfect words?" Leaning forward, she placed her hand on Claudia's shoulder. "When did you get inside my head? That freaks me out a little, not gonna lie."

Blood sprang from Drew's lip, and she stopped her relentless gnawing on it, pressing her finger against the raw spot she'd created. How could she have been so oblivious? Her friends loved her as much as she loved them. Tears won, streaming down her cheeks. She leaned her head against the headrest and covered her face. "I'm sorry, you're right, I should have told you. What if we're too late?"

Reaching over, Claudia grabbed her hand and squeezed it. "Don't think like that, nothing is going to happen to them. We won't let it."

Eerie buzzing erupted in the car as notifications flooded all three phones in unison. Drew pulled her phone out of her dress pocket to see an alert warning the residents of Atlas Cliffs to stay in their homes. An armed criminal was at large.

"This might be good news." Piper's phone lit up the back seat. "The police will be all over this, probably before we get there. It's going to be okay." Her phone buzzed again as she placed a hand on Drew's shoulder. "Well, I spoke too soon. Taj said a tree is down, blocking the main road. He thinks we're still at the yacht club."

Sloan wouldn't let the police take him in without a fight. She needed to be there and stop him. She reached for the amulet, and a surge of energy pulsed through her. Reciting the summoning spell in her mind, she begged for help from someone, anyone who might be on the other side. Heat emanated from the jewel as a vibrant light pulsed from its core. A sign reflected in the headlights showed a seldom used narrow road, a shortcut she hadn't used in years. "Take the road right there. It'll save at least ten minutes."

"That's right along the coast. What if it's washed out?" Claudia's hands shook as she slowed the car down and leaned forward, peering through the pouring rain. She pulled over, staring straight ahead.

Drew could take the car by herself and leave them behind. With the tree blocking the road, Taj would be forced to turn around, and the police would have to do the same. No helicopter was flying in these conditions. She turned around in her seat. "Get out and let me go. Call Grant," she glanced back at Piper, "or get Taj to come get you."

"Hell no," Piper said.

"Absolutely not." Claudia's eyes narrowed, creasing her forehead. She turned to look at Piper and back at Drew. "Did what I just say not sink in? We do this together, or we all go back. Believe me, I know he's a horrible, horrible man." Tears pricked her eyes. "But he's my father. When he sees me, he'll stop. He won't hurt anyone."

"Remember the warehouse?" Drew snapped, unable to stop herself. "You showed up and he still—"

"I'll make him listen. He'll turn himself in. He must still love me, right? I was his little girl. Doesn't that mean something?" Slamming her foot down on the gas, Claudia steered down the dark road, turning her high beams on. Tears streamed down her face as she angrily wiped them with the back of her hand.

This was the Claudia she knew. Everyone else saw the girl who put up stone walls and acted like nothing got to her. But that's all it was, an act to hide the horrendous amount of pain beneath the surface. Claudia's father was incapable of love, and he never would be. There'd be only one way to stop Dominic Sloan and it wouldn't be through love for his daughter.

With each jarring bump, the car sent sheets of water spraying along its sides, as the powerful surf surged against the barrier and encroached upon the road. Sirens faded into the distance as the lighthouse came into view, its beacon rotating, not missing a beat, oblivious to the turmoil ensuing below. As Claudia rounded the turn and drove over the bridge to Neptune Point, the car's tail end swayed from side to side. She slowed down, gripping the wheel, and steered away from the railing, averting a potential disaster into the churning sea below.

White water sprayed over the bridge, coating the car, making it impossible for the wipers to keep the window clear. "I can't see anything," Claudia exclaimed, high-pitched with fear.

The headlights pierced through the darkness, illuminating the vehicles parked on the side of the road. Angled down the ditch, tucked within wild overgrown bushes, was the rusted station wagon Sloan had parked outside the Tough Cookie.

But a brick dropped in her stomach when Nico's car came into view, standing out like Aurora's beacon underneath a canopy of blowing trees.

"Pull over." Drew gripped the door handle as she fumbled with her seatbelt, flinging the door open.

The car jolted to a sudden stop, and Drew collided with the dash as she stumbled outside. An onslaught of torrential rain and forceful wind threatened to sweep her away as it soaked into her dress and hair. Trees creaked and branches snapped under the pressure of the howling wind. She couldn't see the main road as darkness hung over it.

No flashing lights, no sirens. No help had arrived.

A car door shut, and Piper stood beside her, shielding her face with bare arms. "What now?"

She gripped Piper's arms. "Stay here and wait for the police." Not looking back, she tore over the hill toward the new keeper's house. Large tarps broke free from the ropes binding them to heavy machinery, and plastic flapped against metal, cutting through the air as she scanned the field of overgrown seagrass-covered hills leading to the cliffs.

Aurora's beacon rotated, casting dark shadows. With each step forward, her sneakers sank into the drenched mud and seagrass. Her wet hair dripped down her back and over her shoulders, her dress weighed down with water. Wind lashed her face, and she shivered uncontrollably. A loud cracking echoed over the howling wind as a tree crashed to the ground.

Claudia and Piper yelled from behind her. If Sloan hurt Nico, she wouldn't let him walk away from Neptune Point. A life without Nico was... No. She couldn't think about it.

Approaching the house, she leaped up to the floorboards of a new porch. She turned the knob, finding the door locked, and peered into the windows as rain pelted her face and arms.

Out of breath, Claudia and Piper stomped down the hill to where she stood.

"You were supposed to stay back to wait for the police," she called out over her shoulder.

"Drew, were you not listening? We told you all or nothing!" Piper yelled.

Claudia held her jacket closed with both hands. "I don't see them anywhere."

"They're not here. I have to find him." She couldn't hide the panic in her voice.

Hopping off the porch, Drew ran around the house, peering through windows. The lighthouse edged the cliffs, looming overhead the closer she stepped toward it.

"Where are they, Jack?" she screamed up at the lighthouse landing, her voice sucked up into the storm. Waves thundered against the rocky cliffs so hard they sprayed seawater toward the lighthouse. The vast expanse of ocean water submerged boulders, which had remained untouched by the sea until now.

Claudia stumbled from behind her, cursing. "They're going to be okay. If my father's here, he'll want to escape, he won't kill Nico, or his own son. He would've done that a long time ago. Let's wait for the police to get here. I'm sure they're fine. They have to be."

Drew spun around, blinking away rain and tears. Claudia's blonde hair clung to her face as she stood with her arms crossed, watching Drew, panic filling her own eyes. Piper hugged herself, shivering.

The cars were up there. Nico was here. Dominic Sloan was here.

"I'm checking the lighthouse," Drew said.

Piper and Claudia followed as Drew raced toward the lighthouse. The wind carried distant voices, echoing through the air. Angry voices. Sloan had the power to steal everything from her in a blink, and she'd do anything to stop him. Drew pulled Piper and Claudia behind a run-down shed. "Stay here. Please stay here."

Claudia grabbed her and held her so tight her breath caught. "Don't you get it? I don't want anything to happen to you either. If he hurt Shane and Nico—"

Holding Claudia's arms, she pulled back to look in her face. "The police are on their way. Go up and meet them, show them where we are. We're in this together, just like you said."

Wiping her face, Claudia's eyes darted from up the hill and back to Drew. "My brother's there. I'm coming with you."

"We're doing this together." Piper trudged ahead toward the lighthouse, leaving them behind.

"Jesus, Piper, wait!" Charging through the rain and wind, she reached Piper's side with Claudia trailing her, and they moved forward.

Light rotated in a slow, steady rhythm, illuminating the landing of the lighthouse. The figure of a man emerged, his long coat billowing in the wind and his hat casting a shadow over his face. Leaning over the rail, Jack lifted his arm and pointed to the lighthouse entrance below.

Thirty-Four

Rain pelted Drew's face, stinging like shards of glass cutting her skin. The howling wind shifted into a high-pitched wheezing, thrashing her hair against her face. Forceful gusts of wind moved like a freight train, tearing limbs off trees, sending them flying into the raging ocean. Waves crashed over the rocks, moving higher and closer, slapping the side of the lighthouse facing the ocean.

Tearing away from Piper and Claudia, Drew released the clumps of her sopping wet dress from her fist. She sank into the mud as she navigated over sharp rocks toward the lighthouse entrance.

A fire burned in her lungs, and her heart raced, sending blood pumping along her temples. The amulet thrummed against her neck, and she gripped the jewel as the spinning thread of light thickened, glowing brighter, seeping into her hands. As shadows shifted, voices echoed from the top of the lighthouse, distorted by the wind.

If Nico was in there, he had to be okay.

The water surged around her legs, rising to her thighs before receding, only to surge back again with unrelenting force. Her deadened nerves over her thigh tingled in reaction to the cold water as she escaped the rising water and grabbed the lighthouse door. Nico's unmistakable yell sent fear coursing through her like ice in her veins.

A shot rang out as she sloshed through water at the bottom of the winding staircase. Scooping up handfuls of her dress, she gripped the railing and tore up the winding metal staircase, taking them two at a time. As she rounded the top, an expansive landing surrounded her, with thick glass doors hanging open.

Shane stood in front of Nico, holding him back as he yelled at his father. With black duffel bags resting at his feet, Dominic Sloan raised a gun in Nico's direction, and Nick DeSarro moved in front of him, holding his hands up.

Gripping the railing, Drew fixated on the gun and wrapped her fingers around the amulet, begging for help. She stepped closer, torn between charging at Sloan and screaming her rage.

Shane turned away from Nico and advanced at his father. "Take the money and get the fuck out of here."

Anger boiled over, her hands burning as magic erupted underneath her skin.

Just a few more steps..

"How could you do this?" Nico shoved past Shane, standing inches from his own father. His torn shirt clung to his chest as it rose and fell in quick bursts.

As she ascended the remaining steps, her anger unraveled like a pulled grenade pin, fueling her with a fierce determination to protect Nico with her life. She had something Dominic Sloan didn't. A sisterhood of centuries old magic flowing through her. As she reached the top and crossed the landing, a raven swept past her and landed on the staircase railing.

Nico's eyes widened in terror, and he rushed toward her.

Sloan's lips curled into a sinister smile. "Good evening Miss Harlow, so happy you could join us."

Swallowing to keep her throat from closing over in panic, she advanced closer to Sloan. "We had a deal. You promised you would leave them alone if I kept him at that damn party."

Sloan shrugged. "Promises are meant to be broken. You, of all people, should know that. You'll have a front row seat, I see." His arm stiffened as he aimed the gun at Nico.

Not Nico!

She tried to shield him, but he pushed her aside, moving in front of her with his back to Sloan, defenseless. "No, Drew!"

Shane reached for his monster of a father's arm, and Sloan shook his gun at him, his wild eyes glaring between Nico and Shane. "One more step, and son or not, you die."

"You murdered my mother, why not send me to be with her? Fucking asshole!" Shane spat.

Grabbing Shane by his shirt, Nick DeSarro shoved him back, facing Sloan as he created a barrier between Sloan and the boys. "I've done everything you asked. You're free. So, fuck off and let them go."

Nico's hands grasped her arms. "What are you doing here?" he grumbled in a hushed voice.

"I love you." Tears blurred her vision, but she wiped her eyes. The tingling sensation spread across her skin like wildfire, and her hands felt like they would erupt into flames. Sloan's death was the only way to bring peace. She couldn't survive losing Nico or anyone else she loved. Pulling away from Nico's grip, she stepped toward Sloan, slowly raising her hands.

Sirens screeched in the distance, growing louder.

"Drew!" Taj's voice echoed from somewhere below.

"Party's over, back up," Sloan boomed, cracking the gun across Nick DeSarro's face.

Nico charged. Shane grabbed Nico's arms, yanking him back as Sloan cocked the gun with a steady hand. A confident, steady hand.

With magic coaxing her forward, she edged past Nico, not letting Sloan out of her sight. Buzzing rang in Drew's ears, and her lungs expanded, letting in a flow of warm air. Fireworks exploded in her chest, emitting sparkles along her skin. She stepped in front of the three men and raised her hands toward Sloan.

He leveled the barrel of the gun at her with his finger poised on the trigger. "Your turn to die, witch," he snarled like a wild animal. "My sister will be in hell to greet you, but as promised, not before you watch the life leave *his* body."

Sloan's arm snapped towards Nico with unexpected speed, catching Drew off guard—a scream ripping through her as she threw herself in front of him. Nick DeSarro launched himself in front of them both as gunfire erupted, echoing off the lighthouse walls.

"Dad, no!" Nico wrapped his arms around his father, guiding him to the floor as Shane stepped forward to cover them from more gunfire.

She rushed to Nico's side as blood gushed from his father's chest, down the front of his body, soaking his shirt. "Stay with us." She took his hand, concentrating on the burning magic coursing through her to save him.

"Pressure!" Shane hollered, tearing open Nick's shirt as he hovered over him. He shrugged off his jacket, applying it to the open wound and pushing down with both hands.

Nico's father released her hand, giving it a gentle pat before gripping his son's hand. He lifted his head toward Sloan. "Leave. You're free. Don't hurt them." Tears trickled down the sides of his face as his head fell back, the light slowly fading from his eyes.

"Stay with me, Dad, don't die, please don't die." Nico's voice cracked as he cradled his father's head.

Nick gripped his son's hand to his chest. "I'm sorry for everything, son. I love you. Tell Simon and Mom... I'll never stop loving them." His voice strained, and his grip on Nico's hand weakened. He inhaled a final sharp breath and his eyes glazed over, staring blankly at the ceiling, his body growing still.

Drew's head echoed with a piercing screech, her focus shifting to Dominic Sloan. He'd intended that bullet to kill Nico, and she'd been too slow to stop him. He would not get another chance. She advanced toward Sloan and his lips stretched over bared teeth, shifting the barrel of the gun turned on her.

"Stop!" Nico rushed from behind her, but she moved too fast and crossed the landing until she was inches from Sloan.

Aurora emerged from an ethereal light. She placed her hands on Drew's shoulders, sending a wave of magic washing over her, unlike anything she had ever experienced. "Your turn," Aurora's calm voice resounded beside her.

Sloan's face contorted into a sinister grimace as his finger tightened around the trigger. Drew's hands sparked with fiery magic as she extended them, releasing her power toward him. Sloan jerked back, and another shot rang out, casting a brilliant glow across the lighthouse landing.

An explosion of fire slammed into her stomach, sucking the breath from her lungs. Beads of light flooded her vision as she collapsed to the ground. Warm liquid oozed from her torso down her legs.

"No!" Nico's scream echoed through the lighthouse, loud enough to awaken the dead.

With a graceful flap of its wings, the raven landed on her chest, its mournful screech resonating in her ears. Firm hands pushed down on her, and Nico took her face in his hands. Tears filled his eyes and ran down his face as anguished shouts for help escaped his lips.

But she lost control. Her eyes blinked in slow motion until she plunged into an abyss of darkness. Her lungs stopped trying to gasp for air that wouldn't come. The familiar voices surrounding her faded, and desperate wails fell silent. The only sound was the slow, erratic thumping of her heartbeat.

Slow. Fading. Nothing.

Memories flickered through her mind like a home movie.

Five years old and baking cookies with Gran.

Falling off her bike and running to her father so he could place a Band-Aid on her injured knee and kiss it better.

Blowing out the candles on her tenth birthday with the cake Nico helped Gran make for her.

Nico counting his money to buy his first surfboard and sharing with her until she could buy her own.

Fires on the beach with Piper.

Walking the halls of Atlas Cliffs High school, laughing with Piper.

Shane.

College.

Gran's death.

Claudia standing by her side and squeezing her hand when Joelle bolted from her house after her horrific confession about Ori.

Home... Nico. It always came back to Nico.

The bright light at the end of the tunnel beckoned her, its warmth embracing her as she crossed into a new realm.

Is this dying?

"I never thought I'd say this to you, but yes," said a gentle voice. She'd know that voice anywhere.

A breeze billowed through her hair as she turned her head. Ori's crystal blue eyes held her with love. He embodied an angelic presence, but he was undeniably Ori. She ran to him, embracing him as tightly as she could. "I miss you so much. All the time."

"How could you not?" His pale complexion glowed as light wrapped around him.

"What are you doing here?"

"I belong here, you don't."

The serene expanse of the ocean greeted her as her toes sank into the soft sand. "This doesn't look like Jupiter Cove beach, but it feels like it." It was the same place she'd seen Gran when she'd come to her in a dream. Only Gran had died. "Am I dead?"

His smile faded. "I'm afraid so."

"How did you know?"

"When my best human friend's soul wanders, you better believe I'm going to know about it."

The peace inside of her calmed every nerve, but an ache gripped her heart, digging its fingers in like razors. "Nico needs me. This isn't supposed to happen."

"This was definitely not supposed to happen. It's not your time." Ori placed his hands on her shoulders as Aurora had done. "You need to focus on what you want. Where you want to be. And it's not here. Not now. Let's get you back in your body."

"I don't know how."

Ori looked around. "Listen to what your soul hears."

"My soul abandoned me. I hear nothing."

Ori closed his eyes. "Not true. Listen, Drew. Really listen. Who is the one person who can reach you when no one else can? That's who you focus on. You've got to work with me here. I can't do this part for you."

She closed her eyes as the gentle breeze brushed her face. The warmth surrounded her in comfort. "But it's so nice here."

"It isn't your time," Ori said.

Nico's voice cut through the silence in her mind. "Don't leave me, please don't leave me."

"Nico?" she whispered.

Ori beamed. "When are you going to get it? I've said it before, and I'll say it again. The guy is in *love* with you."

In an instant, her surroundings shifted and transported her back to the lighthouse landing, with Ori by her side. The scene unfolded before her eyes, echoing the cautionary red substance in the painting. The piercing sound of sirens and faint, urgent orders in the distance accompanied the wind's howl.

Nico hovered over her lifeless body, pinching her nose, desperately trying to breathe life into her dead body on Shane's command between chest compressions. Blood saturated her blue dress, bunched up to her waist as Piper sobbed, holding a rolled-up cloth down on gushing wounds. Claudia was on her knees, sobbing as Drew's blood pooled around her legs.

Shane stopped and held his fingers to the side of her neck. He sat back and rubbed his tearful eyes. "She's gone, man."

"No, keep going! She can't die!" Nico lifted her body and held her against his chest with his blood-covered hands. Piper dropped her hands and wailed. Dominic Sloan was gone, and Nico's father lay a few feet away, not moving. Not breathing.

"Nico's dad—" she said.

"Right here."

She looked up and her eyes met Nick DeSarro's. Heartbreak hung in his gaze. "I'm so sorry. I never thought it would end this way."

"Why did you do it?"

"He threatened my family. No one threatens my family." He stared at her and glanced over his shoulder at the raging sea beyond the lighthouse. "I don't have much time."

"Ori? What's happening to him?"

"He's got no reason to be stuck. Not like I did. He has you," Ori said. "And you have him."

She followed Ori's gaze toward Taj as he rounded the top of the staircase. He tore off his jacket and tossed it to the side, dropping in front of Nico as he held her body.

And then it hit her.

Breathe life.

Taj had brought the seagull back from death.

Nick DeSarro rubbed his chin. "I gave you the key to the safe. Everything you need will be there." He turned to her, his eyes locking onto hers with intensity. "You're strong, Drew Harlow. I've always known it. You, Nico, Shane, Claudia. You're not your family's mistakes. The cycle ends here." He looked at Ori and held his arms out in front of him. "What is that warm pull?"

"Just go with it, dude. It's paradise, I promise. I'll see you on the other side."

Nick wrapped his arms around Nico's back, holding both Nico and Drew's lifeless body before stepping away. "Take care of each other. I love you both." A swirl of light spun around him, and he glanced over his shoulder. "Do me a favor? Make sure my boys know how proud I am of them. And tell Maria, it's always been her. I can't remember a time I didn't love that woman." He nodded with a smile as he disappeared.

Paramedics arrived at the bottom of the staircase as Taj begged Nico to let her go. "Trust me, Nico, I can help. Look at me, man. I'm *like her. Trust* me." Taj grabbed Nico's arm, but he refused to let her go as he cried.

Piper gripped Nico's arm in desperation and yelled to Claudia to help. Piper and Claudia forcefully separated Drew's body from Nico's embrace, pleading with him to trust Taj.

Coated in blood from his hands to his elbows, Nico surrendered, held up by the girls as Shane stood beside him with his hand on Nico's back.

Placing the blue stone on Drew's still chest, Taj closed his eyes, muttering words under his breath. The spell from his dream, from Aurora. Purple light flowed from his hands and encompassed him, swirling over Drew's body. A force tugged at her, dragging her away from Ori as her arms transitioned into a translucent ghostly appearance. Her lungs expanded in small bursts, taking in quick gulps of air. And the *pain*. A horrendous, sharp, burning pain exploded over her body. "Something's happening, Ori."

A grin spread across Ori's face as he smoothed his blond hair off his face. "You're damn right it is. You're going back my human friend. It's a whole lot of love with a big dose of magic. Go with it and don't forget to say hi once in a while."

A rush of blood slowly pulsed in her ears, a faint thump growing stronger, sending a swish of heat radiating from her chest. Gravity no longer held her feet on the ground, and they lifted, sending her into a gradual fall, her arms reaching for something to hold. Her shallow breaths quickened in brief gasps, desperate for air. A fluttering of stars filled her vision, and she shut her eyes. She collided into her body with the impact of breaking the surface of the water. She sucked in air, wheezing as her hands searched for a lifeline. Arms wrapped around her and lifted her off the ground. Blinking her eyes open, she caught sight of Nico's face. His dark eyes met hers as paramedics charged up the stairs and someone placed an oxygen mask on her face.

Nico lowered his face, just inches away from hers, as he carried her down the stairs. "I've got you."

Paramedics and police in rain gear surrounded them. An authoritative voice called out, "Give us space!"

She couldn't feel her hands or legs as a chill ran through her body. Racked with uncontrollable shivers, the sensation of being disconnected from her own body returned with a mesmerizing display of dancing stars in her vision. As her eyelids drooped closed, all light faded away, immersing her in complete darkness.

THIRTY-FIVE

Machines beeped in a steady rhythm. Drew winced as pain radiated from her abdomen, shooting through her back. Afraid to open her eyes, she wiggled her toes and fingers against the rough fabric stretched tightly over her. She didn't feel like herself. The weight of emptiness overwhelmed her, disconnecting her from the pulse of the living world. A tube hung from her nose; she could feel it when she swallowed. The smell of rubbing alcohol and disinfectant surrounded her. She attempted to raise her hand, but her arm was like a block of lead, restrained by tubes dangling from her hand.

I'm in a hospital bed. Taj brought me back from the dead.

A soft touch grazed her face, prompting her to open her eyes and squint against the blinding light framing Gran's face. "You're a survivor, dear. You did what you had to do. Cling to these words like the air you breathe." With a smile on her face, Gran extended her hands, running them over her, the warmth radiating from her fingertips, before dissipating into a shimmering mist.

Come back! Please. I don't want to be alone.

She attempted to form words, but they refused to come out, and her mouth was so dry she struggled to swallow.

Desperate for human contact, she clutched the bedsheets, trying to lift her head, and a soft hand reached out to hold hers.

A chair scraped along the floor, and Piper's blotchy face came into view, leaning over her. "I'm here. We thought we lost you." Her eyes filled with tears as she gripped Drew's hand.

Drew opened her mouth to talk, but only a hushed whisper escaped.

"Don't talk, it's okay. Your dad dragged Nico to the cafeteria to eat something. He hasn't left you in days."

Days? Her eyes widened, burning with tears. How long had she been here? Nico's dad... no, no, no. It couldn't be real.

Sobs caught in her throat, and the ache stretched from her stomach to settle in her chest.

"I know. I know," Piper cried softly as she pressed her forehead against Drew's. "I know."

Drew tried to squeeze Piper's hand, but her fingers were too weak to use any strength. "Sloan," she rasped.

Piper leaned closer and dropped her voice. "He's dead. Whatever you did, you sent him over the railing, and they found him on the rocks. He can't hurt anyone ever again."

I killed him. I killed a man, glimpsed the other side, and came back. Am I a monster too?

The tears ran over her face onto the pillow, stinging her cheeks. Chills racked her body, sending shooting pain down her legs, and Piper reached for a button attached to the bed. "I'm getting a nurse."

Nico's father was the only reason Nico had escaped death. How could she feel such relief knowing his dad was dead?

"She's awake," Piper said, looking toward the door.

Danny appeared beside her, his eyebrows pulled together as he eyed tubes and pressed buttons on a machine. Inflating with air, the cuff attached to her arm constricted. He made notes and depressed a syringe into her IV tube. Two large bags of clear fluid hung on a metal pole beside her.

"I gave you pain meds." He placed his hand on her arm and exhaled. "It's good to see you back, Drew, we've missed you." He tucked the blanket around her. "Are you cold?"

Tears stung her cheeks, and her nose ran, but she couldn't lift her hand. Grabbing a tissue, Danny dabbed her cheeks and wiped her nose as his own eyes welled with tears. "Just rest. You're safe. I'm here all evening, and you've got a crew who've moved into the lobby." His lips quivered as he smiled and patted her hand. "I'll get a warm blanket," he said to Piper as he left.

Her entire body trembled, and she dragged her hands to her neck, every inch more painful. She couldn't sit up without feeling like her abdomen would tear open. The amulet was gone, along with the butterfly necklace Nico had given her. "Piper," she gasped through tears.

She didn't want to be dead, but the warm place with Ori would be better than this hell.

Piper took Drew's hands. "What can I do?"

Drew pointed to her neck. "Where is it?"

"Nico has them, don't worry." Piper glanced over her shoulder. "Taj is here. He wants to see you." Piper squeezed Taj's hand and left the room, closing the door behind her with a soft click.

Taj pulled a chair close and leaned on the edge of the bed. He observed her with bloodshot eyes and a slight rosiness blotched his brown skin like he'd been crying. "You *died*. You were dead in my arms."

Her fingers found his hand. "You brought me back." Her words came out quiet and hoarse.

"The woman was there."

"Aurora."

"The dream came true, and I'm scared it's going to happen again." His soulful eyes held hers as she struggled to keep them open. "You're just waking up from death, and I shouldn't be bugging you, but I couldn't leave until I was sure you made it. I couldn't leave." He held his other hand up. "The magic isn't as strong, but I can feel it waiting, you know? Just in case."

She tried to squeeze his hand. "Always there."

"Always," he said.

She would be dead if it weren't for Taj. She'd be on the other side with Ori, but there'd be no peace, only heartache. If she'd crossed over, she would be a wandering lost soul stuck in between forever as she watched Nico and everyone she loved move on with their lives. No one would be able to see her, or help her find her paradise, would they?

Taj had saved her life.

"Thank you." She cleared her throat, and the tube moved, making her flinch. Her tears traced a path along her skin, leaving behind a damp trail as they landed on the pillow. "I owe you everything."

He leaned closer to her. "You owe me nothing except getting your ass better and out of this place. Don't leave me alone with all this magic shit."

"Your mom—" Her eyes widened.

"Mom's okay. She's just worried about her found-daughter." With a smile, he wiped his eyes.

"I'll help you," she said. "With magic shit."

"Focus on getting better first."

"She's awake?" Nico charged into the room and rushed to the other side of the bed.

"Like literally ten minutes ago," Piper said, trailing behind him.

Taj squeezed her hand and stood. "He needs to see you more than I do." He hugged Piper and left the room.

Nico brushed her hair off her face, letting his hand linger as he kissed her forehead. Her trembling fingers reached for his hand. "I'm so... I'm just so sorry, oh my God," she choked through tears.

He closed his eyes and wiped away a tear as it ran along his cheek. "I need you to be okay. That's what we do now. Hear me?"

She bit her bottom lip, and her teeth broke through the chapped skin—the taste of blood touching her tongue. So much blood.

Danny returned, opening a folded flannel blanket and draped it over her. Heat seeped into her skin down to her flesh, calming the agitated shivering. "I'm here all evening and can answer questions if you have them, okay?" He eyed Nico and Piper. "I'll check in soon."

Hands rested on her feet, and she strained to lift her head. Nico pressed a button and the head of the bed lifted for her. Gray had overtaken the red in her father's beard, and his eyes were bloodshot and puffy. A fresh wave of tears cascaded down Drew's cheeks.

Piper patted Drew's leg and left the room, closing the door behind her.

"I'll give you some time." Nico's fingers slipped through hers, but with a trembling hand, she tightened her grip. She couldn't let him go.

"Stay, Nico." Gabe sat in the chair, scraping it along the floor until he could rest his elbows on the bed. "They don't know how you lived through that. The bullet... I can't." His eyes averted from hers. "Your friends told me about Celeste's boy, Taj? I don't know what goes on outside of *this* life, but I owe him. I owe him more than I'll ever have to give. Because..." He shook his head and his eyes met hers. "You're all I have in this world. I love you, kid. Losing you would break me, I won't survive it. I'm not leaving again."

"Love you, Dad," she whispered through her sore throat.

"I'm helping Jasper with the bakery—he'll come by later he said, and Henry's been at my place. He's a good dog, I like him."

A small smile cracked her dry lips and faded as she locked eyes with Nico. His gaze held a heartbreak that intertwined with her soul in a tangled web. Nick's message for Maria echoed in her mind. She tugged Nico's hand, trying to articulate through the tube in her throat. "Your mom..."

Nico crouched beside her. "She came to see you this morning, but she's staying with my aunt. They're planning Dad's funeral." Nico's jaw tightened, and he rose, glancing at Drew's father before facing away from them. His shoulders shook as he held a fist against his mouth. She tried to push herself up and get off the bed to go to him and hold him in her arms, but her body betrayed her, refusing to budge as excruciating pain shot through her.

"Don't try to get up." Her father pushed the chair back and got up. He crossed around the foot of the bed to where Nico stood. Placing his hands on Nico's shoulders, he pulled him into a tight hug as Nico cried.

Your dad loved you so much.

The weight of Nico's dad's last words lingered in her mind, his loss leaving an unmendable hole.

Her dad released Nico and kissed Drew's forehead. "I'll be right back." He nodded to Nico as he left the room and let the door click shut behind him.

Nico faced her. "I'm sorry—"

"For what? Come here."

"What are you doing?"

She pushed the blanket aside and placed her hand on the bed. "Lay with me."

He hesitated, eyeing her broken body. She didn't care about the stains of dried blood on the hospital shirt or the tube coming out of her most intimate part. This was life, real and raw.

"Are you sure?" He eyed the tube. "What if I pull something by mistake and hurt you?"

"You won't hurt me, and they'll fix it. I trust you." Her throat was sore from talking, and she patted the spot beside her on the bed.

He pressed his hands on the small hospital bed, and sat, shifting to look at her. "You sure you're okay?"

"The pain meds are kicking in." She swallowed, adjusting to the tube running down her throat.

Lifting his legs, he slowly settled on his side, facing her as she lay on her back. She held his hand, reaching with the other arm, attached to IV tubes, to grasp his arm.

"I don't want to hurt you," he said, resisting.

"Give me your arm."

As he extended his arm, she carefully guided it across until it found its place against her chest. She trailed her fingers over his skin and turned her head to gaze into his intense brown eyes, solidifying the magnetic connection pulsing between them. Somehow, they would have to get through this. "I've got you," she said.

He gripped her fingers tightly. "I've got you too."

Thirty-Six

"Do you need help in there?" Celeste called from the other side of the hospital bathroom door.

"I'm done." Maneuvering the IV pole out of the cramped bathroom, Drew opened the door and made her way back to the bed, her flip-flops shuffling against the floor, with Celeste's reassuring hold on her arm.

Three days had passed, and her body worked at healing itself with slow progress. She never expected doctors and nurses to give her such high praise for simply walking or urinating on her own without a catheter. Her throat had been tender since they removed the nose tube draining fluid from her abdomen, and her incision remained raw and painful, with frequent gauze changes. But she'd started eating again, and her body held itself together. She went through the daily motions with the doctors and nurses, answering their questions about passing gas and following their instructions to take deep breaths as they poked and prodded.

If only my mind could heal as fast.

Nighttime was different. When night fell, the nightmares and gnawing sadness consumed her. And Nico tried so hard to keep it together every time he entered the hospital room, but he was falling apart. How could he not be? She would do anything to get out of the hospital and be home for Nick's funeral. But what she wasn't telling him, what she held deep inside, was the constant fear the monster would return. Flashbacks of dying hit her at random moments, stealing her breath all over again and terror sent blood rushing to her head, its dizzying grip forcing her to focus on anything tangible she could grasp. If not for Ori and Taj, she would have died. What if death sought her again? How many times could someone survive being shot in their lifetime before their luck ran out?

Celeste wheeled the IV pole to the head of the bed as Drew sat on the edge, letting her feet dangle. "Thanks for coming, but who's watching the store?"

"I took a personal time this morning."

"You don't get personal time when you own a business." Stabbing pain shot through her torso. "Ouch, fuck." She clutched her stomach and glanced up at Celeste. "Sorry."

"I've heard worse, Drew." Celeste smiled and grabbed a brush and set to work untangling Drew's wet hair, section by section. "Actually, your father took me for breakfast."

"My dad? Really? I didn't know you two knew each other."

"We didn't until this happened." With precise fingers, Celeste pulled at a knot in Drew's hair. "He was sweet, just wanted to say thank you, that's all. He's worried about you."

The constant tugging on her scalp didn't bother her—she was just grateful to have clean hair. "I know he is, but I'll be fine. How's Taj?"

"He's okay, you know, trying to process things." Celeste stopped moving the brush through Drew's hair. "I never wanted this for him. I did everything to keep this life away a long time ago."

"What do you mean?"

"There's an old spell I used when he was little, and I thought it worked. He never showed signs of magic, no interest."

"A *spell*?" Drew reached for Celeste's wrist, taking the brush from her and placing it on the side table.

Celeste fluffed Drew's hair with her fingers before sitting beside her on the hospital bed. "It's like a barrier, keeps the child from inheriting the magic from the closest generation. Clearly, it wears off."

She couldn't remember a time she didn't see the dead, but Gran had acted like she'd never known about Drew's gift. Had she used a spell and assumed it had worked? "Did you ever tell him about it?"

"Not until that first night at the hospital when they brought you in on death's door. We waited hours while you were in surgery." Celeste shifted her gaze and dabbed her eyes with her fingertips. "Your life was hanging by a thread, and he told me what happened. Everyone in that lighthouse saw you die and come back to life too long after a reasonable amount of time, if you know what I'm saying."

Drew's memory had gone fuzzy beyond being carried out of the lighthouse in the pouring rain in Nico's arms. "I saw the other side."

Celeste angled her head back and narrowed her gaze at Drew. "What did you see?"

"I was with Ori, and it was beautiful." She wished Ori could be with her now. He had a way of calming the storm spiraling inside her. "But it changed, and I was back there, watching them try to revive me. I saw my body, and Taj came... and the light surrounded us. He brought me back from the dead. That's what your son did for me. I'll never be able to repay him."

Celeste blinked fast, wiping tears as they fell. "I didn't realize you'd crossed through the veil."

"It was warm and beautiful, and I wasn't scared, but that's not what worries me. I took a life, Celeste. Dominic Sloan is *dead* because of me."

"That's not what I heard. He had a heart attack and fell to his death."

"You don't believe that."

Celeste shrugged. "That man deserved what happened to him. It was him or you, Nico, Shane, and Lord knows anyone else who was there that night. Good riddance."

"But I used magic for harm—"

"Absolutely not." Celeste embraced her, wrapping her in a comforting embrace.

Drew took a deep breath, savoring the delicate floral fragrance of her perfume, a welcome contrast to the sterile hospital smells of bleach and cafeteria food.

Releasing her, Celeste tilted her head to the side, her silk headband shimmering under the fluorescent lights. "You saved people, including yourself, from harm."

"What if he comes back?"

"Have you seen him?" Celeste scanned the hospital room.

"No, do you think I will? What should I do?"

"We cross that bridge if... *if* that happens, but it won't. That man is gone."

She'd lived in fear for too long. She had to let it go. Dominic Sloan had committed murders, and he was dead.

But I murdered someone too. What does that make me?

She closed her eyes and shifted her thoughts to Nico and recovering enough to get out of the hospital as she hugged Celeste. Her entire torso throbbed with pain, and she could swear something was oozing from somewhere, but she squeezed tighter. She loved this woman like a mother. "I love you, Celeste. Thanks for being here."

Celeste rubbed Drew's back. "Always, child. Always."

A rhythmic tapping on the door interrupted the moment and a stalky man with a shiny bald head and wild hair on each side walked in, thumbing through a chart and grabbing a pen from his lab coat pocket. "Harlow. Yes, of course." He glanced up at her and removed his glasses, hooking them onto the neckline of his shirt.

"That's my cue, honey. Time to cut this personal day short, but I won't be far. Call me if you need anything." Celeste grabbed her purse, nodding to the doctor on her way out.

"There are people waiting to see you, so I'll keep this short," he said.

People came and went all day long, keeping her thoughts from diving into despair. But when darkness fell, it was different, very different. Eerie and unsettling. "When can I go home?"

The doctor cleared his throat and tapped the pen over the chart. His eyebrows moved as he read, matching the tufts of hair on each side of his head. "This isn't your first gunshot wound, I see. I'll be honest with you, given the wounds you came in with, it's a miracle you're alive."

I'm all too aware.

Before her fear spun out of control again, she forced a deep inhale, trying to steady her breathing. "I really just need to get back home."

With a compassionate expression, he tore his eyes away from the chart and turned his attention to her. "I'm signing off on your discharge for tomorrow. It's a small town, everyone knows everybody, and I know you have a funeral to attend. Physically? You'll heal. You are healing, you beat the medical odds. I'm more concerned about your mental health. This man—I refuse to say his name—the violence he's inflicted on you and good people in this town is more than a human should endure over the course of a lifetime, and yet here you are, barely twenty." He reached into his pocket and handed her a pamphlet with a business card stapled to it. "She specializes in trauma, PTSD, anxiety, and I cannot let you leave my care without recommending someone to talk to."

Drew chewed her lip, her fingers trembling as she took the pamphlet. The same therapist she'd seen the last time. The logo on the front displayed rays of sunlight through dark clouds.

How could she tell this woman she'd killed the man who'd shot her with magic? The man who had terrorized her family was dead by her own hands, and with all her superhuman power, she still couldn't save Nico's father in the crossfire. "Thank you." With the doctor watching her in silence, it was the only response that came to her mind.

He stood, tucking the pen in his chest pocket and the chart under his arm. "We'll take out the IV today, get you prescriptions for pain to take home, and follow-up appointments—the staples should be good to come out next week." He paused and looked around the room, his gaze falling on a clear plastic bag in the corner with the blue dress stuffed inside. The dress soaked with her blood.

A shiver crawled down her spine, and she pulled the blanket over her legs as he continued. "I knew your grandmother. A generous, kind woman. Do you have someone to help you at home now? I want to be sure you have support, especially for the next four to six weeks. If not, I can arrange—"

"I won't be alone. I'll figure it out."

He exchanged discharge information with a nurse as she came in and completed an assessment and vitals, and they both exited the room, leaving the door open. Hushed chatter escaped from the nurse's station, and someone mopped the floor in the hallway, sending a strong smell of bleach wafting in. Dull throbbing extended from her wound, reaching her back and traveling down her legs.

She lifted her legs onto the bed, clinging to the sheet as she lay back. Loneliness crept inside her chest like a hollow ache and her eyes burned as she directed her attention to the single window in the room. Sunshine beamed into the small room in stark contrast to the stone gray inside her head. Her phone buzzed, and she tried to reach it from its perch on the side table, but her fingers sent it flying across the floor. She sat up too fast and recoiled as pain shot through her like Sloan's bullet hitting her all over again.

She lost the battle against her tears, and they stung her cheeks. Collapsing back on the bed, she clutched a hand on her torso to keep it from coming apart. If no one was around to hear, she would unleash a scream of such magnitude that it would strip her of her ability to speak.

Thirty-Seven

Shane strode into her hospital room, retrieved her phone, and handed it to her. Sliding a chair beside the bed, he took a seat and rested his elbows on the armrests. As his somber expression deepened, his once bright blue eyes faded to a shade of gray. "I had to see you. I'm going out of my mind."

She closed her eyes, and the tears pooling coursed down her cheeks. "You and me both."

"I'm training to be an EMT, but it doesn't take an expert to see that you *died*. You were dead for too long to come back. I thought it was all over, and I keep seeing your face, pale and gray, and the blood." Shane paused and sighed. "Look, I'm sorry for bringing that up, this isn't about me, I just... I don't know what to say or do. I still don't. And now funerals are being planned."

"Funerals?" she choked through tears.

"Claudia and her mom got stuck planning a burial, nothing more, but I'm not going. We all know you did us a favor."

"What do you mean?"

Shane leaned forward and lowered his voice. "Oh come on, he didn't just fall over the railing, he was pushed with some freak force that came out of you."

"He was going kill me." Her breath hitched, and she swallowed, struggling for enough saliva to soothe her dry throat.

"Of course he was. I just wish I'd been the one to do it. I tried to get the gun he knocked out of Nick's hand before he kicked it over the edge. I don't get it, why not take the money and leave? His obsession with that damn lighthouse." He shook his head. "Maybe none of this would've happened if Nico and I hadn't followed his father."

More secrets. She was unaware that Nico and Shane had followed his father; Nico hadn't said a word about it. He never wanted her involved any more than she wanted him to know about Sloan's invasion inside the bakery.

"When did you follow Nico's dad? Where?"

"None of it matters now, so I'm just going to tell you. The asshole hid bags of money in the tunnels underneath the house out there, they had to be there for over a year, since before he went to prison. Imagine if we'd known that piece of information. Nico overheard his dad on the phone and found out he was going to Neptune Point while half the town was at the party." Shane sat back against the seat and glanced toward the door before continuing. "We both agreed to keep you out of it... he didn't want you going to that party, but as soon as he was sure you wouldn't leave, we took off out there expecting to find Nick and maybe another guy, not Sloan. We thought they were getting the money to meet Sloan somewhere... The plan was to call the police when we got the information. And then shit went down. It all went wrong."

The screen shots on Nico's phone had warned them of the day, and now the media headlines called it the perfect storm for a killer. No one expected the storm to cause so much damage, but no one had ever expected Sloan's return to Atlas Cliffs. He was supposed to rot in prison forever.

Her phone buzzed again, and she wiped her eyes to read Nico's messages. He was late, but he'd be there as soon as he could.

Her fingers fumbled over the screen as she texted him back, letting him know not to hurry. He'd already spent so much time with her in the hospital, and his family needed him.

Shane folded his hands together and bounced his knees as he sat. "Nico?"

"He's running late."

"If it weren't for Nick DeSarro sacrificing his own life, it'd be Nico's funeral."

She snapped her head to the side and glared at him the best she could with her head fuzzy from the latest dose of pain medication. "Do you think I don't know that? I wasn't fast enough to save him. I've got magic in my body, and I couldn't save him."

Shane exhaled through pursed lips. "And I'm an asshole."

"I killed someone and I'm not sad about it, so maybe I'm the asshole. I was ready for him, I had him, I wanted to do it, to make him pay for every horrible thing he ever did. I hesitated and Nico's dad is gone—" Her chest heaved as she struggled to catch her breath, tears streaming down her face.

Shane grasped her hand. Her initial reaction was to pull her hand away, but the pained expression etched on his face stopped her. He lowered his voice. "I thought I'd never see you again, never talk to you again."

"I wish I knew what to say, Shane. I can't think straight, and this is all just too much—"

"You don't have to say anything." He tilted his head to the side. "Nico would be as good as dead if you'd died that night. I saw it all over him. As much as I wish you loved me like you do him, I don't want a life without you in it. If all we are is friends, I can live with that."

She let her head flop back against the pillow. "We already tried that; it doesn't work."

"Well, maybe shit has changed."

It sure has.

He released her hand and sat back in the chair again. "You know how many times I wonder if Dominic Sloan never came into our lives, never killed my mom, never stole time from me, from us, would we have made it?"

She didn't have to wonder. The one person her thoughts gravitated to was the one who dominated her heart, and that person was never Shane. "Fate would've stepped in."

"You believe in all that?"

"I didn't use to, but shit has changed."

"It sure has," he said with a sad smile. He folded his hands over his chest, and his knees resumed their rhythmic bouncing.

Nico stepped into the room, his eyes shifting from Drew to Shane. He ran a hand through his damp hair. His brown eyes had lost their light, and shadows cast a tired look beneath them.

Shane moved to get up from the chair, but Nico stopped him with a hand gesture. "It's okay."

Drew supported herself with her elbows and threw the blanket off her legs to get up. Pain moved with her, and she clenched her fists and flinched. Shane gripped the armrests, and Nico stepped closer.

"Don't help me, I can do this. I *have* to do this if I'm going home tomorrow."

"Are you sure that's a good idea—"

"It's the best idea. The best." She held the bed, letting her socked feet touch the floor as she stood. Shane rose from the chair, exchanging a look with Nico.

"Stop looking at me like that. I'm healing, the doctor even said so. And the pain is better." She gasped and held her breath as another wave of burning pain sank into her abdomen.

"I can see that," Nico said drily.

She reached behind her, feeling for the ties of the hospital shirt to make sure her ass wasn't on display, but Celeste had tied the ties to perfection. Nico approached, his hands ready to catch her, but she steadied herself, wrapping her arms around his waist. "Is there anything I can do?" Her gaze met his as he lifted a wet strand of her hair.

"You got to wash your hair." A small smile softened his desperately sad eyes.

"Celeste came."

"I'm gonna go and let you two do whatever it is you two do." Shane headed for the door, and she released her hands from Nico as a pang of guilt swept through her. Perhaps it was guilt for not helping him enough, or for saying the wrong things to him, or not forgiving him fast enough to be his friend. She didn't know why she ached for Shane, but she did. "Shane?"

He halted with a slow pivot. Rolling the IV pole, she scuffled toward him and wrapped her arms around him in a hug.

His body relaxed, and his arms tightened around her back. "I'm glad you're still here."

"I am too." She let him go, and he opened the door to leave. "If you still want to do the friendship thing, I'm in," she said.

"Friendship sounds good." He glanced at Nico, who had settled into a chair, engrossed in his phone.

She knew better. Nico might appear unfazed, and he would never try to control her or who she was friends with, but he'd be listening to every word between her and Shane. If his ex-girlfriend, Nicki, was the one standing in this room, Drew would respond in the same way.

Except shit has changed.

Nico dropped his phone to his lap as she made her way back to the bed. The display on his screen revealed a list of apartments in town. He was searching for a place to live. He gripped the arms of the chair like he was about to stand. "You sure you don't need my help?"

"Dead sure."

"Too soon, Drew."

Her cheeks flushed. "I'm so sorry."

"That was my lame attempt at acting like everything's okay, but it doesn't feel like I'll ever be okay again."

She sat on the edge of the bed. "We're going to get through this together."

"I'm betting on it." Rising from his seat, he leaned down in front of her, his hands cradling her face. Their eyes locked, and she grasped his wrists, feeling the strong pulse beneath her touch. Her heart rate quickened, reassuring her it still pumped life through her veins.

She hadn't kissed Nico in days or held him the way she wanted to. Desire to be close to him consumed her—to wrap herself up in him so he could chase away her pain, easing his grief in return. She wanted to pull him over her, letting the weight of his body push her into the mattress and crush her in warmth and love, escaping the hell they were living. His mouth found hers and her lips moved with his. Her hands moved around his neck, and he kissed her deeper. A wince escaped her lips between them, and he tore himself away. "Did I hurt you?"

"No, it's not you."

He sat beside her. "Maybe you shouldn't rush to go home tomorrow. Give it a couple more days—"

She took his hand in her lap, interlacing her fingers with his. "I'm going home tomorrow, and I'm going to be by your side for your dad's funeral. I promise you I'm good. I'm alive, healing more every day... Dad's around to help, so is Jasper.

Nothing to worry about." She pulled on the hideous hospital shirt. "Did you bring clothes?"

"Piper wouldn't let me. She texted from your bedroom and said she was taking care of it."

"Probably a good idea."

He stretched his legs out and crossed his feet at his ankles. "She told me you were having nightmares."

Drew fought off a wince. She hadn't wanted Nico to know. "They'll pass." Unless she had exceeded the trauma threshold and it had permanently shattered her.

"You can talk to me about stuff. I'm not as fragile as you think." He lifted her hand from her lap and traced a finger over her skin. "No more secrets, remember?".

Her chest tightened. He had kept his share of secrets from her. "Why didn't you tell me about you and Shane planning to follow your dad the night of the party?"

Releasing her hand, he folded his arms across his chest, his gaze locked onto hers. "Why didn't you tell me he showed up at the bakery?"

She clenched her lip between her teeth. "He threatened to kill you. He threatened all of you if I didn't keep you out of his way."

Nico exhaled and his hands dropped to his lap. "I just need for us to be *us* still, somehow. The, you and I who trust each other and maybe we disagree, but we talk, and we figure shit out. It's the one normal thing I've got right now."

She raised her eyebrows. "This is normal?"

"It is to me."

She curled the corner of the blanket in her fingers. "The nightmares... I see his face, and it's scary, and I feel like I'm dying again. But I hate telling you about it because of everything you're going through."

He wrapped his arm around her. "Want me to stay tonight? They won't say anything—"

"No, I'll be all right. Someone comes in every hour anyway." The memory of Sloan's sinister smile and the glint of his gun played over and over in her mind, and she fought to suppress it. "What about Henry? Is he okay?"

"He's awesome, because of Gabe. He stepped in and just started helping with stuff at the garage, fixing cars, the books, you name it, he's doing it."

"My dad? How?" He visited her every day, but never mentioned a word about taking on any responsibilities beyond Henry, the house, and the bakery.

"He's just *there* a lot, but it's been good. I don't know how I'd keep it going without him."

"I just assumed he was getting ready to head back on a boat somewhere." He'd always devoted himself to constant preparation for his next trip out to sea.

"If he's got plans to go, he sure hasn't mentioned it to me." Nico dropped his arm from her shoulders.

"Is my dad qualified to work on cars?"

Nico smiled. "Yup. That's what I said when he offered to help. He told me he started on cars before switching to marine engineering... He's just doing the work."

What else did she not know about her father?

"And he's taking care of Henry every day?"

"It's a group effort, so you might not have a dog to go home to," Nico said. "Henry is like the extended family dog now, a therapy dog. We should get him one of those vests."

She glanced up at him. "Can we do that?"

"I don't know." He leaned back and reached into the pocket of his jeans. "I meant to give these back to you sooner."

He handed her the amulet, and she held it in her hands before draping the silver chain over her head. "Where's the butterfly?"

"Turn around." He held the delicate chain with the butterfly pendant, letting it dangle along her neck.

Moving her hair aside, he fastened the clasp. A shiver trailed down her back as his fingers grazed her neck. The amulet mingled with the butterfly again, exactly where it belonged, like a small piece of herself had returned. She turned back to face him. "Thank you."

Taking her hand in his, he traced his thumb back and forth over it, his gaze on his feet. "It doesn't feel real yet. I just miss him so much it hurts, and I'm pissed at myself for leaving things the way I did. If I didn't go out there... He died because of me."

"He died to save you."

He raised his head and blinked his dark lashes as he gazed at her. His lip quivered and he bit down on it. "What did you see, when you were gone?"

"Everything." She told him about Ori and how she found her way back into her body.

"Do you remember what Dad said to you?"

"I'll never forget it. He hugged you." As she repeated Nico's dad's words, his voice echoed in her ears. "'Take care of each other. I love you both. Tell Maria it's always been her. I can't remember a time I didn't love that woman.'"

"And he isn't stuck here?" Nico's eyes widened with hope.

"No. But it's good when they're not stuck. It means they're okay, you know? At peace. And he isn't alone. Ori helped him cross over."

The faint whispers of Nick DeSarro's words lingered in her thoughts. *You have the key to the safe. Everything you need will be in there. You're not your family's mistakes. The cycle ends here.*

"Do you still have the key?"

The timing didn't feel right, so she kept the last part to herself, unsure of why she held back. Maybe because she hadn't processed Nick's words herself. Ori's death by her own mother still haunted her, and she was desperate to sever the ties binding her to Joelle.

He held up the silver key dangling from his key chain. "Right here."

"It's for a safe. Your dad wanted you to know that everything you need will be in there."

"The safe in his office is the only safe I know of." Not letting go of her hand, Nico rubbed his face with his other hand. "You think he'll ever come back?"

"If he does, I promise I'll bring him to you."

They rarely came back, but Jules had appeared to warn her, and Enid had been there when Celeste burned down the old Keeper's house. Gran hadn't been a stranger to her, either. Drew had crossed over, but still didn't know all the secrets to the other side.

Thirty-Eight

With a skilled touch, a nurse removed the IV tube from Drew's arm. Rubbing the taped, gauze-covered spot, Drew enjoyed the liberation of being freed from the medication leash—one step closer to going home. Nico moved from his place near the window to sit in the chair beside her bed.

Piper scooted through the door as the nurse rolled the pole out of the room, the remnants swaying from the hooks. "If I'm interrupting, tell me to go away."

"Did you bring clean clothes?" Drew asked.

Piper opened the door wide enough to step in and hold up a duffel bag. "Of course. I did a load of laundry and brought you comfy clothes for tomorrow. Do you have room for three more? We've got to be quick while the nurses are busy switching shifts, or they'll kick us all out." She swung the door all the way open, and Jasper walked in with Claudia, Shane trailing behind her.

With a box perched in one hand, Jasper gave her a gentle squeeze with the other. "Since you can eat real food again, I come bearing gifts. I left a box at the nurse's station, but these"—he opened the box revealing cookies frosted with *you're one tough cookie* on the top—"are for you."

Drew took a cookie and sat back, raising the head of the bed. The sweet frosting awakened her dulled tastebuds as she bit into the soft dough, reminding her of happier times with Gran at the Tough Cookie.

Claudia hung back, quiet, as she eyed Drew and gawked around the small room. Her gaze landed on the dress in the bag. "You still have the dress?" She picked up the clear plastic with both hands and turned it over. Shane threw daggers at her with his eyes and crossed his arms.

After everything that had happened, and not one visit, the dress was the first thing Claudia focused on?

"It's covered in blood. I'll pay you back for it." Drew's stomach tightened, rejecting the cookie. The memory of the deafening gunshot boom and Sloan's scream echoed in her ears, sending burning pain through her, and she clutched the edge of the bed.

"Really, Claudia?" Piper plopped the duffel bag at Drew's feet and glared at Claudia.

"Jesus." Nico stood and approached Claudia. "Give it to me. I'll burn it and give you every cent back." A muscle twitched along his jaw as he held his hand out.

Claudia gripped the bag tighter. "I lost my father too." Tears filled her voice.

As he stood in front of her, Nico's face reddened. "Your father was a monster who murdered your boyfriend's sister, Shane's mother, his own brother and sister, my dad, and if it weren't for Taj, we'd be burying Drew this week, too."

"If he's a monster, what does that make me and Shane?" Claudia's lips quivered as she talked. "Or what about you, Drew? We all saw what you did, and it sure didn't look human."

"What about Drew?" Piper's fists clenched at her sides as she moved toward Claudia.

Shane took the bag from Claudia and tossed it to the floor. "Why are you doing this? That asshole didn't give a shit about you or anyone. We need to leave."

Exerting all her strength, Drew sat up, swinging her legs over the bed, and stood, gripping the rail for support. The room fell silent, all eyes fixed on her. She stood tall, trying to project bravery and resilience, despite the damage lingering deep inside. "You're right, I killed your father. And my mother hit someone with her car and took off, leaving him to die. Does that make me a monster? Like him? Like her?" Tears streamed down her cheeks, relieving the lump in her throat. She covered her mouth as Jasper sank into a chair, holding his face in his hands. "I'm so sorry, J. I didn't mean—"

He lifted his hand. "Don't, I get it."

"I don't know what you are. A *witch*?" Claudia's face was inches away from Drew, her eyes glistening with unshed tears as she wrung her trembling hands against her stomach.

"Shane's right, you need to leave." With a gentle nudge, Nico moved in between Claudia and Drew.

"No, it's okay," Drew said. Claudia's lashing out had nothing to do with her and everything to do with a profound rage toward her inhumane father. If pushed aside long enough, heartache festered until it spread, no matter who caused it, and Claudia's had just ruptured to the surface.

A few tears slipped out of Claudia's eyes and down her red cheeks, and she sniffed, wiping her nose with the back of her hand. She stepped back and folded her arms across her chest. "Am I a monster because I have his DNA in my body? Is Shane? What part of him do we have?"

"I am nothing like him," Shane said through gritted teeth, "and neither are you."

The solemn faces in the small hospital room observed Drew as she took a deep breath and held the bed rail. If she'd never felt the deep searing pain of grief and heartache, she might lash back, defensive. But Claudia was just voicing the shattered fear and anger Drew had observed in Nico, Shane, and everyone who witnessed the horror that unfolded in the lighthouse that night.

We're all broken pieces of our fucked-up families.

Nick DeSarro's serene face as he left her and crossed beyond the veil with Ori to whatever paradise awaited filled her mind, and his last words echoed in her mind again. "We are not our family's mistakes. The cycle ends here, with us. We're not *monsters*, we're good people, we try. That's what matters, right? Claudia, you're kind and generous, and *nothing* like him. You hear me? Nothing like him." The lump grew back, and she blinked away more tears pooling in her eyes.

Claudia's face crumpled, and she fell apart, her body shaking uncontrollably as she wept. Letting go of the bed rail, Drew embraced her, and she buried her face against Drew's chest. A visceral, stabbing pain bit down across Drew's abdomen and she flinched. Claudia pulled back, wiping her eyes. "Oh my God, your stomach, your fucking gunshot, what did I do—"

"You didn't do anything." Drew pressed her arm over her stomach and gave her a reassuring smile.

Nico handed Claudia tissues, and she blew her nose. "I hate him," she said between snorts.

"I do too." Shane looked at Nico. "And I'm sorry this happened to you, to your family."

Nico nodded. "Me too. I just don't really know where to go from here."

"We'll help you get through it." Claudia sniffed as the tears started again. "We all just have to get through it."

Reaching for him, Drew squeezed his hand as she yanked tissues from the box with the other to dab her eyes and wipe her running nose.

Jasper reached for the box, his face blotchy. "Pass that over here, please."

"Jesus Christ," Piper chimed in through sobs. Colliding with Claudia's back, she wrapped her arms around her. "You drive me nuts, but you'll never be like him. You're one of us."

Claudia's tearful eyes widened as she glanced behind her and patted Piper's hands. "I never thought I'd see the day you'd hug me."

Piper let her go, straightening her back and smoothing her pink-haired ponytail. "Hell must've frozen over."

The bag with the bloody dress sat on the floor where Shane had tossed it.

"I'm burning that dress, but I will pay you for it." Drew collapsed back on the bed, cursing the relentless throbbing pain as she tucked her feet in the bunched-up blanket. Nico pulled it over her, crouching beside the bed as Danny opened the door like a burst of sunshine decked in scrubs. With a tiny paper cup in one hand and a plastic cup filled with water, ice, and a bendy straw in the other, he walked up to Drew.

"Just thought I'd come in and let you all know visiting hours are over before someone else beats me to it. Voices carry through doors around here, and I had to tell them you were all beloved family members, just catching up before they sent security in." Danny stopped in his tracks and scanned their faces. "All that is wild and free, what did I just miss?" Placing the water filled cup on a bedside tray, he took Drew's wrist and checked her hospital bracelet before handing her the tiny paper cup containing two pills. "Pain meds time," he said. "Thanks for bringing treats, J. You're making a name for yourself around here." With a smile on his face, he leaned in towards Jasper, their lips meeting in an affectionate kiss.

Jasper had found his match with Danny. She should've told Ori Jasper was okay, but maybe Ori already knew.

Claudia leaned down with caution and hugged Drew. "Thank you for not hating me."

"Never." Drew hugged her back.

"You ready, Shane?" Claudia pulled a compact mirror from her small purse hanging off her shoulder. It could be an expensive brand name, but if someone offered Drew a million dollars to name it, she'd walk away with nothing. Wiping mascara from under her eyes with her fingers, Claudia made a face. "Straight home, Shane. I'm a mess."

"I have nowhere to be," he said.

"Where's Leah been hiding out?" Piper asked the question crossing Drew's mind, but she hadn't wanted to bring it up.

Drew had assumed Leah had gone back home, and it didn't matter to her either way. Her response to Shane's betrayal had shifted away from the hurt to indifference.

Shit has changed.

Shane stood halfway between the hallway and the room. "She's back at my place—well, mine until Claudia takes it back or rents it out."

"Stay as long as you want, I'm not kicking you out. At least we haven't scared her away yet." Claudia reached into her purse and grabbed a set of keys with a heart-shaped keychain. She eyed Nico before turning to leave. "We'll be at your dad's funeral. Let me know if I can help with anything." Giving Shane's arm a tug, she led him into the hallway.

Drew twisted her wavy, red hair to the side as Danny straightened out the blankets and adjusted her pillows. "I'll come back for your vitals. Can I bring you toast or something?"

"No, I'm good." Her eyes grew heavy, and her head was fuzzy with exhaustion.

Jasper got up and brushed the hair from her eyes. "Your dad's bringing you home tomorrow, right?"

She nodded as a rush of weariness swept over her.

Following Danny out of the room, Jasper glanced over his shoulder. "I'll see you at home." He grinned. "That feels damn good to say."

Piper plopped into the chair on one side of Drew, and Nico settled into the chair opposite. Piper tilted her head back and exhaled through her lips. "Nico, go home and do what you gotta do. I can stay for a while."

"You don't need to. I'll stay."

Drew turned her head to the side to face him. "Go home and be with your mom and brother. One more sleep and I'm out of here. I'm good, I promise."

With hesitation, he kissed her goodbye and left her side, shutting the hospital room door behind him.

Piper stretched her legs out, propping her feet up on the bed, and Drew pressed a button on the side to lower the head of the bed. "Can I ask you something and you tell me honestly what you think?"

"This sounds good, and yes, when have I not given you complete honesty?" Piper said.

"That's one of the million reasons we're friends."

"Spill it. What deep secret is brewing in your red head?"

"Nico."

Piper scrunched her face. "Nico?" Her eyes grew wide. "Don't you dare break up with him again—"

"No, God no. The opposite, sort of."

Sliding her feet off the bed, Piper pulled the chair close. "I'm listening, but does this rhyme with carriage?"

"Absolutely not. I don't need a piece of paper to tell me who I'm committed to, or who I love. Maybe someday, but not yet, anyway." She chewed her lip and toyed with the edge of the bedsheet. "Nico's mom has to be out of the house at the end of the month and he's been looking for an apartment, but I'm thinking I might ask him if he wants to move in."

"Live with you in your house, together?" A smile spread across Piper's face.

"Is it too soon? I'm not even twenty yet. I shouldn't, should I? But why do I want to?"

"Because you love him, that's why. And, okay, sure, you're young, but so what? You're also technically adults now, and you've been through a hell of a lot more shit than most grown ass people." Piper flopped back in the chair and folded her hands across her chest, tapping her thumbs together. "Let me ask you a question, and you answer without thinking. I know this is a stretch for you, but you've got this."

"Gee, thanks for the vote of confidence."

"It's what I do," Piper said. "Ready?"

Drew braced herself for Piper's big question. "Ready."

"Kick the bullshit out of your mind."

"Consider it sort of kicked."

"Drew Harlow. My bestie. Nico's about to have no place to live and he wouldn't dare ask his girlfriend who he loves, because the guy is too used to taking care of everything on his own—by the way, remind you of anyone?"

"Is this your big question?"

Piper sat up and leaned forward, inches from Drew. "You meet your future self, years, maybe decades from now. Who is your partner?"

"Nico." No hesitation in her mind, but who knew what the future held? No one could guarantee anything, not even her. A witch with magic. It didn't take long for her overthinking brain to resurface.

"You have your answer." Piper brushed her legs with her hands in a grand gesture. "My work here is done."

"That's not an answer. I don't know where my future self will be. She might be dead at this rate."

Piper's face turned serious. "Don't even go there. Do what your heart wants, your mind can catch up later. What are you waiting for? Some magic age to determine if you're old enough for love? If things change, adjust. But for now, do what your heart wants."

"Who does your heart want?" Drew yawned, her eyelids getting heavier.

"I've got what I want, Taj. And I'm happy. If that changes, I'll deal with it. And turns out he's got magical hands." Piper burst out into a fit of giggles.

Drew laughed with her, defenseless against Piper's contagious laugh. She held a pillow against her sore torso and took deep breaths as her eyes watered.

Piper wiped her eyes and covered her mouth. "I'm so sorry. I shouldn't be laughing in a time like this, but if I don't laugh, I might bawl my eyes out."

Silence filled the room as they regained composure. Drew's body succumbed to sleepiness and her arms and legs weighed heavy against the bed.

Piper stood and tucked her phone in her pocket. "I should let you get some sleep, but I'm happy you're going home tomorrow. I can imagine how awful this is with Nico's dad gone, and so much has happened, but if I lost you that night, it'd be like a piece of me was ripped out, you know?" This time, the tears filling Piper's eyes weren't from laughing.

"I know." A tear escaped and slid down the side of Drew's face.

Bending over the bed, Piper extended her arms, wrapping them around Drew. Embracing her back, Drew squeezed as hard as her tired arms could. Piper was her family, and she didn't know what she'd do without her, either.

Opening the door to leave, Piper glanced over her shoulder. "Don't forget, do—"

"What my heart wants."

My heart wants to be with Nico and make plans with him, future stuff.

Alone in the hospital room for one more night, Drew let her eyes fall shut. As she drifted into a restless sleep, the chatter from the hallway faded into the distance.

Darkness swept around her like the waves at Neptune Point. Water covered her feet, rushing around her calves. She lifted the cascading layers of dress to her waist. The dress transformed her into a graceful woman of power, like Aurora. She couldn't let the water touch it and ruin the beautiful fabric. Ascending the winding stairs, she ran her fingers along the cement wall, stopping at an oval window. The sea raged, surging toward the lighthouse and slamming into the sides. She stumbled backward, gripping the railing as her upper body leaned over and she stared down into the dark abyss at the bottom, lightened only by the white-water flooding over the floor. Screams tore out from above, and the dress slipped through her fingers as she ran up the staircase. A deafening boom followed by screams echoed over the howling wind at the top.

Her own scream wretched from her soul into the night air as she reached the top. Dominic Sloan towered over Nico's lifeless body. He threw his head back and laughed before flames consumed him.

Bolting upright, crying and gasping for air to fill her empty lungs, Drew brushed damp strands of sweat-soaked hair off her face. She squinted in the dark void around her to get her bearings.

I'm in the hospital. It was just a dream.

"It's a shame you didn't die." The deep grinding voice pierced the silence.

Fumbling in the darkness and shaking uncontrollably, she found the metal chain above her head. As she pulled it to turn on the overhead light, a sharp twinge of pain shot through her, and she cradled her stomach. But she'd know that voice anywhere.

Terror clamped down on her chest as icy air curled in puffs of mist with every shallow breath in front of her. "Who's here?"

It's him. He's back.

Saying his name would bring the nightmare to life, intensifying the horror. Her fingernails dug into her skin, leaving behind a physical reminder of the undeniable truth. She was awake and the voice she heard belonged to him.

"You can't get rid of me that easily, Miss Harlow." Dominic Sloan swirled into existence as he appeared in front of the window.

Thirty-Nine

Drew squished the bloodied dress wrapped in the plastic bag into the duffel bag and zipped it up. If she never looked at it again, it would be too soon. She had never been so happy to trade in her hospital wear for actual clothing. Piper knew what she was doing when she'd packed an oversized V-neck t-shirt and shorts with an elastic waist.

As she perched on the edge of the bed, she attempted to remove the hospital bracelet, but it wouldn't tear and was too tight to pull over her hand. She ripped the tape and gauze off the IV site and tossed it in the trash can.

I need to get out of this place.

Sloan had returned, and unless she did something, he would continue to torment her forever. Lifting the amulet, she untangled the butterfly pendant from the chain. The black jewel exuded an unsettling stillness, and she shook it, trying to wake it up, but nothing happened.

This wouldn't be the same as helping the dead make peace and cross over. Getting rid of Sloan would require a certain set of banishing-a-witch-hunter skill, and neither the amulet nor her body were cooperating.

As the ceiling creaked, cool air rushed into the room, covering her arms in goosebumps. Where was he hiding? She should've known he would come back from the dead to haunt her. He would take pleasure in torturing her.

Nico pushed a wheelchair into the room. "Are you ready?"

"I don't need that."

"The nurse told me you needed it." He pushed it closer. "Think of it this way, it'll just get us out of here faster." He tapped the seat. "I don't have the energy to argue. I can carry you if you—"

"Too soon, Nico." The last time he carried her, she was bleeding to death. But with his father's funeral tomorrow, she refused to drain an ounce of whatever energy he had left. She plopped her ass in the seat and slid the bag onto her lap.

"Do you have everything? Prescription?"

She shook a white paper bag, and the bottle rattled inside. "The hospital pharmacy filled it."

"Your dad signed everything. He's pulling the truck up to the front doors." He pushed her into the hallway and looked back, scanning the room. "You sure you're not leaving anything behind?"

I wish I was leaving someone behind.

"I've got everything I need."

Sloan's return from the dead was on the tip of her tongue, but she held back from him. Damn the secrets she couldn't bring herself to say.

Grabbing the duffel bag with one hand, Nico helped her out of the chair with the other. He folded it up and left it with the others in the lobby as she stepped through the automatic glass doors. She squinted against the intense brightness of the sunlight. The warmth enveloped her; the oppressive humidity had subsided, and a gentle breeze tickled her skin.

The calm after the storm. If they only knew it wasn't over yet.

Her father rushed to her side and opened the passenger door to the large cab, settling her in the front as Nico took the back. He stretched the seatbelt across her chest, and she touched his hand. "Dad, I can do it, I'm fine."

He nodded and shut the door, rubbing his unruly, gray-streaked red beard. He crossed the front of the truck and got in the driver's seat, starting the truck's engine. The air conditioning blasted through the vents, and he turned it down as he drove away from the hospital.

Nico's knees pushed against the seat behind her, and his hand rubbed the side of her arm. The side mirror reflected a far-off expression on his face as he stared out the window.

Covering her mouth, she sucked in a breath and swallowed a lump in her throat as tears welled. She would shove her own pain down and help Nico through his dad's funeral, like he'd done for her with Gran, with Shane's disappearance, with everything.

Lowering her hand, she placed it on top of his, and their eyes locked in the mirror. Their fingers intertwined and his grip tightened.

Seagulls soared over the waterfront as the truck rounded the turn onto the highway. A trailer carrying a damaged boat passed by, and power trucks lined residential streets. Workers donning reflective clothing and chain saws hacked apart downed trees. Drew rolled down the window and the salty air rolled into the cab. "There's so much damage." She turned to her father. "The house! Is the house okay?"

"It's fine. A few of Gran's trees in the back came down, but we took care of them. We stacked the wood behind the shed. The power came back on what, two days ago, Nico?" Gabe eyed Nico in the rearview mirror.

"Yeah. Downtown was fine," Nico said. "J's been really busy at the bakery making extra food for people. I told him not to worry about the service tomorrow, but he said he's got it taken care of."

She'd been ten minutes away inside a hospital, but she may have been hiding out on another planet. "Why didn't anyone tell me?"

"You would've checked yourself out of the hospital early," Nico said without hesitation.

He wasn't wrong.

"Well, I'm here now. I'm back." As they passed by, she couldn't tear her eyes away from the sight of the downed trees and damaged houses.

"He's lucky he's already dead," Drew's father muttered. "He got off easy, if you ask me."

Sloan got off way too easily, in her opinion, since he had gained the ability to haunt her from the other side.

The truck's tires crunched as they rolled over sand and pebbles scattered across the coastal road, and remnants of branches had blown over the front yard. Jasper's van was gone, but Nico had his car parked beside hers in the driveway.

Nico got out and opened her door before she had a chance to try. Her father grabbed the bag with her belongings from the back and headed for the front door as Nico helped her down from the cab of the truck. Her feet touched the ground and her knees buckled, almost giving out. She grabbed the door frame and Nico's arm wrapped around her waist. "Not quite ready for a run on the beach just yet," she said.

"Ya think?"

He led her to the front porch, but she insisted on taking the stairs alone. Gran's gemstones sparkled in the sun, winking at her; time to reinforce the protection spell to keep him out.

Gabe unlocked the front door. "I hope you're ready. Your biggest fan missed you."

Henry bounded onto the porch, whining as his tail wagged, slapping the porch swing. "Hi sweet puppy." She reached for him and flinched, gripping her stomach as she crouched down and sat on the wooden floorboards. She took Henry's furry face in her hands and kissed his head as he licked her cheek. "I missed you." Scratching behind his ears, she put her arms around his neck and hugged him. He'd filled out since she'd been in the hospital and his ribs no longer protruded against his skin. His eyes were brighter and his fur shiny. He looked healthy. "Thanks for taking such good care of him."

"He made it easy." Her dad took the bag inside and puttered around.

Nico sat beside her on the deck as Henry hopped down the stairs and took off running around the yard, settling on the grass with a stick. Nico observed her through his dark lashes, and tingles covered her skin. "You okay?"

"I will be." She tucked her hand in his. "If there's something you need, don't be scared to ask, okay?"

"I'm not sure I even know what that is. I'm walking around in a daze, you know? Like what the fuck just happened to my life? Dad's dead, Mom's a mess, my brother's the dutiful son trying to help and keep Mom sane, and then there's me. Keeping a business going so I have *something*. I keep thinking he'll walk out of the office, or up the stairs above the garage." He ran his hands through his hair and looked away from her, wiping a hand over his eyes.

Sadness settled around her like a weighted blanket pushing down on her chest. She'd give anything to take away Nico's pain. But grief didn't work that way. It was a deep, personal ache no one could touch or make go away. She scooted up next to him, wrapping her arms around his waist and rested her head against him. He kissed the top of her head and rubbed her arm. "I'm so sorry," she whispered.

As the sun lowered in the sky, late afternoon transitioned into early evening. Drew sat on the porch swing with Henry at her feet. Dishes clanged from inside as Nico and Jasper cleaned up.

Dominic Sloan's torturous ghost drifted to the edges of her mind, but surrounded by this much love was like being armed with a superpower, and she focused on keeping him away.

For now.

She had a feeling that he'd be back again as soon as nighttime settled around her. A sudden shiver ran through her, contrasting with the warmth of the evening.

She had died and came back to life, but Sloan had too. Except this time, he might actually be the death of her.

The screen door slammed, shaking her out of her stupor, and her father stepped onto the porch and leaned against the railing, giving it a gentle shake. "This needs to be tightened up, too. I'll add it to my list."

"I can fix it. I've done it before for Gran with that toolbox in the shed filled with every tool imaginable."

"You know how to use them?" he asked."I figure out what I need. What I don't know, I find a video online."

Her dad chuckled. "More things about my daughter I didn't know."

She was so grateful she hadn't shut him out when he'd come back into her life. If she'd let anger dictate her decisions, she might not have had this chance to connect with him again. And if she took anything from Nico's tragic loss, she loved her father and wanted him to know how proud she was to have a relationship with him. "I love you, Dad. I'm glad you're here."

His work boots echoed on the porch as he sat on the swing beside her. "I'm glad you said that, because I wanted to talk to you about a couple things."

"I'm not sure I can do serious right now, and this feels serious."

"It is, but not bad. At least I don't think so, but let's get rid of the one shitty part first."

She narrowed her eyes at him. "All right, let's have it."

"Your mother called me, and I told her what happened. She wants to talk to you, but I told her to go through me until you're ready. She's got my cell number, which I'll probably regret, but I'll deal with her."

Exhaling a deep breath through pursed lips, Drew let her head fall back. "I disconnected the house phone so she couldn't call."

"Nico told me."

"What's the rest? If that's the shitty part, does it get better?"

"I'm taking a break, Drew."

"From what?"

"I'm done going away, leaving here. I'm applying for a local job, as long as management approves, of course." Using his foot, he pushed the swing with a gentle motion.

What was he talking about? "But you love working on boats, being on the water, living like the wanderer you very much are. You'll be bored here."

"Boredom doesn't get enough credit. How could I possibly be bored in this goddamn town?"

A laugh escaped her, and she clasped her hand over her mouth. How could she laugh when Nico's world was crumbling, the pain from her *second* gunshot wound was still too fresh for her to comprehend, and the torment from her attacker lingered even in his death? She was on the verge of losing it—she'd exhausted herself with tears, leaving her feeling empty and numb. At least the laugh made her feel something more than heartache. "What's the job, Dad?"

"DeSarro's garage."

Shit was changing.

"Does he know? Have you talked to him?"

"I mentioned it tonight, inside." Her dad leaned forward with his elbows on his knees as he tilted his head to gaze across the road. He absently patted Henry sitting at his feet as he spoke. "Nico's a good man with a lot on his shoulders. He needs help, but won't ask for it, and I'm not talking about pity-help. He'd be doing me a favor, and by helping me stay in town so I get to see my family more, maybe it helps him, too."

So much for exhausting herself with tears. She blinked, and they spilled down her face, leaving a trail of stinging warmth on her cheeks.

Her dad hugged her, and she came undone, crying against his chest. Holding onto her, he sat back against the swing, cradling her in his arms like he'd done when she was a little girl. "It'll be okay," he said. "Might take a bit, but we'll get there."

The screened door opened, and Nico stepped out and retreated. "Sorry to interrupt—"

"You're not, come out." Her dad gestured to him as he stood. "I'm heading out, but I'll be at the service tomorrow."

She wiped her face and sat up as Nico stepped onto the porch, eyeing her face. Henry followed her father to the truck, and he bent down to scratch Henry's head before commanding the dog to sit as he hopped in the truck, driving away with a wave.

Nico sat beside her and stretched his legs out. He called Henry back, and the dog came running with his tail wagging. "I hate leaving you like this, but Mom is at the house with my aunt, and Simon and his girlfriend are there."

She took his hand. "Go be with your family. I'm home, I'm good." She forced a smile. Would the constant fear ever leave her? She'd been through so damn much her mind was envious of her body's ability to heal. But she had work to do, starting with a protection spell, and the painting sitting upstairs. If she could find a way to bring Aurora back to her, maybe the witch could help with the dead-Sloan situation.

Nico leaned close and kissed her. She wrapped her arms around his arm as his hand rested on her leg. His lips lingered on hers for a few seconds, and she longed for time to freeze.

He rose from the swing, sending it in a gentle sway. Turning around at the bottom of the porch steps, he leaned against the rail, and it shifted under his weight. He gripped the ledge and gave it a quick shake, knitting his brows together. If he mentioned fixing that rail, an inappropriate laugh would escape her again, and guilt would smack her in the face with the weight of the tragedy he was carrying.

But his dark eyes met hers, and he hesitated. "I can come back later."

"You can come back anytime you want, I'll be here."

With a double tap on the railing and a smile forming on his lips, his charming dimple made its appearance. "I'll see you later. It feels good to say that."

With a thunderous rumble, the engine roared to life. He backed out of the driveway and sped away.

God, I love him.

FORTY

Henry followed Drew into the house, and she shut the door. He grabbed a stuffed toy, squeaking it as he bit down. A pedestal fan rattled as it circulated air through the living room, and the lingering smells of charcoal and barbecue sauce clung to her senses.

I'm home.

Soft snoring pulled her attention to Gran's reclining chair, where Jasper slept with his head slumped against his propped hand. The past week had brought an unprecedented level of business to The Tough Cookie, and Taj had told her he and Piper were managing with a new hire.

Going back to work, to the Tough Cookie, should feel like home. The bakery held Gran's essence, but the thought of stepping back into that place made her feel sick to her stomach. *He* had been in there, invading her safe space. He'd threatened her and everyone she loved.

Don't let panic win, breathe.

Henry squeaked the toy again, and Jasper shifted in the seat but didn't wake. In an effort to keep Henry quiet and push her building anxiety aside, she grabbed the toy from him and squeezed its tough fabric.

The searing pain across her abdomen had subsided to a dull throb, providing some relief as long as she remained still. She'd resisted taking pain pills to stay alert for Sloan's return. What she planned to do about him, she wasn't sure, but he'd be back, and there was no way she was letting him remain glued to her side for months on end. He needed to go to whatever realm wanted him. She imagined that place to be a black hole that sucked up horrible souls.

The staircase taunted her, and with each step, a flutter of pain crept back in. Thirteen steps up to get to Celeste's concoction of vervain and frankincense, and thirteen back down to sprinkle it along the front door to re-ignite the fading protection spell.

No big deal.

She clung to the railing, her hands sweating as she painstakingly made her way up, determined to reach the top. How else was she going to heal and get back to her witchy self?

Henry bounded up the stairs, his limp no longer affecting him, and his tail wagging. He whined and hopped back down the top three, like a cheerleader edging her forward.

"I'm coming, I'm coming."

Why does it have to hurt so goddam much?

Out of breath, she collapsed on the top step of the hallway. Henry licked her hand and sat beside her. "I did it." She pushed herself up and set to work, rummaging through the cabinet in her art room, and grabbed three black tourmaline stones.

The painting sat untouched in the corner, staring at her, beckoning for her attention. The crimson streaks over the landing had extended down the lighthouse stairs, leaving a vivid trail. She traced her fingers along the pools of red blending with the flooded bottom steps, and pulled her hand away, but her fingertips were dry.

With the stones in one hand, she grabbed a small spray bottle out of the cabinet. Its powdery scent wafted out, mingling with the sight of tiny pink flowers floating inside. Spraying the windowsill, she released a deep breath and visualized a protective mesh covering the house. She tore a piece of paper out of the notebook on her desk and a pen from the drawer and wrote two names. She wasn't taking any chances on getting the name part in the spell wrong.

Dominic Sloan
Ben Morana

Flicking a lighter, she ignited a rosemary-white sage incense and stuck the lighter in her shorts pocket. Henry hopped up on the chair and held his head low.

"It's okay, nothing's going to hurt you." She scratched behind his ear.

A piercing evergreen scent mixed with the comforting pungent of sage in curls of smoke. With one incense holder on the windowsill, she descended the stairs—Henry, her constant shadow. Gripping the railing for support, she carried a burning incense and two black stones in her other hand as smoke trailed behind her, ignoring the pain with every fiber of her being.

Jasper's snores kept in rhythm with the fan as she walked by. She flung the front door open and stepped outside. The sun was setting over the horizon, and clouds dotted the sky. Waves crashed and fell, echoing from across the road as the tide moved in. Cicadas mirrored the gentle humming in her ears as her palms tingled and the amulet thrummed along her neck, reactivated with the magic coursing through her. It lacked the same intensity as it had under Aurora's touch, but her intention behind the words she spoke would give the spell power.

With a flick of her thumb, she ignited the lighter, and a dancing flame emerged. Holding the piece of paper with the two names over the fire, she recited the spell as the paper burned to ash and blew away. "Sisterhood of protection, wrap safety around my home. Build a barrier, keeping him alone."

She tried to release the tension in her shoulders by stretching her neck, but the stubborn tightness persisted. Rustling shook Gran's lilac trees, and she froze. The amulet stopped pulsating, but a thread of light spun in its center. A sleek raven leaped off a branch, into the air and soared toward the porch. The railing shook when it landed, gripping the wood with its clawed feet. Staring at her, the raven tilted its head, its eyes as black and shiny as obsidian.

"He's back," she said.

Its beak opened wide, and a shrill screech filled the air.

She lit another incense and stuck the end in the soil of one of Gran's planters. "Consider showing yourself. How does a conversation I can't have with a bird who can't speak help me?"

The raven cocked its head and flapped its wings.

"Forget it." Turning her back on the raven, she reached for the door.

"She is still here to help, but you need one more to banish him." The raspy voice reached deep into her soul.

As she spun around, a stabbing pain shot across her stomach to her back, and she doubled over, breaking out in a cold sweat along her neck and forehead.

Jack shuffled closer, appearing human. His wild hair swept across his weathered face, and his eyes sparkled underneath the rim of his hat. He reached out, and she fought the urge to back away. This was Jack Morana, and he had never harmed her.

With calculated, cautious movements, he placed his hands over hers as they rested on her midsection, and he glanced up at her with tears in his eyes. "I am sorry he hurt you." His voice rasped as though he had to clear his throat but couldn't.

"I hurt him back." A surge of anger overshadowed her fears as she considered the consequences of killing someone with magic.

Jack transformed from the subtle human form into the ghost she had encountered many times. He bowed his head in a slow nod. "Help death find him and you will be free."

"You said I need one more. Who?"

His gaze scanned over her, and he raised his hand. The sleeve of his long coat slid down his arm, revealing his skeletal hand. "You help the dead. He breathes life with light."

She inched closer, her sweaty hands slipping from the death grip she had on her T-shirt. "Who?"

But she knew. "Breathe life" could only mean one person: Taj.

Jack lifted his bony hand and tipped his hat. A swirling mist spun into sleek feathers and once again, he took the shape of the raven flew and away.

FORTY-ONE

Henry settled himself in the chair of her art room, dropping his head to his paws while Drew stood in front of the painting. The scarlet streaks splattered across the canvas ignited a fiery anger within her. Sloan had stolen a piece of her she could never get back. Her body would heal, but the scars would forever serve as a painful reminder of the torment she endured at the hands of someone perpetuated by senseless hatred. He had injected panic and terror, robbing her of any sense of safety.

Now. What am I going to do about it? I'm going to get rid of this disgusting excuse for a human, and he will never hurt me again.

If Taj represented life and light, she would embody darkness and end the man who wanted her dead for being a witch, her truth. A swirl of light erupted in the center of the amulet, creating a spotlight over the painting. If Sloan was destined to become a witch hunter on the other side, there was one person who could help her harness enough magic to defeat him. *Aurora.*

The spell Celeste had taught her edged into her mind, and she surrendered as it came to her. "I summon thee, spirit of the sea, whose name bears light to guide those in need." A burst of sweetness tickled her tongue, and a tingling sensation cascaded over her palms. "I summon thee, spirit of the sea, whose name bears light to guide those in need."

A sudden gust of icy air spun around her, whipping her hair across her face. In a flurry of black, singed layers, Aurora appeared surrounded in a purple glow. "Embrace that power, young witch. It shall serve you well." Her expression turned serious, and her bright eyes darkened.

Drew's anger resurfaced. "How could you let Nico's dad die? If you helped me sooner, if you stepped in, I could've saved him!"

Stepping back, Aurora tilted her head to the side, her gaze softening. "His actions led him astray; no one could save him."

"But if you'd just given me your power a moment sooner, I could've stopped it."

"His fate was never to be in your hands. You are mistaken. The magic force flowing through you is your own. My presence was merely the guidance you required to use it."

Drew held the amulet away from her neck, the light spiraling out of control. "But this—"

"Is all you." A gentle glow radiated from Aurora's face as she tapped the pendant, emphasizing the contrast between her pale finger and the dark onyx gem.

"If it's all me, isn't it my fault Nico's dad is dead? I *died*, Aurora. If it wasn't for you helping Taj bring me back, I'd be dead too. And he's back for me, what if he wins? When can I stop fighting?"

"No. No!" Aurora's hands flew up to Drew's face, cupping her cheeks.

As if struck by lightning, a jolt of electricity surged through Drew from her feet to her head, blinding her in a sea of radiant white light. Back on the lighthouse landing, the memories of the horror came rushing back, like a wave crashing against the rocks. She squirmed, trying to pull away, but Aurora's magic overpowered her, holding her in place.

"I can't live through it again." Drew's throat burned and tears sprang free.

"It is a mere glimpse of his sacrifice. You must see the destiny that would have unfolded."

As the vision flowed through Aurora, an alternative scene unraveled in Drew's mind. Shane and Nico's angry screams reverberated through the air, surrounding her. Drew tore up the winding staircase as Nick DeSarro stepped between them, the memory revealing itself with an eerie sense of déjà vu. As she endured the terror all over again, her stomach lurched and her legs threatened to give out beneath her, reminding her she was home and not inside the lighthouse. Sloan pointed the gun, and a shot fired from the barrel toward Nico and his father.

But the events in the vision revealed a different ending. Drew's magic surged through her, and as she saved Nico's father, a deathly wail tore from him before everything fell silent.

Nico lay dead on the landing. Blood surrounded his lifeless body as she threw herself on top of him.

The air left Drew's lungs as Aurora dropped her hands.

Grasping at her throat, Drew stepped back. "Why did you show me this?"

"It was Nico or his father, and he chose his son's fate. You did not cause the death of your love's father." Aurora circled Drew and approached the painting. "My magic may possess the gift to mend, but it cannot breathe life. The young man permitted me to share my light, amplifying his power to save your life, but fate will always intervene."

"If fate stepped in and brought Taj to me so he could save my life, and my destiny wasn't death that night, what would've happened if he hadn't shown up?" Drew's voice trembled.

"You would wander as one of the dead who you assist with finding their freedom." Like a haunting melody, Aurora's voice weaved together a chilling blend of angelic tones and a sense of impending dread. "You would have become one of them, searching for a witch possessing the same gift as you."

Wandering Souls were those who died when it wasn't part of their destiny. They were the ones who needed peace to cross over, and Drew helped them find their paradise. "There are more like me?"

A faint smile curved Aurora's lips, barely noticeable but filled with warmth. "There are others like you, who walk with the dead, as there are others like him, who channel the light, breathing life. And you will require his help." She raised a pale arm of bones covered in blistered flesh toward the canvas perched on the easel. "Finish it."

"I can't. There's too much blood, and I don't know what to do next. It's like the blood wants to consume the painting, it's suffocating." *I'm suffocating.* Tiny stars danced in her vision as rising panic clenched around her chest, and she took a deep breath.

With a wave of Aurora's hand, the blood evaporated off the canvas into the air and vanished. She grasped the amulet around Drew's neck and leaned close. Opening her mouth, she breathed the purple light into the jewel and let it rest against Drew's neck.

"Finish it the way only you know how. Show destiny how you want the story to unfold." Aurora disappeared, leaving her words a faint whisper against Drew's ear.

Henry was asleep in the chair as though nothing had happened. Her heart pounded in her chest, and she gripped the desk to settle her rolling stomach and itching nerves. The canvas sat on the easel, waiting. She'd started painting the blank canvas after the holidays before she went back to school. It was supposed to be a sunset over Jupiter Cove beach. But when the sun went down, she painted like someone possessed. The ocean grew wild, and the lighthouse emerged before she hit a wall, and waves of fear consumed her. The piece of art had always struck her as a premonition, a dark omen, a stark warning. Magic had been the catalyst that brought it into existence, and magic would be the force that brought it to its finality.

Twisting her hair into a messy bun, she set to work, wetting a sponge, and placing it on the box-style paint palette. While fixated on the canvas, she placed palette paper on top and emptied the water from the corners of the palette into a metal bucket. Using her artist knife, she mixed the darkest shade of gray with black and white.

Finish it.

The amulet cast light over the canvas as she worked. Heat pouring from the jewel warmed her neck, and she pulled it from against her skin, so it rested over her shirt. Her hands moved faster than her mind could keep up. She switched to a detail brush and pulled the chair up close, sitting on the edge of the seat. Without stopping, she painted with her soul, bringing Aurora to life on the landing of the lighthouse. Shades of purple surrounded the ghost with faint swirls of faded green, and the raven perched, waiting with claws in a death grip on the railing as wind hurled its wings. Water moved along the floor at the bottom, creeping toward the first step.

Drew clutched the amulet, and it reacted under her fingers. Movement caught her eye, and she leaned in closer, a faint smell of ammonia tickling her nose.

Did Aurora blink?

"It's almost midnight. What in the *hell* are you doing?" Jasper yawned and rubbed his tired eyes.

Turning too fast, she gasped in pain. Paint coated her shirt and hands and had splattered over her bare legs. "Painting."

"I can see that. The better question is, shouldn't you be resting or asleep?" Stepping closer, Jasper wiped her face with his thumb. "You're covered." He removed the paint from his thumb with his other hand.

"It's a long story, but I had to finish it." Her entire torso and back throbbed in pain. She dropped the paintbrush on the tray, and sat on the chair, stirring Henry from his slumber. He yawned with a whine and nudged her hand with sleepy eyes.

Jasper folded his arms across his chest and scrunched his face as he stared at the painting. "It's the most stunning work I've ever seen. Who is she?" He pointed at Aurora.

"Aurora."

"The lighthouse witch-woman? She's beautiful... magical."

"That, she is."

I'm going to need that magic to get rid of Sloan.

Jasper spun the desk chair around and sat. "I promised Nico I'd look after you," he said through another yawn. "I don't know what happened, I just crashed. It's been so busy, and Nico's poor dad, and almost losing you." His eyes watered and he rubbed them. "It's too much, and it's not even happening to me."

She stood, clutching her abdomen—the incision had healed beyond pulling apart, but when the pain became unbearable, the weight and warmth of her arm somehow helped her feel like she could hold herself together.

Jasper leaped up from the chair. "Have you taken anything for pain?"

She extended her arms and embraced him. He smelled of baked bread and cookies, reminding her of Gran. "Thanks for taking care of the bakery. I appreciate you, J."He hugged her back, being careful not to squeeze too tight. "You're my family and I love you. I don't know what I would've done if you hadn't pulled through this." Releasing her, he stepped back and rubbed his eyes again. "Are you hungry? I can make you something."

"Go to bed. I'm going to take a shower and go to bed, too."

"Just promise to wake me up if you need anything. I locked the doors downstairs."

If only locking the doors was enough to keep Sloan's ghost away.

Jasper headed to his room, closing the door with a click. Henry followed her down the hall and settled on her bed as she headed for the bathroom.

She ran the shower, letting the water run hot until steam billowed over the curtain. Her reflection in the mirror appeared much different compared to the night of the party. She yanked the elastic from her hair and stripped off her clothes. Dark blood marked the gauze bandage covering her incision. She picked at the tape, peeling it off her skin and tossed the old bandage in the trash. Silver metal held the thin line of reddened flesh taut, and although tender, it didn't show signs of reopening. The source of her pain reached much deeper than what could be visible on her skin.

Pulling the shower curtain closed, she stood underneath the hot water, letting it soothe her skin as it streamed over her head and along her body. Remnants of blood tinged the water pink as it trickled off her abdomen and down the drain. She shampooed her hair and scrubbed the paint off her skin, savoring the fresh scent of the soap. Washing in a hospital bathroom sink couldn't compare, and the day of the party had been the last time she'd taken a full shower. The scorching hot water stung her skin, but it provided a small sense of relief, making her feel a little more like herself. *Alive*.

She turned the water off and stepped onto the plush bathmat. The air collided with her burning skin, sending shivers over her body. She dried off and wrapped the towel around her, running her fingers through her hair. A flashback of the gunshot and Sloan's bone-chilling scream as he fell to his death flooded her mind, and she gripped the counter. She lifted a hand and wiped steam off the mirror. Loneliness filled her green eyes, their depths reflecting the weight of unspoken dark secrets.

I have to tell someone about Sloan. I can't do this alone.

She tore herself away from the mirror, turning the light off as she opened the door and headed for her bedroom, illuminated by a bedside lamp. She rummaged through her drawers and pulled on a tank top and a pair of shorts. Grabbing the paper bag from the hospital, she sat on the edge of the bed and leaned back, drying the incision before placing a fresh gauze across it and taping the edges like the nurse had taught her. She took the bottle of pain pills out and had her hand on the lid to open it. Her abdomen throbbed in relentless pain, but if she took one, she'd sleep and have nightmares, or worse. She tossed the bottle on her night table and lowered herself onto the bed.

Henry edged close to her, and she buried her face against his neck. "It's going to be okay. I'm alive, I survived, I'll keep surviving."

It didn't matter that Henry couldn't understand a word she said. Talking to him made the ache of loneliness less painful.

Her skin prickled with goosebumps, and she pulled a hoodie Nico had left behind over her head, breathing his familiar scent. As she reached for her phone, a sharp, throbbing pain shot through her body, and the phone slipped through her fingers onto the floor.

Headlights illuminated her bedroom as if a cavalry had arrived, accompanied by the familiar rumbling engine. She hadn't expected to see Nico until his father's funeral and prepared for a night alone—she'd gotten good at being alone. But she didn't want to be. She needed him more than she wanted to admit. She needed him to pull her from the pit of darkness, threatening to drown her.

Henry beat her to the front door, bounding outside and down the steps to greet Nico as he got out of his car. Drew flipped on the outside light as he strolled up to the porch, his face somber and his brown eyes so sad her heart broke a little more.

"I know it's late, I wasn't going to come, and I messaged but—"

"I was in the shower."

Trudging up the porch steps, he stuck his keys in his jeans pocket and leaned against the door frame. "I just needed to see you."

She wrapped her arms around his waist and hugged him, pressing her cheek against his chest. His embrace gave her a solitary moment of safety and calm. "I need you too."

Henry rushed inside after them, but as she closed the door, an icy breeze curled around her face, and movement across the road caught her eye. With the door open a crack, she caught sight of Dominic Sloan's shadowed silhouette looming under the streetlamp. Each slow stride brought him to the end of her driveway. With deformed, bloodied fingers, he raised his hand and waved. The protection spell had to work, it had to keep him out. Her hands gripped the door, but she couldn't tear her eyes away from him.

"What are you looking at?" Nico turned his back to her and kicked his sneakers off.

"Nothing," she said.

In a flash of movement, Sloan charged toward her in a blur, moving faster than any human ever could. Her thumping heart reverberated in her throat as she slammed the door and threw the deadbolt. His face appeared in the oval window. His eyes were as dark as ink, lacking any trace of white, and his mouth gaped open, emitting a screech resembling a train halting on metal tracks. She yanked the curtain across the window and covered her mouth to keep from screaming.

Please work, please keep him out.

"Everything okay?" Nico pushed the curtain aside.

Sloan was gone.

"Did you see something out there?" he said.

"It was just a shadow," she lied. "I'm on edge, I guess."

Nico took her hand and led her upstairs, but she let go to hold on to the railing the rest of the way up.

"Did you take something?" He followed her into her bedroom and shut the door. "You look like you're in a lot of pain. Take one of those pills."

"I don't need one."

"You're being stubborn."

I can't take one in case that monster returns tonight.

"I just need rest and I'll be okay, promise."

"Prove it." Flicking the side table light off, he pulled back the blankets and collapsed onto the bed, still wearing a T-shirt and jeans. "Come and rest with me."

She gnawed her bottom lip, resisting the temptation to ignore the ghost lurking outside and lose herself in Nico. "You make it very hard to say no."

"Good."

Letting out a groan, Henry hopped up and curled into a ball at the foot of the bed.

"See? He gets it," Nico said.

She flinched as she lowered herself onto the bed, turning on her side to face him. The moonlight cast a glow over his features, and she ran a finger along his jawline, stopping at the indent of his dimple.

His eyes closed. "Rest, Drew."

She scooted closer, ignoring her body's protests of pain, until she could feel his warm breath on her face. Her lips grazed his, and she hesitated. Was he serious about the rest thing? His mouth moved against hers and he kissed her, running his hand over her arm. He leaned his head away from her, breaking contact, and smiled. "Is that my sweater?"

"I was cold."

"You're also hurting. You need rest, or you won't get better."

The relentless pain radiated across her abdomen and down her legs. "What about you?"

"What about me?"

"Are you..." *He was not okay, or fine.* "Surviving?"

He covered her with a blanket and held her in his arms as she adjusted her position, so her back was against his chest. "I'm surviving."

She traced her fingers along his hand. "I'm glad you came."

His lips moved against her head. "I love you."

"I love you too."

She'd always believed a soul-bending love would never be part of her destiny. How could it when the dead consumed a huge part of her life? Who would want to be a part of her world? But nothing could pierce her heart the way losing Nico would. She had to tell him about Sloan, no more secrets... but he'd be powerless to do anything, and what if telling him his father's killer was back from the dead sent him into a downward spiral?

Forty-Two

A squirrel dashed across the lush green backyard and mourning doves cooed as if they knew about the funeral and were summoned. She scanned the trees for a sign of Sloan's ghost, but he preferred to torture her with his visits at night.

The wrap-around deck of Nico's family home bustled with people holding mugs and dabbing their eyes with napkins. His brother made his rounds, shaking hands and expressing thanks for attending the funeral. With puffy, red eyes, he glanced down at Drew sitting in a wicker chair and squeezed her hand before returning to the house.

Using the arms of the chair, Drew pushed herself up and tugged at the hem of the black sundress she'd borrowed from Piper, keeping the length from creeping above her knees. She masked her grimace at the twinge of pain coursing through her and glided the screened door open. Stepping inside, a steady hum of chatter mixed with tears and the smell of coffee greeted her. Jasper replenished plates of sandwiches on the dining room table, straightening the napkins, and clearing dirty dishes. A woman passed by, stopping to pat her arm. "Such a tragedy. You're lucky to be alive, I hear."

Smile and nod. If one more person said those words to her, she thought she might scream. Luck played no part in this horrific situation. Sloan's power extended from behind bars, allowing him to be a mastermind controlling people on the outside, and Nico's dad had once again gotten caught in the tangled web. Nico's father died to save his son, and she died to get rid of Sloan, but no one would ever understand. Plagued with nightmares and hunted by the living dead, the last thing she felt was lucky.

As Drew navigated her way through the kitchen, Leah and Shane stood near the entrance to the living room, engrossed in conversation and holding hands. Drew hadn't seen him since the hospital and staying true to her "let's try being friends" mindset, she skirted around the large island, and approached them. Leah leaned closer to Shane and wrapped her other hand around his arm.

Shane's gaze fell on Drew's midsection. "How are you?"

"Better." She forced a small smile, trying to chase the awkwardness away. Could they really be friends after everything that had happened between them? Not a problem to solve today.

"I'm sorry for everything that's happened to you guys," Leah said. Her fingers twisted Shane's shirtsleeve, but he didn't appear to notice.

"Thank you." Drew searched the sides of the dress for pockets, clasping her fingers together in front of her when she realized there were none. The awkwardness hung in the air between the three of them. "I appreciate you coming."

"Actually, I was just going to say bye to Nico and his mom before we leave." Shane slipped his hands in his pockets as Leah gripped his arm. "Leah's heading back to Boston later."

"I've got work, so..." Leah's voice trailed off.

"Are you leaving too?" Drew's curiosity overtook the awkwardness.

"I'm sticking around to help Claudia and her mom. It's only four weeks and they pay me well."

"I'm sure I'll see you around." Drew shifted her gaze to Leah. "Have a safe trip back." Beads of sweat formed on her back and under her arms. Seeking refuge from the discomfort, and searching for Nico, she escaped to the spacious living room with its high ceilings and open windows, letting in the invigorating ocean air.

Claudia's mother, Anna Tate, caught sight of Drew and approached. "How do you think one ends up with a murderer for a husband?"

Well, shit. How does one respond to that?

"I, um. I really don't know." Drew's mind was in a battle between putting on a polite face in a room full of gawking locals and the crushing awkwardness. Anna Tate had married and had children with Sloan, oblivious to his secret life, leaving Drew struggling with a correct response to that loaded question.

Anna's eyes widened as she sipped from the coffee mug in her hands and wiped a lipstick smudge off the rim. "I'm happy he's dead."

He's not as dead as you think.

"I don't know if Claudia has told you yet," Anna continued, "but every single one of your paintings sold that night. Every last one. Be prepared, because my daughter is persistent, she'll ask for more. There's a real demand for your art. This is good."

Anna's words terrified her and thrilled her at the same time. Drew never expected her artwork to captivate people so much that they would want to hang it on their walls. "I'll do my best, thanks for letting me know."

"Of course." Anna placed her cup on a small table beside them. "Drew, I've known you since you were little. Maddie loved you so much, all she wanted was for you to be raised with love. People probably say it all the time, but she'd be proud of you. Heck, I'm proud of you. And I'm over the moon that Claudia has you in her life."

"I feel the same about her."

Placing her manicured hands on Drew's shoulders, Anna's eyes watered. "If there is anything you need, call me, I'll be there. Just know this."

Drew struggled to find the right words, but the sincerity in Anna's embrace spoke volumes. "Okay," she said, her voice barely above a whisper.

As Anna walked away, Drew had a clear view of Nico. Locals she recognized had him cornered as they put their hands on his face and hugged him. He held his composure, but she caught glimpses of the breakdown that so desperately wanted to come out. She maneuvered through the dispersing crowd of people until she reached him. She placed her hand on his back, and he reached behind him, his fingers intertwining with hers. His eyes locked on hers and lowered his voice. "They're starting to leave."

"You've almost made it," she said. "Only a little bit to go."

"I'm not sure how." His eyebrows furrowed.

"Something else takes over, I think. Gets you through." She leaned against him as his mother approached.

Maria tilted her head and clutched her chest. She wrapped her arms around both and stepped back. "None of you should have gotten involved in this mess. Goddamn that man. I don't know what we'd do if you hadn't pulled through."

"I'm so sorry, Maria." Drew had said the words so many times, they'd lost their meaning. But she *was* sorry Nick was gone, sorry she couldn't save him, sorry for the pain they were all going through, and sorry Sloan still haunted her.

Nico's mom pulled Drew into a hug, stealing a glance at Nico as one of the local mechanics who'd worked with his father dragged his attention away from them. She leaned close to Drew. "You saw him, didn't you? Did he say anything to you that night?" She sniffed back tears.

Drew wasn't sure how much Maria knew about her unique gift, but if she let that stop her from helping the dead, no one would find peace.

"Don't look at me like that, Drew. I know. I know what you see, and I'm not afraid of it." Maria secured a loose strand of her dark hair into the ponytail at the back of her neck. "If anyone is going to talk to me beyond the grave, it would be my husband." A tear slid down her rosy cheek and she wiped it away.

Nick DeSarro had known what he was doing with the message for Maria. She was a rare one who believed in messages from the dead, and his words hadn't left Drew's mind. How could she when the moment Nico had uttered similar words to her, everything had changed between them, shifting the course of their relationship? "He wanted me to tell you, his exact words were, 'it's always been her. I can't remember a time I didn't love that woman.'"

A smile broke through Maria's tears. "I can't believe he's gone. I wish I could have him back for one moment more, just one. Leave nothing unsaid, trust me on that. Life likes to mess with us, doesn't it?"

"Sure does." Drew took a deep breath, gathering all her strength to hold back the wave of emotions threatening to overwhelm her. "I wish I had more to give you—"

"Oh, darling, you've given me so much." Maria kissed Drew's cheek. "You're part of this family." She gave Drew's shoulder a pat before being swept away by the hugs and condolences of friends.

Piper sidled up to Drew, gulping from a mug. "Is it bad that I've just poured a mickey of rum in a cup of coffee?"

"You won't get any judgment from me."

"How are you doing?" Piper lowered the mug from her face.

"I don't know, as good as can be I guess. Nico—"

"Not him, *you*. You died, too, only you got to come back and his dad didn't. Just saying, that's heavy shit to deal with."

Sloan's back.

The words burned inside her, ready to spill out, but she couldn't let them. Not here in the middle of the funeral's aftermath. As she opened her mouth to tell Piper everything was okay, a cascade of other words poured out uncontrollably. "I feel scared all the time, looking over my shoulder, waiting for something horrible to happen. The gunshot echoes in my head, waking me up in the middle of the night, covered in sweat, my body tingling like I'm not in it anymore. I don't think I'll ever by okay again, not fully, and I'm terrified Nico's going to see me differently when he finds out and it'll all be over." The weight of releasing pain she'd been carrying caught up to her and tears spilled over her cheeks.

"Jesus." Piper set the mug on the nearest table and yanked Drew into a tight hug. "You are not okay, but you will be. I'll make sure of it. Whatever you need."

Drew nodded as the tears caught in her throat. "I'm so grateful for you, what would I do without you?"

Leaning back, Piper used both hands to wipe the tears off Drew's face. "The same thing I'd do without you. Live a miserable, boring, lonely existence pining for a best friend, but no one would measure up because we're like soul mates."

A laugh escaped, cutting through Drew's tears, and she sniffed to avoid a runny nose.

Piper pointed across the room. "Hey, did you see who your dad's been talking to for the last hour?"

In the corner of the living room, Celeste and her father engaged in a hushed conversation, their heads bent close together. As her dad fidgeted with his suit jacket sleeves—the suit had to be decades old and the only one he owned—Celeste plucked something off the lapel.

"She said he took her for breakfast, maybe they're friends now?" Drew had never seen her father in a romantic relationship... She'd never witnessed him having any sort of social life.

"Maybe they're more than friends." Piper made air quotes with her fingers.

"I'm gonna stop you right there. That's my dad and I just can't with this conversation."

Piper shrugged. "Celeste is the coolest person ever, I can see it."

As though he sensed Piper and Drew talking about him, her father glanced up and waved as he and Celeste approached.

"Incoming," Piper muttered with a smile.

"I'm going to head out unless you need me to stick around," her dad said as Celeste hugged Piper before embracing Drew.

"Have you seen Taj?" Celeste asked.

"He's with J," Piper said. "I'll come with you."

Giving Drew a wink, Piper trailed Celeste through the living room toward the dining area.

"If you want me to stay, or run to the house and let Henry out, I don't mind." Her dad unfastened the two buttons of his jacket. "This thing is too small, I feel like I can't breathe. It's a jacket for funerals, and I'm over it." He struggled as he tugged the sleeves.

Drew helped him slide the jacket off his shoulders. "Throw it out."

He furrowed his brows, and the sun through the window highlighted the freckles along his nose resembling hers. "You think so?" he asked.

"Or donate it, but you need to get rid of it either way."

A newfound contentment radiated from him as he laughed and bunched the jacket in his hands.

"You and Celeste seem to get along well," she said, aiming for a teasing tone but falling flat.

A serious expression settled on his face, and the lines around his eyes deepened. "You okay, kid? I'm worried about you."

"I think I will be, eventually." *Maybe not, but I sure hope so.* Fighting back tears, she tilted her head to glance at the ceiling before meeting her dad's concerned eyes.

"Anna Tate is helping me find a condo," he said. "I'm not going away anymore."

"You could move into the house if you need a place to stay. Technically, it was your home."

"Not for a long time, too long. That house is all yours now. It's what Mom wanted, and it feels right. It's for your future."

Her present and future clashed, leaving her unable to see beyond the day.

"If you need me for anything, call me, deal?"

She tried to hug him and recoiled as a flash of pain cut through her. "Deal."

Gently, he embraced her and patted her back. "Go home and get some rest. We'll just keep going and let time do the rest, whatever the hell that means."

Releasing her, he kissed the top of her head before heading for the front door. Leaving everyone else either inside or on the back deck, she followed him outside and waved goodbye.

As she turned to go inside, a sudden rush of frigid air surrounded her, pulling like a vacuum and stealing the air from her lungs. Gasping for breath, she clutched her throat and gripped the iron railing. A dark mist churned across the front yard, rustling the leaves of a large red maple near the center of the property.

Sloan materialized and closed the distance between them with purposeful steps. Cloaked in shadows, his features were barely visible as she backed up, pressing herself against the door. There was no protection spell here, nothing to keep him away. Wrapping her fingers around the amulet, she recited the spell, and an explosion of tingling surged through her hands and light swirled from inside the jewel.

He threw his head back and released a sinister laugh before glaring at her with vacant eyes. "This isn't over."

As the swirling mist curled skyward and disappeared, birds scattered in all directions with panicked chirping.

She stepped away from the door as Celeste strolled outside. She scanned the front yard and adjusted her purse over her shoulder. "What just happened here?"

"Nothing."

"*Nothing*." Celeste raised her eyebrows as she observed Drew's face. "Sure doesn't feel like nothing. Are you all right?"

"Just tired." *So tired.*

Cupping Drew's face in her hands, Celeste pursed her lips as a look of concern crossed her face. "Are you sleeping?"

"Not really," Drew said. Why couldn't she say the words?

Sloan's back. He's back and I don't know how to get rid of him.

"What are you holding back, Drew?" Celeste's hands dropped to her sides. "Do you have a *ghost* problem?"

"Yes," she exhaled, relieved to be asked. "He's back."

Her chest heaved with a loud sob, and Celeste embraced her. Drew wept in Celeste's arms, shoving aside the waves of pain coursing through her. Pulling away, she confided the encounters with Sloan to Celeste and told her about the protection spell she'd reinforced on the house.

"The asshole came back, and you've got no portal to send him through like the witch hunter." Celeste placed her hands on each of Drew's arms. "There's got to be another way."

"How? I reunite the dead with people who love them or find justice so they can move on. No one loves that disgusting man, no one misses him, and how can I give him justice when I'm the one who killed him?"

"We're going to need a spell, a good one. Use the book, you can do this," Celeste said. "You've done the impossible before, you'll do it again."

"What if I can't?" Her bones ached with dull fatigue.

Celeste tilted her head to the side and her curls draped over her shoulder. "You *can*. If he hasn't hurt you yet, I'm betting he doesn't have the power to do a damn thing."

"I can't survive on a bet, Celeste."

"Let me work some of my own magic and see what I can come up with. Does Taj know?"

"No one knows."

"You might have to change that," Celeste said, slightly disapproving.

"I'm not telling anyone. Nico buried his dad today, I can't." The sound of clanging dishes echoed from inside. "I should go help." Drew wiped her face.

Celeste released a deep exhale. "We'll figure this out; the spell will hold on the house, and in the meantime, try to rest for a bit. And consider telling your friends, they love you. Despite what you insist on telling yourself, you don't have to be alone with this." She squeezed her arm before heading toward her car, leaving Drew with her secrets, pulling her down like a rip current, dragging her deeper into its darkness, with no end in sight.

Forty-Three

The front door of Nico's house swung open, and the hushed conversations of the lingering guests ceased, replaced by their footsteps echoing on the steps as they made their way to their vehicles. Grabbing the door before it could close, Drew headed inside to join Piper and Taj with helping Jasper gather dishes off tables around the living room. Her insides burned as she pushed her body beyond its healing limits.

Nico and Simon stood alongside Maria and her sister in the entryway, surrounded by the last of Nick DeSarro's friends, and said their tearful goodbyes. Drew hung her head, her body trembling with the weight of more tears. The suffocating grief for Nico's family and her own self-pity left her struggling to breathe. She needed to escape everyone and lock herself away with the spell book, immersing herself in magic until she had a solid plan to get rid of Sloan and his menacing threats for good. Celeste was wrong. Telling her friends would do nothing to help except make them all worry about fixing a massive problem they wouldn't have the power to solve.

Claudia and Piper loaded the dishwasher and wiped up countertops as Drew made her way onto the back deck and lowered herself into an empty wicker chair. She sank into the cushions as a raven soared across the backyard and landed on the oak tree's branches. She wiped her eyes, averting her gaze from him. What good was a magical ghost-raven if he couldn't do anything to help her?

The screen door glided open, and Taj emerged, settling in the seat next to her. He drummed his thumbs to an imaginary beat on the arms of the chair and scanned the backyard. "I saw you talking to my mom out front earlier and I just wondered, you know, if there's anything you might feel like sharing with someone who's also got an in with the other side. Anything at all?"

"Not really." She spoke slowly as she tried to unravel the hidden meaning behind his words. "Why?"

He stopped drumming on the chair and observed her with raised eyebrows. "Seriously, Drew? Seriously. After all we've just been through, you say nothing?"

A cool breeze pierced the warm air, sending goosebumps over her skin. Had Celeste told him about Sloan already? "I don't know what you're getting at."

"Yes, you do. He's back, isn't he?" Taj lowered his voice and glanced at the door. "Sloan?"

"You've seen him?" she asked, shocked.

"I don't see them like you can, you know this. But after nights of nothing, the nightmares are back and it's all him, back here, at your place, and it ends with him threatening me to *come back*. Either he's resurrected from the dead or I'm losing it."

"You're not losing it." She let her head rest against the back of the chair and wrapped her arms around her stomach to ease the relentless aching.

"That's what I thought. How do we get rid of him so I can get some damn sleep?"

"I'm working on that part." It was time to shatter Taj's world again and pull him back into her chaotic one. She eyed him as his expression turned thoughtful. Who was she kidding? He had already become entangled in the world of the dead and magic—it had never belonged to her, anyway. Aurora's message about him being life and light popped into her mind. "I'm probably going to need your help."

"I had a feeling." Taj sat back in the chair, and it creaked under his weight. "You need to tell me when this stuff happens, especially when I saved your ass. We're in this together from now on, you know what I'm saying?"

Her head flopped to the side and met his frustrated gaze. "Don't tell Nico, not with everything—"

"I won't. I won't. Does this shit get any easier? I'm tired. What happens when I'm back at university? People will think I've lost my mind."

"If it makes you feel any better, you really have an amazing gift, even when you don't think so," she said. "I can hardly keep Gran's flowers alive, and you brought back a dead seagull and saved *me*. I wouldn't be sitting here if it wasn't for you."

With his elbow on the armrest, he supported his chin in his hand. "Wish I could say I'm there, but right now, this sucks."

"Right now, everything sucks."

Taj raised his hand in a fist, and she reciprocated with a fist bump, as one by one, Piper, Claudia, and Jasper filed outside onto the deck. Clouds rolled in, blocking the late afternoon sun as a cool ocean breeze swept through.

The screen door slid open again, and Nico stepped outside, unbuttoning the top buttons of his white dress shirt and rolling up the sleeves as he leaned against the door frame. All eyes fell on him. "Thanks for today." His tired eyes met Drew's, and she offered a strained smile.

Piper gave him a hug. "What else can we do to help?"

"You've already done it," Nico said. "Simon's staying for a few days to help finish packing the house to be out by the end of the month, but that's it."

"That's still a few weeks left, we'll help," Piper said.

Seated on a patio chair, Claudia crossed her legs. "Where's your mom going to live?"

"My aunt's place about an hour away." Nico ran his hand through his messy hair, dragging it across his face. "She got a storage unit until she buys a house."

Claudia clasped her fingers together in her lap. "Perfect, I'll start looking—"

"We don't need your—"

"It isn't charity." Claudia uncrossed her legs and stood, smoothing out her skirt. "Let me do this, please? Send me your mom's number and I'll call her."

"All right, she'd appreciate that," Nico said.

Drew had created some of her best memories on this deck with Piper while Taj and Nico strummed their guitars. Her gaze lifted to the stairs leading above the garage, triggering thoughts of their most intimate moments wrapped in each other's arms. It would all come to an end.

Claudia held her phone and stood. "I have to go meet Grant, but I'll see you all later." Descending the stairs off the deck and onto the grass, she paused and glanced up at Nico. "Where does that leave you? Will you go with your mom?"

Drew sat upright in the chair, gripping the edge of the seat, but said nothing.

He'll stay with me.

The words hung on the tip of her tongue, begging to be released, but she kept them locked inside. Every step they took forward together would make the pain so much worse if he decided to leave. What was wrong with her?

The surrounding conversation faded as Gran's voice twilled in her ears. "He's not going anywhere. Keeping all this inside is a mistake. Stop being so afraid to ask what your heart wants." A blue butterfly danced over the deck and flew over her head, landing on a hanging basket of flowers.

Her gaze swept across the yard in search of Gran, but as she tuned back into the conversation, Jasper was discussing the various apartments he had considered.

"Living at my aunt's is out for me. I can't be that far from the garage and run the business, and I still have to finish my apprenticeship." Nico's eyes landed on Drew as he pushed away from the door with his hands in his pockets. "I'll find something."

"I can help with that too. I have an in on places before they're advertised. I'll message you some." Claudia waved as she walked around the side of the house to the driveway.

Taj rose from his seat, and Piper leaned down to hug Drew. "We'll leave you two," she whispered. Standing, she gestured to Jasper and Taj. "Ready? Are you just going home, J?"

"My van is at the Tough Cookie, and I have a few things to finish up if you guys can drop me off there." Jasper eyed Drew. "I'll be back home soon."

"We'll drop you off, J, easy." Piper wrapped her arms around Taj, and he planted a kiss on her lips before releasing her. She gestured to Nico. "If you or your mom need anything, I'm in, okay?" She followed Jasper toward the car, tapping Drew's arm as she passed. "That goes for you too."

Taj trailed behind and glanced up at her. "We'll talk later?"

"Sure," Drew said.

But not until she spent time alone with the spell book and armed herself with the power to ship Dominic Sloan to whatever hellish place on the other side held a reservation for his deadly asshole self.

Nico sat beside her. "What's that about?"

"He has questions, and I told him I'd help."

"Can he see them, like you? Or just bring people back."

"It's complicated. Really complicated." She gnawed her lower lip raw and locked eyes with him.

"I can handle complicated, I'm listening."

"I've got nothing to say," she said.

His jaw tensed, and he sat back. "Right, of course. You don't have to shut me out. I'm not new here, I know you, and I can tell you're having a hard time."

"I'm fine, I am." Her voice increased an octave, and she cleared her throat.

Change the subject, ask him about the living situation.

"I need to talk to you about something," she said.

Nico shifted in the wicker seat. "This doesn't sound good. You're nervous."

Her teeth pressed into her lip. "I am nervous."

"Why? It's just me."

"Exactly. It's *you.*"

Reaching across the arms of the chairs, he gently brushed his thumb against her lip. "What is it?"

"You're looking for an apartment."

"I've got a few options. I'll find something in town, it'll be good, don't worry about that." He glanced at the garage. "It'll be better than up there, bigger." He took a deep breath. "I opened the safe last night before I came over, and I was going to tell you about it, but I just couldn't do it."

"If you want me to tell you stuff, you have to do the same with me."

He hesitated, and she fidgeted with the hem of her dress as tension stilled the air between them. "What was in the safe?"

"Everything," Nico said. "Printed screen shots of his phone, details about getting Sloan a gun, starting the riot... a legal deed to the property at Neptune Point belonging to Claudia, the seller is a name I've never seen before, but the place belongs to her."

He paused again, and she caught herself holding her breath as the seconds ticked by in silence.

In a hushed tone, he continued. "There's almost three hundred thousand dollars in cash with a note from my dad. I'll give Claudia the property stuff, and I'm thinking of keeping the money for my mom, Simon, and me. The police can have the rest." He leaned forward and rubbed his face. "But what if it's all Sloan's illegal money? Am I an awful person if I keep it?"

The line separating right and wrong had blurred so much, she almost couldn't recognize it anymore, but Nico was far from an awful person. Relief washed over her as discussing living arrangements faded into the back of her mind. "What did the note say?"

He pulled it out of his pocket and handed it to her. "See for yourself."

She unfolded the paper and smoothed it flat.

Son,

If you're reading this, I'm gone. I know I've let you down, I've let the family down. No amount of sorry will fix that. I did what needed to be done to protect you all. I was in too deep for too long. There's no digging out of that without someone dying, but better me than you. The money in here is mine, and that's all you need to know. It's not a lot, but it'll be enough to help Simon and Mom and let you keep the garage and find a place of your own. I swear on your life everything I did was to keep you safe. I printed everything I had on my phone. Do with it what you want.

Tell your mom I'll love her forever.

Tell your brother I'm proud of him and I love him.

Nico, you're free of my shitty mistakes. You're a better man than I ever could be.

I love you, son.

Dad

Swallowing the lump in her throat, she refolded the paper, careful not to tear it, and handed it back to him. "He had your dad trapped. I'm so sorry."

"What should I do with this?"

"I won't judge you no matter what you decide, Nico." She gripped his hand, lacing her fingers with his. "You're a good man and I love you."

"What kind of person would I be if I keep the money?" Tears filled his eyes, dampening his lashes as he glanced down at her.

"A grieving son who is just trying to survive his dad's death, help his family, and build a life for himself. Whatever you decide, I'm behind you. Does your mom know?"

"Not yet." His gaze moved downwards, focusing on their intertwined hands. "Was apartment hunting all you wanted to talk to me about?"

Her teeth found her lip again. "Yeah, that's it."

They sat for a moment longer before Drew got up and tugged Nico's hand for him to join her. He held the door open as she cut through the house and said goodbye to Maria and Simon and his girlfriend. He followed her outside to her car. "I can come home with you until J gets back so you're not alone."

She had her dog waiting for her and a dead man to take care of. "He'll be home soon enough. Don't worry about me, I'm doing better, and I can be alone, trust me." As soon as the words left her mouth, she regretted them. She'd always been good on her own, but she didn't *want* to be alone, not without Nico. She loved him. Closing herself off in the worst possible time was a flaw she struggled to overcome.

Nico opened her driver's side door. "Believe me, I know you can."

Ignoring the pain in her torso, she held onto the door frame and kissed him. He wrapped his arms around her as they parted. "Thanks for being here today."

"I wouldn't want to be anywhere else."

She climbed into the car and pulled her dress from draping over the edge as shut the door and stuck the keys in the ignition. Nico headed inside as she drove away.

The raven flew past her car along the coastal road toward her house. The graceful bird let out a screech as she rolled down the window. Sloan appeared out of nowhere and stood in the middle of the road. She slammed on the brakes, gripping the wheel with white-knuckled hands. If he was in human form, the bumper would knock into his legs, but he contorted his head from side to side as he wagged a finger back and forth.

She wanted to collapse on the ground screaming but slammed on the gas and sped forward toward home, slicing through his ghost, sending him into a flurry of smoke as a shrill ringing pierced her ears and panic constricted her chest.

FORTY-FOUR

Dark clouds painted the sky a somber gray, and raindrops fell in a sporadic rhythm, bouncing off the car and hitting her face as she stepped out. With her heart pounding in her chest, Drew sprinted up the porch steps and opened the door. Henry bolted from the house and relieved himself, sniffing the air with his ears perked on alert. A growl rumbled from his belly, and he barked at the air.

No one was on the road and the driveway was empty except for her parked car, but the feeling of being watched crept over her, making her skin crawl. As she stood on the threshold, a chill surrounded her, and her exhaled breaths formed spirals of fog.

She clutched the amulet, and it warmed beneath her fingertips. "Henry, come!"

Growling, Henry positioned himself at her feet. Gray smoke twisted and churned along the driveway, moving closer until its acrid scent invaded her nostrils and filled her lungs, forcing her to cough.

He's here.

"Using magic for murder isn't a classy move." Sloan materialized and with unnatural, distorted movements, he approached the bottom of the porch steps. Dark blood resembling tar clung to one side of his face.

Grabbing Henry's collar, she ushered him inside and pulled the door, leaving it ajar behind her. With her eyes fixed on Sloan, pent up rage pushed her forward and she advanced to the edge of the porch. "It's nothing compared to the magic I'll use to get you the fuck out of my life."

"Such a nasty mouth." His smirk contrasted with the disturbing emptiness in his unblinking eyes, and the eerie stillness of his tilted head evoked a sense of foreboding, as if he had emerged from a mysterious underworld.

Henry's barking intensified from inside the house and Sloan suddenly paced back and forth. His wild eyes snapped up to glare at her. "I'm never leaving, and you will join me."

"I'm not going anywhere with you."

A sinister laugh escaped him, foreshadowing a death omen, and dark smoke snaked around her neck like icy fingers brushing against her skin. Stepping back against the door, she wrapped her fingers around the door handle. There was a time she'd believed the wandering couldn't hurt her, but that was before the witch hunter had attacked.

"If you don't return to the place where you made the ill-fated decision it to snuff out my life, I will make your life hell until you do." When he spoke, his voice reached depths that defied the limits of human vocal cords. "You put me here, you *will* join me."

Struggling to stand, she tightened her grip on the door, her legs trembling beneath her. "I will kill you again and again to keep you from ever hurting me or anyone else."

Sloan stopped pacing, looming closer near the bottom of the stairs. A heavy force pressed against her chest, making it difficult to move. She recited the spell of protection, and the amulet vibrated along her neck. Henry scratched at the door, pushing his nose through the gap, and she stepped her foot inside to block him.

With a sudden burst of speed, Sloan rushed toward her. A sharp pain sliced through her stomach, and she yanked the door shut and clutched her abdomen. Clenching his hand into a fist, he bared his teeth like a beast and let out a high-pitched howl.

An unbearable heat throbbed from her pelvis to her neck, as if someone had pressed a live flame into her flesh, melting the tissue. Cries of pain tore through her as she collapsed onto the porch, cradling herself. Tearing her hand from her body, she reached up to her neck and held the amulet, letting it dangle from the silver chain. The thread of light in the center shimmered and cast a dazzling purple beam directly at him. The air filled with a dense cloud of blackened smoke, obscuring his figure until he was gone.

"Leave me the fuck alone!"

Lying on the porch, Drew struggled to catch her breath as Henry's barks resonated from the house.

The witch hunter had resurfaced as Dominic Sloan.

Rolling to the side, she propped herself against the house and reached up to open the door. Henry sprinted outside with his tail wagging. He stepped onto her lap with his front paws and licked her face. "He's gone." But he had until the end of time to torture her if she didn't do something.

Her dress slipped down her thighs as she bent her knees to her chest, and she shivered as a cool sea breeze chilled her exposed skin. Blood trickled down her leg and her fingers brushed against a scrape over her knee. She needed to change out of the damn dress she had on and grab the spell book.

Her stomach burned as she hurried up the stairs with Henry at her heels, gritting her teeth through the pain, but rest wasn't an option.

Tearing off the black sundress, she pulled on the first pair of shorts and T-shirt that her hands touched on top of her dresser. Tossing her phone across the bed, she padded down the hallway into her art studio. As she grabbed a handful of candles, a lighter, and the spell book from the shelf, Aurora's hand moved on the painting, and she stopped.

"If you hear me, now would be a good time to show yourself." The painting stilled; the only sounds were Henry's panting at her feet and the fan's cage rattling as it swayed back and forth. With a sudden snap, the cage broke open, exposing the blades as they spun. Balancing the magic supplies in her arms, she yanked the plug from the wall and silence enveloped the room as she headed back to her bedroom.

"Sorry, bud, you stay out here." She shut the door, leaving Henry in the hallway alone.

Spreading the book on her bed, Drew flipped pages until she found the first warning. She read aloud. "'Darkness awaits those who cause harm. Light returns after breaking ties that bind death to life.'"

She had to break the ties binding death to life. Sloan, the dead, and she was life. First part of the puzzle, solved. But *how?*

Searching through the book, she stumbled across the spell Taj had used to bring her back from death. The memory of the night she died resurfaced with vivid clarity, and his words echoed in her ears. *Call the quarters. Seek shelter from the storm. Seek bravery in the face of death, breathe in life.*

Her heart raced, sending blood pumping in her ears. Her fingers traced the tingling sensation on her thigh, a painful reminder of the first gunshot wound Sloan had inflicted on her, before moving up to her midsection. He had to die, *really* die.

It's my turn for vengeance, asshole.

She arranged the pillar candles on her dresser and the windowsill and flicked the lighter, igniting a flame on each one, pausing when she came to the last candle in front of her vanity. Releasing her thumb off the lighter, she let it slip through her fingers onto the dresser and held her hand over the wick.

Focusing on the fiery anger that Sloan evoked, she envisioned flames rising higher and higher. The palm of her hands burned with a scorching intensity, and she held her hand over the wick. A flash of light sparked, and a tiny flame danced, rising until it touched her skin. She flinched, pulling her hand away and rubbing her tender skin. The searing burn provided a strange sense of relief, distracting her from the constant fear and panic that consumed her.

She sat on the bed with the spell book and held her hands over a blank page. Focusing every ounce of magic coursing through her, she begged for a spell to rid her of Sloan's ghost.

The candlelight flickered, and purple letters formed across the page, the edges curling with an artistic flair.

You walk with the dead.

He channels the light, breathing life.

You will need his help.

Those had been Aurora's words.

"I walk with the dead and he channels the light, but how will that help me bring Sloan's death? His *real* death? I need my life back. Please help me make him go away, *please*." Her eyes burned with tears, and her head ached.

She and Taj were opposites. The yin and yang... *balance.* How could she take the blurred line between the living and the dead, send Sloan through it, and lock it tight?

Fatigue consumed Drew's body, begging her to curl up in bed and sleep for days. She held her abdomen and leaned over the book.

"Don't give up, you can do this." She turned back to the first warning. *Darkness awaits those who cause harm*—Sloan was a murderer stuck in darkness, it had to be him. *Light returns after breaking ties that bind death to life.* How could the light be returned? Unless Taj was the key to send Sloan away to the other side forever.

A relentless thumping drummed in her ears, and she clutched her hands over her temples. Sweat pricked behind her neck, and she grabbed an elastic off the side table, gathering her hair into a pile on top of her head.

She held her hands over the book and tried again, asking for a spell, anything to send Sloan away.

The rain tapped against the window and seeped through the screen, dousing the flame of the candle on the windowsill.

Nothing is working.

A housefly buzzed around her head, landing on the book, and she swatted it away. Gusts of wind sent the curtains whipping against the wall, and the pages fluttered out of control.

Why isn't it working?

She slammed her hands on the book as tears streamed down her face, suppressing the pent-up scream trapped inside her body.

A soft rapping at the door startled her. "Drew? Are you okay in there?" Jasper's soft voice called from the hallway.

"I'm fine, leave me alone," she choked through tears.

Closing the book, she hurled it across the room and flung herself on the bed as the door creaked open.

"I'm all for privacy, but it's been hours, and you're not answering messages."

Drew buried her face in the pillow.

"Can I blow out the candles before the house burns down?"

"I don't care." Gasping, she held in a crying fit that was desperate to break free.

Sweet smoke laced with vanilla filled the room as Jasper blew out the candles, but she averted her eyes, not wanting him to see her on the verge of a breakdown.

"Can I call someone? Nico? Piper? Celeste—"

"No. No, please, J. I need to be alone." Henry bolted into the room and hopped up on the bed, settling at her feet.

"Can I get you something?"

"I don't want anything, just please go. Can you take Henry with you? He'll need his supper."

"Drew—"

She sat up too fast and the pain that coursed through her sent black spots into her vision. The prescription bottle sitting on the side table beckoned for her attention. She had slammed into her breaking point. The grief, the flashbacks of death, the constant predatorial haunting...

I'm just so tired.

Jasper stood near the bed, tears filling his eyes as he watched her. "I can't leave you like *this*."

Wiping her running nose with the back of her hand, she shoved the blankets aside and climbed underneath them. "I'm just really tired. Please let me sleep." Turning on her side, she pulled the duvet over her head.

"I'm coming back in here to check on you."

"Close the door," she said.

Jasper called to Henry, and the bed shook as he leaped off. With a gentle click, the door closed, isolating her from the world. Fumbling with the bottle, she popped one of the pills and gulped stale water from a glass. She sank back under the covers, sobbing with ragged breaths before she succumbed to a tormented sleep plagued with nightmares.

FORTY-FIVE

A glimmer of light penetrated through Drew's closed eyes, illuminating the darkness. The deceptive warmth of the blanket cocoon embraced her, lulling her into a false sense of security; she couldn't bring herself to climb out. The bed shifted near her feet, and she extended an arm from under her safety net to find Henry curled up. Struggling to open her puffy eyes, she met Henry's puppy-dog gaze, and his tail wagged in delight as he showered her with affection. She'd kicked him out of her room, and he still loved her and wanted to be close to her. Guilt smacked her in the chest, triggering a fresh surge of tears from a well she believed had run dry.

Movement near the window startled her, and she threw the blanket off her head, finding the bedroom door ajar. Wiping her eyes, she turned onto her side, clutching her aching midsection. Nico placed his phone beside him on the window bench.

"What are you doing here?" Her voice emerged hoarse, and she cleared her throat.

"J called this morning."

"Why would he do that?"

Leaning forward with his elbows on his knees, Nico rubbed his face before lifting his head and clasping his hands together between his legs. "I almost came over last night after you didn't message me back, but when I texted J, he said you were sleeping... and then I found out this morning he didn't want to leave you home alone because you were up crying all night."

"I told him not to call anyone, I was tired." She sat up with her back against the pillows and crossed her arms.

"That's not how he saw it." With a quick glance, Nico surveyed the room. He bent down and picked up the spell book, placing it on her dresser before settling back on the bench. "What's going on?"

"Nothing's going on—"

He exhaled and covered his mouth as his knee bounced. "Stop, Drew. No more hiding stuff."

"I'm not." She averted her eyes and patted Henry, letting her fingers run along his soft ears. How could she tell him the man who murdered his father was back, and she didn't know how to fix it?

"Why are you lying to me?" He sounded hurt. "This is us, remember? We don't lie to each other."

Her head snapped up and her tired eyes locked with his anguished expression. "You lied to me the night of the party. Why didn't you tell me you and Shane planned to go out to the Point after your dad?"

"I didn't lie. I chose not to tell you so you didn't follow me out there and get hurt." His knee stopped bouncing, and he rubbed the back of his neck. "Why didn't you tell me Sloan was in the bakery that day threatening you? You could've said something and he never would have known. We could have done something about it together."

Biting her lip to keep it from quivering, she sniffed and wiped her eyes. "I was scared."

"Jesus, so was I." Nico got up and sat on the bed, and she bent her knees to make space for him. "I'm sorry for taking off that night, it was the biggest mistake of my life."

"Don't say that, you did what you thought you had to." Letting the blankets fall away, she wrapped her arms around her legs, ignoring her aching body. Perhaps if she'd told the police, and no one had gone to the lighthouse that night,

Nico's father might be alive, and Sloan would be a free man, back in prison, or as dead as he was now. Or destiny would have still intervened, weaving invisible threads leading to the same fate. "I'm sorry I didn't go to the police." She wiped the tears as they cascaded over her cheeks.

"What happened here last night, why all the candles and magic?" He traced his finger along her scraped knee, where the blood had dried. "J said he'd never seen you so upset before, he was worried. Why didn't you call me?"

"I can't, I don't know what to do, nothing worked." She blinked away tears.

Nico took her hand, and she released her grip from around her knees. "You're not making sense. What's got you so freaked out?"

"I'm terrified of everything, of what I can do, what I've done, who I am. I'm scared of losing you, of never being able to just be a regular person with regular problems..." Her palms burned and sweat pricked her skin. She let go of Nico's hand and swung her legs over the side of the bed.

He slid close to her, wrapping her in his arms. "I *lost* you that night and I never want to go through that again, never. If Taj didn't do whatever the fuck he did and I had to live without you? You can't lose me. I love you too much for that."

"You really want to know?" She let her head rest against his chest. "No more secrets?"

"I can handle it, all of it." His chin grazed the top of her head as he spoke.

"Sloan's back from the dead and I don't know how to get rid of him."

Nico's body tensed as he held her, and she pulled away. Staring toward the window, his eyes grew distant. "Where is he?"

"He can't get in the house. A spell is keeping him out." *Tell him everything.* "He wants me to go back... *there.* I think that's where I can send him away."

Jerking out of his stupor, Nico eyed her, his forehead creased. "Go back where? The lighthouse? You're not going anywhere near him, he'll kill you!"

Fear and sadness etched across his face, but there was another emotion in his expression, something darker mirroring her own the night before.

Rage.

"I'm sorry, Nico, but you don't get to decide. If I don't go back, he'll never leave me alone. I have to get rid of him." Rising on unsteady legs, she opened the window to let air into the stuffy room. She leaned against the windowsill, searching the road for Sloan, but he was nowhere in sight.

Nico got up and stood beside her. "What if he hurts you and I never see you again?"

"I won't let him. I'll just make a plan with Taj and Celeste—"

"You told them, but you didn't tell me?" The hurt was evident in his voice.

When she spun around, she flinched through piercing pain. Henry hopped off the bed and rushed to her, circling her legs. She gave him a reassuring pat on the head.

He reached for her; his arms poised to catch her if she stumbled. "Shit, I'm sorry." His gaze shifted down toward her stomach. "You're bleeding, are you okay?"

Lifting her shirt, she revealed a small spot of blood that had soaked through the gauze and stained the fabric. "Yeah, I think it's fine, just sore."

"Should it still be bleeding? Where's that bag with the gauze stuff, let me try to fix it."

She took his hands, guiding him away from the wound across her abdomen. "Celeste came outside after I saw Sloan at your house yesterday. I was upset, and I told her he was back. And Taj... he found out on his own. Without Taj, this won't work, he has to know. I need him to help me send him back." Nico's brown eyes locked on hers as she spoke. "I didn't know how to tell you, Nico. How do you tell someone their dad's murderer is back from the dead?" Heat rose to her cheeks and tears burned her eyes again.

"He was at my house on the day of Dad's funeral?" Nico's jaw clenched. "I hate him. I've never hated someone so much, but I hate him, what he's done, what he's taken."

She let go of Nico's hands and wiped away the steady flow of tears from her cheeks. "I hate him too. He scares the hell out of me."

He embraced her in his arms, holding her close. "Nothing can happen to you, I won't lose you again. Tell me what to do and I'll do it."

She slid her arms around his back, gripping the soft fabric of his t-shirt in her fingers. "You're already doing it, just being here."

"What's next? You're bleeding, you need rest. You can't go chasing after a dead asshole who's trying to kill you." He held her tighter, and she leaned against him, shutting her eyes, inhaling him, wishing she could melt into him.

"I have to go see Celeste and Taj."

"Promise me you'll tell me when you go back out there?"

No more secrets, and no promises she couldn't keep. "I promise."

Stepping away from him, she picked up the spell book again and opened it to Aurora's message. Drew walked with the dead and Taj was light. She had no choice but to drag herself out of the despair hole she'd fallen into.

She had a murderer to re-kill.

Forty-Six

Clouds had stolen the sunny day and rain created a symphony tapping on the roof of Drew's car as she parked behind Little Mysteries. Clutching the spell book, she yanked the hood of her rain jacket over her head and sprinted through the rain to bang on the metal service door.

The door flung open with a forceful swing, and Celeste gestured for Drew to come inside. "Do you ever answer your phone? I messaged, I called—"

"I had a bit of a..." *A complete and total sink into the darkest depths of misery.* "It wasn't a good night."

Emerging from a room off the small hallway, Taj stepped around them to lock the door. "I get that, I'd be curled up in a corner days ago."

As Drew lowered her hood, rain droplets scattered to the floor. "I'm not going to bed tonight until he's gone, and I need your help. I brought the book."

"I've had enough witch school the past two days to know I'm over it." Taj's forehead creased as he shifted his gaze from Drew to the book in her hands.

She gripped the book tighter. "I need you, Taj—"

"And I will help you, because you're my girlfriend's best friend, you've grown on me, and between getting to know you over the last year and that god-awful night in the lighthouse terrified I couldn't bring you back from the dead"—he took a deep breath—"I care about you. But I'm gonna need a break after all this. I mean it, no more murder, no more dead guys, none of it."

A bittersweet smile tugged at her lips. "I care about you too." Trusting people and believing in their support had been the toughest lesson she had to learn and relearn. But discovering Taj was more like her than she ever could have imagined released the tight ball that had wound in her stomach.

"All right, honey, if tonight's the night, bring that book in here, I have an idea." Celeste adjusted the ties of her wraparound blouse and sashayed through the beaded curtain into the back room. "Taj might be the healing light, and you might walk with the dead, but you're going to need a plan and a big dose of magic if this is going to work."

Drew chased after her, flipping the book open to find Aurora's words from the night before. "You remembered her words? She sent them through the book last night." Pushing the beads aside, she stepped into the room as Celeste lit a row of pedestal candles.

Taj trailed behind with his hands in his pockets. "Don't get too excited, you haven't heard her plan yet."

"It'll work." Celeste closed her eyes and took a deep breath, extinguishing the match with a soft exhale.

"Any plan is better than mine," Drew said.

"You're used to this, how bad can yours be?" Taj leaned with his elbows on the wooden table.

"Nonexistent, that's how." Drew spread the book on the table, turning to Aurora's first warning, before Sloan's return to her life. "I never get used to this." As she hovered over the crimson words, a tingling energy pulsed off the pages and crackled in the air around her. The magic Taj had used to bring her back from death flowed through her soul and under her skin like an invisible current.

Just like the Sisterhood had done with her, she and Taj would be an unstoppable force. She vowed to erase

Sloan—*Ben Morana*, from existence, not just for her, but for Enid and Ezra, Iris, Jules, and Nick DeSarro.

Drew traced her fingers along Aurora's message, and the scarlet letters illuminated like blazing flames. "What if this is something? 'Darkness awaits those who cause harm. Light returns after breaking ties that bind death to life.' Isn't that what all this is about? Breaking the ties that bind death, Sloan, to life, in this case, me."

Celeste sat on a stool beside the table, her intense eyes glowing amber in the dim light.

"What's your idea?" Drew couldn't hide the hope in her tone. "Reopen the portal somehow and kick his dead ass to hang out with Hathorne so they can suffer for eternity together?"

"Sounds good to me, how do we do that?" Taj angled the book toward him, and sparks flew from his fingers as he touched the pages. "Are you seeing this?" He held his hands out in front of him before slowly reaching for the book and turning the pages. "This one. 'Call the quarters. Seek shelter from the storm. Seek bravery in the face of death, breathe in life.' Can we use this one again?"

"We don't want to breathe life anywhere near that despicable man." Celeste raised a transparent, cylindrical crystal and allowed it to dangle from its chain. "He will never have peace, not in the way you're used to giving them, Drew, because his killer is free to live, as she should be." The crystal spun in circles, and she gripped it in her hand and eyed Drew. "You did the world a favor, what had to be done."

"What am I missing?" Taj said.

The amulet radiated heat, sending a vibration along her neck, and Drew clasped it. "When they're stuck in between the living and dead, I help them find justice or reunite with someone so they can be free and cross over to find their paradise." Ori's voice echoed in her mind, and a heavy ache settled in her chest and along her skin. She shook it off and refocused on Taj. "Sloan can't have either. He needs something else, dark and twisted." The witch hunter's ulcerated face haunted the corners of her mind.

"Revenge." Taj glanced around the room and candlelight flickered in his eyes. "So what do we do? How does the portal work?"

"It was called a moon gate," Drew said. "A portal into a black hole where the sisterhood helped me send the witch hunter, but it's closed, and I don't know if Aurora can open it again."

"A door that should remain closed with cement." Celeste furrowed her brows, causing lines to form on her forehead.

"But if she did open it, we could give your witch hunter a friend, right? It's got to be lonely in purgatory." Taj's gaze remained fixed on the spell book as the pages fluttered from his grasp, coming to rest on an empty page. "Okay, that's cool."

The blank page shimmered like scattered glitter, and Drew placed her hand over it. Sparkles lifted off the page and clung to her skin before disappearing. Magic stirred inside her like a fuse igniting a string of fireworks. "If Aurora opened it once, she could do it again, Celeste."

"And you'll have a hundred more problems than one angry spirit," Celeste said. "It's not that simple."

"Then we make it simple. We find another way." Fatigue weighed every inch of Drew's body down. Leaning against the counter, she hugged herself as the bandage on her abdomen shifted.

Taj slid a stool near her. "Are you sure you can do this?"

"I have to." She sat on the stool and bent over the book.

Rising from her seat, Celeste wandered around the room, her hand hovering over each candle, sending the flames dancing. "Sloan wants you dead, but he doesn't know that you already died, doesn't know about Taj's lifeline... He doesn't know a damn thing except getting you back out there... back to the lighthouse where his soul is connected, so he can drag you with him."

"What are you saying?" The ball in Drew's stomach knotted again. "How do you know all this?"

Celeste stepped toward the table. "You have your connections, and I have mine. And she knows her brother all too well."

"You saw Enid?" The knot coiled tighter and spread into her chest.

Taj glanced at Drew. "You wanted a plan, she's got one for you."

"I don't see them, I hear them. It took a day of spell work, and I burned through all the sage in the store, but she came through." Celeste sat beside Drew. "Sloan is stuck in the darkness, but a door will open when he's ready."

"He'll never be ready—"

"He will when he thinks you're joining him. Go to his place, where he wants you, and let him *show* you, let him think he's won. If he believes he can trap you with him, he'll release his hold and the door will open." Celeste glanced at Taj. "You've got a secret weapon. Taj is the light to break the tie and keep you on this side. He'll be your lifeline, your tether to keep you from death. And Sloan, can cross over."

"To where exactly?" Taj asked.

"Some things are better left unknown." Celeste handed Drew a piece of paper covered in scribbled writing. "I wrote Enid's words for you."

The first half of the page contained words and fragmented phrases like, "Ezra" and "the calm sea", growing darker the further down the page she read, "day on the boat", "he found out I'm a witch", and "my mother is here". At the bottom of the page, a single sentence, written in bold with a black pen, grabbed her attention. Drew cleared her throat and read aloud. "'Focus on the place that my brother holds close, and the spell you need will appear.'"

Dominic Sloan was a horrible monster who held nothing but hate close to his heart.

But even villains have weaknesses, and before his life spiraled out of control, before he was Dominic Sloan... He was Ben Morana, and he had a safe haven.

She raked her bottom lip with her teeth. "He was a boy who grew up in the Keeper's house at Neptune Point, but that house is gone. He was angry it burned down, that's why he had a new one built."

Holding the blue stone that Drew had given him at the party—the one he'd placed on her still chest at the lighthouse—Taj watched as a purple light surrounded it. "The lighthouse is where he died and where his grandfather's ghost still lives." The light swirled in his palms, and a purple glow radiated from the amulet that merged beautifully with Taj's.

"Someone wants our attention." He pointed at the book as dark purple lettering scrawled across the page.

Drew raised her hand over the book, and Taj held his alongside hers. The light transformed into a feathery texture, rustling pages as letters spun and dropped, their purple ink sinking into the paper, forming one word at a time.

Join together, light of life, light of death, light of love.

Illuminate the destined path;
Return to brave the storm,
Return to cast away spirit.

Gold lines interlaced, forming a triangle, melting behind the words.

Drew rested her hands on the table. "I guess that's our spell."

"We ready to do this?" Taj said.

"We have to be." She stood and stretched her neck from side to side. She took a deep breath. "Let's go back to the lighthouse."

Celeste reached for her purse and rummaged until she retrieved a set of keys. "Blessed mother nature, help me."

"Mom, we've got this," Taj said.

"You don't have to come, Celeste—"

"Have we just met? I'm not letting you do this alone, and I'm sure as hell not letting my son join you alone." Raising a hand over the candles, the flames rose and vanished, leaving a trail of smoke curling into the air. Celeste took a handful of smooth, black stones from a basket on a shelf and tucked them into her pocket. As she reached into the cabinet, her hand closed around a black cord adorned with a unique stone, its surface marked with tiny holes. She fastened it around Taj's neck, ensuring it was secure. "It's a hag stone, nothing but goodness can pass through. Don't take this off until it's over."

Taj shot Drew a look but remained silent, letting his mother do what she needed to do.

Smart move. I wouldn't dare say a word either.

With a firm grasp on the stone, Celeste shut her eyes and pressed it into her palm, unleashing it with a forceful exhale. "I'll create a barrier, a circle of protection, but I can't hold it for long." She pulled Taj into a tight hug and stepped back. "Drew will get close to Sloan's ghost. You won't see him, but be alert, listen, you'll know when the time is right, you use the light like a rope, tying her to life. It's all about focus and intention." She clasped her keys in her palm. "Let's get this over with."

Drew closed the book, whispering the spell over and over again as she followed Celeste and Taj toward her car.

Ben Morana was going home.

FORTY-SEVEN

With each rotation of the lighthouse beacon, a magnetic pull coerced Drew back to Neptune Point as Celeste and Taj followed in a separate vehicle across the bridge. Panic surged through her, mimicking the relentless crashing of waves against the rocks below.

She parked her car on a sandy patch of seagrass and rolled the window up. Celeste and Taj stepped outside and stood overlooking the construction of the Keeper's house, but she remained frozen on the driver's side with her hand on the door handle, concentrating on her shallow breaths.

Aurora. Enid and Ezra. Iris, Jack, Ben Morana... Her pulse raced. They'd all died here, but so had she. And now she was back again.

She couldn't do it. She was frozen, unable to leave the car. What if he won and she ended up stuck with him in his hellish eternity? And what about Nico? They had said no more secrets.

Once she left the car behind, cell service would end. Lifting her butt off the seat, she pulled her phone from her back pocket and frantically searched for Nico's last message. She typed out a reply and reread it with her thumb hovering over the send button.

I'm at the Point with Taj & Celeste. We have a plan, I'll call you when it's over.

I love you.

She pressed send as she swung the car door open and climbed out. The rain had diminished to a mist. Seagulls swarmed the cliffs, casting shadows as they swooped down to scavenge through seaweed and mud. Dusk settled and traces of light still clung to the clouded sky, but daylight would surrender to darkness soon. For decades, Sloan's madness had unleashed devastation and ruin, sweeping her up in its relentless grasp for the past two years, but she was done being a pawn or victim in his games. This had better work.

Taj held his phone up. "They know we're here, I won't lie to Piper."

"I just told Nico," she said.

Celeste started down the hill. "Then we better get moving before the calvary arrives, because you know they're coming."

The water had receded from the lighthouse entrance, leaving behind a landscape of rocks, boulders, and a mess of tangled seaweed. With each gust of wind, drizzle soaked her face, mixed with spray off the water, leaving a salty taste on her lips. With a firm grip, Drew tugged at the door handle and it opened without resistance.

Distant screams and gunfire echoed in her ears as she stepped inside. Gripping the railing, she ascended the stairs, triggering haunting images of pooled blood surrounding Nick's body. She blinked and the gruesome scene of Nico clutching her own dead body appeared in her mind. The blood soaked through the elegant gown as it draped over the unforgiving cement floor. Overwhelmed by a wave of nausea, she leaned over the railing, taking deep breaths.

Celeste stopped behind her and rubbed her back. "You can do this, we're with you. Breathe."

Slowing her breathing, Drew clutched the railing, letting the cool metal soothe her burning skin. She regained her composure and kept moving as Taj passed her.

"How do we get him here?" Taj's voice bounced off the cement walls.

Drew's steps faltered as she rounded the top, her eyes meeting Sloan's intense gaze as he hovered near the railing. Fueled by anger, her pace quickened, and anger turned into rage as she ascended to the top. "He's already here."

"How nice." Sloan's sinister smile didn't reach his vacant stare. "The three witches of Atlas Cliffs."

Celeste muttered as she set up a circle of stones on the floor and splashed liquid from a black bottle over them. "Do not let him steal your focus, this won't hold for long."

Taj stepped closer to Sloan. "I hear him but can't see him. You hear me, asshole? You're going down."

Drew grabbed Taj's arm and pulled him back as Sloan advanced near Taj, cocking his head from side to side.

Sloan's terrifying, stoic eyes bore into him with a piercing glare. "Such a shame to drag a son into this world." He clicked his tongue as he extended his hand toward Taj.

Celeste pushed aside stones, creating a break in the circle, and stepped inside. "Will you two get in here before that man gives me a heart attack? All I feel is rage and death."

"It's probably mine." Drew intervened with her hands raised as she stepped between Taj and Sloan. A bright light swirled from the amulet, transmitting a luminous along the length of the iron railing. "You want me to join you, is that what you want?"

"This is going to be too easy." Sloan loomed an arm's length away from her. "You took everything from me, you do not get to live," he seethed with rage.

"If you're doing this, take my hand. Once he pulls you away, I don't think I can stop him." Taj's voice wavered from behind her.

"Step one foot in this circle, just one, so we can keep you here," Celeste called.

"Let me do this," Drew said.

A hand clasped her arm and gave a gentle tug, forcing her to back up. Celeste's wide eyes met hers. "Just one foot, you stubborn girl. Please, work with me here."

Every muscle in Drew's aching body wanted to tear Sloan apart, but if he won, she would be lost forever. She stepped over the dark stones and a sharp current swept through her body.

Sloan's unblinking gaze fixed on her. He raised a hand near her face, moving his contorted fingers, and another wave of nausea rose to her throat.

"Will you let me share something with you?" His words flowed out as if he was taming a wild beast.

Here we go.

"You have nothing I want to see." She reached her hand back until she found Taj's firm grip. "You need to go."

"That's where you're wrong, Miss Harlow. You will see." Sloan lunged forward and clung to her face with both hands. Scalding fire engulfed his hands, spreading a burning heat down her throat and delivering an electric shock to her chest. Arms grabbed her, trying to pull her away from his grasp, but she couldn't move, and he held tighter.

"Don't let go," Taj said, his voice sounding far away.

Silence crashed down on her head, drowning out the noise in her ears, and images collided together, infiltrating her mind. Enid's cries pierced the quiet as she held a dead raven in her arms with Ezra crouched at her side. Aurora materialized in a burst of light, clutching the amulet in her hand, the silver chain draped across her arm. She lifted the jewel and slipped it over Enid's head, breathing life into the black gem. Enid set the bird on the ground and covered its heart with her hands, whispering incomprehensible words as she leaned closer.

The raven's chest fluttered and twitched. In a sudden movement, it extended its wings and rose into the air, emitting a screech at the movement behind them. A young Ben Morana stood at the top of the landing, witnessing the scene unfold. As Enid and Ezra cheered and hugged, Ben narrowed his eyes with a reddened face and pursed lips.

Images flashed and faded to black, one after the other, sending sharp pains through her chest. The scene shifted from Ben on a small boat with Enid and Ezra to him standing alone on the hull, staring out at the ocean. The visuals transitioned to their parents in tears, holding onto two coffins at the funeral.

Unable to breathe, Drew released Taj's hand and clawed at the amulet. Taj's panicked voice pierced the deafening silence, summoning Aurora and reciting the spell. The amulet flashed a purple light, and she fell to the floor, gasping for air. Overwhelmed by Sloan's hold on her, a dizzying sensation overcame her, chilling her blood. As the air left her lungs, she fought to breathe.

Celeste swooped in, dragging her inside the circle of stones as she choked and coughed.

"The spell, say it with me! Join together, light of life, light of death, light of love, illuminate the destined path."

"This town is mine," Sloan seethed. "You aren't welcome here, not near my family." He lunged toward her, but the impact against Celeste's protection circle repelled him.

Taj held his hands up, and a burst of light enveloped him, extending over Drew and Celeste. Aurora appeared, her ethereal glow illuminating the darkness. "Join together, light of life, light of death, light of love. Illuminate the destined path, return to brave the storm, return to cast away spirit."

Aurora hovered over Sloan, and Drew moved near her. "Please, open the gate and send him back."

"It is not possible without a full moon, and we cannot protect ourselves against such an unleash of that world." Smoke shimmered off Aurora's singed dress and hair as she ran her fingers along the railing. "The veil has dropped. He *will* walk through when the missing piece arrives. Light, death. There is no love."

"That man has no love," Taj said.

The door screeched open from below and footsteps thudded up the staircase. Piper and Nico burst onto the landing, panting from the exertion, followed by Shane and Claudia.

"He comes back from the dead, and you don't tell us?" Piper shouted, her chest heaving.

Nico sprinted toward Drew, stepping over the stones without disturbing them, easily crossing the barrier. "Where is he?"

Sloan paced along the circle like a beast stalking his prey. "You can't stay there all night." He stabbed a finger at the circle and retreated. "Your power is leaving, how convenient for me." He paused in front of Nico and his dark holes for eyes fell on Drew. "How do you think Mr. DeSarro would feel if he knew his precious son is dating a witch? Despicable."

Aurora observed him with her hands clasped together, and Drew stepped a foot over the stones. "Do something. Please."

"There is nothing I can do for him," Aurora's ethereal voice reverberated against the lighthouse walls. "You have everything you need to show him his path right here. What must happen for you to realize your own power?"

Taj reached for Piper, gesturing for Shane and Claudia to join them. "I don't know what else to do. The spell isn't working."

Drew clutched the amulet, willing it to give her a sign or a message. "Light of life, light of death... light of *love*. We need one more." She spun around, stepping back inside the crowded circle. "We need love to complete the spell."

"We're fucked." Shane folded his arms across his chest and stepped outside of the circle. "Where is he? Where are you, you piece of shit asshole!"

Sloan's figure transitioned into a dark shadow as he squeezed his hand into a fist in front of Shane. Gripping his head, Shane dropped to the ground, writhing in pain.

"Stop!" Drew stepped over the barrier, tripping on the stones, sending them scattering across the floor. She gave Nico's fingers a reassuring squeeze as she slipped out of his desperate grasp.

Releasing his hold on Shane, Sloan faced her with a sinister smile. "Party's over so soon?"

"Don't do this, Dad." Claudia charged toward Drew, directing her gaze in the same direction. "You loved me once, didn't you? When I was a little girl, remember? You let me sit at your desk and pretend I owned the company. I used to draw pictures of ice-cream sundaes, and you'd hang them on your door. We'd go every Friday." She inched forward, reaching her trembling hands out to the void in front of her.

A glimmer of light flickered in Sloan's eyes, and he stood frozen and captivated by his daughter. "You wanted every topping they had, and I never let you."

Drew nodded to Claudia and repeated his words, staying at her side as she inched closer to her father.

"Keep going, it's working," Drew said.

"Remember when that boy tripped me with his tennis racket? You were so angry..." Claudia's eyes scanned the landing as she moved forward, nearing the railing. "I thought you might kill him, but you didn't, Dad. You were mad because he hurt me, your little girl. You love me, don't you?"

"You don't love me. You don't understand me." The darkness seeped back into Sloan's eyes and Drew grasped Claudia's arm, repeating his words as Taj rushed to her other side.

Taj muttered the spell under his breath, and Claudia glanced at him. He said it again, and this time she joined in.

Sloan released a thunderous yell, and the floor beneath him creaked. "What are you trying to do to me? You never loved me."

Drew relayed Sloan's words for Claudia.

The raven soared over the landing and with a powerful flap of its wings, gracefully landed on the railing outside the open glass door.

"You were my dad, I loved you! I loved you so much. I loved you and you hurt me. You hurt so many, and I hate that I ever loved you." Hyperventilating sobs erupted from Claudia as Shane stepped forward to wrap his arms around his sister.

In a flutter of black feathers, the raven vanished, and Jack appeared in its place. "Time to go, grandson. Your hate is not welcome here." Jack tipped his hat to Drew. "Your turn."

She linked arms with Taj and Claudia. "Join together, light of life, light of death, light of love. Illuminate the destined path so he can return to brave the storm."

The three of them chanted the spell repeatedly, their voices falling into a rhythmic pattern together.

Sloan's expression contorted with rage as a swirling kaleidoscope vortex materialized beside Jack. With a sudden burst of speed, Sloan rushed toward her, his fingers gripping her arms with a burning intensity as he dragged her toward the whirlwind.

"You did this to yourself, you're on your own asshole." Drew yanked her arms out of Sloan's grasp as Taj tightened his grip on her. A burst of light spun from Taj's hand and wrapped around her arm, preventing Sloan from dragging her with him.

Drew yelled out the spell one last time and a bright purple hand-shaped light encircled Dominic Sloan. The veil spun smaller and smaller until it disintegrated into wisps of gray smoke and erupted into a shower of ash. The wind swept through like a mournful messenger, carrying his ashes away.

"He can't hurt you anymore." Jack shuffled toward the railing, his footsteps scraping along the floor. His ghostly appearance faded as he adjusted his long coat and smoothed his wild hair, revealing human-like features. But his eyes held an angelic sparkle within his weathered face.

"Why don't you cross over, Jack? Maybe I can help—"

He raised his hand, and the coat slid back, exposing his iridescent skin. "I know my way home."

Once a source of fear, Jack's presence now provided her with a sense of safety and protection. She threw her arms around him, but he hesitated before he returned the hug with a gentle pat on her back.

"Thank you." Drew released him and stepped back as her eyes met Nico's concerned gaze.

"Bestie, as exciting as all this is, don't forget we can't see a damn thing," Piper said.

Taj shifted his focus from Drew to Piper. "Raven guy... Jack is here, they're just having a moment."

Jack cast a quick glance around the room, observing her friends, his eyes glancing at Shane before lingering on Claudia.

As he moved toward her, his silhouette rippled like water. "My family?"

Drew offered her hand to Shane and Claudia. "Want to meet your great grandfather before he leaves?"

Shane shook his head and stuffed his hands in his pockets. "I can't, this isn't meant for me."

Shifting her gaze from Shane to Drew, Claudia rubbed her arms. "I don't know, is he like... is he like my dad?" Her voice quivered.

"Nothing like him. He's protected and watched over me for a while now. It's okay." Drew linked her arm with Jack's as Claudia took her hand.

Gasping, Claudia's eyes pricked with tears. "Wow, I don't know what to say. Nice to meet you."

For the first time since Drew had met him, a smile settled on Jack's face. "This place is yours now. I know it will be in good hands."

He took Claudia's hand in his, and she looked him in the eyes, determined. "I won't let anything bad happen here again."

He let go of Claudia's hand and tipped his hat to Drew. "You know where to find me."

Jack vanished in a blur of haze, leaving behind the raven perched on the railing. With a swift, graceful motion, he spread his wings and leaped off the lighthouse, soaring into the night sky.

Forty-Eight

As the rain tapered off, stars emerged through the clouds. Drew steered along the coastal road toward home and pulled into her driveway, with Nico trailing behind her, the loud Chevelle's engine cutting off as he parked. The motion light clicked on, illuminating the front door as it swung open, and in a flash, Henry dashed outside, followed by Jasper and Danny.

Jasper's shoulders dropped, and he let out a heavy sigh when she stepped out of the car, crouching down to pet Henry. "Is he gone? For real this time?"

"It's over." Fatigue sank through the ache in her skin, down to her bones as she stood.

Claudia's luxurious sedan glided to a stop along the road, and she sauntered up the driveway with Shane and headed toward the porch. "I don't want to go home yet."

Sitting on the grass with his arms over bent knees, Shane called Henry over. The dog obliged, wagging his tail as Shane scratched his belly. "Is this the stray dog you adopted?"

"I think he adopted me." Drew eased her weary body onto the porch step and Nico sat beside her. As she let her head rest against his shoulder, he lifted his arm and wrapped it around her, pulling her closer.

"When did he come back?" Shane asked.

Nico glanced down at her, waiting for her to respond to Shane's question.

"The night before I got out of the hospital. I fell asleep after Piper left and when I woke up... he was there." A shiver crawled up her back, and she fought the urge to scan the road for Sloan's ghost again. He was gone. Really gone.

"I'm lowkey pissed at you for not saying something." Shane stretched his legs out on the grass as Henry settled beside him with a stick.

"You'll have to get over it. I couldn't say anything." She looked at Nico. "Not until the funeral was over."

Dropping his arm, Nico fidgeted with his hands, and she interlocked her fingers with his. A small smile graced his lips.

A car sped along the road and turned into the driveway. Doors slammed as Piper and Taj got out and walked hand in hand toward the porch.

"How's your mom?" Drew asked.

"She's tired, but okay," Taj said. "We made a solid team tonight, didn't we?"

"The best." Having friends who shared her ability for the supernatural offered a sense of comfort. "I couldn't have done it without you."

Taj extended his fist, and she bumped her fist against his.

Releasing Taj's hand, Piper rested against the railing. "Drew, I love you, you're my best friend, but I'm sick to death of you not telling me when shit's going down. I'm not dragging it out of you anymore." She gestured a hand back and forth between them. "We trust each other?"

"Of course, with my life." She had this coming, no more secrets. Piper was her best friend in the world.

"Stop trying to do it all on your own." Leaning down, Piper gave her a quick squeeze.

"I hear you," Drew whispered.

Taking her sweater off, Claudia laid it on the ground and sat beside Shane. "You think people will know us forever as the kids of those notorious criminals from Atlas Cliffs?" Her gaze quickly shifted to Nico. "I didn't mean your dad was—"

"I know what you meant." Nico's hand slipped out of Drew's grasp. "Maybe they will, maybe they won't, but it doesn't matter what people think. My dad wasn't a bad man, he just made shit life decisions that got him killed. He's gone, and there's not a fucking thing I can do about it." He wiped his eyes and shifted his gaze away.

A light breeze blew Piper's hair in her face, and she twisted the pink strands to the side. She furrowed her brows and the silver hoop in her eyebrow shifted. "I don't care what anyone thinks. You're all my family, and I care about you." She glanced at Claudia's shocked face. "Yes, even you, Claudia. I love you guys, and if anyone says anything bad about any of you, I'll just have to fight them." A mischievous smile graced her lips.

Nico draped his arm back over Drew's shoulder, and she reached up, grasping his fingers. "We can't control who our families are or what they do. Nico's dad told me we're not our family's mistakes, and I believe him," she said. "And this is our town too, it's home. People talk, but I don't care." She locked eyes with Nico.

"If I had a drink in my hand, I'd cheers to that." Piper held up her empty hand, her fingers curled into the shape of a cup. "Is it too late to have a fire on the beach?" She glanced at Drew. "Just an idea, but if you're too sore, we can leave. I'm wound as tight as the bun in my mother's hair when she has court, and trust me, that's not a good thing."

Danny laughed. "It's never been more obvious that you and J are related than at this moment."

"Welcome to the family, Dan." Piper's smile widened.

"I know a dress we could use as kindling." Claudia picked at chipped polish on one of her fingernails.

"It's your call, Drew. If you want a fire, I'm in." Nico dropped his arm and stretched his legs out.

"Let's burn that dress." Grabbing hold of the porch railing, Drew stood and headed inside.

Her body protested, begging her to go to bed, but she fought back with each step up the stairs. She didn't want that bloody dress in her house for another day, and a bonfire on Jupiter Cove Beach always soothed every nerve in her body.

If only this pain would go away.

The screen door creaked open and closed. "Let me help." Claudia linked arms with Drew, and they ascended the stairs together. "I would've gotten it, you know. You're never going to heal if you don't rest."

"I'll make up for it." Drew headed into the art room and opened the closet. Claudia gasped as Drew reached for the plastic bag containing the dress and she clutched the amulet, prepared to strike. The jewel was motionless in her palm, its surface cool to the touch. No one was there. "You almost gave me a heart attack."

"Sorry..." Claudia stared at the painting, her hands covering her mouth. "Holy shit, you finished it. This is... I need this." She plucked it off the easel and held it up. "Please tell me I can hang this in the gallery, Drew, come on."

She'd captured memories of death and sadness of the night Nico lost his father. The painting brought her own mortality to the surface and would forever remind her of what it felt like to die, glimpse the other side, and by an unexplained miracle from a world she'd never understand, return to the living.

And she didn't need it in her house anymore.

"You can have it," she said. "Maybe someone will fall in love with Aurora."

Placing the canvas back on the easel, Claudia hugged Drew, taking the dress bag from her hands. "I know I can be... *a lot* sometimes, but thanks for sticking around and not giving up on me. For seeing something the others don't."

"I could say the same to you."

"We just might be friends for life." Claudia beamed.

"I'm counting on it."

Claudia held the dress up. "Burning party?"

"Yes, please."

As Claudia headed down the stairs and outside, a hushed voice caught Drew's attention and she froze as she reached for the door.

"Are you coming?" Claudia called out from the porch.

"I'll be right there." Drew tracked the source of the voice as it grew louder, leading her from the kitchen to the den.

The clock's chimes rang out and stopped. Recognition set in as the familiar man's voice spoke again. Warmth radiated through her chest, like a soothing embrace. "Ori? Where are you?"

"I brought a few friends who wanted to say thank you." Clad in the same Subline T-shirt and jeans, Ori's pale skin radiated with glowing light, but he was human enough for her to hug him.

Enid held Ezra's hand as Jules and Iris materialized before her in ethereal, ghost-like silhouettes. Their faces beamed with love, holding an energy that stole her breath away. But before Drew could say anything, they gave a gentle wave and disappeared.

Ori looked around the room. "And now, the real reason I'm here. There's one more."

Nick DeSarro emerged beside Ori. A rush of goosebumps covered her skin as her eyes blurred with tears.

I promised Nico if he ever came back...

"You can't leave until—"

"He's coming." Ori tucked loose strands of blond hair behind his ears.

"Drew? You okay?" Nico stopped at the entrance to the den. "Claudia said you were still inside." His gaze met hers and he rushed over, placing both of his hands on her shoulders. "What's wrong?"

"Your dad's here. I think he just wants to say goodbye to you."

Nico's gaze lifted from hers as he searched the room. "I don't see him."

Drew clasped her hand with Nico's and extended her other hand toward his father to bridge the gap. Nick DeSarro placed his hand in hers and his golden light surrounded the three of them.

Nico blinked back tears, but one escaped and trickled down his cheek. "Dad? You're really here?"

"I'm here, but I don't have much time. I love you, I'm proud as hell of you, and I'm so sorry, I'd take it all back if I could, do everything differently."

Nico's fingers tightened as they interlaced with Drew's and his bottom lip quivered. "I know, I'm not mad at you. I love you too."

A tidal wave of fatigue crashed over Drew as she focused on keeping their connection, but Nico's dad's hand slipped away. "He's leaving, Nico, I'm sorry, I can't hold on."

"Tell your mom and brother I love them." Nick DeSarro smiled as he nodded toward Drew. "You're loved son. That's all that matters, trust me."

"I miss you, Dad."

The connection drifted and faded as Nick vanished. Releasing Drew's hand, Nico collapsed to the chair near the window. He leaned forward with his head in his hands and spoke through muffled tears, "I can't believe you can do that. I don't know what to say, thank you doesn't feel right, it's not enough."

Crouching beside him, Drew wrapped her arms around him. "I love you," she said with her face against his hair.

The clock chimes rang again, and Ori clasped his hands together. "My turn. You braved the storms and you're still standing. You did good." Light surrounded him as his silhouette faded. "Tell J I'm really happy for him. Danny's great."

"Will I see you again?"

"If my best human friend needs me, I'll find a way to come." Ori's voice drifted into a whisper as he vanished.

"I didn't realize you had company." Nico lifted his head, wiping his tired eyes, and the dimple she adored so much appeared on his face.

"I guess unexpected company is just one of those strange parts of my life I can't control."

"Keeps it interesting," he said.

"It doesn't freak you out?"

"Oh, it freaks me out sometimes, but it doesn't scare me. Nothing's gonna scare me away, if that's what you mean." Rising to his feet, Nico held her face with his hands and kissed her, letting his lips linger on hers. "You know how many people would die to get the chance that you just gave me?"

Savoring the moment, she leaned against him, silencing him as the kiss deepened. "Company," she said against his lips, breaking the connection, and lifted her gaze to his.

"Huh?" His hands trailed down her bare arms, sending shivers along her skin.

"The beach? They're all waiting down there."

"Maybe they won't notice we aren't there?"

"They'll definitely notice and come looking for us." She stepped out of his arms, her hand gripping his as she pulled him toward the door. "Can you stay tonight?"

"I'm not going anywhere tonight."

The walls she'd constructed around herself to keep her heart from getting broken, holding secrets and hindering trust collapsed, and she breathed deeper than she had in weeks.

FORTY-NINE

Small waves rolled and crashed over the sand, dragging a cacophony of pebbles into the depths of the sea as Danny and Jasper strolled along the beach sipping wine from stainless-steel cups. Taj threw more deadwood into the fire, sending the flames dancing skyward, and Piper engaged in a game of fetch with Henry, tossing a stick and laughing as he brought it back to her.

Positioning herself on the sand between Nico's legs, Drew leaned her back against his chest. She dug her bare feet into the sand and rested her arms on his outstretched legs. Jupiter Cove beach, once a refuge for calming her frayed nerves, had shifted into a haven for creating memories with friends—for healing.

She never could have imagined a scenario where she'd be together with Nico and Shane, but the two of them chatted about cars, the garage, and college. Her relationship with Shane had begun with a rush of first love butterflies, spiraling into grief and shifting into an ex-boyfriend who had devastated her, broken her heart, and betrayed her. But somehow, after everything they'd been through, they'd salvaged a friendship. They'd fallen into an unspoken understanding, and maybe it would always be this way, or one day they'd drift apart, but for now, it was peaceful.

Claudia, sitting in the dirt wearing white, would be a rare sighting, but she got up and brushed sand off her romper without flinching. Drew smiled at the shift in the popular girl who she had once loathed.

Change didn't always have to be a bad thing.

Holding the plastic bag with the bloody dress, Claudia hovered over Drew. "Are you ready for this?"

She took Claudia's outstretched hand and rose to her feet. The motion intensified the constant burning in her mid-section and it shifted into sharp pain. With a deep breath, she tore open the bag, pulling the dress out and let it drape to the ground in front of her.

Pushing off the beach, Nico's eyes lingered on her while he brushed the sand off his jeans. Henry lay near Drew's feet as Piper and Shane gathered closer to the fire.

She touched the dark stains soaked into the light fabric. "It's just a dress. Why does seeing it with all the blood... why does it hurt so much?"

Tossing another piece of wood into the crackling fire, Taj crossed the sand to stand next to her. "Because it's pretty and was supposed to be a night you escaped your regular life, got all dressed up, and had fun, you know? But it turned into a nightmare from hell. And this dress with all that blood represents your death. That shit is pain, trauma. It's dark, and it hurts. You get to take all that back tonight." He surveyed the dried blood, stained and splattered, creating a horrifying contrast against the blue fabric. "You survived." As he spoke, the fire cast a golden amber glow in his eyes, giving them a mesmerizing intensity. The energy he radiated was unlike anything she had experienced before, even surpassing the energy of his mother. He embodied light.

As she held the dress, tingling scattered in a flurry along her palms. "I only survived because of you, and I'll never be able to thank you, not ever. What you did for me and my family." She caught Nico's pained expression. "It was brave, and I literally owe you my life."

"Yeah you do." In a playful gesture, he tossed his hand in the air. "I'm just playing. You owe me nothing and I'd do it again." He displayed his hands with his palms up. "It's nowhere near as strong, but I can still feel it under my skin sometimes."

"That doesn't really go away. I think it sticks around in case we need it." Drew clutched the dress as she lowered her hands and the flowing skirt cascaded over the sand.

With a sudden snap, a log released a shower of sparks around the campfire, and Drew jumped.

"I think the fire is trying to tell you something." Piper gestured to the dress.

Trudging through the sand, Drew held up the dress. The wind caught the fabric and twirled the layers of skirt around. "You sure you're okay with this, Claudia?"

"If you don't do it, I will." Claudia's mouth twisted into a sly smile.

"Do you need to say some kind of spell?" Nico stepped closer, positioning himself by her side.

"Not this time." Drew raised the dress as high as she could, allowing the flames to devour the hem, and set it free. Flames consumed the dress, turning it into ashes, and a sudden shower of bright glitter scattered into the air. "Did you see that?" She spun around.

Taj laughed and shrugged his shoulders. "Just a tiny spell."

With the fire extinguished, Shane and Claudia left in one car and Piper and Taj headed home in another. Drew and Nico trailed Jasper and Danny back to the house. Henry bounded ahead, triggering the flood light to switch on.

Nico yawned and stretched his neck from side to side.

"How are you?" she asked.

"Tired." He laced his fingers with hers as they walked up the driveway. "Really tired."

The weight of fatigue settled back in as she stepped inside the house, replacing the rush of adrenaline that had kept her going all day. Her skin prickled with a burning sensation beneath the bandage on her abdomen, and she lifted her shirt to examine a fresh blood spot forming on the white gauze.

Unzipping his sweater, Danny eyed her. "I can take a look if you want, up to you."

She was afraid to know what was happening under the gauze pad. "You're off duty."

"I don't mind, I've got everything I need." He held up a bag of supplies.

"You came prepared?" she said.

"I always come prepared." Danny rolled his eyes and smiled. "And J mentioned you might need them."

"He knows you well." Nico yawned again as he sat on the arm of the sofa.

She gently touched her fingers to the wound and more blood saturated the pad. "It hurts and I'm scared to see what's under there."

Rising from the sofa, Nico approached for a closer look. "Jesus, Drew." With wide eyes, he directed his attention to Danny. "Is she okay? She shouldn't be bleeding anymore, right?"

Tilting his head to the side, Danny scrunched his face as he eyed her mid-section. "If you're comfortable, I can check it out, clean it up, and change the bandage."

Danny's presence had become as comfortable to her as Jasper's, like family.

"Want me to lie on the couch?" She moved toward the sofa.

"You choose. I just need to wash up." He wandered down the small hallway to the bathroom and turned the tap on.

Drew lay on the couch and Nico placed a pillow under her head as Danny returned with a pair of surgical gloves on.

She laughed. "Do you just carry those around with you?"

"All the time." Danny released a dramatic sigh. "I told you; I came prepared. Let's see this." The tape stuck to his glove as he pulled back the bandage with expert fingers.

"Is it bad?" She propped up on her elbows.

Nico's reaction was not disgust, but concern. He neither flinched nor averted his eyes, shifting his attention from Drew to Danny. "Is she okay?"

"She's going to be just fine, don't worry. How's the pain, Drew?"

It's an excruciating, horrible, relentless burning. "It's sort of tolerable."

"Where are those pain pills?" Nico said.

She surrendered to her body's relentless demands for rest. "Upstairs on the table by my bed."

"This will be cold." With precise and delicate movements, Danny applied a gauze ball soaked in a soothing substance across the incision. "When is your follow-up?"

"Next week," she said. "Why, is something wrong?"

He secured a clean bandage with its own tape by gently pressing it onto her skin. As he took off his glove, he turned it inside out and tucked the discarded bandage, then removed the other glove. "I know it feels terrible, but as far as I can see, it's healing well. I'm assuming those staples will come out at your appointment."

"Thank you." She tugged the hem of her shirt back over her stomach and sat up as Nico handed her a pill and a glass of water.

Carrying the used supplies to the kitchen, Danny returned with Jasper and a plate of deli meat, cheese, and crackers. "Hungry?" Jasper beamed.

The four of them sat around the coffee table, engaged in small talk about the bakery and plans for the rest of the summer, pausing as they savored each bite. The in between moments of silence embraced her, punctuated by the fluttering of curtains as a gentle breeze danced through the living room window.

Drew's eyes grew heavy and watered as a yawn escaped. Standing up, she braced her hand on the sofa, trying to steady herself against the sudden wave of dizziness. "I need to go to bed."

Nico stood and stretched as he followed her up the stairs. The darkness of the bedroom soothed her throbbing head as she discarded her clothes and yanked the first clean tank top she could find over her head. She collapsed on the unmade bed as Nico took off his jeans and T-shirt and climbed in next to her. He lifted his arm, and she nestled against him, letting the heat from his chest relax her aching body.

"Better?" he said with his lips against her head.

"Much better."

"I didn't think we'd get through today."

"Me neither, but we're here now."

He yanked a blanket over them. "Can we just stay like this?"

"I'm counting on it." Her eyes closed, plunging her into a quiet darkness without fear. Nico's breathing shifted into a slow rise and fall against her.

We're going to be okay. We're home.

She pulled the blanket up to her chin and gave in to sleep.

FIFTY

A cool ocean breeze relieved the early evening heat as Drew arrived at DeSarro's Auto Repair and Restoration. As she approached the open garage doors, seagulls cried out above the noise of clanging and buzzing tools. With the garage door open at the back of the building, the view reached all the way to the other side, where music played from a speaker.

She'd finished her first shift back to work after spending the past week doing nothing but resting at home, and the cooped-up weight of restless energy lifted. Her reliance on pain-numbing medication had vanished, allowing her to move faster and without a persistent ache, but the nightmares still plagued her. On the most intense nights, she woke up, gasping for air, haunted by the suffocating grip of death all over again. Nico had convinced her to make the call and schedule an appointment with the therapist.

Her father emerged from underneath a car on a lift and slid his safety goggles on the top of his head. He eyed the Tough Cookie embroidery on her shirt. "You're not supposed to go back to work until next week. It's Friday, why not give it the weekend?" Worry creased around his eyes.

A smile crossed her face. She enjoyed having him around to worry about her. "Hello to you too."

He rubbed his beard and shook his head. "You sure you're up to it?"

"More than sure. Staples are gone, the doctor said things are healing well, and I need to get back to work. I can't sit home anymore." As she watched her dad hard at work in Nico's garage, a swell of pride filled her, but the constant call of ships from across the road brought a sense of unease. The sea was bound to lure him back sooner or later. "So, are you liking the new job, or do you miss all... of that?" She gestured toward the shipyard.

His work boots shuffled along the cement floor as he moved closer, eyeing the shipyard. He placed his hands on her shoulders. "I'm not leaving. I've got too much keeping me here, it's where I need to be, where I want to be." He slipped his goggles back over his eyes and bent down under the car. "And it's nice to work for management who aren't assholes. Nico's back there." He pointed to the restoration bay.

Drew scooted close to the wall toward the back. Hunched over a sleek sports car, Nico wiped his hands on a rag, tucking it into the back pocket of his coveralls. She waved as he glanced up at her, his dimple indenting the sweet spot on his cheek as he smiled. He walked toward her, grabbing his phone to turn the music down and leaned down to kiss her. The scent of grease and car shampoo clung to him, but it only made her want to pull him closer.

"How was it today?" he asked.

"Good to be back, how are you?"

"Work helps. I finished this beauty." He glanced at the car. "The client picks it up tomorrow."

"It's like a piece of art," she said. Every detail of the restored car showcased Nico's meticulous work. He poured his soul into his work the way she did in her paintings.

He placed a spray bottle and a large container on a metal shelf. "Mom's all packed. She's leaving tomorrow and I'll drive the U-Haul to my aunt's house for her on Sunday. I can stay in our house until the end of the month."

"That's only a couple of weeks."

Just ask him. If he's not ready, he'll say no, and everything will stay the same. No big deal.

The clattering tools stopped, and her dad peeked his head around the car. "Nico? Someone's here to see you. Front of the shop."

"That was fast," Nico said. "I made the call this morning, but didn't think she'd come until next week."

"What call?"

Taking her hand, he led her through the garage into the waiting area of the shop.

Sergeant Porter crouched down and rubbed Henry's belly as he rolled over on a plush dog bed. The corner of the waiting room had been transformed into a dog haven with food and water dishes, and a leash dangling from a hook. Her father hadn't exaggerated when he'd told her how much he enjoyed looking after Henry.

The sergeant stood and straightened the belt on her police uniform and shook Nico's hand. He had given the Neptune Point property document to Claudia and mentioned his plan to hand over the contents of the safe to the police, but she hadn't expected him to call so soon. That money could help him with the business, help pay for his brother's college, and set his mom up with a new place—all the things Nick DeSarro would have wanted for his family. But it was not her decision to make.

A look of compassion crossed Sergeant Porter's face as she looked at Drew. "I'm so sorry. This should never have happened to you, to any of you, again. What a complete shitshow."

"Did something else happen, is everything okay?" Thoughts of worry and fear spiraled with a barrage of what ifs. What if Nico was in trouble, or one of Sloan's men was after them, making a bomb...

"It's okay, promise." Nico positioned himself beside Drew and gave her hand a squeeze.

Nico led Sergeant Porter into the back office and Drew trailed behind with Henry at her heels. The door of the safe hung open and papers rested inside with a stack of cash. This was really happening.

Sergeant Porter pulled on a pair of gloves and retrieved a plastic bag marked evidence. She set to work, taking papers out of the safe and placing them into the bag. Nico gave Porter the letter his father had left for him.

"What are you doing?" Drew gripped Nico's arm.

"Trust me."

The sergeant eyed them both and handed the letter back to him. "Thank you for telling us about this. Your dad knew what he was doing when he printed the phone messages. We'll be able to piece together one hell of a massive puzzle."

Drew wanted to piece together where Nico's mind had been when he made the life-altering decision to hand over the substantial amount of cash his father had stashed for him.

Not. My. Decision.

She gnawed her bottom lip as Nico and Sergeant Porter talked about the evidence in the safe. "What's going to happen next?"

Sergeant Porter took off her gloves and glanced from Nico to Drew. "I have everything I need from here, and as discussed with Mr. DeSarro on the phone, this money was his father's earned through the business, and not part of this case." She glanced at Nico. "And I've never seen a letter."

Drew released her lip as her mouth dropped open. "But you just..."

Nico shook his head.

What in the hell did I just witness?

Drew resisted the sudden urge to hug Valerie Porter.

"I do this work to put away bad people and protect the good ones." With the evidence bag in hand, Sergeant Porter turned toward Drew. "I thought you'd be interested to know, according to the autopsy report, Dominic Sloan suffered a heart attack and fell off the lighthouse landing. Sounds to me like karma won."

"I killed him." The words slipped from Drew's lips without a moment's hesitation, right past common sense. Maybe she should've taken a moment to consider their impact, but Porter understood her more than others would, and Drew *trusted* this woman.

With a clenched jaw, Nico gripped her arm, his terrified gaze focused on her. Tools banged against metal from the garage, shattering the stillness in the office.

Sergeant Porter tilted her head to the side, accentuating defined cheekbones and a sparkle in her warm eyes. "If that monster didn't die that night, the three of us wouldn't be having this conversation. Drew, you did not kill that man, we have proof of that, so do me a favor and never say those words again, hear me?"

"Loud and clear," she said, grimacing.

Nico exhaled softly as shoulders dropped and she squeezed his hand.

Defending herself and everyone she loved didn't make her a killer or a monster. It made her human. But had the dominos been lining up for months, waiting to fall since Sloan had gone to prison? "He started a riot and escaped, but how did he get so far unnoticed? And why did it take so long for the police to catch him?"

"With help on the outside," Porter said. "That and he beat one of the guards within an inch of his life, wore his uniform and stole his gun and ID card. We determined he walked out around 4 on Saturday before the sun came up, with a decoy and three others waiting to pick him up." She eyed Nico.

"Dad was the getaway driver." Nico sat on the edge of the desk in the small office and crossed his arms. "I just found out."

Sergeant Porter leaned against the door frame. "Your dad was backed into a corner; he was blackmailed, Nico. He either helped Sloan escape or put his family in danger. He got in too deep a long time ago."

"What happened to the others? Are they still out there?" Fear crept into Drew's chest. Would she have to look over her shoulder again?

"Of the three others, one is in police custody awaiting trial, and the other two are deceased. Sloan shot both before arriving at the lighthouse."

"Dad was number four." Nico rubbed his eyes and exhaled.

Sergeant Porter's radio chirped from its place on her chest, and she responded. "I have to go, but if either of you needs anything, you have my number. Don't think twice about using it."

Nico stood and opened the door. Henry bounded into the waiting room, and the Sergeant gave him a pat on his head as she headed outside, driving away in her police car.

Wrapping her arms around Nico's waist, Drew let her forehead drop to his chest, and he rubbed her back. "You did good," she said.

"We both did."

With his tail wagging, Henry jumped up and Drew kneeled to give him a hug. The dog lived in blissful ignorance, giving unconditional love, and all he wanted in return was a belly scratch, some attention, and food and water. She grabbed the leash from the hook and clicked it on his collar. "It's like his second home here."

"Your dad set it up. Henry is like our mascot, customers love him." Nico crouched down to scratch Henry behind the ears. His back and arms flexed with every movement, revealing his strength. His arms had carried her out of the lighthouse to the ambulance. What if she hadn't come back from death? Would she be a restless soul looking on without him knowing she was here? When would these thoughts stop haunting her? A shiver trailed along her skin, raising the hairs on her arms.

Nico's phone buzzed, and he stood, taking it out of his pocket. He swiped his fingers across the screen and glanced at her. "You want to go to Maze tonight? Next of Kin is playing, Taj and Piper are already there."

No. I just want to be alone with you and make up for the past two weeks of hell.

"Sure," she said.

Hesitating for a few seconds, he tore his gaze away from her and typed on his phone before tucking it back into his pocket. He rummaged in a drawer for a set of keys. "I'll finish up here and head home to shower. I've got to help Mom with a few things, but I can be at your place for 7:30, 8?"

"I'll be ready."

Nico followed Drew outside and opened her car door for Henry, who leaped into the back seat. They both reached for the driver's side door handle, and she paused as his fingers lingered on hers. His lips curved into an irresistible, dimpled smile as his eyes crinkled with a fixed gaze on her. She let go of the handle, letting him open the door for her.

Her father waved as the garage door lowered, and Drew returned the gesture as she got in and started the car. She rolled the window down and let the salty ocean air flow through the car. Driving away, she stole a glance at Nico in the rearview mirror as he sauntered back to the garage, dragging a hand through his tousled dark hair.

The knot of an unmade decision in her stomach intensified, and she did the first thing that came to her mind. Called Piper.

A guitar wailed in the background, and a symbol crashed over the car's Bluetooth speakers. "Hang on, it's too loud in here, I'm going outside." As Piper talked, the background noise faded into a gentle hush. "Talk to me."

"What's wrong with me?"

"I don't have that kind of time." Piper's contagious laughter broke free.

"I'm serious," Drew said through laughter. "What am I doing?"

"You know I'm joking, I'll be serious. What are we talking about?"

"I still haven't talked to him." With one hand on the steering wheel, Drew freed her hair from its ponytail with the other and rubbed her head as she drove through downtown. So much had changed, and so much had happened to them, and between them. She knew what she wanted, but what if he didn't want the same thing? "He's between two places and has to decide by the end of next week so he can move in for August first, and I want to tell him to say no and move in with me, but what if he thinks it's too soon... If he does, it's fine, I'm good on my own, it isn't about that."

"Okay, the first thing you do is breathe." Piper said. "We all know you're good on your own, but it doesn't mean you have to be. This isn't about *that* at all. If this is what you want and it feels right, just talk to him. This is Nico, for Christ's sake. Strong, amazing, sweet, Nico. He wouldn't hurt you to save the world if it was on fire."

"I'll talk to him when it's the right time." With his paws on the console, Henry wedged himself between the seats, and Drew rolled down the back window for him to stick his head out.

"The right time my ass, talk to him, Drew. You came back from the dead for fuck's sake, you're in love with a great guy who loves you back, and so what if he says no? He won't, but if he does, you said it yourself, you'll be fine, but at least he'll know how you feel. No secrets, remember?"

Drew released an audible sigh. "You're frustrated with me."

"I'm frustrated *for* you," Piper said.

"*I'm* frustrated with me." Drew approached the coastal road toward home. "After all the death, pain, fear... the anxiety... I actually know what I want, but I'm too scared to ask for it. It's like I'm driving down the road to self-sabotage and I can't get off it. And the worst part is I'm aware it's happening, and I feel like pushing him away again, but why?" Tears pricked her eyes and her nose burned as she sniffed them back. "What's wrong with me?"

"Drew, there is nothing *wrong* with you. You had Gran, and she loved you like her own daughter, but you grew up doing everything on your own. You had a house to look after before you were a teenager and shit to worry about that no kid ever should, and I don't just mean the, 'I see dead people stuff.'" Piper hesitated, and a low hum of chatter sounded through the phone. "I think pushing people away, *self-preservation,* was the only way you knew how to survive, and it's turned into a deep-rooted, knee-jerk instinct."

"So, I'm screwed." Drew wiped tears off her face and put both hands on the wheel as she rounded the turn, closer to home.

"No, you're *aware*, and you called me to talk about it before doing something you'll regret, good choice by the way. I love you, you're like the sister I never had but always needed. I've seen you battle forces bigger than humanity and survive. Take that power, tell fear to go fuck itself, and ask for what you want. Talk to him."

Drew burst into laughter, a snort escaping as tears stung her cheeks. "The Piper effect in full force."

"Exactly—I'm coming, one sec." Piper called, her voice muffled. "I'm being beckoned by a hot drummer. Will you be okay?"

"I think so." Henry reappeared between the console, and she scratched his head. "Thanks, Piper."

"You might be a Ghost Whisperer, but I'm the Drew Whisperer, it's what I do." Piper called out to someone again, her voice echoing through the car before releasing the call.

The sun descended over the ocean, painting the clouds pink as Drew pulled into the driveway and closed the windows. Jasper had left a light on inside for her, knowing she was anxious about coming home to a dark house.

The wooden railing gave way beneath her grasp as she ascended the porch stairs, and she crouched down for a closer look—fixing it wouldn't take much effort. She headed for the shed and opened the door; the hinges creaking in protest as she slid inside and grabbed the toolbox. Matching a screwdriver with the loose screw, she tightened the metal brace holding the post on the porch until the railing stood firm and unwavering in its sturdiness. With a satisfying snap of the toolbox clasp, she locked the screwdriver away and returned it to the shed.

I can fix things, keep a family business going, attend college... take care of a dog.

"Henry, come." She opened the door and stepped inside as Henry abandoned his stick and ran to her.

Collapsing on the sofa, she let her head fall back as the ocean breeze flowed through the window and blended with the fan's circulating air. Henry bounded onto the couch, curling up underneath her bent legs.

Reaching down, she ran her fingers over Henry's velvety soft ears. He snuggled closer and shut his eyes with a groan. She craved art and college, but her heart always longed for home, not just the place, but all of it. Her friends, family, the ocean... and Nico, intertwined with it all, always.

FIFTY-ONE

Drew emerged from the bathroom, and the lingering steam from the shower evaporated. Water dripped from her hair as she headed down the hallway into her bedroom, and she squeezed the wet strands in a towel. Henry lifted his head off his front paws and greeted her with a wag of his tail as she sat beside him on the bed. She had thirty minutes before Nico picked her up for Maze, and she struggled to hurry and get ready, uninterested in a night of loud music and socializing.

Facing the mirror, she angled the heat from the dryer over her scalp, running her fingers through her hair as Henry rolled onto his side, covering his face with his paws. Her sun-kissed skin had lost its glow, and her freckles had faded away from the lack of sunlight over the past couple of weeks. She turned off the hair dryer and tamed her wild red waves with her fingers before sweeping mascara over her lashes and applying lip gloss.

I look like me again.

Pulling the curtains closed, she let the towel fall to the floor and dressed in a pair of white shorts and a soft, short-sleeved shirt the same shade of green as her eyes. The amulet dangled motionless along the neckline, cool and still. She wrapped her fingers around the jewel as she turned around to take in her appearance before heading downstairs. She would go to Maze with Nico and have fun—they needed *fun*. And when they returned home, she'd be ready to talk to him.

The distinct rumble of the Chevelle's engine filled her driveway before it shut off, and Henry jumped off the bed, barking. She followed him down the stairs to the front door and peered through the small window. Leaning against the house, Nico had his back to the door, his eyes fixated on something across the road. As she opened the front door, he pushed away from the house and spun around.

With his hands in his pockets, he took the few steps toward her, closing the distance between them. His hair was still damp, and he'd changed into a white T-shirt and jeans. His eyes wandered over her. "You're beautiful."

The scent of his shampoo and cologne hung in the night air, reawakening senses in her that had gone numb over the past two weeks. His intoxicating presence overwhelmed her, and she threw her arms around him, holding him against her. His arms embraced her back, and he rested his chin on her head. "Everything all right over here?"

"Yes." Her voice emerged as a muffled whisper against his chest. Releasing him, she sat on the porch swing and leaned forward with her elbows on her knees.

He pulled the front door closed and crouched in front of her. "You sure about that?"

I can't wait to talk to him, I just have to be brave, and tell him what I want. It'll be easy...

Her heart raced, and she fidgeted with the cushion on the swing. "How did it go with your mom?"

He took a seat beside her. The swing swayed under his weight, and he stretched his legs out, controlling the motion with his foot. "I told her about the money, gave it all to her."

"Is she okay?"

"She was shocked, but I told her about Sergeant Porter and everything else. She wants the three of us to split it."

"I admire your mom, she's strong." Drew placed her hand over his and he laced his fingers with hers.

"So are you."

"I need to talk to you," she blurted. When her gaze met his, worry creased his forehead.

"Shit. I knew something was up since that day on my deck after Dad's funeral, but I was afraid to ask." Nico let go of her hand and sat up, bending his knees like he might get up and leave. "Are you breaking up with me?"

"What? No. Not at all." She placed her hand on his leg. "Why do you think that?"

He tilted his head, his eyes meeting hers with an inquisitive gaze. "I know you, Drew, and when you get quiet, I worry. Last time you wanted to run away from this town and I was the first to go. After everything that's happened and after today at the garage, you just seemed off or something... I can't explain it."

"Did you sign a lease yet?"

He knitted his brows together and leaned back, observing her. "A lease? That's random."

"The apartment you were looking at, the roommate, your living situation. Did you make anything official?"

"That's next week's problem, but I can show you the one I chose. You can come see it if you want, but you didn't seem interested, so I—"

"Don't do it. The apartment." Trying to hold back tears, she swallowed the lump in her throat as her emotions surged. Taking a deep breath, she relaxed the grip she had on his leg. "Live here with me."

"I'm not moving in here because I need a place to live, and you feel bad for me. That's not how I want this to go at all. I can take care of this on my own. I *am* taking care of this on my own." He took her hand before she pulled it away from his leg.

Clasping her fingers with his, she locked eyes with his and shook her head. "That's not why I'm asking. I want us to live here together, not out of pity, not even to help you. I want this to be our home because I'm in love with you. Maybe we're too young, and I know my life is unpredictable wild chaos that's far from simple... and if this isn't something you want, please just tell me. Don't live here because you think you need to take care of me or anything like that, because I can take care of myself, I just—"

"Breathe." He placed her hand on his chest, and she inhaled, releasing her breath as the steady rhythm of his heartbeat thumped under her palm. Her skin tingled with a magical energy, the sensation pulsating through her fingertips.

A smile played on his lips. "I don't want simple. I want real, intense, unpredictable, beautiful... I want you because every part of me loves every part of you, and I'm not too young to know my feelings won't change." His calloused thumb traced over her hand, sending goosebumps along her skin. "Don't ask me how I know, it's not something I can explain. Just trust me."

"I trust you with my life."

"Are you sure about this?" he said. "I promise if I get my own place, we'll still be us. If you want more time, I can wait if that's what you want."

Her eyes blurred with tears, her vision clearing as they escaped over her cheek. "Nico DeSarro. Will you move into this sort of maintained, needs work, but pretty cool house with me?"

"How in the hell do I say no to that?" Brushing away her tears, his hands radiated warmth against her cheeks as he brought her face closer to his.

Desire surged through her, igniting a tingling sensation that danced across her skin, creating a perfect blend of excitement and calm. She longed to spend hours in his arms.

Their lips collided, and the urgency in their kiss heightened. Her eyes blinked open at him, breaking their connection. "I don't want to go out tonight."

"Me neither." He stood, taking her hands and with a gentle tug, pulled her off the swing, sending it swaying.

With their fingers intertwined, he opened the door and led her inside, her grip on his arm firm as he locked the door behind them. Henry leaped off the sofa, and Nico gave him a quick scratch on his head as he led Drew upstairs into her darkened bedroom. He closed the door, shutting the world outside.

She lifted his shirt over his head, running her fingers over his chest. With his gaze fixed on her, he gently slipped off her shirt, his touch sending a tingling sensation over her skin. Her heart raced and breaths quickened as she held his face with her hands and kissed him, seeking their familiar connection. Breaking away from him, his rapid breaths tickled her face as their lips hovered inches apart.

If she hadn't survived that night, she'd never have another moment like this with Nico again, and the ache to be with him overwhelmed her. Taking his hand, she guided him down onto the bed with her and they lay facing each other as he brushed his fingers along her arm.

"Are you sure this is okay?" Moonlight streamed through the window, illuminating his face as he spoke. "If you're still in too much pain—"

She pressed her lips against his. "This is perfect," she said between kisses.

Leaning over her, he trailed delicate kisses along her neck and down her body. His lips lingered on the scar across her abdomen, forever etched in her body, and he lifted his head to face her and held her against him. "I love you," he said.

"I love you." She ran her hands along his back, up to his neck.

He brushed her hair away from her eyes before leaning in closer, capturing her lips in a passionate kiss. Their hands explored each other's bodies, and she clung to him as they collapsed against the bed, entangled together.

She traced a path of kisses along his jawline, and he hugged her tighter. As he rolled onto his back, she nestled close to him. His heartbeat beneath her ear steadied her breathing, easing her tired mind.

So, this is what soul-bending love feels like.

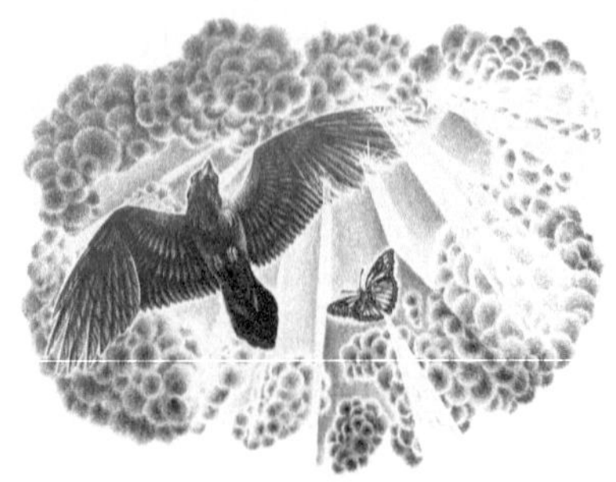

FIFTY-TWO

With the end of August approaching faster than Drew wanted to admit, the sun hung lower in the sky and scorching heat shifted to cooler days and nights. The back deck of her home bustled with friends and family. Nico's mom joined Drew's dad and Celeste at the barbecue, their laughter filling the air as they grilled plates of chicken, sausages, and burgers.

Sliding the screen door open, Drew walked into the kitchen to grab a pitcher of iced tea.

Jasper stood at the counter, using Gran's wooden salad tongs to mix dressing into an oversized salad bowl. "The new pastry chef is a miracle; do you know how long I've waited to have a Saturday off?"

"She's pretty great, and if I haven't told you lately, I appreciate you and all the Saturdays you work." Drew sliced lemons and added the wedges into the glass pitcher.

Jasper grabbed a fork and tasted a bite of salad. With a dramatic flair, he brought his fingers to his lips, mimicking the chef's kiss gesture. "This is good." He dropped the fork into the sink and eyed her. "There's something I need to talk to you about before it gets brought up outside."

"Should I sit down for this?" She gave the iced tea a final stir and placed the spoon on the counter.

"No, but I should." He took a seat on the nearest stool.

"You bought that house, didn't you?"

He smiled at her. "Are you psychic, too?"

"I'm observant." She'd been preparing for this. The stack of home decorating magazines and houses circled on real estate flyers, and endless real estate appointments had been a dead giveaway. She gave him a hug, and he embraced her with a pat on her back. "Congratulations, J. I'm happy for you, this is a good thing."

"I think the place is Ori approved," he said, releasing her.

"Oh yeah?"

"Don't laugh, but one of the bedrooms has a constellation accent wall—they're all named. Bet you can't guess the constellation in the center."

Ori's face materialized in her mind. "I don't know much about astrology, but I sure know Orion the Hunter."

"Bingo." Jasper stood and exhaled.

"He's happy for you, too."

"You telling me about what he said... it made taking this step feel right." Jasper's gaze wandered around the kitchen. "I *am* happy. I found my family in this town, and I never thought I'd have all this."

"I'll miss having you around—"

"Please, you don't need me living here, especially not *now*." He laughed.

"I'm serious." She picked up the container of iced tea with a smile.

"Don't worry, I'll be around. Your dad is connecting us with someone to do the renovations, maybe that's how you knew."

"I promise you, he didn't tell me. But Dad wouldn't say a word until you told him he could, not even to me."

"Your dad's awesome." Jasper slid off the stool and grabbed the salad from the counter as Danny slid the door open for them.

Drew positioned the iced tea next to the salad on the big rectangular table while Claudia instructed Grant to take the wrapped canvases to his car so she wouldn't leave them behind. Sitting at the head of the table with poise, she poured herself a tall glass of iced tea and crossed her legs. "Are you sure I can't get one more painting out of you before you're gone to college?"

"We're leaving for vacation tomorrow and I'm heading to Boston once we're back." Drew threw a ball for Henry, and he tore across the backyard after it. "I'll work on a piece at school and bring it home for you."

"Where are you guys going exactly?" Claudia twirled the ice in her glass with a straw.

"Wherever the wind blows them." Piper held up her hands in a grand gesture as Taj handed her a plate with a sausage in a bun and a baked potato wrapped in foil.

"I don't know how you can just travel without a plan." Claudia grabbed the tongs and filled her bowl with salad.

Shane eyed Claudia while balancing a plate stacked with two burgers on his lap in a wooden Adirondack chair. "Not everyone needs every minute of their day organized, that's how."

"Are you sure you need to go back to Boston tonight?" Claudia glanced over at Shane. "There's still a week left—"

"My dad wants to hang out... I miss him. We're gonna catch a ball game or something. And Leah wants me to come home. My life's in Boston." Shane glanced at Drew as he bit into his burger. "You'll go back the weekend after your vacation, right?"

"Probably the Sunday before classes start." Drew sat next to Nico at the table and scooped potato salad and a piece of chicken on a paper plate, feeling Shane's eyes on her. Friendship was going okay, but an air of awkwardness still lingered between them. She refused to let it bother her. If Nico could get over it, she could as well.

Nico leaned back in his chair to toss the ball across the yard for Henry again. Drew's father sat beside him, and Nico let his arm drape along the back of Drew's chair. "Are you sure about this week? There's a delivery on Thursday, and someone's dropping off a 60s Continental that's in rough shape for when I'm back, but I wrote everything in the book."

"Go, have fun, and stop worrying," Gabe said between bites.

Nico's mom sat across from Nico and Drew, savoring a glass of wine. "I can help, too. It's only an hour away, and I don't mind the drive."

"Thanks, Mom, I gave your number to Gabe in case," Nico said.

Drew's father wiped his mouth with a napkin and stood to pull out a chair for Celeste to sit beside him. They had been inseparable, and although her father claimed they were just friends, an undeniable chemistry radiated from them whenever they were in each other's presence. Drew loved them both, and if a relationship developed between her dad and Celeste, how could she not be anything but happy for them?

"J's got the bakery under control and I'll manage the garage," Gabe said. "It'll still be standing when you get back. You have my word." He took a long drink from his beer, the condensation trickling down the bottle as he glanced at Jasper and Danny. "I've got a plan for your renovations. Remind me to share everything with you later."

Jasper and Danny nodded, their smiles brighter than the late afternoon sun. Jasper smoothed out his white linen shirt. "Who can do the work, Mr. Harlow?"

"Please call me Gabe, I can't do the mister stuff." Her father nodded toward Grant. "The Salingers."

A gust of wind tossed a strand of Claudia's hair in her face as she ate her salad and Grant brushed it away. With her fork in mid-air, she kissed his cheek.

"My father has a crew ready," Grant said. "He won't let you down."

"I'm not worried." Danny's eyes flickered to the smart watch around his wrist. "I hate to cut this short, but I've got to run and get ready for work." His eyes watered as he glanced at Drew and Jasper. "Thanks for today and for welcoming me into this family you all have."

Pushing the plastic chair back, Drew stood and hugged him. "We're lucky to have you."

With a wave, Danny headed inside the house, with Jasper following him.

"It'll be quiet around here when you all go back to college," Celeste placed her hand on the back of Taj's chair. "It always makes me a little sad."

"Oh, we'll be back. We always come back." As Piper played with a strand of hair, she blinked her doe eyes at Taj. "I'm just happy you're not upset Taj is coming to New York."

Celeste laughed. "Silly girl, he doesn't listen to me, this is all Taj. But just so you know, I wouldn't stand in his way for anything, and it's good for him to spend time with his father."

"You sure you don't want big city life, Mom?" Taj asked. "The band scene will be fire, and you could set up your shop."

Celeste reached for the glass pitcher of iced tea, but Drew's dad grabbed it first and filled her glass. "I don't want big city life, this is home." She reached across the table and patted Drew's hand, exchanging a wordless connection with a knowing look.

Atlas Cliffs had an invisible tether connecting Celeste and Drew to the town, clinging to them like glitter on skin. Perhaps the same mysterious force would forever have a hold on each person gathered around the table. The coastal hometown she'd once been desperate to leave behind was her haven.

Jasper returned and sat back down, his eyes sparkling with excitement as he gushed about his new home renovations. Laughter filled the backyard as conversations carried on into the evening. With the night winding down, the last of the sunset cast a pink glow over the horizon, and everyone worked together to clean up before heading home.

Drew followed Nico as they made their way to the front porch with his mom. Maria embraced Drew, holding her cheeks in both hands, kissing each one. "I love you like a daughter." She turned to Nico and hugged him. "Come over for dinner when you get back and I'll give you a bunch of meals for your freezer."

Nico held his mom's car door open for her. "I don't need you to do that—"

"I'm doing it anyway." Maria settled in the driver's seat and started the car. "Have fun, and check in, even if it's just a text to say you're alive and everything's all right. That's all I ask."

"Of course," Nico said.

Maria stuck her hand out the window and waved as she drove away, and Nico glanced down at Drew. "Did she tell you she's buying a house near my aunt's place? It's pretty nice."

"She did, and she also said you could move back home if ever you needed to." She leaned into him and planted a soft, lingering kiss on his lips.

"Not a chance." He wrapped his arms around her.

Stepping outside, Claudia handed Grant an empty bag and her purse. Her heeled sandals echoed on the porch steps as she approached Drew. "Well, enjoy this trip to… wherever it is you end up going." Unlocking her car with the flick of a button on her keychain, she gave Drew a quick hug goodbye.

"You make it sound like we're not coming back."

Rolling her eyes, Claudia began listing things off on her fingers as she walked toward her car. "Oh, you'll be back. I'm planning a fall party, we've got another artist's work to feature with yours, and I also need to do a welcome to the gallery thing, and then there's the holidays—"

"Bye, Claudia." Drew smiled and waved. As much as she loved bringing everyone together, her focus was on the road trip with Nico the next day.

Claudia climbed in the passenger side, taking her purse from Grant before he shut the door and got in the driver's side. "I'll message you soon," she called out the window as they drove away.

"Are we having a fire tonight?" Piper stepped onto the porch with Taj and sat on the swing, toying with her eyebrow ring.

Shane emerged from the house with his hands in his pockets. "I can't. I'm heading home." He wore a thoughtful expression and positioned himself in front of Nico.

Drew chewed her bottom lip and released it, waiting for what was coming next as the two eyed each other.

Nico spoke first. "Be safe."

"If you weren't such a good guy…" Shane took his keys from his pocket and twirled them around his finger. "It's hard to not like you, I can't do it." His focus shifted to Drew. "I hope we can all still hang out once in a while. Maybe in Boston or back here again."

The time she'd spent in a relationship with Shane had faded into a collection of bittersweet memories, blending in euphoria, grief, heartache, and betrayal, but after everything they'd been through, she would keep her promise to try friendship. "I think we could figure something out."

"Sounds good… later, Nico." Shane called over his shoulder as he walked away.

"Later." Nico watched Shane leave, but he appeared calm and unbothered as he opened the door for Henry.

Perhaps it was strange that the man she loved and the one she'd left behind coexisted with an odd harmony in her life, but their circumstances *were* strange.

Drew's dad followed Celeste down the porch steps. He wrapped an arm around Drew, giving her a kiss on the forehead. "See ya, kid."

"I'll drive Mom home and come back," Taj said.

"I'm happy to give you a lift if Taj wants to stay." Her dad opened the passenger door of his truck with a nod to Celeste.

"I'm happy to take you up on that." Celeste placed her hand on Piper's shoulder. "See you soon, honey."

Taj and Piper locked eyes as he smiled at her. Piper lived in spontaneity and adventure, but Drew would bet the amulet around her neck that Piper was as captivated with Taj as he was with her. She admired Piper's fearlessness, diving headfirst into what she wanted. She enjoyed the adventure, no matter how short or long it lasted.

Henry sprinted from the house, zooming around the front lawn as Nico stepped onto the porch, closing the door behind him.

"And then there were four." Piper rose from the swing and slid her arm around Taj's waist, tucking her hand into his back pocket.

The gentle surf of the ocean beckoned, its rhythmic waves crashing against the shore, as the four of them descended the stone steps to Jupiter Cove Beach for one of summer's last bonfires.

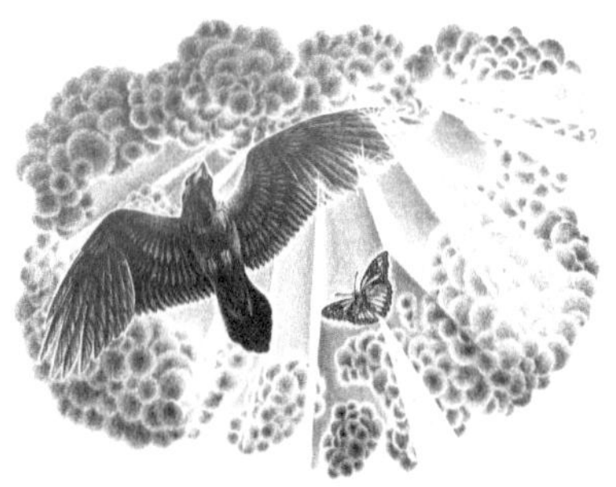

Fifty-Three

With the sun streaming through her bedroom window, Drew leaned over the plush seat and pushed the curtains apart. Nico threw a ball for Henry as he packed the trunk of the Chevelle for their weeklong getaway. They planned to embrace spontaneity and drive along the coast, renting surfboards when they could, and staying at small town motels or a campground when they got tired. A whole week stretched ahead, free from work, people, and responsibilities.

The wandering souls on the other side had kept their distance... for now. The stillness never lasted long, but life wouldn't wait, and she wanted to *live*.

Her necklace snagged in her hair, and she angled her head down to untangle the butterfly necklace from the amulet. She unraveled the fine silver chain apart from the amulet and slipped the pendant over her head. The stone came to life in her hand, unleashing a radiant thread of light spiraling upward before disappearing. A slight burn spread through her hands, leaving a tingling sensation and a fading energy on her skin.

What would happen if she took it off for a while? There had been a time when the amulet hadn't belonged to her, and she'd survived. Gran had given the jewel to her in her death—a gift from Enid. The amulet had protected her from forces beyond this world, but danger no longer threatened her.

Holding the delicate butterfly charm in her fingers, she glided it back and forth along the chain and let it rest against her skin as she stood in front of the mirror. The gift Nico had given her looked pretty on its own, like it belonged in the contours of her neckline.

A small jewelry box Gran had given her when she was a little girl remained untouched on top of her dresser. She wiped the accumulated dust covering the pink floral pattern and opened the square box. The rotating mechanism clicked as the ballerina spun in time with the enchanting classical tune. She'd never been to a ballet or taken a dance class, but she used to bring the musical box to bed with her on nights she couldn't sleep. That had been a long time ago, and it had become an overlooked part of her bedroom décor.

Lifting the chain, she let the amulet swing. Icy air caressed her cheeks and her breath formed a mist in front of her, curling around the black gem, but the crackling of energy was light and familiar. Love overwhelmed her, leaving her breathless.

Gran.

A warm hand pressed against her back. "You're taking it off?" Gran appeared, bathed in a warm light.

"I have to try life without it. I need to trust that I'll be okay with just... *me.*"

"Aye, you will. The road is clear, for now. But promise me you'll keep it close. In case there's ever a time you need an extra boost, you hear?" Gran's eyes sparkled as her gaze turned toward the window. "I see your paths finally aligned."

Drew followed her gaze. Nico was crouched down with Henry on the lawn. "I love him, Gran. Maybe it's wrong for me to drag him into this strange life of mine, but I can't imagine us not together."

Gran's face beamed, and her eyes shimmered like flickering candles. "That young man isn't being dragged anywhere. As much as he's a part of your destiny, you are a part of his. Trust me, my dear." She winked.

Drew clutched the amulet in her palm. "I miss you."

"And I miss you. But you've found another like you in Taj, and his journey is just beginning." Taking Drew's hand, Gran turned it over, revealing the amulet resting in her palm. As Gran traced the amulet with her finger, light flickered inside, spinning into a burst of rainbow colors. She closed Drew's fingers over it and wrapped her glowing arms around her.

Warmth covered Drew's head, cascading down her body like water, filling her with a deep sense of peace as the music box song slowed to a stop, ending the tiny ballerina's dance.

"You will never be alone. If you call, someone will always come. You can put the amulet to bed, but never lose it." Gran's voice faded as she disappeared.

A blue butterfly landed on the window, and Drew reached out and touched the screen. With elegant wings fluttering, the butterfly danced away and vanished from sight.

She dabbed the corners of her eyes with the sleeve of her shirt, and took a deep breath, releasing the bond with the amulet. The spinning light curled from the jewel and absorbed into her skin with a tingling warmth. She placed it among Gran's costume jewelry in the box and closed the lid with a click.

Locking the front door, Drew flung her backpack over her shoulder, shielding her eyes as she made her way toward Nico. Henry ran around her and jumped up on her legs, and she reached down and patted his back. Nico leaned against the car with the trunk open. As she wiped dog hair off his black T-shirt, he slid the backpack off her shoulder and tossed it alongside sleeping bags, a tent, Henry's dog food, and a propane camping stove. It was the first time she'd ever gone away with Nico before, and her heart raced with anticipation.

He closed the trunk and opened the passenger door, calling to Henry as he pushed the seat forward so the dog could hop in the back. Adjusting the passenger seat back into place, he squinted against the blinding sunlight, his eyes shifting from shades of brown to amber hazel. His head tilted, and a warm smile graced his face, highlighting the captivating dimple on his cheek. The way he looked at her reminded her of the day they'd reconnected on Jupiter Beach almost two years ago. She'd been surfing alone, still mourning Shane's loss, wiping out on her board when Nico showed up on the water.

I didn't know it then, but that was the day everything changed.

Maybe Gran was right, and their paths had always been destined to align. Magic pulsed through Drew's world. Perhaps, against all odds, fate had woven her life together with Nico's, and regardless of the decisions made along the way, she would still end up right here, at home, with him. She'd grown up believing real, soul-bending love didn't exist—and if so, it sure didn't last.

She had sharpened her skill of keeping people at a distance and had forced herself into a sad contentment with loneliness, but not anymore. Shane had opened the door, cracked her walls, and offered her a glimpse of what love could feel like, but Nico was the exception to everything else.

His smile faded as he stepped closer to her, furrowing his brow as he placed his hands on her arms. "Are you okay? You got quiet and you look like you're gonna cry. Is it the trip? We don't have to go—"

"You need to know how much I love you, and what having you here means to me." A gust of ocean air blew, and she brushed careless strands of hair off his eyes.

"I feel the same about you."

"I just... I want you to know that I'm happy here, with you."

He looked around and settled his gaze back on her. "Is something happening that I should know about?"

"Nothing. I guess I was just having a moment or something."

"Or something..." His fingers grazed her skin as he touched the butterfly charm dangling from her neck. "You took off the amulet."

"It's taking a break. Don't worry, it'll be there if I need it."

Once again, the dimple resurfaced as his lips curved into a half smile. "What's worrying going to do, right?"

Rising onto her tiptoes, she pressed her lips against his, their mouths moving in sync as his warm breath caressed her skin. Her fingers curled around the fabric of his shirt and pulled him closer. The kiss held an unspoken promise as they pulled apart, their eyes locked in a silent understanding.

His arms encircled her waist, and he lifted her off the ground. As he spun her toward the car, she threw her arms around his neck, his laughter mixing with her playful scream echoing through the air. Letting go of grief and heartache might not always be possible, but moments like this gave her hope.

Henry barked from the back seat with his tail wagging as Nico set Drew back down next to the passenger side door. The smooth leather warmed her bare legs as she yanked the door shut. Henry stuck his head between the center console, and she scratched his ears. Settling into the driver's seat, Nico brought the engine roaring to life.

He slid a pair of sunglasses over his eyes and rested his arm on the door frame as he faced her. With each gust of wind through the open windows, her hair swept across her face, obscuring her smile in the reflection of his glasses.

"Ready?" He smiled.

Over the past week, he had been doing a lot more of that.

She leaned against the seat, sweeping her hair off her face. "More than ready."

The house disappeared behind them as the car rumbled along the coastal road. She extended her hand out of the window, letting the ocean breeze glide across her open palm.

Faced with death, grief, and loss, time had always been said to be the ultimate healer. The passing of time dulled the suffocating pain, but it couldn't heal all wounds. The wounds might scar over with time, but the skin would always remain sensitive and tender, re-opening with the sharp jab of a certain smell, a song, or a memory.

This would forever be Drew Harlow's path, all of it. The weird and wonderful, scary and stunning, beautiful and dark, with flawed and unique perfection. Society's definition of *normal* might not apply to her, but normal was overrated, and she'd take her version of normal anytime, anywhere.

Character Art

ARTIST: ALEXANDRA HUTAN

Alexandra Hutan brought Drew Harlow to life using pencil and charcoal, and I wanted to share this stunning art with you...

Acknowledgements

I'm going to miss the characters of Atlas Cliffs. Pouring myself into these stories over the past four years has been consuming, but I've found my passion for writing and publishing, and I'm not giving up now.

Writing a book is a solitary, in-your-head process, but these books would never have seen the light of day without the support of incredible people I've met along the way. Where do I start with Braving Storms? It's the longest book I've written, but the story needed to be told the way the characters wanted me to tell it.

Thank you to my Beta Readers. You were the first to lay eyes on this manuscript, and I devoured your feedback—it was beyond valuable and I appreciate you so much!

Kayla Ramoutar, my editor. Three books into my author journey and now you're stuck with me for as long as you want. Working with you has been like collaborating with a good friend who is cheering me on, seeing potential beyond my self-doubt, and pushing me to "squeeze every last bit of goodness this novel can be out of [me]".

To Natasha Mackenzie, thank you for bringing my vision for Drew to life on the cover of Braving Storms, wrapping up the Atlas Cliffs series. I'm grateful for your patience and talent throughout the process of each book cover in this series.

The talented audiobook narrator, Victoria Connolly. I am so excited and grateful that our paths have merged. I cannot wait to hear the magic you'll bring to Seeking Haven and Braving Storms in the coming months.

Whitney Law of New Ink Book Services, these chapter headings are everything! All four pieces captured the story arcs beautifully, but the final chapter heading hit close to my heart—thank you so much.

The world of Bookstagram introduced me to character art, and Alexandra Hutan brought Drew Harlow to life beyond the book covers. Thank you, Alexandra! She's stunning, and I can't wait to have prints available for readers soon.

To my ARC Readers, a special thank you for being part of this journey, sharing posts, reader thoughts, reviews, and reaching out with encouragement and, more importantly, your friendship. I appreciate you so much. Please know you've made a lasting impression on me and will always have a place on my author team for future projects.

If you know me, you know I love being on Bookstagram and Booktok, and some connections I've made turned into lasting friendships. Sara Flanagan, thank you for helping me brainstorm taglines for Braving Storms, and writing that captivating one-liner that ended up on the cover. Your support with all things social media and navigating the indie author world means so much to me, and I adore you. Jaclyn Kot, I always feel lighter after our conversations. Thank you for your advice and friendship. Tess Watters, thanks for being my sounding board and bringing some laughter into my life when this business feels overwhelming. I love our banter and the fierce support we share. Abby Mei, a marketing collaboration that turned into friendship. You're a light in the Bookstagram community, and I'm so happy we connected. Kamy Lavin, always an author cheerleader and friend, supporting so many of us. I'm excited for you to publish your debut—there are wonderful things coming your way!

Thank you to my family, and close friends who feel like family. A special nod to my oldest, Lucien, who challenges me to just write the story and stop overthinking every sentence to get the movie reel playing in my head onto the pages.

To the readers who have reached out, and whom I've connected with over our mutual obsession with books. I never dreamed that my fictional stories about ghosts and magic could lead to beautiful friendships. Thank you, I am humbled, and I appreciate you.

I worried that once this series was complete, I would be at a loss for what to do next, but my mind is already overflowing with more stories than I can keep up with. I'm working on a prequel to the Atlas Cliffs series, and a romantic thriller coming in 2025, which is a brand-new challenge, stepping outside of my genre, and I'm excited to share details as soon as I can.

Until next time, thank you for being a part of my author journey. This one is for you, because I couldn't do this without you.

Angela

Also by Angela van Liempt

Find out how it all began for Drew Harlow in Wandering Souls...

Continue Drew's journey in Seeking Haven... A silver medal winner in the 2024 Readers' Favorite Book Awards for the Young Adult, Paranormal category. https://readersfavorite.com/2024-award-contest-winners.htm#seeking-haven

Angela van Liempt is a small-town girl with big dreams. Music inspires her and she creates a playlist for every book she writes. The Atlas Cliffs series emerged from her curiosity with the paranormal, but along the way, she discovered a passion for weaving romance into her stories.

She lives on the east coast of Canada with her family and her beloved dog, Harley, otherwise known as 'Pippy' or 'Harley-Quinn'. A lover of the ocean, full moons, and sunsets, she'd choose to be barefoot on a beach any day over big city life. Escaping into fictional coastal towns with characters who feel like real people is one of her favorite pastimes.

Follow for writing updates, book playlists and more!

https://linktr.ee/angeladvl

https://www.instagram.com/angela_vanliempt

https://www.tiktok.com/@angelavl_author